...ico, ...atre ...eare Company and at Ronnie Scott's among others, ... s in London with her family.

Visit www.AuthorTracker.co.uk for exclusive updates on Christie Dickason

'*The Firemaster's Mistress* is that rare historical novel: utterly congruent with history and successful as a work of fiction. It tells the story of an engaging man betrayed both by his own honour and his love for a Roman Catholic woman. His skills with explosives lead him into the very heart of the conspiracy, walking a difficult line with plotters, spymasters, and his own fears.'

PHILIPPA GREGORY

'*The Firemaster's Mistress* explores the political astuteness of the King's minister Robert Cecil, and is a tour de force on many levels. Primarily a love story set against the backdrop of 17th-century terrorism, this relates a tragedy that puts you on the rack in its literary quest for the truth about November 5.' *Oxford Times*

'Historical fiction, but far too rich and intelligent to be a mere bodice ripper. It couldn't be more topical as it re-creates London in the grip of a terrorist plot … a rich mix of romance, suspense, adventure and lightly worn knowledge.' KATE SAUNDERS, *The Times*

'… A racy read … reveals the principal actors to be models of conspirators everywhere: single-minded, ideologically driven, careless of their own and others lives, believers for the wrong reasons in the efficacy of a single violent blow to change the course of history … so strangely does it resonate with our own times … sometimes one is momentarily unsure whether one is in 1605 or 2005 as one read... ...al Times*

Also by Christie Dickason

The Lady Tree
Quicksilver
The Memory Palace

CHRISTIE DICKASON

The Firemaster's Mistress

HARPER

This novel is entirely a work of fiction.
The names, characters and incidents portrayed in it are
the work of the author's imagination. Any resemblance to
actual persons, living or dead, events or localities is
entirely coincidental.

Harper
An imprint of HarperCollins*Publishers*
77–85 Fulham Palace Road,
Hammersmith, London W6 8JB

www.harpercollins.co.uk

This paperback edition 2006
4

First published in Great Britain by
HarperCollins*Publishers* 2005

Copyright © Christie Dickason 2005

Christie Dickason asserts the moral right to
be identified as the author of this work

A catalogue record for this book is
available from the British Library

ISBN-13: 978-0-00-718068-4
ISBN-10: 0-00-718068-3

Set in Meridien

Printed and bound in Great Britain by
Clays Ltd, St Ives plc

For John

MY THANKS

When you're trying to build a complex imaginary world that is not of your own time, you need help. At the top of my long list of people to thank for theirs are:

Joy Chamberlain, my editor at HarperCollins, lethally perceptive, gentle, and right; *Lynne Drew*, Publishing Director, at the helm; *Robert Kirby*, my agent at PFD; *Alan Hayes*, retired fisherman with an encyclopaedic memory, at The Brighton Fishing Museum, where hoggies can still be found; *Tom French*, my son, for help with computers and the chemistry of bombilations; *John*, my husband, Artificer and Fixer, whose ability to quote by heart and illuminate most of Shakespeare gave me the original (mysterious) Francis Quoynt (See Richard II, Act 2, Scene 1, l.277); *Stephen Wyatt*, writer and friend, on whom I depend for 'What if you . . . ?' and 'Have you considered . . . ?', my first and last resort; *Peter Bonsall*, for giving me a research base and writing space in Brighton/Brighthelmstone; *Abigail Faulkner* (BBC editor) and *Lucy Wolf* for background information on the culture of the period; *Will Le Fleming*, of Historic Royal Palaces, likewise, but for costume most of all; *Helen Poole*, Director of Research, Sussex Heritage, for her generous gift of time and information; Sussex Heritage and National Trust Volunteers at

Michelham Priory (including *Joyce Bruce* and *Mary Murray*), Baddesley Clinton (*Alan Langstaff, Rachel Smith, John Jarman* and *Mary Denby*), and Coughton Court, among many other places. Invaluable people, full of facts and historical gossip; *Jeremy Preston* of Richmond and Sheen Libraries for his constant support and help with my research; *Emma Faulkner* for textual advice; *John Fox*, Sue Gill and Welfare State International, whose handbook 'Engineers of the Imagination' gave me much of the hard stuff I needed in order to imagine an early seventeenth-century fireworks display; *Stephen Bashford* and Prince Research Consultants for information on gunpowder, both in the making and in history; *the staff of the Public Records Office*, Kew, most of all those in Document Retrieval, who persisted when most people would have given up and made it possible for me to have the thrill of seeing original letters and state papers, including the signed confessions of Guy Fawkes and the mysterious Monteagle letter. Thanks also to the Royal Gunpowder Factory, Waltham Abbey, Essex; Chilworth Gunpowder Mills, Chilworth, Surrey; and The London Library, without which I wouldn't know where to begin.

Among the many books I read while doing my research, I would like to call attention to *The Gunpowder Plot* by Antonia Fraser, in which she argues that there are few unambiguous facts about the episode. I am particularly grateful to her detailed, combative and deliciously readable examination of alternative historical possibilities that allowed me to confirm the interstices into which I have imagined my story. (Needless to say, she bears no responsibility for any of my possible misinterpretations of her work.)

For readers interested in both the historical details and the gaps, there are notes and a chronology of The Gunpowder Plot at the back.

THE MAJOR CHARACTERS

Real

Robert Cecil, Earl of Salisbury, the English Secretary of State

Sir Francis Bacon, cousin of Robert Cecil

Father Gerard, the Jesuit Superior of English Catholics

Mary Frith, a cross-dressing, pipe-smoking pimp and fence (mythologized by Dekker and Middleton as 'Moll Cutpurse'). I have slightly adjusted her likely age.

The Gunpowder Treason Plotters

Robert Catesby

Thomas Percy

Tom Wintour

Rob Wintour

Kit Wright

Jack Wright

John Grant

Robert Keyes

Thomas Bates (retainer to Robert Catesby)

Guy Fawkes (Yorkshireman, mercenary soldier, converted to Catholicism)

Sir Everard Digby

Sir Ambrose Rookwood

The English Royal Family

King James I of England & VI of Scotland, succeeded
   Elizabeth I in 1603, crowned in London in May 1604
Anne of Bohemia, Queen to James, a Catholic convert
Henry, Prince of Wales, aged 14 years
Princess Elizabeth, aged 11 years
Charles, Duke of York, aged 5 years, Later Charles I
Princess Mary, infant, the first of the royal children to be
   born in England.

Invented (perhaps)

Kate Peach, the only surviving member of a Catholic
   artisan family
Francis Quoynt, a firemaster, the last in a long dynasty of
   military firemasters and siege engineers
Boomer Quoynt, Francis's father, also a firemaster
Hugh Traylor, a London merchant and speculator
Robert Stuart
Father Jerome, Jesuit priest
Hammick, gentleman and neighbour to the Quoynts

Places

Most of the places in *The Firemaster's Mistress* are real, or
based on real places. Brighthelmstone is the old name for
Brighton, for example. For more details, please see notes at
end of the book.

N.B. If I show people as I conclude them to have been as a
result of my research, it does not mean that I always agree
with them. Part of the imaginative struggle in writing
about an historical period is dealing with the distortion
caused by the filter of our own modern sensibilities.

On the other hand, I find that the seventeenth century hovers on the barely conscious edge of our own experience. While the medieval mentality feels utterly foreign to me, I suspect that most of us could get through a day in the early seventeenth century and feel that we pretty much understood the people around us. We could make some sense of their lives. We would recognize and share both their pleasures and their terrors. I fear that we would also find much to recognize in their politics.

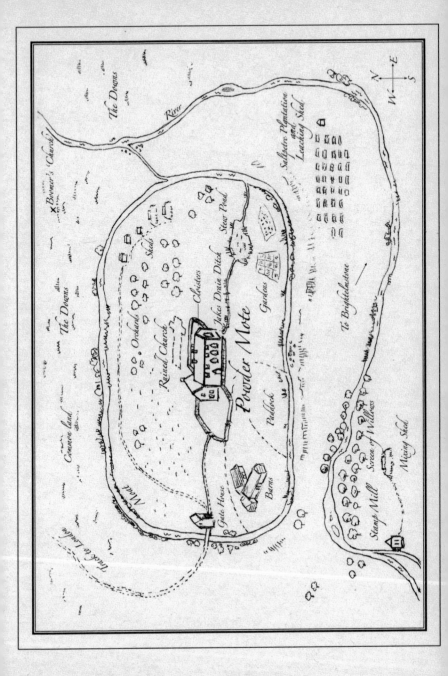

PART ONE

FLINT AND STEEL

*'But men must know, that in this theatre of man's life
it is reserved only for God and angels to be lookers on.'*

Francis Bacon, Advancement of Learning *(1605)*

PROLOGUE

Brighthelmstone, Sussex. March 1605

His hair stood on end as the wave washed in over him. As the wave sank back, his hair flattened against his head like dark seaweed on a rock, glistening and dripping in the morning sun. The next wave lifted him a little higher onto the rough shingle beach. He was a young man lying face down in the water, with the red weathered neck, strong arms and callused hands of a fisherman. The honey-coloured pebbles had scraped away the skin of his face.

A village dog found him. Another fisherman, pulling up his traps, rowed in to see what the dog was barking at.

'He would go out alone!' cried his eighteen-year-old, pregnant wife, trembling with the rage so often flung after the dead by those they have left behind. 'Why did he go out alone?'

'Yes, that's Shelvy,' said the fisherman Peter Mawes, when shown the body of his elder son. Mawes had already lost his wife and did not speak again for two days.

Peter's younger son, Jem, knew that his brother had not been fishing on the night he drowned, but he kept his mouth firmly shut for a number of reasons. Instead, Jem wept alone on the beach at night, on the stretch of shingle where his brother's body was found.

If only I had stayed . . . He sucked in air between clenched teeth and pounded his thigh with his fist in helpless fury.

'Jem Mawes?' Pale hair moved in the darkness.

'Sir! Master Quoynt!' Jem scrambled to his feet.

The voice and hair belonged to the owner of Powder Mote, an estate northwest of Brighthelmstone. Boomer Quoynt, tall, broad-shouldered and lean, in his early fifties, with silver hair and eyes that were light blue when they could be seen. Coming off his clothes, and blown towards Jem on the sea breeze to prod at the back of his throat, drifted the reason the Quoynts were feared locally as something between wizards and hangmen. The smell of gunpowder.

Of course, both Jem and his brother had disobeyed strict orders from their parents to stay away from Powder Mote. Like all the other village children, they spied on the Quoynts and their dangerous work. Shelvy even became a companion in crime of Boomer's son Francis for several years before their fathers called them, respectively, to fishing and war. Jem, nine years younger than his brother, remained in awe of both father and son.

Even so, he quite liked Boomer Quoynt. The man was surprisingly easy company, given his age, fearsome reputation and somewhat military air of authority. Jem was certain that the men under Boomer's command must have liked him.

On the beach, Boomer Quoynt offered all the appropriate condolences. Then he startled Jem with an unexpected question.

'May I see your brother's body?'

The young fisherman was laid out on the table in his father's cottage. While Shelvy's silent father and astonished brother watched, Boomer's fingers explored behind the bandage that held Shelvy's mouth shut.

The next day, Boomer went back to stare at the sleek waves rolling smoothly onto the beach where the body was found.

The wide-beamed hoggies of Brighthelmstone were beached on the day the little fishing village buried Shelvy Mawes. There was no inquiry.

Fishermen drowned. It was a brutal fact of a hard way of life. Only Boomer Quoynt questioned how Shelvy died, but he kept his doubts to himself. It occurred to no one, not even to Boomer, that Shelvy might be the first victim of a plot to kill, in a single terrible blow, the King, his heir, ministers, lords, and most of the Members of Parliament – all the most powerful men in England. As well as any of the powerless who happened to get in the way.

1

Kate Peach worked hard to keep her life under control. This morning, she was feeling a cautious sense of success. Her small lodgings were immaculately clean. She had orders for seven pairs of gloves, at seven shillings each, from four local Southwark whores and three innkeepers' wives, not counting the unfinished hawking glove on her lap.

Although the glove would be worn by a mere smith to fly a common kestrel, its silver embroidery and twisted fringe were rich enough for a gentleman's falcon or nobleman's eagle. Kate did not see why only fine ladies and gentlemen should enjoy the small luxuries that let you pretend for a moment or two that life was better than you knew it to be.

Furthermore, unlike fine ladies, the whores didn't ask whether she was a member of the Glovers' Guild. Unlike many fine ladies, they also paid on delivery, just as they themselves expected to be paid.

As she did every morning, Kate sat on a stool at the window with her father's thick leather apron over her long thighs, her broad elegant shoulders curved tenderly above her work. With her awl, she punched holes in the edge of the gauntlet and lined these up with the holes in the edge of the wrist.

The two pieces of thick leather slipped. Her needle stuck.

When she pushed it with the hard leather pad she wore in her palm, the needle snapped.

Her peace of mind felt suddenly fragile.

It's only a broken needle, she told herself.

She turned to the window to look at the Thames. She could spend hours staring blankly at the changing colours and patterns of the water. Today the surface was choppy. The sun struck bright sparks on the crests of the slate-green ripples.

Slate-green like his eyes. The thought slipped through her guard like a dagger thrust.

'Kate!'

Gratefully, she set aside the glove and pushed open her window.

'Broken meats again this morning, duck?' called Peg the Pie from the street below. 'Still warm from the oven . . . Hot pies!' she bellowed to a passer-by.

Kate tied her purse to her girdle and ran down the narrow stairs of the tenements above The Little Rose. The stink of piss in the staircase still made it hard for her to think the best of her present life, even after more than a year, but she no longer noticed the smell of stale beer rising from the inn at street level.

In the street, she handed over her ha'penny. As always, Peg gave her all the broken pies. Then, instead of climbing back up to her lodgings, Kate went to stand beside the Thames while her tongue savoured the warm succulence of minced mutton spiced with cinnamon, cloves and nutmeg. The breeze played with a loose curl of her dark hair.

Compared to that of many others on Bankside, her life was quite tolerable. But only as a passing-through life. Though she had enough to eat and was blessed with lodgings on the top floor, with a window that opened onto the river instead of a narrow, foetid alley, she meant to leave

Southwark as soon as possible. The price she paid for her tolerable life was becoming intolerable.

'Wainfleet oysters,' cried a woman with a basket over her arm. 'Oysters!'

'Buy fine apples,' called another. 'Morning, Kate.'

Kate waved at the apple-seller, then licked her fingers, smelling the stink of tanned leather on her skin under the mutton.

With half a dozen slightly bruised apples and the rest of the pie fragments in her apron, Kate set off as she did every day, down Bankside, past the water mill on the river at Bank End and into Clink Street.

Men looked at her as she walked past, tall and moving with deer-like precision, her skirt snapping like a flag. She was not beautiful in the pale, plucked fashion of the day, but handsome, like a lovely youth, with a long straight nose and large watchful black eyes. The skin of her hands and face was faintly touched with copper, as she no longer bothered to wear a hat in the sun.

She refused to trouble herself any longer about a great many things. Why waste time fending off small disasters like freckles when the worst you can imagine has already happened?

At the Clink prison, she stooped to pass the apples and broken pies down through the bars to the reaching hands of the debtors locked in the underground cells. They were given no food but what they could pay for, or was brought by their families or by well-wishers like Kate. Some of them starved to death.

'Bless you, mistress. God bless you and keep you out of our company.'

'Amen,' she murmured. She stood up and shook the last crumbs from her apron through the bars. She did not speak to the prisoners.

Others brought food to the prisoners as an act of charity. For Kate, the gift was a preventative charm. As long as she could still give, she felt she had not yet fallen into total ruin.

She was not hard-hearted. On the contrary, her heart felt fragile, always close to tearing. It would hold, so long as she did not wear it out further with everyday use.

Being so close to the Bridge, Kate decided to cross to the City to buy another needle. Her heartbeat quickened. She disliked London Bridge. Going onto it was like entering a deep chasm. She always felt that she must cross quickly before something could happen.

She pushed through the crowds that jammed the narrow roadway. The noise was deafening. On either side, buildings three- or four-storeys high trapped and magnified the racket. In places, these buildings spanned the road entirely, with bridges called *hautpas* creating murky, echoing tunnels beneath. Vendors shouted from the open fronts of their shops. *'What d'you lack? What d'you lack?'* Dogs barked. Buyers haggled. Cattle lowed plaintively as they were driven across to the knives of Smithfield. Their herders bellowed. The hoofs of horses drummed.

Even so, Kate could hear the rush of the falls below her. The tide had just turned. High water was trying to escape downriver through the narrow arches of the bridge, made even narrower by the boat-shaped starlings on which the arches stood.

She wondered if she were the only person in this jostling crowd to feel the wild crashing and tossing beneath their feet. They pretended that the Bridge was an ordinary market street, while under them everything slipped away, out of control.

'What d'you lack? What d'you lack?'

She paused at a mercer's shop to turn over hanks of silver wire and golden threads on the narrow counter that hung out into the road. While the crowds pushed past her, she fingered the hanging stranded silks that framed the shop's open front with rich ochres, blues and reds. But she hadn't brought a sample to match for the right shade of blue silk she needed. She would have to go back and get it.

With relief, she turned to leave, but when a gap between the houses allowed an open view of the river, she forced herself to the wooden rail to look straight down at the turbulent slide of the water into the teeth of the Bridge.

Boatmen, for a wager, sometimes tried to run these falls, ten feet at high water. More often than not, the river split the hulls of their boats then spat up the broken men into the Pool of London as it spat up dead cats and unwanted babes.

A faint sweet stench drifted down from the butchered limbs and severed heads displayed on spikes on the roof of the Great Stone Gate. Upstream, the wakes of hundreds of wherries scratched the smooth, glinting, muscular surface of the Thames before it curved out of sight around the Lambeth marshes. Through her feet, Kate felt the current crashing and tossing below her.

Having tested herself enough for today, she left the rail and walked quickly back towards Southwark and The Bank. She was still in the dark, crowded tunnel beneath the Great Stone Gate when the roadway quivered under her feet. She felt a thud, as if someone had clubbed her.

2

A man lurched into Kate, knocking her off balance. Fine debris rained down from the roof of the tunnel onto her shoulders and head. The people around her seemed to be screaming, but, deafened by the explosion, she heard only a thick roaring in her ears.

A deep internal shift told her that the world had just changed in some significant way, though she did not yet know how. Her mind went blank, while her animal self prepared to survive.

The panic-stricken crowd carried her towards the Southwark end of the bridge. Between the heads in front of her, Kate saw a line of men blocking the way off the Bridge Foot, waving the crowd back.

The front of the crowd stopped and tried to turn. The back of the crowd still piled forward. Crushed between them, Kate struggled to breathe. The currents forced her first one way, then another. In the dark tunnel beneath the Great Stone Gate, she lost all sense of direction. Desperately, she craned her head for a glimpse of light to show her the way off the Bridge.

Someone was clawing at her arm. A terrified face stared up at her wildly then sank out of sight behind some knees. A willow pannier scratched her cheek. Something snagged the back of her hair. The crowd heaved. A thick strand of hair was torn from her scalp.

Then a weight suddenly crushed her left foot and pinned her in place. She began to fall but found herself jammed, half-reclining, between a short fat man who stank of horses and two women who looked as terrified as she was beginning to feel. Their racing heartbeats jolted against her ribs. Their panting breath was hot on her face.

Her hearing returned. Screams began to pound at her ears until the air felt solid with terror.

The weight lifted from her foot. Just as she regained her balance, an elbow knocked the wind out of her. Doubled over, gasping for breath, she felt clawing hands and hot breath on her neck as someone tried to climb up onto her back.

All she could see now were boots. Legs. Skirts. Someone's hand on the ground under a boot. Blood on the ground.

The climber's knee dug into her back. Hands gripped her hair.

Holy Mother Mary, help me!

She imagined falling, her ribs cracking, her skull crushed like that hand. She heaved upright with all her strength, dislodged the climber and pushed between two male backs to try to escape. There she stuck again, lodged against sweating flesh and bone, her nose filled with the sharp stink of panic.

Her waist hurt. At first she thought it was a knife.

Apron strings. Skirt caught.

She forced her hand behind her, found the apron strings, prayed, and pulled. Her apron disappeared, as if it had taken on independent life, slithering through the massed bodies back towards the City. Then she tried to untie the points that fastened the front of her overskirt to her bodice.

Her fingers slipped. She couldn't reach the back ties. Her ribs flattened as her bodice strained backwards, pulled by the yards of heavy wool. Then the string points at the back snapped. She gasped, able to breathe again. But she still could not move. Her skirt still hauled at her ankles. She fumbled in her petticoat placket for the strings of the padded bumroll that made a little ledge of her skirts just below her waist. She yanked.

The curved sausage of wool-stuffed linen slid down her legs. Now as slim and unencumbered as a boy, she stepped out of her skirt and wriggled like a minnow to the front of the heaving mass of bodies.

Two constables had just finished locking a chain across the Bridge Foot. 'Go back! Back!' they shouted. 'No one comes through. There may be more explosions.'

'My house! I must go to my house!' a woman was screaming at the constables.

'No one comes through,' they repeated.

Kate leaned against the wall just inside the Great Stone Gate to catch her breath. The entrance to The Bear Inn was on the Bridge side of the locked chain. The landlord stood in his doorway, gaping along St Olaf's Street. Kate followed his gaze. South of the Bridge, along the river, smoke rose from beyond St Olaf's Dock. In the street she saw a fair head moving quickly away. Then he was gone, swallowed by the smoke before she could cry out his name. She was no longer certain that she had seen him.

While the publican's attention was still on the street, Kate slipped past him into the tavern. The excited patrons jostled at the front windows or tended to those injured in the street by flying splinters and glass.

'An explosion . . .!'

'. . . One of the Bridge House warehouses!'

With a final glance at the distracted landlord, and at his wife who was trying to soothe a screaming child, Kate slipped into the landlord's private chambers at the rear of The Bear.

Their back door led into a tiny passage running between the inn and its adjoining tenements. From the passage, she turned into Bear Alley. Another right turn and she was in the open air beside the river, outside the chain. Her throat felt swollen and dry. Her heart thudded. Her chest was tight. The air she sucked at was full of dust.

She felt very odd. A little shaky. Slightly dreamy, as if someone else had almost died under the feet of the crowd.

A sound like the roaring of the water added its voice to the clamour from the Bridge. She smelled smoke now, and burnt sugar, roasted corn, charred meat, and a faint, nostril-flaring tang like the firing of a gun.

That last smell had conjured up the hallucination of a bright head in St Olaf's Street, she was certain. If she saw him in her dreams at night, why not during the day as well?

In the past two years, ever since he had left for Flanders, she had trained herself not to think of Francis Quoynt. Every morning, her reason erased any dreams of his long, lean warmth, his clever, beautiful hands, his sleepy smile and pale hair as fine as a duckling's down.

But her reason had no defence against the power of a smell.

An erotic perfume. The loss of her maidenhead had smelled of it. Passion had smelled of it. Tenderness had smelled of it. And long hours of intimate talk, imagining a future together. But so, too, had disbelief, humiliation and despair.

Gunpowder.

She sank down onto the top step of some narrow water stairs and embraced her knees with both arms. Her scalp burned where the hair had been torn out. Her foot throbbed. She had lost her shoe. The top of her instep was already turning purple.

She felt urgently for her purse, which had been tied to her belt. It was gone, and two precious shillings with it.

Shoe gone. Apron gone. Overskirt gone. Purse gone. She felt hollow with loss.

She stood up abruptly. The dazed, brittle shell of Kate Peach limped back along the Bank towards her lodgings at The Little Rose, one shoe off and one shoe on, wearing only her bodice and shift. Hobble, hobble. Past The Castle, The Gun, The Antelope, The Bull's Head, and other inns, hostelries, taverns and ordinaries that made up the half-mile or so of the old Southwark stews. Many of them still let out rooms by the hour to trulls and their marks.

Kate looked neither left nor right. In recent years, every crack of space between the inns and every yard behind them had been filled with packed tenements where people slept in heaps and the homeless nested. At this moment, she lacked the strength to meet even one pair of hungry, desperate eyes. Or worse, to see the light of recognition.

'An eager punk!' cried a drunk in delight as Kate passed. 'Half-naked and ready for work. Aren't you cold? Over here! Pretty rabbit. Pretty rabbit. I'll warm you up.'

'Go lick a fig,' said Kate, astonished that she could find words at all.

She wanted only to reach the safe calm of her lodgings. Unlike the smell of gunpowder, no instinct slipped past the guard of reason to warn her that the explosion at Bridge House had just changed the direction of her life.

Like Shelvy Mawes, Kate had stumbled by chance into the first unreadable moments of an intended horror that no one could foresee, because it was still unimaginable.

3

Without Which, Nothing

The unimaginable had so many beginnings that the mind of a single man or woman could not have held them all.

In the first part of the previous century, a now-dead English king began to lust for a court waiting-woman and determined to make his doxie into his second wife. Later, in 1587, a fearful Anglican queen beheaded her dangerous royal Catholic cousin. In 1588, an attacking Spanish fleet fled from English waters in humiliation. Trade treaties, personal ambition, religious fervour, persecution, chance and false promises all played a part.

As with most events, the possible causes unrolled endlessly backwards for at least nine hundred years, as far as a meeting at Whitby where church leaders elected to follow the rule of the Church of Rome. Possible cause multiplied and intertwined into a thorn hedge of reasons. Nevertheless, events could not have unfolded as they did if one particular baby had not been born, twenty-three years before, in a small, isolated castle on the Scottish coast north of Berwick.

'It's a boy, mistress!' said the midwife.

The birthing chamber was barely larger than the gilded four-posted bed that almost filled it. The damask bed-hangings lined with cloth-of-silver made a small inner cave. Shutters covered the high, narrow windows. All light came from the fire and six half-burnt beeswax candles. Under the aromatic fragrance of the rosemary and lavender branches burning on the fire, the air held a metallic tang, like the whites of eggs – the smell of birth.

'A healthy boy.' The midwife kept her back turned on the obscenity of the men in the birthing chamber. A dark-haired English captain, his second-in-command and three armed soldiers.

The young mother lay propped on stained, down-filled pillows in linen cases edged with bands of Italian silk. She was a frail-looking creature beside the heavy, carved oak pillars of the bed. Her blonde hair was dark with sweat, her silk shift damp and bloodied. She reached out for her new son. As she bent to kiss the damp feathers of his hair, her eyes were hard with thought. She could hear, faintly, the sound of splintering wood.

On the floor below, English soldiers were prising the walnut panelling from the stone walls, pulling down the tapestries and slitting open the hems. They gutted feather beds and pillows and waded through the snowdrifts of feather and down to break open locked coffers and slice the painted leather panels of the antechamber.

They were not looters. This was a systematic search. The Englishmen did not know what they were looking for, nor how large it might be. But they would know when they found it.

During the birth, the dark-haired captain and his men retreated a few feet to the fireplace, but the captain kept his sharp crow-gaze fixed on the bed, as if he feared some trick or substitution. At the midwife's words, he exchanged a look of triumph with the other officer.

The soldiers, sweating in leather jerkins, waited in the

shadows with their swords. Bloodied rags filled a bowl on the floor beside the bed.

After cutting the cord, the midwife laid a shawl around the young woman's shoulders so that she could put the child to her breast without further exposing herself to male eyes. The woman kept her own eyes on her new son, but her head and neck were braced as if against an executioner's sword. The only sounds were the snap of the fire and the child's suckling.

There was a sudden knock at the door. The woman lifted her head like a deer hearing the hunt. One of the soldiers pulled the midwife away from the bed and another seized the waiting woman who had been helping her.

A jubilant searcher entered. 'We have it! It is hers. Our proof!'

'Let me see!' The captain snatched the letter . . . or the jewel . . . or the signet . . . whatever the newcomer held. He sighed with voluptuous relief.

'Give me the child now, mistress.' He stepped towards the bed.

She made a noise low in her throat and pushed the baby's face into the softness of her breast so that he could not breathe.

'Give him to me! He'll be looked after like a king, I swear.'

She forced her son's head against her body with both hands as if trying to press him back inside her.

With an oath, the English captain leapt forward, hauled her head back by the hair and cut her throat with his sword. At the same time, the soldiers cut those of the waiting woman and the midwife.

4

When news of the explosion reached him, one man, unlike Kate Peach, did feel the possibility of horror quiver in his bones. Paying attention to such quivers was part of what he did.

He was a small man with a twisted back, forty-two years old but scarcely taller than a ten-year-old child. In the Palace of Whitehall in London, he perched on a specially raised stool, hunched over a heavy oak writing table, gazing with opaque eyes at the silver-mounted goose-quill pen he turned in stubby fingers. A blank sheet of paper lay before him.

England was ruled from Whitehall, whatever the Members of Parliament who sat upriver at Westminster Palace might wish to believe. Whitehall was a jumble of old buildings on the north bank of the Thames – apartments, offices, gardens, orchards, kitchens, turreted gateways, great halls, public thoroughfares and a cockpit. It also housed James Stuart, England's new Scottish King. And this small figure on the stool, weighed down by an old-fashioned gown of black silk velvet, was the most powerful man in England after the King.

Robert Cecil, recently made first Earl of Salisbury, was the English Secretary of State and the most successful surviving member of England's leading political dynasty. His father, Lord Burghley, who had been the First Minister and most trusted confidant of the previous ruler, Elizabeth Tudor, had overlooked a handsome first son in order to groom this twisted little second son as his political heir. After Burghley's death, Cecil had served Elizabeth as loyally as his father had done.

At the same time, he also began secret dealings with her most likely successor, James VI of Scotland. When Queen Elizabeth died, Cecil smoothed the way for James and his followers into their new kingdom, which did not entirely welcome the invasion of barely intelligible Scottish barbarians.

Some men called Cecil 'The Deep Dissembler'. Others used even less flattering names. The King called Cecil 'my little beagle', jovially, with an implied pat on the head, as if to deny how much he depended on his First Minister's quiet murmurs into the royal ear. Meanwhile, courtiers whispered that Cecil was the true ruler of England.

Now, Cecil's quick intelligence had already assessed the first vague reports of the morning's explosion. The details lacked substance. The rigour of his mind demanded proof. It takes at least three points to define the direction of a line, and he wanted that third point.

After almost fifty years of war with the Catholic powers on the Continent, England was at last at peace. But after the truce, secret wars continued. One assumed nothing.

Robert Cecil had armies of secretaries to write letters for him, but this letter he had to write himself. If you trust no one, no one can betray you.

He dipped his quill into the silver-rimmed pot of oak-gall ink.

'To Francis Quoynt, The Younger, who was lately in Flanders . . .'

5

After eleven hours in the saddle, Francis Quoynt arrived at Kingston-upon-Thames.

He was wet, tired and in a vile humour. The bay gelding he had exchanged for his own large grey mare in Horsham was muddy to the saddle girth. His boots and breeches were caked.

It was about what he might have expected of a journey that was unwanted, unforeseen, and unexplained. He still could not think why the English Secretary of State had asked for him and not for his father.

'He took no chance of getting the wrong one,' Boomer had said tartly when he saw the letter. Once such a letter would have come for Boomer Quoynt. Now it came for his son.

When Cecil's letter arrived by messenger the night before, Francis had been on the beach secretly testing a new design for a rocket. Far enough from Powder Mote for it to be a secret from his father, at least. Explosives did not lend themselves to absolute secrecy.

As a wave thudded onto the shale at his feet, he watched the streak of light climb the night sky. Held his breath for the decisive heartbeat of silence while the shell decided whether to accept the fire or fall back to earth, dark and silent, pregnant with an unborn explosion.

A sun leapt out of the darkness with a burst of heavenly light barely imaginable in the shadowed human world.

YES!

The explosion echoed off the Downs. The stars from his rocket fell like hot snow. The air around him reeked of burnt gunpowder.

He was absolutely happy.

Wiping his palms on the thighs of his breeches, he listened to the steady heartbeat of the sea and the startled gulls that wheeled above his head.

Only birds screamed. Not horses or men. Not women, nor children. Not pigs, sheep or dogs. This rocket had destroyed neither houses nor lives. It had not peeled off men's skins nor cooked their eyes like hard-boiled eggs. No walls or hostile armies had crumbled.

This is perfect joy, he thought with amazement.

He had bred that heavenly fire. He had shaped that constellation. He felt as God must have felt at the Creation.

'Use more charcoal next time,' called his father's voice unexpectedly out of the darkness. 'Flash wasn't bright enough. And you packed some of the stars too close to the bursting charge.'

Boomer Quoynt's great bulk stood silhouetted against the pale chalk cliff.

'What the devil brings you all the way down here at this hour?' Francis demanded. They both knew that attack was the best defence. With both of them now unemployed after the truce with Spain, they could not afford to burn up precious ingredients merely to feel joy. Francis wondered whether the older man's expert eye had detected the use of the last of their Muscovy rosin. 'Are you spying to see if I learned bad habits while abroad?'

'Don't be an ass, France,' said his father. 'No whorehouses in Brighthelmstone.' He began to pick his way back across the boulder-strewn beach to the bottom of the cliff path. 'Where's your horse? You'd best come back to Powder Mote.'

The beach pebbles clattered in pursuit of retreating waves. The rigging of the beached hoggies rattled a syncopated rhythm. A sheep bleated far up on the downs.

The sounds of peace, thought Francis.

Peace was wasted on most people. He wanted to stay there all night. With no walls around him, no death, no fear. And the smell of only the sea.

'England's at peace,' said Francis. 'Why would anyone need a military firemaster?'

Boomer stretched out his hand for the letter and tilted it towards the firelight. 'I've never liked any reason they give for calling us in peacetime. Perhaps he's heard how prettily you sing and dance and wants to corrupt you into a courtier.'

Francis, who rated himself as a clumsy, paddle-footed clot at dancing, and not much better at singing, took back the letter with a dark look. He read it a last time to memorize the contents, then stooped to throw it into the fire. The firelight turned his ice-pale hair to a warm gold.

'Well,' said Boomer. His thoughtful gaze made Francis feel like his eight-year-old apprentice again, not like a man who had just commanded his own men for two years in the Low Countries. 'A Quoynt is summoned to fly with the eagles again. You must have kept your nose cleaner than I ever did.'

The two fair-haired, long-limbed giants stood side by side near the fire in the great dusty hall, watching Cecil's letter burn. In body, except for the twenty-four years between them, they might have been twins. They were so different in nature, however, that they sometimes stared at each other with the mutual incomprehension of a New World explorer meeting an Algonquin chief.

'Cecil's too small,' Boomer said at last. 'Never trust a small man.'

'No, sir!'

'I'm in earnest.'

'Yes, sir.'

'Why does your civility sometimes make me want to clout you?'

'I couldn't say.'

'Oh, go jerk your yard!'

Francis had been back less than a week and they were already at each other again, the father and son, carrying in their blood not only the height and fair complexion of ancient Viking raiders but something of their flinty, war-like male purpose.

When Francis returned to Powder Mote after his two years in Flanders, he had found the world of the estate very small, the house in need of repair, and his father a little changed. A strange new angry Boomer seemed at times to creep into his father's head, as if Boomer's nightmares had begun to possess his waking self.

His father refused to speak of it. Would not even admit that he dreamed, though he had shouted loudly enough to wake Francis twice since his return.

Thinking about his father's decline made Francis even more uncomfortable than the mud and rain. But so many hours in the saddle gave him little else to do but to think.

His father, also christened Francis, like his own father and grandfather before, from a dynasty of firemaster Quoynts. His father, who had not been called to London. A vast monument of a man. Methodical. Unshakeable. Once the trusted confidant of generals. Once the supreme master of that dangerous lady of the battlefield: gunpowder. A man whose skills had shaped both the outcome of wars and his son's future, until he had one accident too many.

Francis knew that he could never match his father at his best. But, far worse, he was no longer certain that he wanted to.

Francis already had his own nightmares.

Asleep, only two nights before, he had watched his hand burn. His large palm and long, scarred fingers wore a glove of fire. The flames were thick and blue at their roots, stumpy and orange at the tips, like *aqua vitae* flickering over a pudding.

He plunged his hand into the sea. The fire kept burning.

With growing terror, he plunged his hand into the sea again.

Still the hand burned. He could not remember how to put out the flames.

He saw now, as he rode towards Kingston with water dripping off his hat brim and puddling inside his boots, that his dream was a distorted memory from Flanders. The severed hand and forearm of someone caught in one of his blasts, burning amidst the rubble.

Fire. Tunnels. Wormholes. Tight, enclosed spaces. The world of the sapper and of the firemaster who commanded him.

As a large man, Francis had always disliked small places. In the last months before the truce, he had found it harder and harder to steel himself to crawl through siege tunnels to place his own charges, even though he employed miners to dig the things.

But what else could he do? Civilian coal-mining? Blasting out cellars to store turnips?

Along with the disquiet you would expect when about to meet England's most powerful man, Francis felt a cautious excitement. In his head, again and again, he went over his father's final warning. Not for the warning itself but for the words that came with it.

'You've had courage to spare, ever since you could walk,' Boomer had said as Francis mounted to leave. 'But Robert Cecil is dangerous in a way you're not accustomed to.'

In twenty-seven years, his father had never before told him that he was courageous.

'Cecil was betrayed by Nature,' Boomer went on. 'Born so small and twisted, he has had to win everything by his wits. Even his own father's backing. Whereas you, my son, were blessed beyond reason by Nature, in every part. And you've wits enough, but they've never been honed by necessity like his.'

'Sir . . .'

Boomer raised a silencing hand. 'You may be able to bring down a city wall almost as well as I ever did, but you're too honest. That little man can tie truth into knots and convince others they see a straight line.'

Francis still reeled. '. . . *courage to spare* . . .' '. . . *blessed beyond reason* . . .' Such compliments were proof indeed that his father was not entirely himself.

Or that he was very afraid for Francis. Which was also unlike him.

Whispers had once accused Boomer of treasonous Catholic sympathies. For a mercenary, it was said, he showed too much fervour for certain causes, like that of Mary Stuart. But even if these stale rumours had shaken themselves awake again, Francis could see no reason why such sins, even if real, should be visited on the son when the father still lived.

Cecil just might offer him escape from the holes in the roof and the overgrown, suffocating ivy of Powder Mote. And by calling Francis to London, Cecil also gave him the opportunity to look for Kate Peach and learn whether she would still speak to him.

Boomer was right to say that his son had courage to spare.

Francis lived by tweaking the tail of a monstrous, capricious beast. But he had not yet learned to fear politicians.

The landlord of The Trout came out into the drizzle to welcome Francis as if he were royalty, with promises of hot mutton stew and a warm dry bed. The gelding would be groomed and returned safely to Horsham.

Francis nodded at the other drinkers in the inn as he passed through on the way to his chamber. The magic wand of Cecil, he thought, as he stretched his aching back. A fire burning in the grate. Clean windows. And the bulge of warming bricks under the fine wool coverlet on the bed. Altogether cleaner, warmer and in better repair than his own sleeping chamber at home at Powder Mote. Francis went back downstairs to dry out and eat the promised stew.

If his mood had been lighter, he might have been quicker to read the signs. After years of flirting almost daily with death, he generally sensed at once when something was wrong.

Francis pulled off his boots and gave them to a boy to clean. Then he crossed in his stocking feet to the fireplace to offer his breeches to the heat of the fire. Only then did he look again at the three men drinking at a table nearby.

Ordinary enough, on first glance, in patched wool and leather jerkins, like farmers or rural tradesmen. But their faces held suppressed anger and their eyes were bleak.

Francis looked at their hands, the breadth of their shoulders, their boots, and redefined them as unemployed soldiers who had sold their gear for bread.

One of them stared curiously, which was only to be expected when a stranger arrived. But the other two pretended at first not to see him. Then they looked, but quickly looked away again. Francis was certain that they had been expecting him.

The only other guest was a man who sat alone against the far wall with his head down.

Francis nodded and spread his cloak on a bench to dry. He sat.

'You're a big 'un,' said the man in the middle. 'Do you think you're any good in a fight?'

Straight in, thought Francis. No time even to wash the mud from my mouth. He smiled up at the serving girl who brought him his mug of beer.

'I know I am,' he said. 'But feel no need to prove it.' He raised his cup to the three men in a friendly fashion. 'Unless provoked.'

They stared back in silence.

Francis sat quietly, waiting. He was used to challenges from smaller men with something to prove. But this challenge had come too soon. And these were not small men.

'Your bread, sir.' The girl smiled again sweetly, as women generally smiled at Francis. He watched her disappear through the scullery door.

'Keep your eyes off that.' The man in the middle again.

'Looking is free,' Francis said mildly. He could not decide whether the single man by the wall was one of them or not.

The girl reappeared with a wooden bowl.

'Hey, doll,' said the youngest of the three men. 'Give us something nice and juicy, too. I'm sure there's enough to go around.'

The girl flushed and went quickly to the fireplace where she stooped to scrape down the stew from the sides of the earthenware stewpot. Francis glanced again at the single man by the wall. He was staring into his ale pot.

'Mind your tongue,' said Francis. 'She's not a greasy London blowse.'

'Oooh,' said the man in the middle. 'We got us a lah-di-dah messewer come to teach the ignorant country folk how to behave.'

'When they need it. But if you're ignorant country folk, I'm a camel.'

The man pushed himself to his feet, wavering as if drunk. His friends sat up alertly.

'You gelded dandiprat . . .!' He sounded like a bad actor reciting his lines.

Francis readied himself, but the man veered away to the girl at the fireplace, grabbed her and began to fumble up under her skirts. 'By your kind leave, messewer. May I do this?'

The girl exclaimed angrily and dropped the stewpot. As it smashed on the hearth, Francis lunged. Just as the man dropped the skirt and began to rise behind the swinging blow he had intended all along, Francis seized him from behind in a ferocious embrace. He let the man's swing turn them both around.

'Open the door,' he told the girl.

When she did so, Francis heaved the man out into the dark rain. The girl slammed the door with feeling.

'That should cool him down.' Francis walked slowly back to his table, smiling at the man's two companions.

They stared back, on their feet but uncertain now that their leader was gone. After a moment, they sank back again onto the bench. The fourth man now watched with interest, arms folded over his chest.

Francis sat with his back to the door and eyed the two henchmen speculatively. He had calmed enough drunken soldiers to know the smell of boozy breath. The man he had thrown out into the rain was not as drunk as he pretended.

'More ale?' he asked.

The girl nodded and wiped her eyes.

'And some for my friends there.'

She gave them a look of furious scorn but vanished into the scullery. When she had brought the wine and gone again,

Francis lifted his cup to the other two men. Then he set his cup aside, pushed back his empty bowl and took his tobacco pouch from a sack beside him on the bench. He rummaged again and set two small wooden boxes on the table.

He unwrapped a white clay pipe with a larger-than-usual bowl. 'Would one of you be good enough to hand me a light?'

The younger man leapt up to bring him the bowl of coals from the hearth below a pipe rack. He set the bowl at Francis's elbow, where he continued to hover, as Francis had foreseen, just a little too close.

'You're far too kind.' Francis gave him a gentle smile, but his back stiffened. He felt the brush of cold air on his neck.

The eyes at the next table flicked towards the door, then locked back onto Francis.

Slowly and deliberately, he tamped down into the pipe bowl a small paper-wrapped parcel from one box and then several pinches from the other. With the little tongs resting on the edge of the bowl, he picked up one of the red-hot coals. He watched the two men while he fussed at the pipe bowl with his thumb.

Suddenly, they stiffened. The one still at the table opened his mouth in anticipation.

Francis touched the coal to his pipe. He flicked the coal into the face of the man at his elbow, turned on his stool and threw the pipe. There was a blinding flash and the thump of an explosion. Cups rattled on the tables. The man behind him, sword raised to strike, was enveloped in smoke and flames.

He screamed. His sword clattered on the stone floor. Francis swung his cape. The landlord burst through the scullery door, without coat or shoes, his daughter at his heels.

Almost hidden by a cloud of acrid smoke, Francis rolled his attacker on the floor inside the damp cape, beating him with his flattened hand far harder than required to put out the flames. Then he pulled his shaken attacker into a sitting position and brushed away flakes of charred wool.

'Next time, I'll throw it at your face.' Francis turned to the landlord. 'He'll need ointment of lard and marigold for his burns.'

'How did you know he was there?' the younger man quavered.

Francis curled his lip. 'I smelled him.'

When Francis thought to look, the single man had gone.

He sat awake all night in his chamber, back against the wall, loaded pistol on his knees. A little after dawn, he got up, changed into his best suit of clothes and gathered his belongings.

Downstairs, he found the landlord stirring up the fire. The silent onlooker of the night before was already eating his breakfast of watered ale and bread.

'Do you know those men?' Francis asked the landlord, who refused payment for the lodgings.

'Never seen them before.' The landlord kept a wary distance, and pushed away Francis's offered coins as if he thought they too might explode. 'How did you do that last night?'

'It's merely an amusing trick.' Francis glanced out of the window at the Thames, looking for the boat promised in Cecil's letter. Then he stepped out of the smell of stale ale and urine in the corners of the inn into the stillness of the fresh riverside morning.

The rain of the previous day had gone wherever English rain went to lurk in ambush. The sun still struggled to free its roots from Kent. To the northwest, across the Thames, the eagerly ornate, twisted red-brick chimneys of Hampton Court were just catching the first light. The river, still in shadow, ran pewter-coloured and sullen below the bank.

No wartime ambush ever looked more innocent, thought Francis.

In the short time he had been back home at Powder Mote before Cecil's letter arrived, he had imagined that after two years of fighting abroad he would find himself at a loss, a military man without a part to play in the new English peace.

After another moment of watching the sun seep down the Hampton Court chimneys, he went back into the inn to retrieve his sword, left with the landlord for safe-keeping. Protocol forbade the wearing of swords within Whitehall. On the other hand, on the evidence of last night, a man would be a fool to go unarmed in this new peaceable England to which he had returned.

As Francis emerged from the inn again, the silent man from the night before fell in step beside him. 'We're moored just over there.' The man pointed at a small dock a little way downstream. 'I'm your boatman.'

6

Back in her lodgings after the explosion, Kate washed her hands and face in a basin, then leaned forwards to comb the debris out of her abundant black hair.

She put down the comb and stood staring at nothing. She suddenly needed to lie down. Just for a moment.

She woke the next day. The sun was already in the west. Scales of light reflecting from the river quivered on her wall. A mosquito from the marshes crouched on her bare arm. Her slap left a streak of blood on her skin.

She swung herself upright. There was work to do. No time for feebleness.

'Ough!' She grunted with pain as her injured foot touched the floor. Though her foot was now so black and swollen that the toes looked to her like little teats on a cow's udder, it took her weight. Just.

She hopped to her stool and laid her father's leather apron over her thighs. Then she remembered that she never got as far as buying another needle.

She sat looking at the two halves of the broken needle, unable to move. Her world here in this room seemed frozen as if by a deathly spell, while outside her window, boats still bumped against the water stairs, wherry men shouted for customers, dogs barked, and drunks sang out their delight at a fine evening.

'Mooncalf!' She slapped herself lightly several times on both cheeks. She did not need a new needle in order to cut out one of the other pairs of gloves. But she still could not move. She felt a stab of fear that she would stay frozen like this forever, unable ever again to rejoin the everyday world, which felt so impossibly far away.

With effort, she slid down onto the floor and pushed aside a woven reed mat in the middle of the room. With the point of her leather knife, she levered up one of the planks to reveal a secret hiding place under the floor. From this hiding place she lifted out a heavy, leather-bound Missal with brass edges and pressed her hand to the first page, over a list of names.

There they all were. Proof of a former world whose reality she had begun to doubt. With dates of birth and death. The names of her family, a long line of Peaches. And there she was, tied onto the end, flapping like a kite. The only one still flying.

Here were her parents. Father. Mother. And her older brother Luke and younger sister Anne. Only in the Missal could she still find them. Their bodies were lost in an unknown mass grave. Kate herself had written in the dates of their deaths, as there had been no one else left to do it.

Her father's narrow-shouldered handwriting recorded the date of her own birth: '*10 June 1581, a daughter sent by God . . .*'

Katherine Mary Apollonia Peach. Daughter of Master James William Peach, a glover, and Mistress Barbara Martha Peach. Born in Stokewell. Still alive and perplexed as to why.

She stopped her thoughts there. To remember more was still intolerable, even after more than a year. She reached down into the secret hole for her rosary, also salvaged from her former life.

Holy Mother, she thought. Hold me steady. You're all I have left. She was certain that no male deity would understand or forgive her present complex state of sin, both theological and personal.

'*Ave Maria . . .*'

Hail Mary . . . The familiar pattern of the words carried her to another quieter place, where she could escape from Bridge House explosions and memories of Francis Quoynt. From grief, regrets and repentance for her sins. Even from Hugh Traylor, to whom she was supposed to be grateful, and who imagined that she was present inside her body while he was on top of it.

By the time she had recited a half-rosary, that is to say, seventy Aves and seven each of Paternosters and Glorias, she felt a little more like herself. She kissed the rosary, wrapped it again in her mother's best handkerchief and hid it far back under the floor.

The Missal and that small cross, with its ivory image of the crucified Christ, were dangerous. Even owning them put her life at risk. Owning them made her a secret traitor in her own country. Not even Francis had known she was a Catholic. Not even when they were lovers.

Like all English Catholics, Kate was in an impossible bind. If they were to be good Catholics, they must fight for their faith against the Anglican Church and the English Crown, as ordered by the Pope in Rome. If they were loyal English subjects, they betrayed their faith.

The rest of her secret hoard was no less dangerous but almost as comforting. Crossing her legs to make a nest of her shift, she emptied a heavy leather pouch. The coins fell into her lap with a satisfying clatter until they weighed down her shift like a curled-up cat. She stirred them with her fingers, relishing the sound and their dull, cool gleam.

Groats, pennies, tuppences, thrupences, sixpences and

shillings, of base metal and silver. She had found or earned them all.

'Two groats . . . eight . . . thirteen,' she murmured, counting out the coins with long slim fingers. 'One . . . three . . . twelve shillings. Thirteen. And seven.'

She set aside a pile of coins to change for a single gold angel. All that silver in exchange for a single coin the size of a large button. Less satisfying than a lap full of silver coins, but easier to hide.

Kate had seventy-three pounds in gold under her floor, from the labour and scrimping of the past year. But she needed nine hundred pounds to escape her present life. Money to pay for the journey itself, then for a small cottage in Sussex or Lancashire . . . anywhere far enough from London to escape from Hugh Traylor. And for food and coal and all the small expenses you don't remember.

She would also need two gowns: one of plain wool for every day to replace the one she had lost, and one for Sundays, like any respectable woman. Black gowns.

Kate was resolved never again to be trapped by need and gratitude, nor to be beholden to anyone. And there was only one way in which a single female could live her own life with freedom and dignity. Kate meant to become a widow, but without the inconvenience of first having been a wife. With black satin at ten shillings a yard, however, and eighteen yards needed for a gown, plus trimmings and buttons, that was nine pounds just to start.

She reached for a shilling to resume counting. Then she paused again, too weary to lift the coin. Eight hundred and twenty-seven pounds still to find. At that rate, it would take thirteen more years of stitching and scrimping and searching for dropped coins at the water steps to buy back her self-respect and try to save her soul.

In thirteen more years she would be thirty-seven. She

would have forgotten what it was to be respectable. And clean. The grime would no longer wash off her hands. In thirteen years she might not care any longer, and that would be the end of her.

Setting aside the uncounted coins in her lap, she limped to the window, opened the casement and leaned on the sill. The surface of the Thames flashed. Broken light from the setting sun bobbed above a deeper layer of sharp-cornered shadows. Swarms of wherries carried early evening passengers between the City and Southwark, or plied up and down the banks.

She breathed in and waited for the river to lift her spirits.

The air carried wood and coal smoke, stale ale from The Little Rose tavern below her, the stink of night-soil heaps and of sewage in the drainage channels. Rank barnyard odours wafted from the Bear Garden three houses away. Under it all lay the smell of the river. An interesting emptiness tinged around the edges with fish, salt and rotting weed. An emptiness huge enough to suck up all the noise, stink and misery around it and wash them away to dissolve in the unimaginable vastness of the sea.

Kate tucked a loose strand of dark hair behind her ear and leaned on her elbows again, looking down on the tops of the hats and heads in the street two floors below her. Pleasure-seekers of all sorts milled along the Bankside.

Suburb sinners. The world Kate refused to accept as her own.

Men seeking whores. The whores who grasped their sleeves. Men wanting to drink. Or to eat. Or to gamble. Or play bowls. Or smoke in a tavern. Or squeeze up against a woman in the crowd. Or fumble a mistress in the Paris Gardens. Or merely to walk beside the water.

You would think that the horror of yesterday morning had never occurred.

A young whore of barely fourteen years bumped into a man headed into The Little Rose. The girl smiled apologies into the man's eyes while she readjusted the tilt of her bosom and tugged his collar straight. Meanwhile, her nipper sliced the man's belt and made off with both dagger and purse.

Farther down the Bankside, men and women alike shoved and jostled out of the Bear Garden. It's Wednesday, Kate thought with astonishment. She had lost track of the days and slept through the bear-baiting. She must go at once to see if Meg had survived the afternoon.

But before she could move from the window, she saw him in the street. He had turned towards a clamour of oaths and cheers at the water stairs, where two racing wherries had arrived at the same time. The boats rocked dangerously as their passengers competed to vault ashore first. A man fell on the slippery steps. Two men tried to help him to his feet. Others shouted instructions or jeered from the bank.

Kate went cold. Before she could pull back, the man looked up at her window and saw her.

Hobbling, she rushed to hide the money. Scooped up the coins, poured them back into the leather pouch, dropping them in her urgency.

Coins rolled into corners.

No time to chase them. His footsteps mounted the stairs. She stuffed the pouch back under the floor. Replaced the loose board. Pulled the woven matting back into position.

The barred door rattled. Then a fist pounded.

'I know you saw me, bitch. Open the door.'

She dived after a glint beneath her stool, a sixpence. Then spied another by the door. And on the far side of the room, a shilling leaned on edge against the table leg.

'Open the door, do you hear!'

No time for the shilling.

With the two sixpenny pieces hidden in her sweaty fist, Kate lifted the iron bar to admit Hugh Traylor, her protector and some-time lover.

7

'What kept you so long?' He pushed past her, bringing with him a startling blast of rage. He glared around the room then opened the door to the tiny closet that made up the rest of her lodgings.

'I'm not hiding another man,' said Kate.

From the window, Traylor studied the street. Kate had never before seen him looking so ruffled and askew. So unlike his usual sleek and glassy self.

Nor did his abruptness feel like one of his usual games of cat-and-mouse.

She eyed him with apprehension. At least he did not want sex (Praise God!). She always knew as soon as he entered. In any case, it had been clear to her for some time that he now went elsewhere for most of his chilly pleasures. His chief uses for her were otherwise.

'Any letters for me today?' he asked absently.

'I would have said at once.'

He left the window and circled the room with an agitation unlike his usual sharp-edged self-possession.

When they first met, she had thought him handsome, with dark, cool good looks. He was of her height but outweighed her, a man at the end of his prime but not yet out of it. Under his plain black wool doublet and breeches he was thickening through the chest and belly, but he still had the broad shoulders and well-muscled arms and legs of a swordsman. His dark beard and hair were cut short, framing a square face with the assessing eyes of a hungry carnivore.

'Where's your gown?' he demanded suddenly. 'You look like a whore on display in a bawdy-house.'

'It's somewhere in the City, along with my best apron. I lost them both on the Bridge yesterday morning.'

'You were on the Bridge during the explosion?' he asked sharply.

She flinched under the sudden force of his gaze. 'Under the Great Stone Gate.'

'Do any rumours say what caused it?'

Kate shrugged, puzzled by his interest. 'Most opinion favoured an explosion in one of the riverside warehouses.'

He stared at her for a long time, deep in his own thoughts once more.

'Do you mean to give me wine, or not?' he asked abruptly.

Kate went obediently into the little closet where she kept her wine and glasses, making certain that the door was securely propped open before she went in. She had found that she could drive him mad by submitting when he wanted a fight.

Besides providing sex on increasingly rare occasions, Kate also ran errands for Hugh Traylor. She passed on letters that were shoved under her door at night. She exchanged money, foreign for English and vice versa. She collected packets and parcels and held them until he came for them. And, as ordered, she kept her mouth shut.

Just once, wondering what she was embroiled in, she had asked him why he insisted on absolute secrecy. To which he replied that unless she wanted to live on the streets, she should do as she was told, and keep both her mouth and her legs closed.

In exchange, he gave her lodgings at a time when London was flooded with refugees from the wars abroad and from the English countryside. He protected her from arrest and fines for working illegally, outside the Glovers' Guild. And as the purported mistress of a man who clearly had money and influence, she could live alone in reasonable safety, in a world of whores, thieves, players, beggars, homeless soldiers, sailors and rogues of every sort.

It had come about slowly. A year and a half ago, in the first chill of autumn, she had arrived in London from Stokewell, wearing her dead brother's clothes and carrying nothing but her father's tools, two Venetian glasses, the rosary, the Missal, and a ragged gown. She had nothing more. Nothing to trade on. Nothing to barter. No money, family or maidenhead. The previous month was still a large dark hole in her thoughts. She was not yet strong enough to peer into it, and feared that terrible things might begin to slither out when she was not paying attention and let down her guard.

In Southwark, Kate soon saw by example, on every street corner and up every alley, that she had something to trade after all, if only she would. Then she met Mistress Mary Frith – if the title 'Mistress' could be applied to a woman who stood two yards high and always wore men's clothing. Mary also had a face like a loaf of unbaked bread and the small peering eyes of a bear.

To say that they 'met' would be imprecise, however. Mary accosted Kate, who had dug in with her few possessions under a bush in the Paris Gardens, praying to snatch a little sleep without being robbed. She had already lost her purse, the gown and her family's little silver-gilt patten that held the consecrated host during Mass.

Mary took her into the big house, which had once been the manor house before the Paris Gardens became a brothel. 'Look at you!' exclaimed Mary through a cloud of pipe smoke.

'Tits like lovely little melons. Lips made for kissing. Let's have a gawp at your legs . . . No?' She refilled Kate's wine cup and pushed more bread and an apple across the table. 'No matter. After a good bath, duck, we'll make your fortune.'

Surprisingly, Mary did not throw Kate out when she declined to have her fortune made. When Kate also refused to sell any of her father's glove-making tools, Mary offered a red callused hand.

'What could you do for this great paw of mine? You can eat and sleep here for a time for the price of a pair of the finest gloves. I'll swear not to report you to the Glovers' Guild.'

While Kate was making the gloves, carefully not thinking how she had once helped her father, Mary tried several more times to induce her to work as a whore. 'It's a pity I can't change your mind, doll,' she said at last, when the gloves were done and declared to be finer than those of an archbishop. 'But as you're so set on respectability, we must find you a respectable man.'

Mary then introduced Kate to Hugh Traylor. A London merchant and widower, she said. She did not quite say that the man was looking for a new wife, but the unspoken words somehow arrived in Kate's mind as if she had actually heard them.

When she met him, Kate saw the dark good-looks, the still-lean body, and the confident air of a man who knew what he was about. From shyness, fear and need, she did not look clearly into his eyes until it was too late.

It was common enough for older men to marry younger second or third wives when the first had died in childbirth. Duty and mutual interest were firmer ground for marriage than fragile love. Kate had been a dutiful daughter and knew that she could be a dutiful wife.

When she learned better, she settled for being Traylor's

mistress. She was trapped. She hoped that the Holy Mother might understand that one man was less wicked and far safer than many. She considered running away to turn serving maid, but after talking to a few young women in that situation, she learned how vulnerable they were to the fumbling of the master or his sons.

Traylor began to ask her less often for sex and more often for other services, until she began to wonder if the early love-making had not been, for him, chiefly an inconvenience to be got out of the way in order to secure an obedient recruit for his other purposes.

She decided on escape, but on her own terms, not like her dazed flight from Stokewell. So she made illegal gloves and hid gold coins under the floor.

Now, Traylor drained his wineglass, then leaned forward suddenly and picked up the shilling by the chair leg. 'You're careless with your money, Kate. Perhaps I should charge you rent.'

She smiled blandly. 'Then, I would have to charge you for a fuck.'

'But that would make you a real whore.' He bared straw-coloured teeth and tossed the shilling at her. 'Catch.'

She reached and missed. In silence, they watched the coin roll into the fireplace.

'Tut,' he said. 'Clumsy girl. Do sit down. You're too tall to hover. Puts me off my drink.'

She poured herself a glass of wine, sat on the stool and bent all her attention to the ribbon of red that twisted up inside the stem of her glass from the high-shouldered red base to the clear rounded knob that supported the bowl. It was one of six glasses her father had brought back from a trip to Italy to buy gold and silver thread.

'I have urgent employment for you.'

She raised her eyebrows.

'To arrange a meeting. Discreetly.'

'The dark side of commerce?' she asked lightly.

'An acquaintance of mine wants to meet Francis Quoynt.'

Kate spilled her wine. This is one of his cruel jests, she thought wildly. But she had never told Traylor about Francis. It was hideous coincidence.

She glanced at him from the side of her eye as she wiped the wine from her shift with her handkerchief. He was watching her with suppressed glee.

'Get someone else to arrange the meeting,' she said.

'Because he was once your lover?' He smiled at the expression on her face. 'Surely, you didn't imagine I would take you on without looking into your past?'

Yes, she had been fool enough to imagine exactly that.

'Just this once, Hugh. I've never refused you anything before. You must have other doxies who could arrange the meeting for you.'

'Quoynt is newly back from Flanders,' said Traylor as if she had not spoken. 'Without employment, alas, like so many other poor military fellows now that we're at peace with Spain . . . but perhaps you've already met him again and know all this.'

'I won't do it.'

'Ask for him here in Southwark. The place overflows with unemployed soldiers and other rogues. Or he may have skulked off to the family estate . . . Powder Mote or some such name . . . near Brighthelmstone, in Sussex, I believe. It can't be beyond you to find him.'

Again, Kate shook her head.

Traylor stood up. 'Overcome your wounded pride, my sweet. Past history will make your task easier. Guilt should make the man feel obliging – so long as he needn't trouble himself too much.' He smiled at her with satisfaction. 'If you're a good girl, I might even give you money for a new gown.'

With rising fury, Kate understood that he had not chosen her for this task by chance. He will have to do without the pleasure of humiliating me this time, she thought. Of course he knew about Francis!

Kate had learned to escape Traylor by withdrawing into her secret thoughts. Unfortunately, he saw this escape as a stimulating challenge and tracked her like a hunter, reading every broken twig and overturned pebble. She felt him always there behind her, sharp-eyed and inexorable, waiting for a moment of weakness to show him where to close his jaws again.

'Think, Kate. You've much to lose. How will you make gloves if I withdraw my influence? How will you pay rent if I turn you out?' The cold fury with which he had arrived began to edge back into his voice. 'By trading on your bottom on the streets? Assuming that you can find a vacant rat-hole, with all the bumpkins and foreign rabble now crowding into London.'

'Turn me out. I'll take my chances.'

'Find Francis Quoynt,' he snapped, games over. 'Arrange the meeting. But be warned. Soldiers bring back the most vile diseases. Don't be tempted to revisit old joys. I'll most likely kill you if you give me the clap.'

'How dare you!' Provoked past control at last, she rose to her feet. 'You can spy on me and sniff out my past but I will not let you use it to torment me. I will not go looking for Francis Quoynt.'

'You'll do as I say!'

'Not this time.'

Traylor grabbed her by the arms. Kate closed her eyes against a blow. He could not touch her. Only her outer shell.

She could smell him, chilly and metallic like a fish.

'One last time, will you do as I tell you?'

'Never.'

Instead of striking, he dragged her across the floor to the little closet, shoved her in and slammed the door.

She never closed the closet door when she was inside. In the darkness, she heard the bar drop. She drew a steadying breath. 'Open the door, Hugh.'

Nothing happened.

She fumbled for the latch handle. Her hand slid over the place where it should be. The latch handle was gone. Traylor had pulled it out of the door.

He knows about Stokewell, too, she thought with despair. Mary must have blabbed.

She pounded on the door with her fists. She would not think how small the closet was. Nor about the dark. She would not remember that other darkness and what had lain hidden in it.

Pass through! Pass through! she ordered herself.

He would open the door any moment and let her out. She would not beg, would not give him the pleasure of seeing her terror.

The closet was six feet long and four feet wide, without a window. The only light was the bright, threadlike outline of the door.

Traylor did not open the door. There was not enough air. She could not breathe.

Pass through. Wait.

Six feet long and four feet wide. More than enough air . . .

Her resolve broke.

'Hugh?'

There was no reply. Then she heard the outer door of her lodgings slam.

'No,' she whispered. She listened, trying to hear over the thudding of her heart. 'Hugh?' she called again.

He had locked her in and left her to die.

Unreasoning terror, which she had held off in the mob,

gripped the back of her neck with icy fingers.

She bruised her fists against the door. Kicked it. Ran at it to try to break it with her shoulder. She sank to her knees, clutching her arm. 'Please!' she begged the silence on the other side of the door. 'Please let me out. Let me out!' She pounded again. 'Please, God. I can't bear it again.'

The air already felt thicker. She would suffocate. He had left her to die . . . They had left her . . .

The dark hole in her thoughts . . . Past and present folded into each other. She was behind the nailed-up door of the Stokewell cottage. She was back in Stokewell amidst the stomach-turning stink of death.

She could not pass through this moment. She was stuck in it, raw and real, in every fibre of her body. She lay flat on the floor and pressed her face to the crack at the bottom of the door where light and air seeped in.

'Please . . . I'll do what you ask.'

The latch rattled as he reinserted the handle.

'What a rare and pleasing sight,' said Traylor when he had opened the door. 'Kate Peach grovelling at my feet.' He reached down and lifted her up. 'Kate . . . sweet Kate. You didn't really think I would leave you in there?' He brushed back her dark dishevelled hair and leaned forward to lick at her tears. 'My own tame virago. My humbled Amazon queen.' Then he led her tenderly to the stool and refilled her wineglass. 'I knew that you could never resist me for long. Drink, there's a good girl.'

He paced the room, watching her as her terror ebbed and her breathing grew less jagged. Kate stared out of the window, groping her way back to the present and fighting off an absurd gratitude that he had opened the door.

'Better now?' he asked after a time. He stood behind her and stroked her hair. 'Like a crow's wing,' he said. 'As dark as your secret heart.' His hands were heavy on her shoulders.

'You'll find Francis Quoynt? I'm leaving London for a few days. I want to hear that it's done by the time I return.'

Kate gave a stiff nod.

'And you'll ensure that it's nothing to do with me?'

She nodded again.

'You think I'm merely tormenting you,' he said gently. 'You'll learn one day that there's good in what I ask of you. We must all put larger purposes before our own petty concerns.'

8

An eye rolled at Boomer's heels like a dog. He tried to ignore it. Had work to do.

Steady with that powder barrel! he said. Up the cliff we go, and into the dark cellars of the castle. Head down, body bent double to fit into the wormholes of underground passages.

The eye was still there, watching brightly.

A newborn baby began to scream . . .

The thin screams faded as Boomer woke.

He sat up, breathing hard, and stared into the darkness at the end of the four-poster bed.

Safe at Powder Mote. Not in Scotland, after all.

No baby neither. Not here. But in Scotland . . . If the child still lived, it would be twenty-three years old.

His large hand slid out to feel the cold sheet beside him. If only my wife were still here, he thought. I could bury myself in her and forget.

He wished he could remember her as well as he did the other one.

Boomer prayed every night for peaceful sleep. He did not presume to hope for good dreams, just oblivion. Awake was almost as bad as asleep. He could still see the three women with their throats cut. The new mother still in her birthing gown. Fine silk, limp and sticky with her blood. A pearl of milk hanging on her breast.

As a soldier, he had seen many terrible things, but those images infected his mind as if he were burning with fever. Such weakness of will infuriated him. He was, after all, a level-headed man gifted with good sense and blessed by a lack of the imagination that so often unsteadied his son. Furthermore, Boomer was accustomed to command and to being obeyed.

But these miasmas from the past defied his robust will. They closed around him like a swarm of hungry flies. Caught him off-guard in his sleep, where good sense and natural authority could not help him.

How swiftly birth and death crash against each other, he thought. With barely a breath drawn between. Poor mother. Poor babe . . .

Boomer felt too tired to get up, but afraid to sleep. Afraid of the crowded darkness in his head. He let his thoughts drift towards the most alluring, if disquieting, presence in that darkness.

Lovely Mary . . . Mary Stuart, Queen of Scotland at the age of six days. Queen of France by marriage at sixteen. Granddaughter of Henry's sister, Margaret Tudor. A Tudor by legitimate descent, with legitimate claim to the English throne. But a Catholic. Which made her England's enemy.

Sweet Lord, but that pussy had been bewitching, he thought. Enemy or not. Made Anne Boleyn look like a squat little toad. And she was the only woman Boomer had ever met who was tall enough to look him in the eye.

He lay back against his pillows again.

Mary had looked him in the eye. More than once.

And how she could look at a man! Made your cock go as stiff as a cudgel, even if she was a queen. Young bloods and ancient gallants alike fell over their feet offering to fight for her cause.

You among them, Boomer. Once.

But then he turned married man and worked for England once again. And Mary had been deposed in Scotland and made a prisoner of the same royal cousin whom her supporters plotted to assassinate.

You poor, silly woman, thought Boomer. To have encouraged those dangerous gawks. What ailed them all, to be so blind?

Elizabeth had signed Mary's death warrant, as politics and reason said she must. Even though they were cousins. Mary's own cousin killed her – and her friends, through their ambition and plotting, sent her straight to a traitor's death on the scaffold. With that lovely long, white neck . . .

Boomer had tried to help keep the pretty head on that neck. And had found himself in Scotland with a coiled fuse slung on his shoulder, laying gunpowder charges in the castle cellars. Knowing nothing yet of the woman in labour on the top floor. Without the least sense of being present at a beginning.

He thought he knew why he was there. A king's cock . . . If you cut through the fine words and theologizing and went back to that beginning, a king's swollen cock had led to Boomer being in that damp, godforsaken place, helping to destroy treacherous Catholic Scots who would ruin Mary by trying to put her on the English throne.

Her great-uncle, that old lecher Henry, had split with the Pope and given England a new Anglican Church, just so he could set aside his true wife and wed the Great Bitch, Anne Boleyn . . . though that was not quite how the new English bishops explained it.

Boomer sighed. Old religion set against the new. So much trouble to make a queen of The Concubine. And for what, in the end?

His thoughts shifted direction seamlessly, as drifting

thoughts do, with no wrenching of logic. He was back in the castle ditch in Scotland, drawing the end of his fuse towards him through the grille over the drain from the castle privies. He would wade through shit if need be but avoided it whenever possible.

A common blue butterfly dipped briefly down into the ditch then hiccupped up again into the vast blue sky. Pink thrift clung in the cracks of the castle wall. Thyme fringed the outer lip of the ditch. The green straps of hart's-tongue ferns crowded the damp earth at the bottom. Then he heard the baby scream as the soldiers carried it away.

Boomer sat up. In the dark, he felt on the floor beside the bed for his clothes. He pissed into the night-soil pot, then dressed and went in search of his boots.

He hoped that striding along the edge of the dark sea would let him escape his dreams. He should have paid them more attention. Only the dreamer in him saw that his past was a slow fuse. Boomer might have taken his eyes off it, but it still burned, closer and closer to the explosive charge.

That night, he was far more interested in what he discovered on the beach.

9

In disbelief, Francis stood in the early evening light on the narrow, sagging jetty where the boatman had left him. The stink of open sewers, salt marsh and rotting weed assaulted his nose. He looked at the small wharves, loading tackle and moored boats in the mouth of the Wandle, one of the many small rivers that fed the Thames just above London. Then he glanced down wryly at his best doublet, donned for Whitehall. He was glad he had decided to bring his sword.

Below the jetty, the water ran as dark as blood with the discharge from a dye-works just upstream. The flat-paddled wheel of a tide mill creaked and dripped on the far bank.

The wherry had disappeared downstream into the Thames. The homeless of London and Southwark had not yet moved into the dark moist crevices between the commercial buildings. A single skiff heaped with firewood set the moored boats rocking gently on its wake as it slid upstream. On the other side of the Wandle a feral cat lay curled on a roof. Otherwise, Francis seemed to be alone in the backside of commerce after the end of the working day.

The only way off the jetty was through a small, silent warehouse. Francis thought once more of the boatman, who had watched the swordsman's rush last night and not shouted a warning.

He sniffed the air for the sharp whiff of men keyed up to attack but smelled only rotting weeds, raw sewage and coal smoke, along with the sharp tang of brazil wood rasped for dye and the chalky dust of ground fuller's earth. It was a stink thick enough to mask the smell of an attacking army.

The little wicket door cut into the larger loading gate of the warehouse opened silently when he pushed it. He swung it back and forth a few more times on its well-oiled hinges. Beyond the door, the warehouse was dark.

Sword in hand, Francis ducked through the little wicket and walked straight into a cold, clammy, yielding wall. He recoiled, gagging on the stench of rotting bark, stale urine and wet sheep.

He felt again. Damp wool. He was in a forest of hanging fabric, length after length of it, newly dyed, draped over ropes strung from wall to wall, stretching from just above his head to the floor.

A dozen men could be hiding there. In the failing light, he would never see a blade thrust through a length of the cloth. And who would notice blood amongst the stains on a dyer's warehouse floor?

'The stairs are against the right-hand wall,' called a voice from above.

The loft of the warehouse was dimly lit by a single window in the gable end. As his head rose above the loft floor, Francis peered cautiously into the gloom.

'Put up whatever weapon you're undoubtedly holding,' said the small figure seated at a table in the otherwise empty room. 'We're alone.'

'My lord,' stammered Francis, trying to make a reverence and sheath his sword at the same time. 'Quoynt,' he added. 'Sir.'

'I had not expected anyone else.' Robert Cecil was a lump

in the dusk, a small irregular bundle in a plain cloak. A wide-brimmed, unadorned sugar-loaf hat sat on the floor beside him. The English Secretary of State perched on a stool like a child, his toes stretched down for balance on the floor.

Robert Cecil, in person. The man his father called The Deep Dissembler. Recently made Lord Salisbury. Second son of the great statesman Lord Burghley, who had been Lord High Treasurer and the old Queen's most trusted confidant.

Why did such a man need to talk to underlings in a place like this? He had secretaries and armies of other creatures to speak for him while he directed his own voice into the royal ear in the comfort of Whitehall.

Yet here he was, unattended, apparently unguarded.

'I don't often meet in such circumstances,' said Cecil, as if reading Francis's thoughts.

Francis swallowed. 'I'm honoured, my lord.'

'You may change your mind.'

'Never, if I can serve you . . .'

Cecil waved an impatient hand. 'I don't meet men in private to play public games. Consider yourself to have performed all the necessary flattery.'

'Consider it done.' However, Cecil had not yet invited him to sit. 'Plain man-to-man, from now on,' Francis added.

There was a brief silence while he felt Cecil weighing his words.

'How did you find the Low Countries when you left them?' Cecil asked at last.

'Uncommonly peaceful, my lord.'

Cecil snorted delicately. He himself had played a large part in achieving the recent treaty with Spain, after years of war and threatened invasions. He steadied himself on his stool by bracing his short arms on either side of him on the table.

Francis glanced at the man's hands, barely larger than those of a child, then quickly looked away.

The intelligent, veiled eyes studied him through the dusk, noting his unsuitable, over-eager court dress. Francis decided to hold the man's gaze rather than appear to stare at the uneven shoulders or the odd face around those eyes. Even a glance at the forehead might possibly offend. He had never before seen the man close to, and the effect was unsettling. The lower part of Cecil's face seemed to have slipped downwards, as if the wax of his modelling had softened. All his features sagged towards the jaw, leaving behind a vast promontory of brow. It would be easy to overlook the eyes.

'Outward shape reflects inward nature,' people said, forgetting to ask themselves why old Burghley might have chosen this twisted second son over his more comely but stupid heir.

'And how is your noted father?' asked Cecil, with what sounded surprisingly like real interest.

Francis weighed Cecil's tone but heard no threat to Boomer. 'Chafing in forced retirement after an accident,' he ventured. After a moment, he added, 'Your own will undoubtedly be more at peace in Heaven.'

'Let me speak for my own father. I know better than anyone that he achieved one or two things in his life.' Cecil shuffled his toes to balance more comfortably on his stool. 'It's our turn now, Quoynt. Your father served mine well, from time to time. Will his son serve me equally well?'

'Try me.'

'The Quoynts are men for hire,' said Cecil appraisingly. 'Do you have true loyalties, Quoynt? Or only to each new paymaster? How do men judge your good faith?'

'If we were equals, you would not dare ask. I have been a mercenary, but never for England's enemies!' Francis clenched his fists and drew a deep breath. 'What are you trying to say, my lord?'

'Come with me for an evening ride on the river before I say more.'

Cecil shuffled his backside off the stool. Standing, he reached to just below Francis's heart. He began a slow descent of the steep, dark stairs, with one hand braced against the wall. 'I will now, like the devil, lead you up onto a high place and whisper temptation into your ear.'

'I'm no Saviour.'

Cecil heaved himself down the last two steps and vanished between two lengths of wet wool. 'But I don't hear you go on to deny that I might be the devil?' His muffled voice reached back up to Francis on the stairs. 'Do be careful how you answer.'

'Sir, I learned at a very young age how to play with fire.'

Cecil's private wherry slid silently up to the little dock just as the two men arrived.

'Purpose first, temptation after,' said Cecil after the boatman had steadied his descent into the boat. 'But we've some way to go before either.'

The oars splashed and jumped on the water as they turned out into the current and headed down the Thames. They sat knee-to-knee under the arched sailcloth canopy that protected the wherry's passengers, its side panels now rolled up. Cecil faced downriver, perched on a thickly cushioned bench, his face invisible in the shadow of his hat.

In spite of Cecil's question about his loyalty, Francis found his spirits considerably higher than when he had first arrived on the jetty. The privacy of the meeting, the presence of Cecil himself without an intermediary, suggested an uncommon mission. He did not sense a threat from the Secretary of State. He had been testing Cecil as much as Cecil had tested him.

They rode for a long time in silence. Francis thrummed with curiosity as he watched the vast darkness beyond the warm circle of their lantern. The surface of the Thames was punctuated by the small sparks of other lanterns on wherries and the boats of night fishermen. Only a slight thickening of lights hinted at the two lines of the river's banks.

'I wish to beg a favour,' said Cecil suddenly.

'I'm not yet hired, my lord. But a gift of service, by all means.'

'There was an explosion yesterday morning in one of the warehouses used by the Corporation of London, near Bridge House in Southwark.'

'Near St Olaf's Church and wharves?'

'I want to know what you make of it. As a firemaster. Tomorrow, I'll have you appointed a customs clerk, and given a key. Make some excuse to be there – checking bills, inventories – sniff around. I'm sure I don't need to lecture you on discretion.' Cecil settled back again into his preoccupied silence. A fish jumped near the boat.

Francis watched the dark riverbanks flow by, pricked by the lights of houses and lanterns on the foot of water stairs. As the river began to curve eastwards towards the City the overlapping bulks of the Westminster Abbey and Hall appeared on the left. To the right, on the south side of the river, rose the twin towers of Lambeth Palace, with St Mary's Church nearby and the flat darkness of the Lambeth marshes beyond.

Cecil leaned forward, so close that Francis could smell the civet and camphor on his clothes, and anise seed on his breath. He pointed beyond Westminster to the Palace of Whitehall, the residence of the new Scottish King, James, his Danish Queen, Anne, and their royal brood.

'That jumble of buildings holds the future peace of England,' said Cecil. 'A male monarch and his male heir. Fifty years and more, we've had, without dynastic stability. Longer than your lifetime, Quoynt. And mine, for that matter.' His small shape yearned towards the palace. 'Half a century of plots, counter-plots, pretenders and threatened uprisings.'

England had not seen dynastic stability since Henry VIII had broken with Rome and made enemies of the Catholic kingdoms of Europe, as well as a large number of his own subjects, the English Catholics. Then Henry's only son Edward died before he could grow a beard, to be followed by two barren queens, Mary Tudor and then Elizabeth the First.

Mary was desperate for a child but could not have one. She tried again and again, but carried only, for a time, a phantom in her belly.

Elizabeth did not even try. She refused even to marry, let alone to delight her subjects by birthing a (preferably male) heir. The question of who would succeed her on the throne was made even more uneasy by the firm belief of many English that she had no right to be there at all. To all English Catholics, who could not by the tenets of their faith accept Henry's divorce from his first wife, Catherine of Aragon, Elizabeth was his bastard daughter by his concubine Anne Boleyn.

There were more legitimate if less closely related heirs. Henry's distant niece, Arbella Stuart, for one. And Mary Stuart, the Queen of Scotland and France, who was the grand-daughter of Henry's sister, a Tudor by blood, and therefore a cousin to Elizabeth; there was also Mary's son James.

But Arbella lacked a taste for the throne. She was also thought to be too much under the thumb of her ambitious maternal grandmother, Elizabeth Shrewsbury, familiarly known as Bess of Hardwick. And Mary Stuart was a Catholic. Each of them, however, had ambitious followers.

'And always,' continued Cecil passionately, 'always . . . the hot breath of France and Spain blew on our necks as they waited to snatch England back for Rome.'

'Hot lead, too, as I and any other soldier who has served abroad can testify.'

Cecil gave a small grunt of agreement. 'Now we have peace.

And a male ruler who is not a Catholic, with legitimate claim to the throne and two sons. And a daughter, as well, with whom to cement treaties through marriage. And still another royal pup in the pod. But the maggots still gnaw.'

Cecil's fists made small, pale balls on his black silk knees. 'The new reign has already seen two treasonous plots, and traitors like Cobham, Markham, and Tresham. And we're not done with treachery yet. It is my duty to keep the King safe. To keep them all safe.'

Looking at the child-like figure balanced on a padded bench in a small boat in the middle of the Thames, Francis found nothing either improbable or ridiculous in the man's assumption that he was responsible for the safety of the English throne.

'Tell me, Quoynt . . . Do you not wish for our children to grow up in a peace that you and I never knew?'

'Of course, my lord.'

'I want you to help me protect the king.'

'You have only to tell me how.'

'Turn traitor.'

10

Francis felt an unpleasant lurch in his gut. 'Is that an invitation to confess to treason?'

Cecil exhaled impatiently. 'Don't be an ass. I'm asking how far you're willing to serve me.'

'As a traitor?'

'In any capacity.'

'Willing to serve you, my lord, or England?' Francis looked at the man some called The Deep Dissembler, wondering suddenly, how deep? How false?

Cecil stared coldly. 'Are England and I two opposing causes?'

Francis could not see Cecil's eyes, but the Secretary's voice was dry.

'For the sake of debate,' said Cecil, 'say that you doubted my loyalty to the King. Would you still serve me?'

Every shred of reason told Francis to lie. A man's body could disappear in the dark stained waters of the Wandle and not be seen again till Gravesend.

'No, my lord,' he said. 'I would not. And I'm sorry if you hoped for a different answer.'

'You would not serve me, against England's present interests, even if it were for her long-term good?'

How easily he can tie a man into knots, thought Francis. 'No,' he said stubbornly.

'There's advancement and considerable fortune to be had in serving me without question.'

'I should fall on my sword like a Roman! To save the executioner his pains. But still, no. I'm sorry, my lord.'

Cecil leaned forward. 'If the matter were not so grave, I would not deign to defend myself to the likes of you. England and I are the same. I questioned your loyalty earlier only in order to learn whether men would accept you as a plausible traitor. Does that satisfy you?'

I have survived, Francis thought with astonishment. Then he found that he was trembling. A hot flush of anger washed through him, an anger that had been growing ever since Kingston.

'I would be yours then, my lord, if I didn't feel such distaste for your games to test my loyalty. Treachery is a terrible word. I'm not one of your ingenious courtiers. I knock down walls. I set fires. I can't play with such a word as if it were a tennis ball. Why frighten me half to death if you mean to employ me? I'm not a dancing bear to be broken before it can be trained.'

'Temper, temper.'

'Nor do I wish to serve a man who will put my life at risk to test my skill at defending myself. They were your men at The Trout in Kingston, were they not? Did your man pass on a good report? And if I had failed your test, would I now be dead?'

'Silence!' Cecil's voice was quiet but deadly. 'I dislike insolence even more than flattery. Try to guard your tongue when we speak together. Otherwise, I think you will serve very well.'

'I'm amazed that you think so, my lord.'

'No longer "honoured", and so forth?'

'You warned me off all that, did you not?'

Cecil gave an amused grunt.

'Surely,' said Francis, disconcerted by Cecil's amusement, '. . . I've just proved how ill-suited I am for your work. Lord knows, I need employment, but there must be better men for your plausible traitor. Since childhood, I've been told that my face betrays my lies. I can't dissemble. I have a short fuse. I lack social graces . . .'

'I'm sure that you underestimate your powers of duplicity,' said Cecil. 'Most men do. I'm satisfied that you're the right man for my purpose. Do you question my judgement?'

'My lord, believe me, I am not your man.'

Their boat pulled level with the long, low frontage of Whitehall, a hodge-podge of buildings illuminated and subtly changed by royal presence.

'I have it on good report that some new treachery is afoot,' said Cecil, gazing at the kitchens, the Whitehall stairs and the Prince's Lodgings. At the Stone Gallery and the houses fronting the royal orchards. 'I need to learn what.'

They remained silent as the lights of Whitehall dwindled, until the next bend in the river revealed the distant stars of the lights on London Bridge

'Letters can be intercepted,' said Cecil at last. 'But these plotters do not write to each other. They seem to send no messengers. I believe that they must meet in private and write nothing down.'

Treachery, thought Francis unhappily.

'I'm watching all the usual trouble-makers. Always the same Catholics with a grievance. Like Throckmorton, who would insist on making a martyr of himself. And the Jesuits, of course. And those who hide them.'

Cecil looked back towards the vanished lights of Whitehall. 'This plot is something new. It's not your business how I know, but I hear hints. Vague threats of urgent action. But no proof, no details. Not even where to guard against attack.

I want you to find these new traitors. Join them. Tempt them out of cover, whoever they are. Draw them out.'

'You need an intelligencer, not an unemployed firemaster.'

'They will be on guard against intelligencers,' said Cecil. 'Your very unsuitability recommends you.'

'You're too subtle for me, my lord. Please explain.'

'You don't yet know who they are, but you know them. You've worked among them, unwittingly, in the Low Countries. For that's where such vipers make their nests. Where they train, recruit and plot. They will find it easy to trust you, with your reputation as a blunt, honest man. You've worked as a mercenary . . . aren't yoked to any religious or political faction.' Cecil leaned back and turned his face to the dark water. 'It will help that your father is already suspected of having Papist sympathies.'

'Is that a threat?' demanded Francis, half rising. 'Is that the real reason for hiring me? Because I must jump to your tune or else my father suffers? Is this another way to break the dancing bear?'

'You're rocking the boat,' observed Cecil, a little anxiously. 'The current is far too strong to swim ashore. Sit down, Quoynt! I meant just what I said. I don't always speak with a double tongue.'

'I don't need threatening to want to help save the King,' said Francis hotly.

'It's more than the life of the King,' Cecil replied with equal passion. 'I want no more Smithfield fires. Do you understand me? No more Protestant martyrs. I want to end all threat of invasion by Catholic princes and kings. I want unity and peace in which England can heal after those long years of war. The King's life is merely a part of that greater good.'

Francis rubbed his forehead with cold fingertips. The man's sincerity was convincing. 'I'm more accustomed to war than to the subtleties of peace.'

'We're not at peace yet,' Cecil said shortly. 'A treaty merely drives the war underground. You will find yourself still very much at home.'

He told the boatman to pull into the water steps of a large private house hidden behind its walls on the north bank of the Thames. 'You must now find your way up onto the high place without me.'

Francis sat stubbornly on his bench. 'You don't send a man into battle without orders. What must I do here?'

'Enjoy the entertainments.' Cecil sounded far too pleased with himself for Francis's taste. 'We'll speak again in an hour or two.'

'My lord, tell me openly,' Francis begged. 'If my father is not hostage, am I free to refuse?'

'Ask again when you know what your reward might be. I do understand what a costly business treachery can be, not least to the soul,' replied Cecil. 'But I believe I have guessed your price.'

PART TWO

SLOW FUSE

'The Causes and Motives of Seditions are; Innovation in Religion; Taxes; Alteration of Lawes and Customes; Breaking of Priviledges; Generall Oppression; Advancement of unworthy persons; Strangers; Dearths; Disbanded souldiers; Factions growne desperate . . .'

Francis Bacon, 'Of Seditions and Troubles'

'. . . they are the most dangerous Discontentments, where the Feare is greater than the Feeling.'

Francis Bacon, Ibid

11

Boomer had not moved for nine hours. He lay flat on his belly in a small dip in the side of the hill, looking down over the edge of a chalky outcrop. After he had been there for half an hour, three rabbits grazed past his elbow. An hour or so later, a bird landed on his boot. After four hours, he realized that he was enjoying himself.

With a ragged, lop-eared hat over his silver hair and an old patched blanket across his shoulders, he disappeared into the side of the down until you stepped on him. The hat sprouted four sprigs of gorse. The blanket looked as if it had been left out in the rain and snow for an entire winter. Boomer treasured both items. He also wore his old firemaster's boots and belt, made without metal buckles or studs. He carried his knife with the blackened hilt and blade.

Come on, you bastards. Do something.

Below him, Pangdean Place hunkered down on the edge of the sea cliffs. Except for the tops of its brick chimneys, the house was hidden from view by the sides of a shallow valley where a stream, born higher up in the chalk downs, made a run for the sea. Large as it was, the house could be seen only from above, where Boomer lay, or from the sea. You could pass along the beach below the house and never know it was there. It had been empty for twelve years, during which local smugglers had made good use of the caves in the cliffs below the house. Now, it seemed that Pangdean Place had a new tenant. Everyone in Brighthelmstone seemed to know that someone now lived there. No one knew whom.

They must have landed at night, thought Boomer. And provisioned by night as well. Even this far from Brighthelmstone . . . a good half-hour ride . . . someone in that gossip-mill of a village would surely have noticed them arriving overland, by daylight.

Unless he had imagined what he saw last night. From wishful thinking. It gave him an excuse to do this again. He knew that he was enjoying himself far too much.

He tensed and relaxed all his muscles several times, as he had been doing all afternoon. He would not be able to walk home otherwise. In the old days he could lie in ambush for two days and still manage to lift his sword.

The house below him blurred and swam in the late after-noon light. He swivelled his eyeballs and blinked a few times to refresh his sight, then gazed at the grey-green line where sea met a sky filled with inky clouds glowing red on the underside.

He could not stare as he used to, either. Least of all into the setting sun.

Rather than think about his son, called to represent the Quoynts in London, Boomer counted the fishing boats headed for the beach at Brighthelmstone at the end of their working day. Then he counted the other hoggies headed out for night fishing. The scarlet circle of the sun began to flatten against the horizon. Movement flashed across the side of his vision. He looked back down at the house.

Whatever it had been was gone.

Then a groom crossed the part of the stable yard that lay in Boomer's line of sight, carrying a dung fork and bucket.

Nothing more happened while the sun slipped below the

sea. Gulls wheeled on pink-stained wings. As the last hot red sliver disappeared, the sky blushed with a quick, furious radiance.

Two more grooms . . . two different body shapes . . . began to trudge back and forth across the yard.

Though his eyes were now fixed on Pangdean Place, Boomer remained alert to the hillside around him. The nearby grass and bracken rustled, creaked and chirped as the night dwellers of the Downs began to emerge. Gulls and terns, which had been following the fishing boats out at sea, now gathered on their roosts on the cliffs. The air above his head began to cool although the ground still held the sun's warmth. The light would fade quickly now.

Twelve men crossed the yard from the house and vanished into the stables.

Boomer's mouth twitched with satisfaction.

He had not imagined what he thought he saw last night, after all.

Slowly, he began to inch back from his observation point. Then he froze again. Even at this distance from Pangdean Place, he heard several horses snort. The clear air carried a man's voice, giving an order. Listening hard for the sound of hoofs, he began to move down the hillside, sliding between patches of gorse towards the cleft of the little stream.

They exercised them on the beach. Boomer stretched his broad hand across the print in the sand. His fingertips barely spanned it. Even allowing for the leather muffler, it was a big beast.

He measured other prints in the interwoven tracks that scarred the patch of sand. Equally huge.

Like the prints he had found last night by accident, after waking in a cold sweat from another dream. Unable to bear his bed and the confining walls of Powder Mote, he had dressed and walked for the rest of the night, along the tops of the Downs as far as Piddinghoe. Then he dropped down to the sea to return along the shore before the rising tide blocked his way.

The long, straight coast from Shoreham, west of Brighthelmstone, to Newhaven on the river Ouse to the east, offered few havens and lees. The wind attacked unchecked and brought water to his eyes.

Most of the beach was shingle, punctuated by muddy salt marshes where springs seeped and chalk streams emptied into the sea. A ribbon of fine, firm shingle ran along the water's edge at low tide. In places this was worn to sand. When Boomer spied them, the advancing tide had already begun to blur the ribbon of hoofprints that punched black shadows into the dark, wet sand. The tide would wash them away before daylight.

If these prints tonight had not held water to reflect the dim light, Boomer might still have missed them.

He lifted his head to listen. Then, with a glance up and down the beach, he slipped into a crumbly fissure in the cliffs.

Shortly, the riders returned along the beach. They passed Boomer in his cave and headed up a zigzag path towards Pangdean Place. When they were well out of sight, he came out of his cave. He had taken a good look at the horses as they passed.

Why did the new tenant of Pangdean have need of twelve warhorses?

The man who had killed the young fisherman Shelvy Mawes watched Boomer climb up from the beach. Boomer was too far away for his face to be seen, but his height and breadth of shoulder marked him out. The man tried to follow but lost his quarry in the gorse on the hillside.

Headed for Brighthelmstone, the man noted.

He retraced his steps and went down onto the beach. The incoming tide had almost washed away the tracks. The man studied what remained, and the prints of a man's boots. Someone had squatted down beside the line of horses' hoof-prints.

He looked thoughtfully after the vanished invader. That one, too, would need dealing with.

12

Kate stripped naked and took the parts of her other self from the chest below the window. She folded her smock and bodice. Then she laid her palms on the tops of her long slim thighs.

How strange it seemed that her flesh could still be so solid and warm when the spirit that animated it felt so chilly and numb. This body of hers should, by rights, already have been buried for one and a half years, and turned to dust. Like the rest of her family. Father, mother, brother and sister, all together, without her.

But that had not been God's Will for her.

She bent to scratch a mosquito bite on her slim ankle. She was the opposite of a ghost. Her body still walked and itched after its soul had fled.

She stretched out her hands, palm down. Long, strong fingers spread like the branches of a tree. The skin was smooth and faintly bronzed. The nails flushed pink, with pale half-moons at the base. The hands seemed to belong to someone else.

A little cleaner, they might pass as a lady's hands, she thought. Used only for holding posies or plucking a lute.

She turned them over. There was the truth.

Palms stained muddy brown by leather dyes, with green

patches from the hawking glove. Fingertips pitted with needle pricks. A callus between her right thumb and forefinger, where she wore the stiff leather pad to push needles through thick hide. Nothing gentle about these hands now. Nor dainty. They looked just like her father's hands, and her brother's. Who'd have thought it would be Kate and not her brother Luke who ended up with the tools?

If he had lived, Luke would have taken over the glover's trade. The Guild might have accepted him.

She closed her woman's clothes into the chest. No doubt God had a purpose in killing her family, but it escaped her understanding.

Over her bare skin she now put a man's shirt of linen, with long tails and a separate, soft ruffled collar tied on at the neck. Then she tied the points around the bottom of her doublet to the matching strings sewn around the waist of a pair of coarsely woven kersey breeches, her dead brother's everyday slops, wide at the hips and gathered at the knee.

When she wriggled into the assembled suit and tied the front of the doublet, her female body vanished inside a male carapace. She was, in any case, as tall as her brother had been, and almost as wide in the shoulder. The doublet, stiffened with canvas and buckram, disguised her breasts. Small padded rolls, or wings, set into the shoulder seams broadened her silhouette even more. The high collar of the doublet pushed up the ruffled linen shirt collar to conceal her elegantly female throat. Where some men padded their breeches at the top with bombast, Kate had no need. Her own hips filled them out as well as any bran, wool or rag stuffing.

Knitted wool stockings tied up with leather garters. Flat-heeled shoes tied over rounded tongues. Leather belt holding a knife. The pockets in her wide breeches swallowed her purse, her gloves and a handkerchief.

Blessing the new fashion for long hair in men, she let down her own dark curls to fall around her ears and shoulders. A wide-brimmed Dutch felt hat hid her eyes. Gloves that she had made hid her hands.

She had no looking-glass but knew how she must appear – a well-favoured young apprentice with a good leg, not so tall as to attract attention yet tall enough to be left alone by drunks looking for a fight. A young man who could move safely through the streets of Southwark at night when a young woman alone could not.

She strode twice across the room, then stopped with her fists planted on her hips. Though she disliked the reasons for her errand, anticipation lightened her spirits as she trotted down the tenement stairs.

Kate stepped out into the street as her handsome, confident, dead older brother. Jauntily, she strode along the Bankside, freed from the heavy insinuating eyes of men who drank outside the inns. She had no need to be modest in her bearing or else risk being taken for a whore. The thick layers of fabric around her felt, not like a prison, but like a magic robe that made her invisible. Even Traylor might not recognize her.

She waved away the solicitation of a young whore of twelve or thirteen, then called the girl back to give her a shilling. Frowning a little now, she rustled and creaked onwards to the only company in which she dared reveal her double self.

13

At the top of the Bankside stood the Paris Gardens, a cluster of inns, tenements and brothels around the remains of a once-fine house. Curfew had begun. The Bridge was locked. Nevertheless, the streets of Southwark teemed with pleasure-seekers. The City of London, locked safely within its walls at night, had more or less given up trying to enforce order in its lawless Ward Without. Every pleasure and vice could be found in Southwark, day and night. And it suited both saints and sinners alike to know where to find Gomorrah, to be either shunned or relished.

Kate found her quarry in Upper Ground, at the centre of a small crowd of men, taking wagers on a game of bowls set up in the dirt of the street.

'Mary!' called Kate.

'Patience, doll.' Mary Frith palmed a final offer of coins and thrust them into the depths of her voluminous breeches. Then she waved Kate to her. 'Be quick, sweet. I don't dare take my eyes off these cheats.'

'I'll wait.'

'More husbands should say the same.' Mary turned back to the game. 'Get your great foot back on the right side of the line!' she bellowed.

Absently, Kate listened to the thud of the balls in the dust. She tried to think how to explain what she wanted, without either betraying Traylor's part in it or inviting Mary's heavy-handed teasing. She felt cold and a little shivery, as if an ague threatened.

'You look thirsty,' said a voice in her ear. One of the other onlookers. 'Let me help.'

'I'm already taken.' Kate pointed at Mary.

'Lord! Another twisted piece!' He backed away in disgust.

'I need your help,' said Kate, when the game was over and the wagers settled.

'If it pleases my will, my august majesty shall assist thee.' Mary held out a large red-knuckled hand like a cardinal waiting for a kiss on his ring. 'Shall I slit your Master Traylor's gullet and tip him into the Thames . . .'

Mary took a closer look at Kate's face and dropped her arch pose. 'We must stay away from the house,' she said. 'The girls will be all over you, dressed like that.' She hooked her arm through Kate's. 'And I want you for myself.'

She led Kate along Upper Ground, back towards the river. 'Poor Kate, burrowing in the darkness like a little mole. You should poke your pretty snout up into the daylight once in a while. Hazard all, as we eagles do . . .'

'. . . And get shot down,' finished Kate bitterly. 'End up in the stocks or a prison cell.'

'I can endure the occasional stocks or cell better than I could stomach that two-legged dog-turd Traylor.' Mary gazed down her long, flat nose at Kate from under short cinnamon-coloured lashes. 'Flying beats burrowing, in my opinion. And if I'm hanged, someone might at least write a ballad.'

She led Kate along the riverside in the dusk. 'Let's smoke a pipe or two of the nicotian weed at The Falcon. Best tobacco on Bankside . . . How do you, Nicodemus?' she shouted to a

passer-by. 'We must speak.' Then, 'Hola, Kitten Tits!' to a
passing whore.

'Come work for me, Kate, if it's money you want,' Mary
offered as they lit their white clay Dutch pipes with a coal
borrowed from The Falcon. 'I forgive all past refusals.' They
sat on two barrels on the dock, smoking and watching the
wherry men jostling for landing space at the foot of Falcon
Stairs.

'I don't want to die young of the pox.' Kate turned her
head to look at the wherry lanterns beginning to sparkle on
the river.

'I have two most high-born gentlemen of my acquaintance
panting to pay through the nose to have you whip them
while you're dressed as a boy.' Mary waved to a pair of
beggars trotting briskly past. 'Good hunting!' she called.

Kate blew a smoke ring and tried to put her finger through
it before it dissolved.

'I give sound advice, Kate. Change your station. Traylor's
mistress before you also died young.'

'So do many women. Or are you saying something
more?'

'Nothing anyone could prove.' Mary sighed. 'What else
shall we talk of, then? Tell me about this husband of yours.'

Kate dropped her pipe. 'What husband?' Francis Quoynt
floated into her head and was pushed out again sharply.

'Your phantasmagorical mate. The husband who is to die
and leave you a widow, fool! When you finally pluck up
courage to bolt from Traylor.'

'When did I tell you of this?'

Mary waited expectantly.

Kate said nothing.

Mary prompted her. 'Was he tall? Small? Was his prick
straight or curved like a cowcumber? Did he snore? You must

always rehearse your lies till they feel more real than the truth, if you hope to be believed.'

Kate bent to pick up the fragments of her broken pipe from the cobbles, hiding her face.

'Tall,' Mary prodded her. 'Or else you would have made a comical pair . . . At least so . . .' She held her hand a little above her head. 'And fair-haired, the better for the two of you to set each other off. Your darkness against his light. Did he pleasure you?'

'Mary, I beg you, shut up. I've had a devilish two days.'

'And you doted on him so fondly that you could never, ever, love any other man . . . ah, well.' Mary re-crossed her legs and tugged her sword into a more comfortable position. 'What can I do for you, Kate?'

'I need to find Francis Quoynt.' Kate flushed scarlet.

'Blow me!' Mary cocked her large head. 'Old Boomer or his son?'

'Are they both named Francis? I didn't know.'

'Boomer must be fifty-odd years. His son somewhat more than a score.'

'The son, then.' Kate's face still burned.

'What does a respectable widow-to-be want with one of those dangerous fellows?'

'That's not your affair . . . and I don't want him.'

The slab-like face looked amused. 'Everything is my affair. Isn't that why you came to me? Who knows when knights fart and butchers go bankrupt? Why, Mary Frith, of course!' Mary knocked the dottle out of her pipe against the side of her barrel. 'Trade, Kate. Tell me who wants him, if it isn't you.'

'I'll trade when you've something to exchange.'

Mary stared indignantly into the empty bowl of her pipe. Then she snapped the stem and lobbed the two pieces into the river. Her small eyes resumed their close study of Kate's face.

'Well?' Kate stood up.

Mary also rose and enfolded her in a bear hug that smelled of tobacco and sweat. 'Poor Kate. Poor little Kate.' She patted Kate on the back and released her. 'I've heard rumours that someone very like him landed in London not long ago.' She leaned forward again and kissed Kate on the mouth. 'Go home. Sleep. I'll see what else I can learn for you.'

As she left, Kate turned back. 'Mary, did you tell Traylor I once loved Francis Quoynt?'

'Yes,' said Mary, unperturbed. 'But that was before I grew so fond of you.'

There was no need for Kate to ask further. Traylor knew everything. He already knew exactly where to close his jaws, whenever he wished.

14

Francis strolled among the guests with detached disbelief. Cecil had left him at a private party. A few of the guests wandered here in the lowest part of the vast gardens, chiefly in pairs seeking private conversation. Others milled up and down a long, grassy central avenue between two wooden fences. Most people thronged on the wide terrace behind Hungerford House at the far end of the gardens, from which came the faint rise and fall of music.

All that whining catgut would be improved by a good, forthright drum, thought Francis sourly.

A small fair woman in green silk gauze, slashed to show a darker green silk-velvet lining, smiled at the tall, pale-haired stranger.

'Whose friend are you?'

Cursing Cecil for not telling him more, Francis winked and tapped the side of his handsome nose.

'Ah,' she said knowingly. 'It's like that, is it?' She looked him up and down in open invitation.

He nodded, distracted by her rouged nipples, which sat just above the rim of her bodice like two little red eyes peering up at him. He winked again and moved on.

He had been out of England for two years. The Quoynts were no longer close to the men who lived in the great houses that lined the north bank of the Thames. Though Francis could ride and fence as well as any gentleman, he came from middling folk who had, on occasion, fought on the wrong side. Even though she might display herself like a Bankside baggage, a woman wearing such opulent silk gauze and velvet was not for a tradesman like himself, even if he was a tradesman of a very special sort.

Nevertheless, those nipples made his cock twitch. He wondered if she were one of those women excited by the aura of danger around a firemaster. Or one who recoiled.

He walked on. Not many other soldiers or sappers among this silky, beribboned crowd, he thought. Sweet Lord, just smell all that orange water and attar of roses! Why the devil had Cecil set him here among these over-nice, goffered fools? Surely not to sniff out suspected traitors.

No one spoke to him as he walked. He spoke to no one.

'Eagles don't fly in flocks,' Boomer had once told him, explaining a firemaster's isolation. Even as a boy, Francis had seen this merely as a gentle way of saying that other people gave them a wide berth for fear of being blown up.

Suddenly, through the perfumes and burning pitch of the torches, came the familiar whiff of sulphur.

And Francis thought he understood why he was here.

Beyond the right-hand fence lay the kitchen gardens. A grove of short iron launching tubes for rockets sprouted among the carrots. Two twelve-foot posts rose from the cabbages, with a stout double line strung taut between them. From these lines hung two dragons of willow rods and paper, facing each other. A cluster of small rockets projected from their maws and arses.

Toys, thought Francis scornfully. Gunpowder tamed to titillate. I could show them real fireworks.

An army of pyrotechnical assistants bustled behind the

fence. Those who would light the fuses already wore tradi-
tional protective suits of fresh green leaves.

Francis eyed two of them, who needed a haircut and a
shave, and ran his hand over his own short crop which was
already growing out. Fashion was all very well until a shell
blew up in your face and set fire to your curls.

And there was the great man himself. Pyrotechnician and
artificer to the nobility. The one man here who was certain
to know the name Quoynt.

Francis gazed at the pyrotechnician with a rush of loathing.
An arse-licker. A fortunate dabbler who had managed to
seize a monopoly on the civil fireworks of the Court and
nobility. Though he had never sewn a canvas fuse in his life
and bought all his powder because he feared to make his
own.

The man could not bring down a castle wall to save his
life, thought Francis. Nor would he last one moment on a
battlefield. Cecil was badly mistaken if he thought Francis
would take pleasure in the work of such a buffoon.

The pyrotechnician stood in peach-coloured silk, just below
the terrace, instructing a gaggle of bushy green assistants. At
fifty-five, he sported a ribbon on his dyed lovelock like a
blade of twenty.

Francis looked away as if the sight pained his eyes.
However did that creature keep such a tight grip on his
patrons?

He accepted a glass from a passing serving man, noting
absently that the glass was a red-tinted Venetian. He held it
up the light of a torch and wondered what mineral salt had
given the Venetian glassmaker that rich, clear hue.

He began to imagine a shower of red stars falling from a
rocket. Not the yellowish nor greenish nor faintly pink that
were the only achievable colours so far, but a rich, full-hearted
crimson.

He drained the glass, watching the pyrotechnician again. How importantly the man waved his arms.

He held out his glass to be re-filled.

A line of garlands, made from wire wrapped in rags, stretched the length of the gardens behind the dragons. Francis sniffed the air. The pyrotechnician had not even soaked the garlands in oil of nitre before sprinkling them with gunpowder. With mere *aqua vitae*.

To a spattering of applause, a double line of women and boys dressed as sprites in ancient costume emerged from the house, throwing squibs at the feet of the guests. Women screamed as the squibs sparked and writhed and jumped up under skirts. The sprites danced down the avenue between the fences, spreading a pall of greasy smoke from their torches.

Then the first rocket burst into a shower of pale yellow stars.

A second rocket shed faintly pink stars.

The guests buzzed with excitement.

Francis stared about him, indignant that they could be so easily satisfied. The burning garlands would be next, no doubt. Delightful, if you had a taste for smoking rags.

He eased through farthingales and fur-lined cloaks towards the two posts in the cabbage patch, for the *pièce de résistance*.

When their fuses were lit, the two dragons jerked slowly towards each other along the lines, propelled by their nether rockets. Then they jerked apart, now spitting sparks from the rockets in their mouths. Then they advanced once more, farting sparks again. The boom of a maroon marked the end of the battle.

To the disgust of Francis, several women shrieked with delight and at least two fainted in supposed terror.

And these dragons could not even fly.

Francis felt an ignoble pleasure when a woman began to scream that a spark had set her sleeve alight.

'Master Quoynt? Your boat is here.' A serving man stood at his elbow.

Finding that he still held the red glass, Francis tucked it into his pocket to grind up for later experiment and headed for the water gate. As he moved into the shadows, away from the good humour and fellowship that a few moments before he had been scorning, he was attacked by an unexpected and fearful sense of isolation, so strong and so unexpected that he had to pause to think about it.

By turning traitor for Cecil he would be set apart even more than he had been here this evening. He would choose a solitude more absolute than the isolation of the firemaster – the solitude of the liar. Never again able to be entirely frank, not with his comrades, nor with his father, not with Kate Peach, nor with any woman he might come to love. That was not the splendid, sunlit isolation of eagles but a return to crawling alone through underground darkness in the serpentine wormholes of a siege engineer.

He tried to swallow but could not. Then he waved his hand angrily, as if plagued by gnats. He could not grab onto the coat tails of his familiar self. With a sense of falling, he stepped onto the boat waiting for him outside the watergate.

The small passenger, bundled against the evening chill, was almost invisible under the canopy of the waiting boat. In silence they pulled out into the river, just two of the hundreds off to seek pleasure. Music and laughter from the gardens of Hungerford House followed them across the water. Other voices grew louder and faded again as wherries approached and passed. Somewhere behind them a man cried, 'Oars! Oars!'

Cecil leaned forward on his pillow to close the distance between his mouth and Francis's ear. 'So, what did you see from the high place?' he asked quietly.

15

'Fools and fireworks.' Francis had lost patience with metaphor.

'And your opinion of the fireworks?'

'Civility or truth?'

'When I ask a man's opinion, I hope to hear it.'

'Those tricks were already old in my grandfather's time. Squibs. A few salutes and burning rags. The Italians and Chinese put that man to shame.'

'Could you do better?'

'I can imagine better – a true theatre of fire – but I can't pay for it. Pyrotechnics are costly toys. I lack both the money and the occasion to do more than imagine.'

'Didn't you see both theatre and fire back there?' The knees of Cecil's dark silk stockings caught the light of a passing lantern as their boat wove through constellations of other boats on the river.

'I saw *theatre*, my lord. Carpenters' work tricked out with the odd sparks and bangs. Pleasing enough, but earthbound. Fire is far more awesome, noble and dangerous. Those pretty tricks demean it. Fire is lightning trapped on earth. First cousin to the sun. It can become hell unloosed. Was never meant to be the servant of cheap tricks with *aqua vitae* and pitch . . .'

Francis stopped abruptly.

'If you put half that passion into serving me, I will be satisfied.' Cecil tapped Francis on the knee. 'And if you serve me well, I shall satisfy that passion.'

Francis opened his mouth, then closed it again.

'Beginning with honourable retirement from all military duties. With a generous pension . . .'

'But I'm a military firemaster. If you condemn me to civilian coal-mining or to bringing down old barns, I would feel myself punished, not rewarded.' Francis hesitated, then said vehemently, 'I won't go back underground.'

'And I would undertake to become your patron.'

'My patron?'

Cecil had seen the truth about Francis before Francis had grasped it himself.

A little later, Francis stood numbly on the Bankside where Cecil had left him. Hands on his hips, saddlebags at his feet, he stared out at the sequins of light on the water. Behind him jostled a stream of pleasure-seekers with dry throats or stiff pricks. Wandering among them were respectable matrons who guarded their reputations with masks, as well as off-duty watermen, unemployed soldiers, apprentices and the occasional honest man.

Then there were the predators – whores of both sexes, nips, snaps and handkerchief-foisters, pie-sellers, pamphlet-mongers, beggars, peddlers, pimps and gambling touts. They pushed, they shouted, they propositioned and threatened.

Francis heard none of them.

Cecil was the devil, after all. He had reached into Francis's soul and, like a midwife, hauled out thoughts still waiting to be born. Then he breathed life into them. And, with astonished delight, Francis recognized them as his own.

He felt terrified and exhilarated. Raw, aching desire gripped his gut as fiercely as when he had still suffered that first rampant puppy love for anything in skirts.

Possibilities unfurled in his imagination.

He would be able to live in England, not merely visit between bouts of martial employment abroad. He could visit Italy, that Holy Land of European fireworks. Or study with Signor Ruggieri in France. Or even travel to Cathay, the birth-place of gunpowder, where their firemasters were said to make intricate flowers of light bloom in the sky.

He could afford to repair Powder Mote. Insure that his father lived well. Could provide a dignified and comfortable old age for their ancient nurse and housekeeper, old Susannah, who should have retired years ago. Yet he would still be free to pursue his own life, away from Sussex and the smell of pigs and holes in the roof. He could buy his own estate . . . if Cecil did not give him one. He could even marry, in time . . . Kate Peach, for instance. The fancy had taken him once, though now he must wait until he was done with Cecil's work and could be himself again.

'I will become your patron,' Cecil had said. 'Pay for your masterpiece display. I will also see that everyone of note attends. There will be other celebrations . . .'

Francis turned away from the water towards The Elephant, off Long Southwark, where he took lodgings for a week. He sat on the edge of his wool-stuffed mattress, jigging his knees up and down, staring blankly at the two other, still-empty beds.

It was done.

He was to work for Cecil alone, in absolute secrecy, using ciphers for all written communication. He would report each week, while avoiding both Westminster and Whitehall. They would meet only when necessary. The more successful Francis became, the more assiduously he must avoid Cecil, as the English Secretary of State did not consort with traitors.

Francis stripped off his best clothes and dug into his saddlebag for his workaday doublet.

He had tried once more to talk himself out of employment. 'I would prefer a task in which I might hope to succeed,' he had said. 'For both our sakes. You must have a surfeit of plausible villains to choose from.'

'And many plausible villains already serve me very well,' Cecil replied. 'But you're a far harder beast to come by – an implausible villain.'

Francis stuffed his silk stockings into the bottom of a bag, imagining conversation with his father, who might not see turning artificer of fireworks as advancement. For five generations, the Quoynts had been military men.

As for becoming Cecil's spy . . .

Francis dropped the saddlebag and paced the wide planks of the floor. God's teeth! he thought. You're a grown man of twenty-seven. You've commanded your own men, but still fear your father?

After two turns of the small room, he sat on the bed again. He looked down at his fists as he tapped his knuckles together. The passing watch called out that it was nine o'clock and all was well.

He lay back on the bed, swung his legs up and closed his eyes. But still, sleep would not come.

Treason, he thought, testing the word. Traitor.

For a noble cause.

Sleep was impossible. He stood up and put on his cloak, then clapped his hat over his pale harvest moon hair, lighter than gold, warmer than silver.

As he passed the Great Stone Gate of London Bridge, the whiff of decay drifted down from the heads and quartered bodies of executed traitors displayed on its roof. The smell reminded Francis of the one thing Cecil had said that had frightened him more than anything else that evening.

No one would know that he was working for Cecil. The

stakes were too high, Cecil said. There would be no nods and winks to constables or sheriffs. If Francis were swept up with other traitors, Cecil might not be able to help him. And Francis might die a traitor's death.

'I would do my best,' Cecil reassured him. 'Try to survive long enough to reach prison, where things can be arranged. I will, of course, let you know of any raids by my own men, but I don't control Bacon's men.'

Though Francis had witnessed summary executions on the battlefield, he had never attended the formal execution of a traitor in England, nor wished to. The spectacle was held to be salutary for the common populace. Francis, however, found no moral instruction in watching a man cut down from the gibbet while he still breathed, then having his intestines pulled out before his eyes and his severed genitals displayed to the crowd. Then to be butchered like a bullock or ram, as if to say, 'This creature is less than a man.'

This could happen to him if he accepted Cecil's offer.

But he could not let fear make his choices. If he did, he would never light another fuse.

He strode away quickly through the crowds to escape the smell, not noticing how people moved aside to let him pass. They made way for his height, for the forward thrust of his stride, and for the intense concentration of his inward gaze. While none of the Bankside revellers who stepped aside could have put words to their reasons, they let him pass as they would an executioner or a wizard.

For a moment, Francis considered walking to the Holland's Leaguer at the Paris Gardens, to see if the women were still as he remembered: clean, and gifted enough at conversation and music to persuade a man that he was buying more than a cold fumble. But his other passion now commanded him. He wandered without purpose, lost in thoughts stirred up by Cecil.

He saw Cecil whispering in the royal ear. A grateful king, a celebration at court, a royal patron for the new pyrotechnician. Perhaps, one day, Firemaster of England . . . Even his father would have a hard time curling his lip at that.

With Cecil as his patron he could achieve all that his imagination might conjure. No burning rags or moulting garlands. No cut-out dragons jerking into battle whilst farting fire. He would set the sky on fire. Make light in the darkness. He would turn the matériel of war into agents of delight. Like God in the days of Creation, he would make a future coiled in his imagination flower into reality.

When he returned to The Elephant he found a packet on his bed. Inside were a set of keys, a commission from the Bridge Wardens to undertake a check of the warehouse inventories after the explosion, and twenty pounds.

Francis fell asleep at last, in a room smelling of stale tobacco smoke and hops, with the red Venetian glass in his hand, imagining a life spent creating perfect joy.

16

As she returned the next morning from taking food to the debtors in the Clink, Kate felt the tug of a pickpocket but was too slow to seize his wrist. The boy stuck out his tongue and darted away into the crowd. When she searched her pocket to see what he had taken, she found a note.

Mary had written in a large, sprawling hand: '*He lies at the Elephant.*'

Knowing Mary, Kate was certain that the double meaning was intended. She crumpled the note in her fist.

The Elephant was nearby. Francis was nearby. She had no excuse now not to act.

She repeated the message Traylor wanted her to deliver. She would pretend that she was flinging herself off the Bridge and be done with it as fast as possible. But there was also something more, and she knew it. She felt something that was incomprehensibly like hope.

17

Francis stepped suddenly out of the inn. This first sight of him after two years struck Kate a blow under her heart that pushed her off-course from a resolute approach to The Elephant into the shadow of a doorway.

Francis paused in the street, still holding his hat, and lifted his face to the luminous morning sky. The early sun lit his pale hair so that he seemed to shine as brightly as Lucifer, the fiery fallen angel. Close-fitting venetians showed the long, lean curve of his thighs.

Kate looked hungrily at the high angles of his cheekbones, the clean line of his mouth, his strong wrists. She forgot to breathe.

She had never seen anyone so beautiful.

Nor so remote. She could not believe she had ever held that man naked in her arms.

She could not move from the doorway.

Francis set off towards Long Southwark, his long legs slicing the air, head thrust a little forward. Though he wore only a leather jerkin over a linen shirt, his shoulders were as wide as most of the winged and padded doublets of other men in the street. Kate would once have followed those shoulders through fire.

He had seemed to carve a path through life with her in

his wake, not trotting behind like a drudge but moving freely, not needing to mind where she put her feet.

Following cautiously, Kate watched people move aside for him, and saw the admiring glances of other women. Her misery was so fierce that it made her want to be sick in the street.

18

After leaving The Elephant, Francis walked the short distance to Long Southwark market in the wide thoroughfare that led south out of London towards Sussex and Kent. Here, among bundled asparagus, cooped chickens and sweaty cheeses, he bought a short brown wool gown without holes or blood-stains from a tatter-monger. Then he headed back up Long Southwark towards London Bridge, wearing the gown over his second-best shirt as a gesture to clerkhood. Just before the Bridge Foot he turned right into St Olaf's Street towards the Bridge House warehouses, to perform a favour for the English Secretary of State.

Do it now! Kate told herself as she followed him into St Olaf's Street.

Good Heavens, Francis! she would say. Francis Quoynt! What a surprise. By chance, it happens that I have something I must ask of you . . .

With shameful relief, she watched him disappear into the gate to the warehouses. She leaned against a wall near the gate and tried to compose herself. Instead, she found herself remembering how he had looked when asleep, with his arm thrown across his eyes. She could still see the elegant line of that long arm, wrist and hand.

Damnation, she thought with a swoop of despair. Satan's teeth and toenails! I must stop this.

The remembered Francis lowered his arm and smiled at her drowsily, his short hair spiked like the fuzz of a damp chick.

She leaned her forehead against the wall and closed her eyes, recalling how gusts of his warm male smell rose up from the sheets. More than once she had buried her face in the golden fur under his arm to breathe in his smell, foxy but pleasant, like a good wine.

The memory of his smell was so strong that he might have been standing behind her now.

Abruptly, she left her position by the wall and marched back up St Olaf's Street. She had waited long enough. Fate clearly was not going to help them meet that day.

She went to the Long Southwark market and bought wool to replace the skirt lost on the Bridge. And then linen to make a new apron. She hated to part with the money but, while her brother's clothes might serve at night, she needed women's clothes for the day.

A pile of polished apples on a vendor's tray brought her up short. She fumbled in her purse again. Traylor and Francis between them had driven all other concerns out of her head. She bought five slightly bruised apples for a reduced price and set off with long, quick strides for the Bear Garden.

19

A young bear-ward let Kate in through the back gate that opened off a narrow alley that ran at right angles to Bankside.

'Did she survive Wednesday afternoon?' Kate asked urgently.

The boy smiled happily. 'They'll stop baiting her soon if she keeps killing so many dogs . . . won me three shillings, she did. You should have laid some money on her.'

Rewarding him with a dazzling smile in return, Kate crossed the field behind the high-walled amphitheatre where the baiting took place. If it made her a hundred shillings, she could not bet on Meg, she thought. She could not imagine laying a wager on the life or death of another living creature of any kind.

As there was no baiting that day, the main gate across an archway on Bankside was locked. The only other people there besides Kate and the young bear-ward were two grooms feeding the dogs. Kate's arrival sent the dogs into a frenzy. Chained in kennels down the length of both sides of the long rectangular field, they bayed. They howled. They flung themselves against the ends of their chains in a quivering lust to tear her flesh from her bones.

On the far side of the field stood a line of open sheds, sheltering cages. Some of the cages were empty. Some held indistinct growling shapes. A sign above the last cage read 'Caledonian Meg'. A chain rattled in the shadows.

'How does my poor captive queen today?' Kate leaned close to the barred door. The ripe stench made her eyes water. A deep, pungent, metallic stink of dirty fur, stale urine and rotten meat.

A pair of small dark eyes stared dully back.

'It's me.' Kate offered her hand through the bars, holding an apple. 'I'm sorry. I forgot to come on Wednesday night.'

She felt warm breath on her fingers. Heard the creature sniff, then grunt. A cool nose, as delicate and probing as a fingertip, explored her wrist. Then a damp sweep of tongue removed the apple. A chain rattled as the bear sat back on its haunches again.

Kate saw no gashes on Meg's nose. The dogs always went for the hamstrings or the nose. She stood listening to the crunching jaws, beginning to feel a little calmer. Before she offered the second apple, she sniffed it curiously. It smelled cool, elusively fragrant, and comforting. Like nothing else she could think of.

She broke the skin with her teeth. A burst of intense sweetness filled her mouth and nose. Then she gave it to Meg.

After the second apple, the bear remained near the barred door, though its watery eyes peered past Kate at the raging dogs.

'What do you care for broken hearts and humiliation when you have to keep fighting off sharp teeth and snapping jaws?' She offered the third apple.

The long pink tongue swept it neatly off her palm.

'I don't know how you find the strength to live with your enemies always close at hand. I suppose you have no other choice.'

The bear thrust its snout between the bars. Kate looked again for the marks of teeth, then ran her thumb in the direction of the short, dark brown bristly fur.

'Don't lose courage,' she told Caledonian Meg. 'Don't let your attention wander. If you keep winning, they'll grow tired of having their best dogs killed or maimed. You might be retired. The bear in that cage before you survived.'

She gave Meg the last two apples. Then she picked fleas off the snout and cracked them with her nails. 'Imagine if I had an orchard full of apples and took you to live in it. How fat you would become. One day, I will have an orchard of my own, I swear it. "That fine, small orchard belonging to the Widow Peach."'

Neither Hugh Traylor nor Francis Quoynt could be allowed to stop her. She must not let her own attention wander. She had managed ever since Traylor's visit to suppress all memory of her appalling flash of joy when he spoke the name Francis Quoynt.

She sat for a time beside Meg's cage, thinking unhappily about the beautiful, angular, questing, and slightly uneasy man whom she must approach. It wasn't that she was afraid, she told herself. But there were no half-measures with Francis. He swung between making explosions and a total stillness of the soul. He disliked half-answered questions and undertones, preferring to make everyone else slither about on the ice of honesty.

She did not know if she could lie to him. But, for sure, she could not tell him the truth.

Idly scratching behind Meg's jaw, she suddenly saw how to deal with Francis. She rose and bent her face to feel the delicate brush of that searching nose. 'Win next Wednesday afternoon. Stay alive.' She turned away from the cage.

As for you, she said silently to the howling, chain-rattling melee in the kennels. Poisoned meat all around, if I dared.

20

'Why does Customs need to make another list of all stores destroyed in the explosion?' The young warehouse clerk was indignant. He was also sharp-eyed and clearly ambitious. 'I'm already preparing a report for the wardens. From my complete inventory lists.' He eyed the letter of commission, then looked back at Francis. 'I suppose you'll need yet another copy of those lists.'

'I suppose I will.'

And I should have brought something to write with, Francis thought. And should be carrying sheaves of paper under my arm.

He waggled his head at the clerk in a you-know-how-it-is fashion. 'Powerful men don't like to share information with each other – not even inventories. Do you think they care how much time the rest of us spend writing out copies?'

The clerk grunted and vanished through a door in a wall untouched by the blast. He reappeared almost at once. 'How did I know to make an extra set of lists, eh?'

'By the same quick wits that will see you rise to Chief Bridge Warden one day.'

'Pull the other one. I don't know who you really are, but you're clearly nothing to do with the Corporation of London.'

'Why is that?' Francis asked equably.

'If you were, you'd know that a lowly clerk can't aspire to be Chief Warden. Only to be the chief clerk. Wardenship's reserved for City gentlemen.' The clerk gave the letter of commission a little flap, as if drying the ink. 'Don't fear. I won't stand in your way. Not with this. Go on, sniff around. Be my guest. You have keys for any doors that are left.' He handed Francis the folder of papers under his arm. 'You'll need these. If only to make you look like what you say you are.'

Francis opened the folder. The top sheet of paper was densely written with a finely sharpened quill in dark brown ink.

Lists, just as the clerk said. Over a hundred entries on this page alone. Descriptions, quantities, values. Dates delivered and removed. Names of suppliers. Notes to re-order. The stack of paper was nearly two inches thick.

'Those numbers at the top identify the storerooms. Do you want me to come with you to say which building is which? Or, rather, "was which".'

'What do you think I really am?' asked Francis.

'A soldier.'

'Oh?'

'Or a sheriff's man. Isn't that the next reasonable step? To find out why it happened?'

'You're not afraid of being blamed? You'd make a convenient scapegoat.'

'That's why I hope you're good at doing whatever it is you're here to do. If so, you'll learn the truth. Which is that I had nothing to do with it. And any number of other people could have done.'

Francis riffled the pile of paper with his thumb. 'Could anything have been stored without being on these lists?'

'My lists are correct to the last detail.'

'So far as you are informed.'

'I make my own checks,' the clerk said stiffly.

'You open every keg and sack?'

'Of course not. That's unreasonable. But I . . .' When Francis met his eyes, he stopped. Then he shrugged. 'Within reason.'

'Are you ever asked to overlook certain items, for a short time?'

'Never!' The clerk jumped back as if Francis had slapped him. His thin face went red.

'To save the trouble of recording them in and out again almost at once,' Francis continued blandly.

S'death! he thought. That started a hare. He felt cautiously pleased with himself on several counts. To fail as a clerk but be taken as a soldier boded well for the more serious work to come. And the clerk had never questioned his authority, only his disguise.

'Can you show me where the centre of the blast occurred?'

The young man nodded obligingly, his cockiness now muted.

Fallen beams still smouldered. From time to time they creaked and shifted, shedding sparks.

Some salvage work had been attempted the day before, then halted for fear of further explosions and because of the intense heat and remaining pockets of fire. A small party of fire fighters was now pumping water up from the Thames and passing it along bucket chains. Small clouds of steam marked their progress as they worked their way across the ruins from the river towards St Olaf's Street.

Francis stood in the rubble looking for safe paths through the haze of smoke and steam. He was expert at moving around such ruins. From the age of eight, he had helped to create them. His nose had already learned what Cecil wanted to know. The Secretary of State may even have suspected it when he chose Francis to inspect the site of the explosion. The smell was faint now, but unmistakable.

It was sharp and acrid but with something deeply pleasing in it as well. It had been in his nostrils even as he sucked his mother's milk. He knew the odours of its separate parts. He knew its smell and textures as it was mixed. He knew the different forms it could take – serpentine, cake or corned – and how to make each of them. The smell lingered among his clothes, on his skin and in his hair. It was the smell of the mistress to whom he had dedicated his life. The intimate compounding of sulphur, saltpetre and charcoal. Gunpowder.

He retreated to sit on an undamaged keg and study the lists.

No gunpowder.

He went through all the pages again, carefully, all two inches of them. Still found no gunpowder. However, one or two entries might have been false. The 'maize meal', for instance, could be gunpowder under a different name. If no one checked.

He felt eyes on his back and turned to see the clerk watching him.

'Wet your throat?' the clerk called. 'It's almost dinnertime.' He held up a small ale-jug.

Francis had been sitting on the keg for two hours.

He shook his head, thinking that he could now leave. He had learned what Cecil asked him to learn. What the gunpowder was doing there and who put it there were questions for someone else.

On the other hand, he did not want the clerk to imagine that his precious lists were the answer to everything. A young man like that could be useful so long as he was kept under control. And so long as he wasn't a villain.

Francis stood up and picked his way over some charred bricks, broken roof tiles and blackened spade handles to the dead centre of the blast damage. The smell of gunpowder was strongest here.

At the centre lay the ruins of a small brick-walled chamber, next to a larger square shed, now flattened. Francis stared at a lump of mangled iron, trying to decide whether it had been a military mortar of some kind. Or perhaps merely a vast scalding kettle. Or a cistern. Then he realized that he was looking at the remains of a metal bread-oven.

He riffled through the lists again.

The large square shed had been the public bakery the clerk had mentioned. It sold bread, but also gave local people the use of its ovens to bake their own dough.

Francis examined what was left of the wall between the bakery and the smaller storeroom. Flour, he thought. A fine dust hovering in the air. And some poor devil was careless with the fires in the ovens.

A flashover fire. More than enough to set off any gunpowder stored with the flour. Disguised as flour.

What kind of fool did not understand the explosive dangers of fine dust in the air and stored gunpowder next to a bakery?

He nudged aside a section of broken brick wall in case a fragment of barrel or sacking remained. Almost at once, he spied a tatter of burnt cloth under some rubble beyond a smoking beam. He shouted for water. When the fire fighters had steamed a path through the wreckage, Francis squatted down.

Not flour sacking. Wool. Tightly woven. Former colour impossible to tell. He tugged gently. The wool came away between his fingers.

With the toe of his boot, he shifted some of the rubble. 'I've found a body,' he said.

The charred hand was attached to a shrivelled, blackened arm, and the arm to a body under a pile of rubble too large and still too hot to be disturbed. A faint smell of burnt meat seeped out between the broken bricks.

'Who's still missing?' Francis asked the clerk, who was peering over his shoulder.

The young man shook his head and raised his brows at the fire fighters.

They all agreed. No one was missing. Six dead. Four warehouse workers and two local women who had been collecting their bread. And countless injured. But no one missing.

'Perhaps it's a homeless rogue,' suggested the clerk. 'Another Southwark body. You find them in the river and the alleys. Why not here?'

Francis nodded. If the clerk had not noticed that the coat sleeve was made of a fine wool that no homeless rogue was likely to wear, Francis would not point it out. He could think of several more possibilities for the identity of the body. And he had changed his mind. Why the gunpowder was in the bakery store and who had put it there were no longer questions for someone else to answer.

21

'Two small kegs at the most, to judge by the damage.' Francis leaned back to study the Bridge House stores through the dusk from their vantage point on the river.

'Can you be so certain?'

'Within reason.' Francis stretched out his long legs under the seat opposite. He was still stiff from sitting so long on the keg. 'Ten full barrels, for instance, would have flattened Long Southwark, as well as St Olaf's Street, the church, and the first two or three arches of the Bridge.'

Cecil sat hidden under the awning, with the sides rolled down. The boatman from Kingston had just picked Francis up from the stairs at Horseley Down. Now they slid through the Pool of London below London Bridge, under the towering bows of sea-going merchantmen and a single, high-tailed, fat-bellied Dutch galleon. It was only four hours since he had left his message for Cecil.

'Could it have been merely a flashover fire caused by the flour dust, as you described?' asked Cecil.

'It was gunpowder.'

'Gunpowder not officially there?'

Francis shook his head. 'It wasn't shown in the inventories. And the clerk was outraged when I suggested the possibility of unofficial, unlisted stores.'

'Was he lying?'

'I think so. But he aspires. Won't risk his position with the City. He may accept an occasional dob to look the other way, particularly if a gentleman asks. But I don't think he's a smuggler or fence. And I doubt that he'll damn himself by blabbing now.'

'Did you mention gunpowder to anyone?'

'No,' said Francis shortly, irritated that Cecil felt he had to ask.

'The gunpowder wasn't there,' said Cecil after a few moments.

'No, sir, but it had been. Before it exploded.'

'Don't pretend to be slow, Quoynt. The gunpowder was not there.'

Francis stared into the shadows of the awning. 'Sir?'

'It was never there, do you understand me? There's no need to spread alarm. Never alarm the populace unless you can offer them either a solution or revenge. The gunpowder was not there. And from what you say, the only man who might argue otherwise is dead. Do you understand me?'

There was another thoughtful pause. 'Learn who the dead man was.'

'As a favour?' asked Francis.

'I've opened your account.'

22

'*Dear Francis . . .*' wrote Kate. She began again with another piece of paper. '*Dear Master Quoynt . . .*'

Dear God, I loved him, bedded him . . . So, '*Dear Francis*' it will be. She went back to the first piece of paper. '*You may not remember me . . .*'

Too barbed.

'*I wish to assure you that I bear no ill will . . .*'

Too craven.

'*You may wonder why, after so much time . . .*'

She threw down her quill.

It would not work. No man of sense would rush off to meet some stranger for unexplained reasons just because a letter asked him. Least of all Francis, who wanted answers to everything. The letter could be from anyone. Not that a letter from the woman he had deserted two years earlier was likely to be any more persuasive than one from a stranger.

She dropped her head onto her table. There was no escape. She had to meet him and persuade him in person. But this time she would plan her strategy. Prepare in advance. She would be cool, collected. Follow him again, but wait this time until he settled somewhere pleasant, at dinner perhaps. Then approach him, casually. With dignified composure. She had only a few words to say to him, after all.

23

By the next morning, most of the warehouse wreckage had been cleared. A half-dozen merchants and members of the Corporation of London stood here and there in sober but costly clothes, talking to clerks and shaking their heads over lists.

Surviving stores had been neatly stacked. A party of women squatted in the pools of their skirts, picking over fragments of linen from damaged bales.

When Francis spied him, the young clerk was kicking a bag of lime. 'Hard as a rock,' he announced at large. He looked alarmed when he saw Francis. 'Back again?'

'Were any stores undamaged by the fire?'

The clerk seemed to examine the request for an ambush before he answered. 'Almost everything in those two sheds survived, down there at the end.' He pointed. 'Through that gate. But it all stinks of smoke.'

The door of the nearer shed was charred but still solid. The second shed backed onto the first, but stood in a separate courtyard on the far side of a brick wall, facing the river. It might once have been the store for the tidal mill just downstream, before being absorbed into the maze of Bridge House. This second shed had stone walls and a watertight roof. The sixth key on Cecil's ring unlocked the door.

Inside were stacked barrels of aromatic nutmegs and baled wool that smelled of sheep. There were crimson Turkey carpets from Amsterdam. A forest of ash staves. No gunpowder.

Had any gunpowder been stored there it might not have exploded, and Francis just might have been able to hazard a guess as to where it had been made. As it was, he had nothing to guide him but a scrap of fine charred wool.

He locked the storehouse, retraced his steps and unlocked the shed with the charred door. This shed held only stone for repairing the Bridge.

Back in the main yard where the damage was greatest, Francis prowled. The big beams had been taken away. Charred fragments of timber were raked into heaps for removal. He bent to examine a chunk of black wood. It might once have been the stock of a musket. Or it might not. And it could have been stored in any of the wrecked storehouses, then raked here, near to the former bakery. It was not evidence of a secret cache of weapons to go with the exploded powder.

'Where's the body now?' he asked the young clerk.

'In the St Olaf crypt. Waiting to be claimed.' The clerk removed a key from his ring and gave it to a waiting salvage worker. 'But I shouldn't think they'll keep him much longer in this warm weather. Not in the plague months.'

Francis bade him a neutral farewell. It would not hurt to keep the nimmer wondering whether Francis suspected him of anything or not.

A crowd of beggars waited outside the warehouse in St Olaf's Street to fight over the charred cloth, blackened oranges and any other spoiled goods cleared from the ruins.

'My uncle was taller,' Francis told the churchwarden who escorted him down to the crypt. 'Praise be to God.'

This was most likely true, though Francis had never met his father's older brother, who had died on a voyage to Tortuga when Francis was four.

The black, shrivelled corpse lay curled on its side, clenched fists drawn up as if about to box. It was missing a leg and part of the head. The features had flattened into a black mask. Nothing remained of the clothes. Even the scrap of wool had now vanished.

'I don't know if this will tell you anything more,' said the churchwarden, through the handkerchief he held to his nose. 'Found near the body . . . doesn't prove it belonged to him, of course.'

Francis looked at the small silver buckle in the man's palm. From a boot, perhaps, or a narrow leather belt. Too light to have held a sword or the hanger for a rapier. It was finely engraved. Francis held it to the light but could make out only a hairline scroll, no identifying device.

'Made in York,' said the churchwarden. 'There are initials on the back. I showed them to a silversmith.'

Francis picked up the buckle and turned it over. So far, all he could report to Cecil was the corpse had most likely been a gentleman. Or else a thief.

He had no reason to connect this death with that of his boyhood friend, Shelvy Mawes, nor to guess where these deaths were leading. Only with hindsight do the first hints of a pattern become clear to see.

When bells began to ring midday, he decided to go back to the beer houses at Horseley Down, where he could sup in the green shade of the trees and gaze at the river.

Francis walked straight down the river to the leafy gardens at Horseley Down. Alone.

Kate could not have asked for better. She followed him down a path through the trees. She would give him time to sit, just as she had imagined the night before. And to drink a little ale. Give him time to settle, to grow a little mellow. Then she would approach coolly . . .

Francis disappeared.

24

Kate stared at the path ahead of her. One minute he was there, the next minute gone.

She trotted a few steps and stopped to look again. A few drinkers sat at tables under the trees. A hopeful dog was watching a plate of grilled chops.

Francis stepped from behind a tree and grabbed her in a bear hug.

He had noticed the youth behind him soon after leaving the warehouse.

'How now, my lad?' he demanded roughly. Then he felt female breasts under the doublet.

'How dare you attack me?' she countered furiously.

He stared, then released her so suddenly that she staggered. 'Kate! What the devil are you doing following me, and in breeches?'

Kate caught her balance. Didn't fall, thank God. She could not breathe. She heard herself gabbling. 'FrancisIneed-tospeakwithyou . . .' Her face went scarlet. Her voice wobbled. She shook herself like a doused cat and straightened her clothes.

'Kate Peach,' he said, in mixed tones of wonder, delight and alarm. Those slate-coloured eyes stared at her with amazement. His lips parted to speak again. The sun glinted on the golden stubble on his chin. She could still feel the grip of his arms.

'Next Wednesday,' she babbled. 'You must attend the bear-baiting. That's all I wanted. To tell you that.'

He looked dumbfounded, as well he might, watching her make such an ass of herself. Not saying a word to help her out . . . What did she expect him to say, anyway? Please God, just let this be over with!

'Wednesday,' she repeated. 'The bear-baiting. To meet someone. Please go.'

She thought she saw amusement sliding into his eyes.

She bolted without waiting for his answer.

Back in her lodgings, she sat on her bed, arms around her knees, rocking in misery. *You're in a mess now, my girl, a right pestilential taking!*

She squeezed her eyes tight, as if that would wipe out the image of his head outlined against the sun and the sound of his clothing brushing against her own when he released her.

Just as her skirt had brushed his breeches at their first meeting, on a wherry, three and a half years ago. Kate had noticed the faint rustlings before she became fully aware of the man inside the breeches. Then, after a quick, curious glance, she kept her eyes on the gloves in her lap for the rest of the journey.

She was still ignoring him when a gallant, long-fingered hand reached down to help her up onto the water steps. It took her hand, lifted her onto the steps, and did not let go. She did not protest.

With her looks, Kate was used to approaches from strange men. But this hand, so large and warm, felt so right holding hers that she could not bring herself to behave as she knew she should.

He walked with her while she delivered the gloves, then he asked her to come with him to a playhouse.

'What is the play?' she asked stupidly, still trying to comprehend this tall, fair, unknown young man who made her feel unaccountably happy.

'I don't know,' he said. 'But it would give us a chance to sit together without having to speak, while we grow accustomed to each other.'

Kate wiped her eyes now on the sleeve of her brother's shirt. Then she turned her head sharply to the window.

There it was again. She had not imagined it.

A flash of light against her window, the *paff* of a delicate explosion.

Then another.

Francis stood in the street below her window. 'I don't think we've done talking'

'How did you find me?'

'I'm rather better at that game than you are. Will you come down?'

If he still wondered why she was wearing a shirt and breeches, he did not mention it. And Kate was too agitated to wonder why not. The old Francis would have asked at once.

'To The Cardinal's Hat?'

She nodded.

They walked in silence towards the inn, but their cloaks carried on a conversation of wool on wool, with the legs of her loose slops adding a quieter murmur. Their four boots beat an irregular rhythm on the cobbles. Kate looked straight ahead. Francis glanced sideways at the cloak over her breasts.

They sat across a table from each other, enclosed by babble and the clinking of mugs. He watched her with his changeable sea-green eyes, which at that moment were the colour of dark slate.

Kate thought she still saw the earlier amusement. And something a little detached, a little darker than she remembered.

'To old friends.' She lifted her mug with a defiant swagger.

'Yes. We were that, too.' He drank. 'As well as the other.'

Kate inhaled sharply and forgot what she was going to say. She gripped the bench and watched his throat in the smoky light.

He set down his mug. 'I'd like to be flattered that you were following me, but from your face I fear otherwise. Why did you follow me, Kate? What was all that jabber at Horseley Down about Wednesday and bear-baiting?'

She flinched. 'I do things in these slops I would never even conceive of when I'm wearing a skirt. For fun.'

He reached across the table and took her hand. 'Sweet Kate, this is not "for fun" and you know it.'

'Well,' said Kate, pulling against his grip. 'Well.' As she had feared, he was going to keep slicing through all her subterfuge until he was comfortable again. She yanked her hand free. 'Why did you leave me?' She clapped a hand to her mouth. The cry had escaped before she knew.

Francis pressed his fingers to his high forehead as if trying to scrub away a pain. 'I don't know,' he said at last. 'At the time . . . I was overtaken by events. I had a chance to command my own unit of sappers if I could step in at short notice. Thought that I'd be able to see you and explain in person. And then suddenly, we were mustered to sail from Gravesend, with only two days' warning and a scramble to get away. I tried to send a message . . .' He took a deep breath. 'I thought I might have more to offer you as an officer than as my father's apprentice.'

Kate groaned and dropped her face into her hands.

'Are you married, then?' he asked after a moment.

'No. I live alone.' For the most part. Explaining 'the most part' must be avoided at all costs.

'But you're very angry with me still?'

'Angry?' She shook her head. 'Francis, you cannot begin to imagine . . .!'

'Most likely not.' There was a pause. 'I'm sorry.'

As if an apology could put everything right again. Assuming that he cared to put it right.

'I tried to answer your question,' he said. 'Now you answer mine.'

She told him what Traylor wanted, at last.

'And you're the bait,' he said thoughtfully. 'He's a wily one.'

'Please don't humiliate me any further. I manage very well by myself. And I often deliver messages. Not just to you.'

'Who is he?'

'The man you are to meet? I don't know.'

'I meant, the man who asks you to deliver his messages.'

Kate considered all the lies she had prepared to meet that question. She rubbed her cheeks with both hands and settled for partial honesty. 'I'm not allowed to say . . . What's wrong?'

Francis shook his head. 'Why do you ask?'

'You suddenly have an odd look on your face.'

'It's absurd, in the circumstances. But I think I'm jealous of him.'

Their eyes met directly for the first time since they had entered The Cardinal's Hat. Kate feared she would burst into tears. She should have remembered that he would be compelled to answer honestly. 'Compliments can be cruel, Francis, even implied ones.'

She stood up.

Stop me! cried an unreasoning part of her. *Touch me again!*

'I would be most grateful if you would oblige on Wednesday,' she said. 'And attend the bear-baiting.'

He frowned, then opened his mouth.

'Goodbye, Francis,' she said, before he could ask any more questions.

She has changed. It was a mistake to touch her, thought Francis miserably as he watched her tall, elegant shape dart away through the Bankside revellers. The touch had brought the past rushing back. The feel of her smooth thighs, the curve of her bare back. Her smell of cinnamon and honey. Her husky voice. The weight of her black silky hair in his hand. Images he had worn to tatters while falling asleep in his tent or in front of campfires, and used to fuel daydreams of what they might do when he returned to England. If he survived to return.

But, clearly, he could put all that right out of his head again. Their conversation had been full of lumps and thorns. She was still too angry with him even to accept his offer to man her home again. Now that she had delivered her message, it was clear that she wished never to see him again.

And even if she had been warmer, a would-be traitor made a poor prospect as a suitor.

He would go to this bear-baiting of hers all the same. As a courtesy. And, if he were honest, he hungered to know what manner of man or woman Kate Peach wanted him to meet. Then he would leave her alone until he could woo her properly, as she deserved to be wooed.

Assuming that he survived the peace and could induce her to speak to him again.

He called for more ale. An hour or so later, he told himself to haul his thoughts out of his codpiece and get on with his task for Cecil.

25

'Tell me all the scandal I've missed these last two years.' Francis lifted his chin to let the barber scrape under his jaw with the razor.

'Even down in Sussex, you must have noticed that we have a new king.'

Francis waited to speak until the blade was removed from his throat for wiping. 'Down in Sussex, we hear little of how he's been received. What sort of man is he?'

'Well . . .' The barber gripped the end of Francis's nose, tipped his face upward and leaned close to deal with the golden stubble on his upper lip. 'It has been said . . . though I merely pass it on . . . Some naughty man had only to utter it for disrespectful rogues to chorus it all over London. "The Queen is dead," they say. "Now James is quean."'

'Hmph?'

'He has *privadoes*, favourites.' The barber stood back to check his handiwork. He was a short wiry man with a scar slicing through his chin. 'Armies of favourites. Great hulking Scots, who followed him to England in droves. He tosses titles at the pretty dears by the fistful, like sweetmeats.'

'But their lands, profits and taxes remain in Scotland?'

'Sharp as ever, Quoynt. Their titles and privileges suck wealth from us but give nothing back.' The barber looked quickly at his other customers who sat drinking by the window. 'That's what I mind. Not the rest. You and I both saw enough passionate friendships over there, between men with few other pleasures. The King can do as he likes behind closed doors.'

The barber was an old military surgeon, whom Francis had known during his first year in Flanders, when the man served with the same unit of sappers. Most of his early customers after he'd set up as a barber-surgeon in Old Fish Street were also former soldiers. In peacetime, he continued to pull their teeth, let their blood, and dose them for the pox, just as before. But in London he added a range of ointments, perfumes, pomades and purges never seen on the battlefield. He also offered steam baths to ward off the plague.

Francis let his head be turned one way, then the other.

Delicately, the barber flicked away a last patch of stubble. 'So long as he doesn't betray his new subjects for the sake of pleasing everyone else.'

'Everyone else?'

'The Scots. The Spanish. The Catholics. His latest Ganymede. Let your hair grow out into pale gold curls, Quoynt, and I'll douse you with civet and rosewater. We could make you into another royal favourite, no trouble.'

'I do need employment,' said Francis.

'Scrape your teeth?' The barber laid out a row of ivory picks.

By the time he left, Francis knew which old comrades had the clap, which alderman of the parish was losing his hair because of the pox, and which well-known goldsmith and ruthless moneylender was buying aphrodisiacs to pleasure a new young wife. He had also primed the barber to let it drop into the appropriate ears that he, Francis Quoynt, firemaster, had surplus gunpowder to sell, now that the treaty with Spain had dried up the military market. Also, assorted weapons no longer needed on the battlefield. The barber had agreed to keep his own ears open for murmurs that anyone was seeking to buy such things.

Francis had no particular reason to believe that the traitors whom Cecil feared would want to buy either powder or weapons. A single mad assassin might intend to attack with a dagger, for example.

On the other hand, Cecil clearly feared a major conspiracy. And a large body of men meaning to assassinate the King would need arms. If not for the deed itself, they would need them to fight off capture afterwards. For weapons, they needed gunpowder.

Unless they hope to burn down Whitehall, Francis thought, as he stood in Old Fish Street, fingering his unnaturally smooth cheek. Or to poison the water in the conduits as it flows down from Hampstead. Or to shoot the King with a bow and arrow while he's hunting. Or to tamper with his horse. Any of these is also possible.

There were too many possibilities. He felt his thoughts begin to slither on the uncertainties. But gunpowder was his trade. And Cecil had chosen him, knowing that gunpowder was his trade. So gunpowder seemed a good place to start.

He tried to see himself with Cecil's eyes. He was unemployed. He could offer powder for sale. He did own surplus weapons. In trailing this bait, he need hardly lie at all. In fact, from Cecil's point of view, as he guessed it to be, he was ideal.

Hang on to Cecil's certainty, he told himself. It will have to serve in place of your own.

He had been interested to note that the barber did not mention the presence of gunpowder in the Bridge House explosion.

26

After leaving the barber-surgeon, Francis went to the bottom of Long Southwark. He then bought a cup of ale in a number of the many inns and taverns passed by visitors from Surrey, Sussex and Kent on their way to London. More vitally, these places were also patronized by the unofficial intelligencers of London, the hundreds of watermen living in Southwark, who carried thousands of people across the Thames every day and eavesdropped on their passengers.

Southwark also drew the outlaws who could not find shelter inside the City. The City of London had only a feeble grip on its Bridge Ward Without. Any sport, any licence, any wickedness could make its home on Bankside and in the teeming alleys and tenements behind the white-painted facades on the river. Francis reasoned that this list of evils might include treason.

He worked his way up Long Southwark from the Spur, by way of The Christopher, The Bull, The Queen's Head, The Tabard, The George, The Hart and The King's Head. By The Bear, at the southern end of London Bridge the following afternoon, he merely held his cup and pretended to drink.

In each inn, he dropped word of what he offered for sale. He found no immediate buyers. The closest he came to a traitor was a former infantryman turned pimp, who told him feverish tales of Jesuit priests smuggled into England disguised as returning cavalry officers.

'I know, because I've had two of them visit my girls,' he breathed across the table. 'One of them started to pray while he was still at the business. Got carried away and cried out to the Virgin! You can imagine . . .'

When Francis murmured of possible reward for leads to a buyer for his powder and guns, the man's eyes sharpened.

'Some were just found, if you follow me,' said Francis. 'No papers. Easy come, easy go.'

The former soldier winked. 'I've a piece or two I found like that. The other poor bastards didn't need them any longer. Waste not, want not. Where can I find you?'

'Leave word at The Elephant.'

A possible first nibble, he thought. But still no rumours of gunpowder where it should not have been. Nor, interestingly, any mention of the mysterious dead man under the rubble.

After visiting a half-dozen taverns in the City itself, and meeting only booksellers, lawyers, fishmongers and butchers, Francis returned to the lawless riches of Southwark. By early evening on the second day, he ached to swim in the sea to wash off all the smoke, grease and foul breath that had spilled over him. His stomach felt sour, and not just from an excess of ale. His wits were not as sharp as he would have liked when he found a page, in blue livery but without an identifying badge, waiting outside The Elephant to take Francis to his master.

27

'So, you're working for the Little Toad.' Sir Francis Bacon, newly elevated by the King from plain 'Master', had the high forehead, long nose and pointed beard of his cousin, Robert Cecil. But Cecil did not have that waspish edge to his voice.

'Sir?' Francis feigned confusion.

'Come, Quoynt. Your face betrays you. I know you're employed by my cousin. Therefore, you're most likely an ambitious man, filled with an eager alacrity. Be ambitious on my behalf. I will offer better terms.'

'For what, sir?' Francis clung to a pose of earnest, bewildered civility, which would oblige, if only it could.

Bacon brushed away subterfuge with an impatient wave of a well-shaped hand. 'For facts, of course. Tell me what the King's little beagle has set you chasing after.'

In London, Bacon lived at York House, on the bend where the Thames turned to the south just after the open space of Scotland Yard. It was the first in the long string of palaces of noble families, built between the river and The Strand.

The page had led Francis through a small side gate into the walled gardens behind York House. Francis then waited in the setting sun, on a stone bench set amongst neatly clipped box hedges. The soil at the foot of the nearest brick wall was thick with maiden pinks and treacle-coloured columbines. Roses sweetened the evening air.

'God Almighty first planted a garden,' said a voice from behind him. 'Does this place refresh your spirits, Master Quoynt? Or are you a modern man caring only for innovation and utility?'

'A garden's a fine place, sir,' replied Francis, rising to his feet. 'But I lack the touch for growing.'

'From lack of inclination or lack of learning?' Bacon did not seem to want an answer. Hazel eyes as sharp as a ferret's had looked Francis up and down.

'I hear good things of you, Quoynt,' he said now, after his astounding offer of employment.

'Surely not,' Francis murmured. 'Then I must mend my reputation at once.'

'I like the look of you. I would like you among my followers.'

Francis imagined a flash of sexual flirtation. 'You welcome spies as your followers?'

'A man must have all kinds.' Again, that flash. 'The mould of a man's fortune is in his own hands. What say you?'

This man was rated as the finest intellect in England. But he had also served as a counsel for the prosecution in the treason trial of his own patron, Essex. Few people liked him, though many admired him.

'Sir.' Francis searched for words he could speak without also feeling sick with shame. 'Even if I were employed by your cousin, as you seem to believe, my talents have never stretched to spying.'

Though he had avoided a direct lie, he felt his cheeks burning. 'With regret, I must decline your most gracious offer.'

'It was no offer,' snapped Bacon. 'It was a request. Unlike my little cousin, alas, I'm not yet in a position to give orders.'

But give me time, said his tone of voice. And I will be.

His saturnine face closed off. Francis had disappointed. Was dismissed.

Francis tried to decide what Cecil would want him to do. He met Bacon's now chilly eye. 'I may not be placed to spy on Lord Salisbury for you, but I'm quick at ciphers. I can carry messages and keep my eyes open.'

'Interesting colour, your eyes.' Bacon smiled again, but more coldly. The apostrophes of his soft brown moustaches bulged briefly outward around a full lower lip. 'You discover a taste for spying, after all.'

'I prefer to think of it as making myself useful.'

'You're wasted on my cousin,' said Bacon, letting his eyes sweep Francis from head to toe once more.

How did Bacon learn? Francis wondered. Who had seen him with Cecil? He could think of only one man.

'You may go.' Bacon turned away, his long black coat swinging, narrow white ruff bright in the fading light. 'But be warned. Nothing hurts more in a state than that cunning men pass for wise. I am wise. My cousin is merely cunning.'

Francis was in no doubt what he must do next. If he did not tell Cecil that Bacon had asked him to become a double agent, someone else almost surely would. And given the choice, he wanted Cecil as his enemy even less than he wanted Bacon.

He found a public horse-trough, where he tried to wash away both his Southwark drinking and a pair of noble cousins who set spies on each other.

Back at The Elephant, with a letter sent to Cecil, Francis tore a chunk of bread from the loaf beside his wooden bowl and leaned back against the wall, welcoming a quiet moment to reflect.

The dead man at the warehouse. Cecil's order to hide the

truth about the gunpowder. And how to get a grip on the slippery task of finding unknown traitors.

Francis had never before been asked to mine a wall that he could not see, without knowing what shape it took, nor even what country it stood in.

The Elephant was peaceful that evening. Many of the men around him were also lodgers eating their evening meal. He tore off another piece of bread. He would wager that Cecil could have pointed him at suspected traitors but wanted to see first what else Francis might find. Had set him off with an open mind. In Cecil's place, that's what Francis would have done.

As for the dead man in the warehouse . . . he had no idea where to go next . . . Pluto and hell! What had possessed Cecil to choose him?

This question led him on to cursing Cecil for employing him just as Kate Peach had come back into his life.

He saw that he had torn the bread into tiny pieces and rolled each piece into a ball, then arranged the balls in ranks on the tabletop.

He suddenly felt like getting as drunk as an owl. He had done his day's work. There was no need to remain sober like a dutiful intelligencer. He hadn't had a good roar since getting back from Flanders. In the next three weeks he would need to keep his wits about him. This evening might be his last chance to risk cheerful oblivion, for a very long time.

28

Kate cursed and pulled her pillow over her head. Drunks downstairs in The Little Rose were usually thrown out if they made such a racket.

They have been thrown out, she realized. That's in the street.

'*Man!*' bellowed the voice. '. . . *Man is for woman made. And the woman for the man.*'

There was a faint suggestion of melody in the intonation but nothing that Kate would have called music.

A constable would come soon. Or the watch.

She rolled over. Then sighed.

'A pox take you,' she said to the air above her head. 'Why did you have to choose that song? Go disturb someone else.'

'*As the scabbard for the blade, so woman for man is made . . .*'

The drunk seemed settled on the dock outside her window.

'*As the furrow for the plough . . .*'

Kate leapt from her bed and leaned from the window. 'Shog off!' she shouted. 'I'm trying . . .' Her voice faltered. She gripped the sill.

In the street, under the lantern of The Little Rose, Francis grinned up at her. He threw up his arms in triumph. 'You're there after all . . . That's good. Come down to me, sweet Kate . . . sweet-faced Kate . . . sweetheart Kate . . . my *bashket* full of sweets . . .'

She closed the window, climbed back into her bed and curled up into a tight ball.

Dear God, what does he think he's doing to me?

The street was now silent.

The letter appeared on the floor at the top of the stairs outside Kate's door some time during the morning, while she was delivering the finished hawking glove and taking food to the Clink. She picked it up as if it were an adder and dropped it on her table. The sight of his handwriting made her shaky.

She left the letter unread. Reading it would be like talking with him again. It would let his words inside her. It was easier not to read it, but she could not destroy the letter either.

She arrived at the evening somehow, with no memory of the day. She knew that it made no difference whether or not she read the letter. Francis was not a man who let things lie.

29

Only one person would run up those stairs so lightly and so fast. Kate knew who it was before she opened the door.

'I'm going mad,' he said. 'I've been walking all day. I can't work. Can't think. I can't pull my boots on without thinking of you.'

'Please go away,' she managed at last.

'Impossible.' Francis swayed dangerously as if he were still drunk. 'Look, there. My boots are glued to your threshold.' He leaned forward, long arms braced on the doorposts. 'Kate, we must talk.' He looked ill.

Kate stepped back. 'Have you been drinking again?' Then she realized, too late, that she had already gone too far. She had entered into conversation with him when she should have closed the door in his face.

He groaned. 'Haven't you forgiven me? Did none of my abject but sincere grovelling touch your heart?'

'I didn't read your letter,' she said after a moment. 'And you can't come in here,' she added hastily when he dropped his arms from the doorway and stepped forward into her chamber.

He looked around curiously.

'Go!' she shouted. 'You can't come prying . . .'

'Then come out for a walk.' He lunged and caught her

hand. 'I want to know why you didn't read my letter . . .' He paused and looked at her. 'And I want to know . . .'

They looked at each other.

'Pluto and hell,' he muttered.

It's too late altogether, thought Kate. She stood very still and waited, feeling the familiar heat of his hand, holding his slate-coloured gaze.

Their first kiss was firm but quick. And very gentle. Francis hardly touched her. He leaned his head forward as if to drink from an offered cup.

'Oh,' said Kate. His lips . . . his wonderful, familiar smell. In a single instant she abandoned good sense, forgave past wrongs and fell with him into helpless joy.

'Yes.' He gave a deep, shaky sigh. 'It should be "no". But, oh, yes.' He kissed her again, a little less gently. 'Unless you want to stay here, we should go for a walk.'

All pretence had gone. Within twenty strides they were on fire, and agreed on their course.

'Back to your lodgings?' Francis asked.

'No!' She looked about in sudden terror that Traylor might choose to pay another unexpected visit, to ask if she had obeyed him yet.

'I would take you to The Elephant,' said Francis. 'But I can hear the man in the next room combing his beard.'

They stared at each other in frustration. He pulled her into an alley and pressed her against a wall. They kissed feverishly until Kate cried 'No!' and pushed him away. 'Not against a wall like a whore.'

'No,' Francis agreed, with a final regretful kiss. He clamped her to his side with one arm as they walked through Upper Ground. 'Shall I take a room in the Paris Gardens?' he asked.

She turned her head away. 'As if I were a doxie you picked up at the playhouse?'

She could ask Mary to lend them a room. But at such a cost in curiosity, knowing looks and triumphant smiles. The whole venture was too fragile to survive Mary. Later, perhaps, if there were to be a later.

'We could ride through the night to Powder Mote,' said Francis. 'To our estate. There's no one there but my father.'

'I can't leave London,' said Kate.

He gave her a sharp look but did not ask why.

Francis thought he would explode. He would not survive many more hours of walking about hand-in-hand. He wanted to ask her to put her hand inside his breeches but knew that she would pull back if he did. He wanted to put his own hand into the placket of her skirt but was afraid to. Not here on the street, for certain.

Where? For God's sake, where could they go?

He stopped to kiss her, forcing himself to be tender. 'Are you still with me, Kate? You swear that you're not just teasing me?'

'In revenge?'

The anger, hurt and hunger jumbled together in her eyes made him want to weep. If he were a fine London gentleman, he would have friends with great houses and spare chambers to lend to a comrade in dire need. With lighted fires, Turkey carpets, fur coverlets, and doors with secure locks.

He suddenly clapped his hand to his purse. 'I have it,' he cried. 'I had forgot that I am a customs clerk.'

30

Kate watched while Francis's dim shape prowled the warehouse, kicking at bales, prodding bags.

'Over here,' he called. 'A pile of Turkey carpets from Amsterdam.'

She went obediently, feeling her way among the stacks of barrels and bales, to sit primly on the edge of the carpets, her feet hanging just off the floor. She shivered. Now that they were at the point, she felt only terror. But there was no way she could leave. Fate had caught her again. Her will was now irrelevant.

'Oho,' Francis cried in a theatrical ecstasy of discovery, from a far corner. 'Close your eyes, Kate.'

He sounds as uneasy as I feel, she thought, a little comforted that he had not planned for this any more than she had. How could two full-grown, reasonable people be so dead set on plunging into waters that terrified them both?

Because, she answered herself, two other people are making the decisions.

Another Kate, squeezed inside the same body, had taken over. That other Kate told the would-be respectable widow to go hang, while she went plunging around Southwark in search of a bed on which to make love.

'Are your eyes closed?'

'Yes. Not that it makes any difference in this light.'

'Keep them closed.'

She heard him approach in the echoing stillness. Felt him standing in front of her. His hands beginning to unlace her bodice.

'Francis . . .'

'Help me.'

She pulled her arms free. Then she felt his fingers brush her bare skin.

They inhaled at the same time.

He undid the neck of her shift and pushed it down over her shoulders. She felt cool air on her breasts.

'Dear God . . .' he said. 'Oh, sweet Kate.'

He moved a little away from her.

He's leaving me again, she thought with a flash of terror. He's going to kill me . . .

She had left the reasonable world.

A current of air brushed over her. She heard a giant wing flap past her head and felt the softness of fur settle over her bare shoulders.

'Fur rugs from Muscovy,' he whispered in her ear.

This is true, she thought in joyful disbelief as she clung to him, naked at last under the rug with the Turkey carpet prickling her back. I'm here. Not passing through. It really is Francis. His wonderful smell, his lovely mouth, his weight pressing me down again. Oh, the delight. The relief. The rightness of it all.

Francis had promised himself that he would take great care with her. He would be gentle. He would take pains.

But her first gasp, when he touched her neck, began to unravel his good intentions. Then he pulled off her skirts and saw the beautiful pale length of her legs in the shadows and the dark, assertive triangle of her bush.

I don't think she minded my rush of urgency, he thought afterwards, as he reared back up onto his elbows. One of her hands followed, the fingers locked in the hair at the nape of his neck. He turned his head and kissed the soft inside of her raised arm.

'Your hair is longer,' she murmured.

'There's no need now to prevent an enemy soldier from doing what you are doing.'

'But still no beard.' Her other hand gently rubbed the stubble on his chin.

'I might still set it on fire.'

'That hasn't changed with the peace?'

'I still play. . . . Is it too soon if I come into you again?'

She opened her legs a little farther in reply.

I don't care, Kate thought, as they walked back to The Little Rose just before dawn. I'll repent by daylight.

The faint blush in the sky was exquisite. A delicious salty breeze off the river cooled the flush in her cheeks.

'Look,' she said. 'There, over the water. How they all move together.'

They stood silently, arms around each other, entranced by the dark tilting bodies of a flock of small birds.

'I'll come for you tomorrow,' he said.

'Not here.' She kissed him to stop any questions. 'Watch for that youth who keeps following you. I'll meet you at the warehouse tomorrow night.'

31

And she did, dressed this time in her brother's clothes.

Francis leapt from his shadows with joy.

They spoke very little on the Turkey carpets under the fur rug. That second night, they coupled with a desperate hunger then walked back afterwards in silence, holding on to each other as if drowning.

Then, just as they parted, tearing live flesh from live flesh, Kate asked, 'What fur is that rug made of?'

'Hush,' said Francis. She had reminded him that the next day was Wednesday.

Halfway up the dark stars of The Little Rose, Kate, too, remembered. She raced back down. 'Francis?' she called urgently

He turned eagerly in the street.

'Take care tomorrow.'

He returned to kiss her again.

Francis did not fear the morrow. He was, however, interested in Kate's fear.

But he was her champion now. The meeting at the Bear Garden, at first a reluctant duty, had become the lists in which he would challenge and defeat whatever troubled her.

He was certain that he would work out how to deal with

the complications of his new secret life. With Kate's voice still in his ear, her smell in his nostrils and her taste on his tongue, a life of duplicity still posed problems, but they seemed soluble ones.

32

With one hand on the wall to guide her, Kate floated up the dark stairs to her lodgings. She was a fool and did not care in the least. Let cold reason come with daylight. She was happy now.

. . . Fourteen steps, fifteen steps, turn on the landing, past Molly's door . . . sixteen, seventeen . . . She began to fumble in her pocket for her key, then froze.

Her door stood slightly ajar.

'Do come in,' said Traylor's voice. His silhouette stood at the window. 'Where have you been?' he demanded.

'Finding Francis Quoynt, as it happens. How dare you come in when I'm not here?' She looked to see that the matting still covered the hiding place in the floor.

'Into my own rooms?' He sounded amused. 'Why don't you strike a light?'

She felt him watching her as she raked a small coal from the banked fire and blew it into life.

'Did Quoynt agree?'

She lit a candle from the coal.

'Well, what have we here?' Traylor crossed the room to her. An aura of sexual intent flared around him. 'Young Master Peach . . .' He ran a hand down her sleeve. 'I quite like you like this. Why have you never shown me before?

142

Fortunate Master Quoynt. I'm jealous. Have you made love again?'

Her flesh crawled.

'He agreed to go to the bear-baiting.' She backed away, but Traylor followed.

'Good girl. Good Kate. I'm sure that he wanted to make love to you.' He reached for the front of her breeches. 'Let me feel if you're hot and moist from seeing him.'

'I'm bleeding,' she said desperately.

'Then you'd best get on your knees to welcome me.'

She emptied her head of all thoughts of murder and met his eyes blankly. Shaped her lips into a stiff smile. 'I have a fresh jug of ale just over there.' She tried to ease past him, but he stopped her again with a hand on the side of her neck.

'Not that kind of welcome.' He pushed her down onto her knees. He untied his codpiece, then the strings of his breeches. 'You needn't pretend you like it.'

She had stopped pretending many months ago. Unfortunately, her dislike of him, and his power to force her in spite of it, excited him far more than her first months of eager willingness.

She sank down into the depths of her well, into a kind of sleep, leaving only her shadow on the surface. The shadow took his stiff penis in her mouth.

She shivered. The creature on the surface had a wild thought of biting. The muscles of her jaw tightened.

Dear Lord, what was she thinking!

Jolted awake again, she caught herself in time, appalled by how close she had come to total folly.

It's not forever, she told herself. Not forever. Not forever. Just a little longer.

This was nothing compared to those days in the Stokewell house. She would survive this, too.

He clutched her shoulders to hold her steady against his

thrusts. She had only to keep her lips closed around him and try not to gag. Thank God he did not demand a show of passion, like the marks who made the whores laugh in derision. 'How the fools are convinced by false shrieks and moans of ecstasy,' they chortled. 'A man sees what he wants to see.'

Over soon. Over soon.

She pulled back, retching from his final deep thrust, and spat the hot slime onto the floor. He slapped her. Then wiped himself with his handkerchief and tucked himself back inside his breeches.

He sat on the chair. 'I'll have that ale now. And clean the floor.'

The jug rattled on the rim of the glass as she poured.

He had himself under full control again this evening. He was again a block of smooth, slippery stone. Dark and glassy. No cracks. Not like the other night. No chinks tonight, or unexpected crevices. She was always surprised by the fleshy reek of his genitals compared to the sharp chilly pebbles of his eyes.

Thoughts ricocheted inside her skull. She was as tall as he was. And much younger. Though he outweighed her, she did not doubt that she could kill him if she tried. If she picked her moment.

But he was not worth hanging for.

'You glower most charmingly,' he said. 'It warms my heart.'

'You know how to flatter.'

He regarded her with satisfaction. 'My great lump of a tamed she-bear.' He held out the cup for more ale.

She gave it to him and watched him drink. Wolfsbane, she imagined. Or a brew of swamp water and turds.

She knew that she had to run, now, with or without money. Before Francis could learn the kind of whore she had become.

Traylor must never touch her again.

Kate looked at her scissors lying on the worktable. She stood trembling, holding herself still with iron bands, willing him to go before she lost control and thrust the scissors through his heart.

33

Shortly before two o'clock the next afternoon, Francis headed for the Bear Garden flag. The jostling crowd, men and women both, surged around him up the Bankside. Half the city seemed to be pouring across London Bridge into Southwark.

An excited turmoil almost blocked the entrance to the baiting place. Toughs in leather jerkins and armed with pikes huddled around their officer, getting last-minute instructions. People climbed over the movable railings placed on either side of the entrance to hold back the crowds. Bodies lining the riverbank pushed and shoved to get a better view of the water.

'The King is coming!' they cried. 'To see the baiting.'

'There.' Heads craned and arms pointed.

The royal barge approached down the river from the palace at Whitehall, its gilding satisfyingly resplendent in the afternoon sun, banners snapping, oars in perfect unison.

Francis paid and went through the carriage arch of the Bankside inn, down a short, muddy track. The bear pit, an eight-sided, roofless wooden amphitheatre, rose three storeys high. Its rings of seats climbed in tiers, with galleries above. A stout, circular wooden palisade protected the spectators from the beasts that would fight on the sand-covered arena at the centre. The stench of dogs and wild beasts rolled in from the cages and kennels in the field beyond the bear pit.

Francis gazed with his usual curiosity. A few seats were enclosed in boxes, special chairs, like the private pews of a church. An elderly carpenter was hastily nailing garlands of ivy and holm oak above one of these chairs. Just below him, two stewards argued heatedly about which of two pillows would be softer for the royal buttocks.

Francis watched the feverish preparations with amusement. Clearly, the novel condescension of the royal presence at a popular entertainment threw the King's new subjects into a state of high alarm.

Condescension notwithstanding, railings around the royal box separated the press of common bodies from the royal party.

Francis ran his eyes over the gathering crowd for a sign from the person he was to meet. The bear pit was already jammed with spectators of both sexes. Still more were elbowing their way in. Thirteen bears and a bull, the placard had said. The ferocious appetite of peaceful saddlers, tinkers, tailors and clerks for the pleasures of baiting astonished him.

He squeezed himself into a seat near the entrance, on the first tier, from which he could make a swift exit when he had had enough. As a result, he could almost have touched his new sovereign as the man entered the Bear Garden, passing no more than five feet away. A short, stocky, bearded figure preceded by three men-at arms, walking too fast, as if embarrassed. His Majesty lifted a hand almost absently in response to the patchy cheers. James the First of England and Sixth of Scotland was a little disappointing after the grandeur of his barge.

Followed by a posse of attendant lords and gentlemen, the new King stumped up the steps to his box, dropped onto his seat with an audible thump and looked about him. His jaw moved as if he were chewing. His small, close-set eyes studied the startled crowd, which had been expecting at least the warning blast of a herald's trumpet, if not a triple fanfare with drums.

An ugly bastard, Francis thought. Even for a Scot. And, by God, I believe he is wearing a padded doublet for protection against an assassin's knife, just as rumour has it.

'God bless His Majesty,' cried a tentative trio of voices.

The assessment in the King's face gave way to pleasure. He gave a smile of ravishing sweetness.

'Long live His Majesty!' bellowed the gratified crowd.

Then a single man's voice yelled, 'Is the Queen at Mass, then?'

The King's smile faded.

'You sold us to Spain,' cried a second voice, tremulous with daring and passion. 'To Spain, the Scots and the Papists.'

'And yer a bluidy traitor!' a Scottish voice shouted back.

'. . . Scottish barbarians dressed as gentlemen,' muttered a voice behind Francis. '. . . Like bears in doublets.'

Someone else then booed. It was not clear at whom.

A scuffle broke out around the first voices. Six pikemen hustled two men away through the heavy doors that would later admit the beasts.

'They're dog meat now,' cried a wag. Only a few people laughed.

At last, a trumpet sounded. A troupe of flustered singers, clutching sheets of music, rushed onto the sand to sing a hymn of welcome to the new King.

The King, however, sat stony-faced, while his attendants muttered among themselves. Unrest still simmered where the two troublemakers had been sitting.

At the end of the song, an acrobat sprang up from a seat on the front row, vaulted over the palisade and did back-flips around the arena. No one watched him. The word 'treason' buzzed in the air like a plague of horseflies. As did speculation about the likely fate of the two offenders. The execution of traitors offered even finer sport than the killing of bulls, dogs and bears.

Francis bought some hazelnuts from a vendor, with one eye on the crowd. He still saw no sign that anyone recognized him.

He . . . or she . . . had best not make me sit here until dark, he thought. I'd have chosen an alehouse myself.

He could not imagine finding pleasure in the wilful death of any creature. Death might often be the result of his own work, but it was never his chief purpose. And those who died were, for the most part, men like himself who had entered into the contract of war.

The afternoon's baiting began with the bull. Bellowing and shying, the beast was hauled in by six large men and tied to a stout post in the centre of the arena. A revolving ring allowed it to circle around the post. The tips of its horns had been wrapped with leather to keep it from goring the dogs.

One at a time, men paraded three mastiffs on leashes, calling out each dog's name. The air began to hum with the placing of wagers, both among friends and with touts.

At last, the dogs were let off their leashes.

'*Hoo! Hoo!*' shouted the crowd. 'To him, Sable!' 'Take him, Trump!' '*Sa! Sa! Sa!*'

The bull roared and stamped, keeping its head close to the ground so that the dogs could not get under the horns and grab its snout.

Francis gazed up into the afternoon sky and thought about Kate. Tonight at the warehouse. They must talk together more this time. Afterwards.

A pulsing surge in the clamour made him glance down in time to see a dog hit the side of the palisade and tumble into the sand. Its hindquarters dragged as it tried to rise, its back broken.

'One for the bull. A clean toss.'

The owner clubbed the dog and took the body away. The bull was bleeding from a gash on its hind leg and a torn muzzle.

Francis eyed the spectators on either side of him. Still no sign of whoever wanted to meet him. On his left, a short man with heavy muscles in his forearms and red clay under his fingernails was shouting at the two remaining dogs. 'Don't take all day about it. Bite the bastard!'

The man on Francis's right sat with his face in his hands. A backer of the tossed dog, Francis surmised. He cracked a hazelnut with his fingers and ate it.

The bull tossed no more dogs, began to take too many bites to its hindquarters, and was retired. The crowd booed its exit. Francis watched King James pay over with his own royal fingers the wager he had lost. The new regal informality might take many people a time to get used to.

His Majesty declined to bet on the next animal, a Russian bear.

'Harry Hunks. Harry Hunks. Harry Hunks.' The crowd chanted its name.

Like the bull, Harry Hunks was chained to the post. After much roaring and feinting while the dogs lunged and retreated, the bear's claws tore open a dog's belly. Shouts of despair burst out from those who had bet on the dog to survive.

But while the bear was distracted, another dog sprang at it from behind and closed its jaws on the loose skin behind the front leg. For a second the dog hung, swinging two feet above the ground, then the bear's skin tore. The dog fell to the sand and scrambled away while its owner shouted in triumph. Like the bull, the bear was retired to be patched up by its keeper.

Francis dozed through three more bears.

'Put your money on the next bear,' confided the potter on Francis's left, who had noticed his neighbour's earlier glance at his hands. 'Caledonian Meg. A Scottish bear. Smaller than the Russians but even braver than old Harry Hunks. They've kept back some of the best dogs to bait her.' He waved at a tout.

Francis watched the King lay a wager but could not tell whether it was on an English dog or the Scottish bear.

'*Sa! Sa! Sa!* To her!' cried the owners of the dogs.

Caledonian Meg was much smaller than the other bears but quicker. She killed two dogs almost at once and crippled another.

'Yes,' screamed her backers. 'Sweet girl! Oh, you darling!'

'Send the accursed beast back to Scotland,' a man shouted.

'Back where it belongs,' chimed another voice.

There was a rumble of agreement. Looks were exchanged between other spectators. An awkward ripple passed through the crowd. Many looked at the King, then away again quickly. His Majesty stared straight ahead, gripping the arms of his chair.

Two constables raised their eyebrows at each other but could not agree whether or not a further breach had been committed. They moved closer to the source of the shouts.

Caledonian Meg snuffled warily and rocked on her hind legs as a single replacement dog was brought in.

'That's the one!' cried Francis's other neighbour. 'He'll get her by the nose. English Knight. Owned by the Duke of Suffolk. Eight to one, for.'

A great swaggering mastiff circled the arena on its leash, its flat nose striped with white scars from previous battles, its eyes on the bear.

The crowd roared approval. 'The English Knight to take the Scottish bear,' they shouted. 'English Knight! English Knight!'

Francis listened to the undertone as money was laid on the dog. The yells of the crowd held emotions more complex and dangerous than a simple sporting lust for blood.

'A pound on the bear,' he said to the man on his right.

The mastiff was released.

Unlike Harry Hunks and the other bears, Caledonian Meg did not roar as she met the dog's attacks. She seemed instead to contain her force, increasing it by her silence.

Just as containment magnifies an explosion, thought Francis. When it comes.

'Sa! Sa! Sa!'

The mastiff danced closer, made bold by the bear's quiet demeanour. Suddenly, with an audible grunt, Caledonian Meg swung like a boxer, putting her body behind the blow. Her long claws scooped up the mastiff and flung it, writhing and bleeding, over the palisade into a woman's lap.

A roar of rage went up in the amphitheatre. The King, who had half-risen to his feet in triumph, sat down again and stared at the crowd.

The woman screamed and struggled to escape from under the dog, which snapped and howled in pain. Men leapt to the rescue. Spectators began to pelt Meg with apples and nuts.

'Back to Scotland! Back to Scotland!' The chant started with a single lonely voice but quickly gathered force. 'And take your Papist cronies with you!'

Shouts of both outrage and approval replied. Two men exchanged blows. A third one piled in. Francis stood up. Once the constables and pikemen waded into the growing melee they would not be overnice in choosing which collar to grab.

He was not alone in this thought. There was an accelerating rush for the exit. Among those hastening to leave was the royal party. A guard shoved Francis aside just as he stepped down onto the ground. For a moment, with his shoulders crushed against the nose of the man behind him, Francis looked directly into the frightened eyes of his new sovereign as His Majesty was hustled past.

Francis slid into the wake of the royal party and plunged under the arch. As he was spewed back out onto Bankside he felt a hand on his arm.

'You took your time,' Francis said.

'I wouldn't have missed that last bear for anything.' A red-bearded man released Francis's arm and began to walk beside him.

Kate hung out of her window, listening to the shouts and roars from the Bear Garden, trying to follow what was happening, imagining that she could hear Francis shouting among the others.

A bull first. Its roars raised the hair on her arms.

'*Hoo! Hoo!*' That hunting cry, setting the dogs at their prey. But this prey was chained in place so that it could not escape.

And '*Sa! Sa! Sa!*' Urging the fighters on as if they were duellers.

Francis is there, thought Kate. If he were to shout, she might hear him.

If she went there, she might see him, one last time.

Now came a bear.

'*Sa! Sa!*'

Yelps.

More cheers.

Caledonian Meg would be fighting soon.

Fight well, Kate urged silently. Fight well!

She heard a great cheer. Perhaps for Meg, who was a winning bear.

'Scotland . . . Scotland . . .' The shouts sounded angry. The crowd had stopped cheering.

Kate could not think what might have happened.

The hubbub in the street suddenly grew more urgent. Excited people began to pour out of the entrance to the Bear Garden long before the baiting should have finished. Among the first was a tall figure she recognized with certainty like a blow to the chest.

Her eyes followed his unmistakable, thrusting walk until he was swallowed by the crowd. As a result, she almost missed the King's party hurrying towards the water steps.

Clearly something momentous had happened.

She closed her window and ran down the stairs to the back gate of the Bear Garden.

No one answered her knock. She pounded harder.

'Shog off,' said the young dog-groom who came to the gate at last. His eyes were swollen and red. 'We're all arsy-varsy in here. Don't need gawpers.' He sniffed and slammed the gate again.

'I want to speak with Master Gunn,' shouted Kate.

But the gate stayed firmly shut.

34

Francis noted the liquid, slightly doggy eyes in a handsome, sun-cured face. Soft reddish-brown hair curled above the dark russet beard. He was a little cheered by the fact that, though not small, the man stood four inches shorter than Francis. And, therefore, a little shorter than Kate.

A sense of recognition stirred then subsided again. Francis was aware chiefly of an intense dislike. The fellow was too handsome by half, with that ingratiating manner women seemed to like.

'I'm steering us towards drink.' Red Beard returned Francis's close look. 'If you have no objection.'

'So long as we avoid all alehouses with flowers in their names.'

The man raised his brows in anticipation, but Francis ignored this cue to explain.

What is he to Kate? he wondered. Jealousy stabbed like bad digestion.

They stepped out of the way of a carter who was risking his vehicle on the cobbled cliff-edge of the Bankside. Then the man turned into Unicorn Alley and the maze of tenements that grew like a canker in the yards and crevices behind Bankside. After the briefest of pauses, Francis followed.

They both looked back at the mouth of the alley then glanced at each other.

'I'm alone,' Francis assured him.

'So am I, Quoynt.' The russet facial hair split into a white-toothed smile.

Francis scanned the dark doorways, too close on either side. And there were too many windows and lofts just above his head. His eyes swivelled in the near darkness. His ears strained. The muscles of his shoulders twitched.

He knew this man. But how?

They turned again, into an alley scarcely wider than his shoulders, moving away from the lights and crowds towards the open spaces of the Lambeth marshes. A man coughed a few inches from his left ear, on the other side of a wall. A baby screamed in a steady, inexorable rhythm a few feet above him. Francis could hear hubbub and music faint in the distance. Here, in the narrow channel between high tenement walls, all sounds except the closest ones were muffled. The stink of human ordure was intense.

They emerged into Upper Ground outside an alehouse of the roughest sort, behind Paris Gardens.

'In such a disreputable place,' said Red Beard. 'Who will look twice at a pair of old soldiers?'

But were you the sort I wanted under my command? wondered Francis.

'Why meet at the Bear Garden?' he asked.

'I thought it might prove instructive.'

'The baiting?'

'One could call it that. The dogs most certainly pricked up their hackles and growled.'

'And what's your business with me now that I'm instructed?'

Red Beard stepped over a drunk to enter the smoke and

reek of the tavern. The low room throbbed like a drum with raucous laughter.

Francis waited inside the door with his back against the wall until Red Beard wove back towards him, holding high two slopping ale-pots.

'You didn't answer my question,' said Francis.

The man merely smiled and gave a jovial nod. 'To your good health, Quoynt.' He raised his ale.

Francis declined to drink. 'That's twice you've used my name without offering me yours.'

'Guido.'

The name meant nothing but the sense of recognition twitched again. 'True or assumed?'

Guido drank, gazing at Francis over the rim of his pot. 'It's the name I prefer.' He looked about to see that he was not overheard, his eyes lingering on a snoring lout at the next table. 'Didn't it interest you, being so recently returned to England, to see that our little Scottish monarch is not as popular as official report would have us all believe? And to observe that His Majesty's claws are blunter than those of the little Scottish bear.'

'The two men arrested for pointing out that the new Queen is a Papist won't agree about the blunt claws.'

'Those intolerant louts deserve everything they will get.' A flash of real anger lit the doggy eyes.

A Catholic sympathizer, thought Francis. The first break from cover. 'Do you want to buy gunpowder?'

Guido inhaled sharply and pulled in his chin. 'Why do you think that?'

'Do you take me for a fool? Why else would you seek me out? How much do you want?'

Guido stared at him.

Francis rose to his feet. 'Thank you for the drink, Master Guido. You're wasting my time.'

'How much powder do you have?' Guido spoke aggressively, trying to regain control of the conversation.

Something felt awry to Francis. Guido was not the right name. But he could not remember where he had seen the man. There was something tricky and emollient about him, a hungry eagerness that Francis knew he should pity. Instead it made him want to bite Guido's head off. Together with that air of self-important secrecy and a trudging wit . . .

His sense of smell told him to steer clear. The business now concerned his livelihood and reputation. He had fulfilled his promise to Kate and owed her nothing more. He could not imagine how she came to know a creature like this.

'Sit down, Master Quoynt. I beg you.'

'I don't think I can help you,' Francis said. 'We don't hold stocks and our mill is shut down. There's no need to keep it running, with the new truce.'

'Please give me another minute. I didn't expect to plunge straight to details. I hoped merely to meet you, learn what you can offer.'

'A glut of powder was released when the armies were stood down after the treaty. Anyone can buy powder on the Continent for a sixpence. I suggest you look there.'

Guido gave Francis a knowing look. 'We . . .' He corrected himself. '. . . I need the best.'

'You've already bought powder on the Continent,' said Francis with sudden understanding. 'But it was decayed.'

Guido nodded. 'I have some experience with explosives, but mainly as a sapper.'

In other words, thought Francis, you lack the experience to risk remixing decayed powder.

But if Guido had been a sapper, it would at least explain how they might have met.

'Most of the powder was decayed,' said Guido. 'We lost the rest in an accident.'

Francis felt his mind heave with an almost physical effort as two words boiled to the surface.

Bridge House.

He sat down again.

35

'I assume you don't have a licence to import gunpowder yourselves,' Francis said to Guido. 'Don't give me that startled look. Between you and me, licences are just another excuse to extract fees from the poor working man.'

Guido conceded with a shrug but cocked his head as if listening for a false note in the other man's sudden geniality.

'You should have said.' Francis clapped him on the shoulder. 'Next time . . .' He decided not to overstretch his performance by saying 'my friend'. '. . . When you need to import without a licence, come to me first. There are helpful fishermen down on the Sussex coast who can catch the most wondrous things in their nets.'

He felt a quick surge of relief at being able to tell a simple truth. Shelvy Mawes had unloaded a good many odd cargoes into the caves in the chalk cliffs before he drowned. The same cliffs where, as boys, he and Francis had played at being smugglers and buccaneers.

'How much powder do you need?'

Guido narrowed his eyes suspiciously. 'I thought you couldn't help us.'

Francis leaned across the table and spoke under his breath. 'Not legally. So I had to be certain. You might have been an agent of Cecil . . . or Bacon. I need to keep my licence. For at least some of my work.'

Guido stared at him for a very long time. 'Why are you so sure I'm not an agent?'

In a parody of the bluff soldier he was trying to imitate, Francis patted Guido on the arm. 'I trust my sense of smell. I read you as an honest man.'

Guido's mouth twitched with a gratification.

I have just lied and been believed, thought Francis with uneasy astonishment.

'You must meet someone else,' said Guido. 'Before we go further.'

Francis shook his head. 'I'm losing patience. You and I can talk together, can we not, Guido? We may serve others, but we still have minds and tongues of our own.'

Guido bristled. 'I serve no man.'

'There's no shame in serving. I've never ached to be a general.' Francis watched the other man settle his feathers again. 'I need to know if it's worth my time to go further.'

Guido sighed in concession. 'Forty full barrels.'

Four thousand pounds of gunpowder.

Francis whistled softly.

When the watch cried nine o'clock, Kate ran back down the lane at the side of the Bear Garden, past several fornicating couples. To her surprise, the rear gate was now unlocked. The mud was furrowed by cartwheels. She listened to the frantic yelps of the dogs.

She pushed the gate open. The window at the back of the chief bear-ward's hut still glowed with lantern light. The spades kept for shovelling out the stalls, kennels and cages were missing from their usual place against the wall. At the far end end of the field between the two rows of kennels, three dog grooms threw gobbets of meat to the baying hounds. Feeding was very late tonight. Things seemed still to be all arsy-varsy, as the young groom had said earlier.

Kate turned right and followed the wall towards the familiar stink.

Caledonian Meg was gone.

In disbelief, Kate pressed her face against the cold bars of the cage door. 'Meg!' she called softly into the darkness. She listened for the rattle of the chain or the familiar monster sigh.

She heard only hollow, rackety emptiness.

'Master Gunn!' She banged on the lighted window. 'Master Gunn!' She banged again. 'Where's Caledonian Meg?' she demanded when an irate face appeared. 'Was she killed?'

'No such luck.' Gunn began to close the window again. 'Pug off. I'm trying to save a valuable dog she ruined.'

'Where is she?'

'Sold to the first taker. Gone. And good riddance. She lost me the King's patronage this afternoon.'

'Just for injuring a few dogs?'

'For provoking a riot. I hope they make her into a rug.' The window slammed shut.

'Who bought her?' begged Kate. But Gunn had returned to his injured dog.

Kate's eyes felt hot and swollen as she lay in the dark in her little room, trying to sleep.

It's not fair, she thought. Meg was only doing what they wanted her to do.

If she did it well, it was their lookout. When you're attacked, it's natural to fight back. Where's the good in turning the other cheek if you end up dead?

The thought of that bearskin rug made her stomach heave. She was already sick with apprehension. Meg's disappearance merely confirmed the decision she had made after Traylor left her.

A stab of perception showed her the shameful truth. Without prodding, she might have kept on passing through her present life until she died.

Francis slept no better than Kate. After leaving Guido, he had waited for Kate at the warehouse, but she did not come. For a time, part of him was almost relieved. He could not think how to ask her what he now needed to know.

In spite of her prohibition, he then went to The Little Rose. She was not there.

He ran back to the warehouse in terror that he had missed her.

Then, suddenly, he grew furious. He was not a fool. He knew very well why she would not let him come to her lodgings. He had always known but tried not to think of it. Had avoided conversation because he was afraid of what he might hear.

He would not go back to The Little Rose to mope like a lovesick puppy outside her door. He was not yet ready to see the other man. She was out with him now. (*Please, let him not be Guido!*) She had duped him on that pile of Turkey carpets in the warehouse.

Just before dawn, he was striding along the Thames towards Greenwich, still chasing after his thoughts as if they were runaway geese.

The river glowed as if it had trapped the faint dawn light before it could reach the sky. Some of the wherries crisscrossing between London and Southwark still carried their lanterns. Others, already unlit, slid indistinctly like optimistic ghosts, gaining substance with every moment that passed. Mist still blurred the rigging and furled sails in the Pool.

Francis looked blankly at the ghostly masts, lanterns and indistinct hulls of the great sea-going ships anchored in the

Pool of London below the Bridge. The thought of Kate paralysed him into helpless confusion.

She had said that she delivered many messages. Was, in fact, a woman for hire.

What if she had turned whore after he left?

He could not imagine how the dignified daughter of a respectable glove-maker might turn whore. But, if so, he could not deny his own responsibility. Taking her maidenhead. Not making his intentions clear before leaving her. He would prostrate himself at her feet, learn what had happened to her in his absence . . . offer to put right whatever he could.

He was not yet ready to think about the fact that she had arranged a meeting with a former sapper who wanted, together with some mysterious 'we', to buy four thousand pounds of gunpowder. A man who, with his friends, had very likely owned the gunpowder stored illicitly in Bridge House. Kate might even know the name of the dead man.

No jumping to conclusions. He must now be as deliberate and careful in his actions as when laying and setting off an explosive charge. Every move in order. No haste, even when there was much urgency.

The water below him swirled as a fish struck at an insect on the surface.

Where had she been last night? he wondered again. Why didn't she come to the warehouse?

36

At dawn the next morning, Kate found a sack in the closet and began to pack. She gathered up her father's knives. Then she put them back down on the table and looked at the pale crumpled doeskin of an unfinished woman's glove.

She had accepted orders and part-payment for those gloves, as well as several other pairs.

She was not a thief, whatever else she might be.

She listed everything to be done before she left: the doeskin gloves with embroidered cuffs for the wife of the landlord at The Antelope; another pair of women's gloves in yellow goatskin, also with embroidered cuffs and an edging of gold lace. A mending job. A pair of men's riding gloves, no embroidery. A further hawking glove.

Three days, if she burned precious candles to work all night. Three days of avoiding Francis Quoynt, who must not learn what kind of whore she had become.

Her body felt permanently clenched with self-loathing.

If Traylor returned, she would stab him with the scissors and hide him in the closet where he had locked her. And be gone before he could stink enough to draw attention through that reek of beer.

Even without enough money, she must run far enough that neither of them could ever find her.

She finished the doeskin gloves by midday. In spite of her urgency, she gazed with satisfaction at the little silk knots and feather stitching on the cuffs, and smoothed the silky leather with her fingers to leave faint marks on the nap.

Bankside gossip reported gleefully that Mistress Skeat at The Antelope once earned her living on her back in the Paris Gardens. But, as a landlord's wife, the woman now cooked and scrubbed. Either way, in Kate's view she had earned a few luxuries. As had the whore who ordered the yellow goatskin gloves.

The whores were more honest than she was, Kate thought, as she pricked out the patterns on the buttery, saffron-dyed leather. She did not lie to herself about that, at least.

She then patched a pair of red deerskin gloves between the fingers, for one of the boy players at the Globe Theatre. Mid-afternoon, she went out to deliver both pairs of gloves.

'How rich! How fine! What a beautiful silk garden you've made to bloom on the cuffs,' cried Mistress Skeat, the landlord's wife, turning her hands this way and that in delight.

The encounter lifted Kate's spirits enough for her to decide next to brave the Bridge. As she walked along the Bank past the pike ponds, she kept thinking about Mistress Skeat's pleasure, and how the woman had pressed Kate to make a pair of riding gloves for her husband. With hot cheeks, Kate had promised to return for the order when she was not so busy.

She watched the hands swinging by her and assessed the quality of the gloves they wore. She could make gloves as well as any proper glover. Wherever she might go. The Guild could not possibly have spies in every small village in

England. She would make gloves as she made them now, outside the law – doubly damned, both as a Papist and as a woman. There must be custom enough among the rest of the damned.

I truly like to make gloves, she thought suddenly. She could be content to spend the rest of her life keeping her thoughts on gussets, French knots and fringes, and on giving pleasure to women like Mistress Skeat.

Though her brother had been their father's apprentice and would have taken over the workshop, Kate had always helped. And when not helping, she watched. Her father sent her to buy threads and metal wires. He let her cut out the blanks and thread his needles when his sight began to blur.

Along the length of Bankside, men lounged outside the string of inns, taverns and hostelries. The Anchor, The King's Head, The Leopard, The Unicorn, The Rose.

'Coney, coney, come over here,' cried one as Kate passed.

'There's a tall one,' cried another. 'Imagine those legs wrapped around your waist.'

'Bella, bella, bella,' moaned another in mock agony. 'Relief, I beg you.'

She turned her head to the river as if she did not hear. To her left, just above the Bridge, the Thames broke around the starlings that supported the arches. Tumbling skeins of white water thundered into the wheel of the great corn mill in the nearest arch on the Southwark side.

Kate drew a deep breath, readying herself to walk over the roaring waters, to buy more silks as well as spare needles. Ochre, scarlet, crimson, azure, oak-leaf green . . . she would carry secret colours in her runaway bags.

She saw a pale shape in the river just below her, tapping gently against the upstream side of the stone water steps. A human skull, minus jaw, bobbed gently. It was settling onto the mud as the tide flowed away, leaving it trapped behind a rotten mooring post.

Kate climbed down the slippery green steps into the muscular pull of the current, feeling for her footing in the mud. She stretched out a long arm. At the touch of her fingers, the skull bobbed away. She leaned a little farther and hooked a forefinger through the nearest eye-socket.

'What you got?' Three filthy boys with running noses blocked the top of the steps.

She tipped the water from the skull and rinsed off the mud. 'It's mine! So shog off!'

Thank you, Holy Mother, she whispered. The skull was in near-perfect condition. Washed clean of flesh, only a little green with weed.

Wearing her fiercest face, she sloshed up the steps with her wet skirt grabbing and slapping at her ankles. The three boys moved back from this tall, strong-looking, grim-eyed young woman. Nevertheless, she kept an eye on them. Three was a dangerous number; they could work as a pack.

'Your lucky day, duck,' called a waterman who was just pulling in to the stairs.

'A pound for it,' cried one of his passengers.

Kate shook her head and clamped the skull firmly into the crook of her arm. Whoever you were and however you got into the river, you do me a good turn now, she told it.

The stench of decay drifted down from the heads and body parts of executed traitors and other wretches displayed on the roof of the Great Stone Gate. Kate looked up. Her skull might have fallen from there. Or the Bridge Warden might have thrown it into the river to make room for a fresh head.

'What you gonna do with that?' The boys followed her, but she ignored them.

They gave up their chase after a few more yards and

returned to the stairs to circle the new arrivals from the wherries.

'Bitch!' one of them shouted after her.

'Ten shillings,' said the physician.

'Two pounds.' Kate had polished off the faint green sheen of algae. The white bone gleamed in her hand.

'I could have you arrested for grave-robbing.' The physician pressed a scented handkerchief to his mouth as if she stank. His orange-water and frankincense reached her across four feet of waxed floor.

Silently, Kate held his eye. *You don't frighten me. You're a pubic louse, like the rest of your kind.*

When he looked away, she made a cold, assessing survey of the room. You're doing nicely, sir, she thought. That's a costly gown. That cupboard is stacked with brass and pewter.

A manservant, not a mere maid, had answered the door of the substantial house tucked behind Thames Street, near the Glaziers' Hall.

Kate stared again with angry eyes at the posy hung around the physician's neck as protection against the annual summer plague, and wondered if he wore arsenic cakes in his armpits as well.

'Two pounds,' she repeated. He would have it set in silver and sell it for three times as much.

The physician took the skull and turned it in extraordinarily clean, soft hands.

'The plague this summer threatens to be worse than the last,' Kate said. 'Your patients will clamour for such a drinking cup.'

She would wager that he fled from the City every summer. Like all the rest of his kind.

'One pound,' he offered.

She snatched back the skull.

'Thirty shillings then. My final offer.'

'You're not the only physician in London.'

'Thirty-five.'

'Thirty-seven.' Kate kept her hold on the precious skull until he had counted the money into her hand.

As she left, she asked over her shoulder, 'How many have you left to die?'

Back in Thames Street, she hurried past a family of beggars, who clamoured after her with a theatrical display of scurfs, scars and missing limbs.

Thirty-seven shillings, she thought in joyful disbelief. The profits from a month of glove-making. And of hunting for dropped coins by the water steps and in the Long Southwark marketplace. And any other shift she could think of.

What more did she need to assure her that she was right to flee at once?

Thank you, Holy Mother, she breathed. For sending me such a clear sign.

She let a group of shouting apprentices overtake and pass her. Then waited again while termers from the different Inns of Court and Chancery surged past in the other direction. When certain that she was not observed, she retied her purse to her rope belt and tucked it through a slit in her skirt, to lie on top of her petticoat but under the bumroll she had borrowed from the whore living below her at The Little Rose.

Thirty-seven shillings to help start a new life.

She could almost afford to spend a little money on one of her black widow's gowns, she thought, with improper delight. She imagined Traylor arriving to find her chamber empty. And Francis throwing his poxy squibs, or whatever they were, against her window in vain.

Crossing back over the Bridge with those thirty-seven wonderful shillings in her purse and a fragile new sense of purpose, she looked straight down at the turbulent slide of the current. For a few moments, she stayed firmly at the rail while the current crashed and tossed below her, breaking up the evening light like shattered glass.

She was off. Nothing would stop her now.

37

Francis went alone into The Duck and Drake, a city inn near The Strand to which Guido had directed him. Inside the door, he stopped and peered through the smoke. Then he froze.

He saw the man at once. Catesby was as easy as ever to pick out in a crowd, seeming to be lit a little more brightly than the more ordinary mortals around him.

The handsome, amiable face lifted. Francis remembered very well how they had met. He had clasped the finely shaped hand now raised in greeting.

'What do I call you now?' he asked quietly when he reached the table.

'Robin, as always. It's safe enough. We're among friends here.'

Francis took a stool and stared in dismay at his quarry. Facing him across the wooden table sat a broad-shouldered man with lively, intelligent eyes, in his early thirties, only three or four years older than Francis. He was dressed with restraint in sombre gold and brown, but expensive engraved silver buttons edged the front of his doublet. Robert Catesby, a gentleman of the middling sort and a militant Catholic.

Catesby had joined the traitor Essex in an earlier rebellion against the old Queen. Unlike Essex, Catesby escaped with his head, though he had to sell his estate to pay a fine of four thousand marks. In the open throat of his doublet and shirt, he now wore, clear for anyone to see, a gold crucifix on a chain. Wearing a crucifix was forbidden by English law. Around Catesby's neck hung an open challenge to the Anglican authorities.

'Robin,' said Francis uncertainly.

'Welcome, France.' Catesby gave a delighted smile. 'My old comrade in cups and conversation! I've been as edgy as a lover waiting to learn if you would come.'

Francis felt a rush of renewed liking in spite of the circumstances. He smiled and spread his arms. 'Here I am.'

'Well.' Robin Catesby shook his head in happy disbelief. 'Who'd have thought we'd meet again like this? Thank the Lord it's not face-to-face on the battlefield.' He grabbed the skirt of a serving girl. 'Wine for my friend.'

They looked at each other in silence while they waited for her return. They had seen the same things, though from opposite sides of the battlefield. Once, during a chance encounter in Bruges after the truce, they had got drunk together and talked until dawn. They had been enemies on the battlefield but that counted for less that night than being two Englishmen of companionable natures, both soldiers, both away from home. They never met again but the evening in Bruges, though blurred by time, left a lingering warmth.

'Here's to all of us who are victims of the peace,' said Catesby when he had his wine in his hand. 'The heroic firemaster and the intrepid officer. Whatever are we to do with ourselves now, you and I?'

Francis warmed to this easy familiarity as he had in Bruges. 'We could try to live like other men. I may turn farmer.'

Catesby laughed. 'Exchange fireballs and shells for cabbages and turnips?'

'I'm weary of war,' Francis heard himself say.

'As are we all. But what else do we know?' Catesby leaned

forward. 'Be honest, France. At least you still have your land. I've none of my own while Ma's alive. Not since I was forced to sell Chastleton to some Protestant shopkeeper. I no longer have a place as a gentleman. What else am I fit for, but to fight?'

Francis raised his eyebrows at the suppressed anger in Catesby's voice.

Catesby looked down into his drink. 'There are still battles to be fought. Here in England.'

Their eyes met. The rhythm of their meeting changed.

'Bridge House?' Francis asked quietly.

Catesby fumbled at his cup and splashed wine onto the table. 'Explosion heard all the way to Hackney, they say.' He studied Francis for a moment with intent eyes. 'What caused it?'

Francis glanced at the glint of gold inside Catesby's shirt. A black melancholy seized him. He did not want to be there. 'Your gunpowder,' he said.

'Why do you say that gunpowder caused the Bridge House explosion?' Catesby's eyes were now too candid, his mouth uneasy. 'I never heard it named as the cause.'

'Because I went there shortly after the blast. My mother smelled of sulphur and saltpetre when I first suckled at her breast. I learned to corn powder at the age of nine. I'm not likely to mistake the smell of it now.'

They sat in silence for a moment.

'You set Guido to find me, Robin. I think you'd best make the next move.'

Catesby gazed down at the table for a moment, then straightened in decision. He looked Francis in the eye. 'Guido wasn't here to land the stuff. I had to leave it to someone else less experienced with gunpowder. I blame myself for the death.'

Francis nodded with understanding. 'As you doubtless blamed yourself for the death of any of your men.'

'I'm asking you to find more powder for us, France. To replace what was lost in the explosion and the spoiled barrels from abroad.'

'For what purpose?'

'It's best if you don't know.'

'But your purpose will determine which powder you need. Is it fine grain for muskets, for example, or coarse grain for mining walls?'

'It's not for muskets.'

Robin seems to find deviousness as distasteful as I do, thought Francis wryly.

'For mining, then?'

Catesby shrugged. 'That's close enough.'

'Robin! You can tell me that you want me to sell you, illegally, enough gunpowder to supply an infantry regiment. But you can't tell me why? I must know why you need so much. The war is over. We're back in England now.'

'Which England?' Catesby asked, almost too low to be heard.

'How many are there?'

Catesby drew a breath, then shook his head. 'Only one England, of course. You're quite right. But as for the English . . .' He drew lines radiating out of the pool of spilled ale. 'They're of all sorts. Followers of the Church of England. Followers of the Church of Rome. All of them good Catholics.' His voice tightened with emotion. 'Some of those good Catholics hold other good Catholics, like me, to be enemies of England. Must we lose everything merely because we won't swear allegiance to their new, bastard English religion? Because we refuse to turn traitor, as they have done, to the True Church? Which was once the church of every grandfather and grandmother in England. The church even of kings.'

'Please don't say too much,' begged Francis.

'You knew I was Roman when we met in the Low

Countries. I never hid it from you.' Catesby's forefinger sketched a small cross on the tabletop. 'The Crown didn't like the way I said my prayers then and likes it even less now.'

'Robin, I'm a loyal Englishman. And I want to keep my head on my shoulders, my guts inside my belly and my cock between my legs. And you should want the same.'

'The treaty with Spain will ruin us all,' said Catesby. 'The Spanish King has renounced his support for English Catholics. We have been abandoned.'

He clenched both fists on the tabletop. 'We have been doubly betrayed. Scottish James promised us tolerance . . . before his accession. Now, safely on the throne, he has broken those promises, twice. He did not revoke the laws oppressing us. Instead he makes new laws that are even more savage. In February, all Catholics were declared outlaws. Therefore, the King of England is no longer our king. We have lost our allies abroad. All our hope is gone. All we have left is action.'

Francis held up his hand. 'No more, I beg you.'

'I'll tell you frankly, France, we mean to strike a blow that will turn England upside down. And I entreat you to help us.'

Francis stared at Catesby in dismay. 'You shouldn't trust like this, Robin. You don't know me after just one evening in Bruges. I might betray you.'

Catesby shook his head. 'Those open words show you still to be as honest as I remember. I will trust you, France. I must. I'm a desperate man who must now stake everything on trust. As I trust in God's support for the cause of the only True Church.'

'Give me time to think.'

'A little time only. Our need is urgent.'

'And the matter is grave. I can't decide in haste.' Francis looked at Catesby unhappily.

Catesby, instantly calmed by his friend's distress, laid on

Francis's wrist a hand that conveyed both reassurance and good will. 'I like the struggle I see in your face. It tells me that you have a conscience. And I would not have you set aside your conscience for the world. God and Conscience are our only guides. But I trust God to guide your conscience towards our cause.'

'Hellfire and damnation,' muttered Francis. 'Won't you give it up?'

'We no longer have any other choice. English Catholics have become no better than slaves in their own country. Would it ease your decision if I told you how we are pursued, imprisoned, tortured and murdered, even now, under a king who promised tolerance?'

Francis shook his head. 'You've already said far too much.'

38

Blindly, Francis crossed back over London Bridge to Southwark. He was in no doubt on one point. He had found Cecil his first traitors.

But he did not know what to do with them. Finding them had been astonishingly simple. Reporting them was impossible. Because Kate Peach had introduced him to the traitors.

He had snared a woodcock he didn't want.

At a well pump, he splashed water over his face and head. Then he shook himself like a hound, replaced his hat and set off again. Farmers bringing produce to the market stepped aside to let him pass. A few turned to look after the tall figure that moved as if it expected the Red Sea to part before it. Their wives looked too, in thoughtful speculation.

Where Long Southwark dwindled to a wide track between rolling fields and heath, he turned right to escape the oncoming stream of horsemen and carts. In the field ahead, a group of archers were shooting at targets. More than one passer-by had been killed by accidental arrows in such situations. Francis turned again and followed a drainage ditch as he reasoned silently.

Kate had asked Francis to meet Guido before he trailed his bait for traitors through the barber-surgeon. Therefore, Guido could not be one of the men he sought for Cecil.

He saw the flaw in his own logic at once. Reluctantly, he followed reason where it took him next.

Two separate favours had led him to the same place. A favour for Cecil, a favour for Kate. Two lines that should have been parallel met suddenly in Guido and Robin Catesby.

He began a large circle to the east, swinging round to rejoin the river to the south of London.

A week ago, he did not know where to start. Now he had an excess of possible quarry. Guido and Catesby, replacing their decayed powder from abroad and the powder lost in the Bridge House explosion. And Cecil's traitors, for whom he had trailed his bait.

Catesby and Guido and his friends wanted four thousand pounds of good powder. Enough to equip an army. To fire five hundred large field-guns, again and again, all at once. A terrifying amount.

No more than two barrels had caused the damage at the warehouses. Multiplied more than ten times . . . twenty times . . . The blast would flatten Southwark, destroy the Tower of London and much of the City as well. And fling the pieces halfway to Powder Mote. There was no innocent explanation for four thousand pounds.

No matter how he kept turning and twisting the facts, the two lines became a single line.

The simplest answer was most often the right one.

Catesby and Guido were Cecil's traitors.

By Catesby's own confession.

Robin Catesby was doubly dangerous, to himself most of all. Long on courage, short on guile.

Francis tried to imagine delivering him to the rack and then a traitor's death.

And what of Kate?

Francis was certain of only one thing. If he told Cecil how much gunpowder was wanted, even without revealing the names of the would-be buyers, the Secretary of State would call in his entire army of intelligencers. It would not take long.

Once Cecil sniffed the scale of Catesby's ambitions, he would find him, find Guido, and have them both on the rack for the names of their associates. And arrest everyone else he could seize for examination. Kate would be interrogated with a little more courtesy, perhaps, but no less fervour.

Francis stared blindly south across the openness of the Lambeth Marshes, with the narrow ribbon of Southwark at his back.

He could not report Catesby to Cecil yet.

His reason now began obediently to construct excuses for putting off telling Cecil everything he knew.

Firstly, Kate might be innocent. Of treason, at least. Unwittingly tangled. She must be protected until she had a chance to explain. (Reason steered clear of the image of Kate being arrested and learning that Francis was responsible.)

Secondly, so long as they did not have their gunpowder, Guido and Catesby were not truly dangerous. And that much, Francis could control. For all Francis knew, Catesby might be one of those men who satisfied their anger with a constant dreaming of great and terrible deeds, but never took action.

And thirdly, until he delivered their four thousand pounds of powder, he still had the chance to prevent whatever they planned. He might keep them, and any other confederates, from rushing headlong at their own destruction. Preventing their 'Blow' would serve England just as well as handing them over to be butchered. And make Francis a great deal happier.

He reached the first houses at the edge of Bermondsey, convinced that Cecil, with his stated distaste for premature alarm, would be the first to tell him not to leap to conclusions.

A softly muscular sea of grey geese washed raucously past his knees, unnoticed.

He must not wait too long to tell Cecil the truth, however. Not after two meetings with men who should be reported. Not when he had heard treason spoken so baldly.

He must not lie to Cecil or his own head would be in the noose, his body on the butcher's block. The populace weren't the only ones to turn their anger on the nearest object.

If he failed Cecil, even slightly, it could be the end of his hopes for a new life, of escape from Powder Mote and the broken window-frames, and the silted-up fish pond, and the bloody ivy that choked him as it choked the chimneys. His father's old Marian sympathies might be re-examined . . . the threat had been floated.

He turned, scattering the geese as he headed back towards Southwark.

He walked past The Little Rose, where Kate could be seen in the window, sitting with her head bent over her work.

Francis groaned again at the thought of causing her arrest.

'Wait till you can offer the populace either a solution or revenge,' Cecil had said. 'Otherwise they turn their anger on the nearest cause to hand.'

Take a leaf from his book, Francis told himself. Wait. Don't give him Kate as a nearest cause.

He continued up Bankside to The Antelope, where he bought bread and ale and sat at the water's edge, trying to shape the best way to ask the woman who had been his first love if she were a traitor or acting for traitors.

Some considerable time later, he returned to The Elephant and wrote a careful, evasive letter to Cecil. He offered only a single name: 'Guido'. Almost certainly assumed.

No mention of Kate. Nor of Robin Catesby.

He took care not to lie, however. Protecting traitors was treachery.

*   *   *

While he waited for Cecil's reply, Francis decided to watch Kate. With luck, he might soon be able to discount his suspicions without having to confront her. The more he considered the alternative – that she was guilty – the more unthinkable it became. He would sooner cut off his hand than injure her again.

Kate sat stitching. He could see her bent head and the top curve of a pale ear. He imagined rushing up those pungent stairs and taking her on the floor.

At least one of the other lodgers in The Little Rose tenements was a whore, to judge by the number of men who passed through the side door in the alley. If the man who now warmed Kate's bed were among them, Francis would never know.

He ached to see the man, in order to despise him.

The following morning he had a letter back from Cecil. Deciphered, it said: *'I find your message tantalizing but incomplete. Sunset, tomorrow. S.'*

39

On Bankside the watch cried, 'One of the morning.'

Kate sat hunched in her shift over a riding glove of medium-weight, buff-coloured deerskin, as close to the window as she could get. When there was a moon, like now, even the night sky gave off a faint light. Three candles burned on her table. A terrible extravagance, but necessary in the circumstances. Silently, she cursed her own urge for perfection that had led her to suggest gold-edged scallops around the otherwise plain cuffs. Her eyelids drooped.

Only two more nights of working, then she could sleep. Even if under a hedgerow.

She had already wrapped the Missal and two Italian glasses in coarse sacking and sewn her rosary into the lining of her unfinished, new black bodice front.

With the money from the skull, she now had one hundred and twenty-two pounds, six shillings, and five pence under the floor, including four gold Portuguese *crusados*, divided among small leather pouches that she would stitch inside her petticoat. She was almost eight hundred pounds short of what she calculated she would need, but at least she owed nothing.

She thought unhappily about the debtors in the Clink as she secured her thread and clipped it off with her knife. *Holy*

Mother, prod someone into feeding them when I've gone . . . She reached for the basket of gold thread.

A willow hamper with leather shoulder straps sat on the floor ready for her tools. It was large enough to hold them all, including the wooden hands. If she padded the sharp corners with her shawl, she could carry the hamper on her back for as long as it took to find a safe place to alight.

The stairs creaked loudly. Under a foot.

She blew out two of the candles and set them in their usual place on the mantelpiece. She hid the hamper in the closet. Then she listened again.

Silence.

She grabbed her shawl off the bed to cover her shift. Something scratched at the door. Paused. Scratched again.

Kate laid her ear against the door, wondering who it could be. Traylor? Francis? One of the homeless? A thief who would slit her throat for her leather knives?

On Bankside you did not open your door rashly.

She laid her hand on the latch, changed her mind and went to the window. The street below was quiet. The Bridge had closed. Curfew was in force, so far as it ever applied in Southwark. Bankside never slept when the law said it must, but it did subside.

While Kate watched, a two-man wherry slid past upstream, the curtains rolled down to hide its passengers. A dog lifted its leg against a post at the top of the water steps. Out of sight to her right, a man laughed. Footsteps faded.

The landing outside her door remained silent. No more scratching.

Kate shoved her feet into her slippers. As she did so, she realized that she intended to open the door. She picked up the long-bladed shears from her worktable. Listened at the door again for a very long time.

No floorboards squeaked as someone shifted impatiently.

But no groans from the stairs announced a departure neither.

She gripped the shears like a dagger. If this were a vicious jest on Traylor's part . . . If he had sent a brigand, or a man to whom he had cruelly promised her favours . . . Or if Mary's terrible hint about short-lived mistresses was based on fact and he'd simply had enough of her . . . She would strike this time.

She opened the door.

She did not see him at first. Then she looked down.

He sat on the floor just outside her door. Even when he scrambled to his feet, he was scarcely more than half her height.

'Mistress Peach?' he whispered.

Kate peered into the darkness behind him on the stairs.

'Please,' he whispered. 'They're looking for me in Southwark tonight.' With his large shaggy head and brown ragged cloak, he looked, in the dim light, like an amiable bear-cub.

Kate let him in. Then she locked and barred the door. 'Who the devil are you?'

'Nicholas Owen.' He introduced himself diffidently. When Kate said nothing, he added, 'Lay brother and joiner.'

'Lay brother?' Kate stared down at him, dumbfounded. Not a thief or murderer, then. Quite the opposite.

'Of the order of Jesuits.' He set down his heavy bag with obvious relief. 'Did Master Traylor not warn you I was coming?'

'Traylor?' Kate echoed again.

A Jesuit fugitive had been sent to her by Traylor?

'There may not have been time to warn you.' He peered up at her with shrewd eyes. 'Would you rather I left again?'

'I'm sorry,' she said hastily. 'You caught me off-guard.'

I think I'm meant to hide him, she thought wildly. At least

Owen was a very small, gentle-seeming creature, with a large dark head and uncertain smile.

'I'm very grateful to you and to Master Traylor,' Owen said.

'Are the pursuivants close behind you?'

'I don't know. I was warned to leave my last lodgings before they arrived. One of the grooms there may have betrayed me. But I fled by boat to put off the dogs.'

'No one will betray you here.'

'Are you of the Roman faith, then?'

Kate nodded.

Owen looked at the room, then back at her. Kate hoped that he was revising his first, inescapable opinion of a young woman who would open her door to a man on Bankside in the middle of the night, wearing only a thin shift. And it seemed that she might have to revise her own opinion of Traylor, at least in part.

'Not every Catholic, however devout, would take such a grave risk,' said Owen.

Kate's mouth grew dry as the truth of the situation began to sink in. With Owen's entry into her lodgings, she had become an outlaw guilty of a capital crime.

Until now, she had been Papist only in her private thoughts, all damning proof hidden under her floor. Now she was sheltering a member of a banned religious order. The Crown pursued the Jesuits as treasonous devils, the root and cause of the ongoing struggle between Catholics and the new Anglican Church.

She would almost certainly hang if Owen were discovered here.

As she began to grasp this truth, she struggled to grasp, too, how a man like Traylor, capable of almost any cruelty and perversion, could also be a Catholic fighting for his religious faith.

She showed Owen the floor of the little closet into which Traylor had locked her.

A look of unease passed over Brother Owen's face.

'I couldn't sleep in that little place either,' Kate said quickly. 'Take my bed, if you like. I must keep working.'

'You don't have somewhere more hidden?' asked Owen.

She shook her head.

'One day, I must make you such a place.' His bag clanked as he set it on the closet floor. He had brought his own food but accepted a cup of warmed wine. Before he closed the door of the closet, she gave him her night-soil pot and coverlet.

Kate stitched all night, imagining footsteps on the stairs. She looked out of the window again and again, certain that she heard the murmur of men gathering in the street outside The Little Rose. Every time a dog howled in the Bear Garden kennels, she knew absolutely that a party of pursuivants was tracking Master Nicholas Owen, Jesuit and outlaw, who had gone to ground under the protection of the Papist traitor, Katherine Peach.

The next morning, she saw that Owen was indeed as small as she remembered, slightly twisted, but otherwise well-proportioned. His manner, too, was as gentle as it had seemed the night before.

After she gave him breakfast, he sat in silence by the fire, and with incredible speed began to whittle at a small block of wood. His knife winked. Chips and shavings fell onto the cloth he had set on the floor to catch them.

Kate stood by the window, watching the street below. 'You said that one day you must make me a hiding place.'

'That is why I came back to England. To make safe hiding places in walls and under floors, for the holy fathers who risk their lives to celebrate the Roman Mass. And to bring hope and courage to their flock.'

'You're very courageous.'

'You will learn that there is good in what I ask of you,' Traylor had said.

'Oh, no. It's you who hide us that are brave,' replied Owen. 'You. And Master Traylor.'

I'm not brave, thought Kate. Merely far too obedient.

'The holy fathers are the most courageous men in the world,' Owen continued. 'The rest of us must do what we can.'

He worked in silence for a time. 'You have a small secret space under your floor.' He lifted his dark head and smiled at her shocked expression. 'My feet can hear it as I walk.'

'Would anyone else detect it?'

'Not unless they were looking.'

'What can I do?'

'Put a second floor-plank directly under that one, for a start.' He examined his work, two shapes that interlocked. Then he tucked it into his pocket and began another.

Kate took up her patterns and scissors. But the blades kept slipping. She peered again and again from the window. Her ears strained to detect footsteps on the stairs.

Owen kept up his carving even after dark. Kate lit him a candle in addition to her own.

'Do you ever stop working?' she asked.

'Do you?' he replied with a smile. 'This is only play. It helps me to steady my thoughts during long hours of waiting.'

She stood watching the fire and the candle flash off his blade. She realized that she was enjoying his presence. He calmed her in a way she did not understand.

'Do you make double floors?'

'I did once. But the pursuivants have now learned to knock and listen for any hollowness. I must devise new, undetectable ways to hide a man. So he can vanish at once, like a conjuring trick.' Owen snapped his short fingers. 'That makes the problem harder. The Communion vessels are easier. They don't need to breathe.'

She nodded, listening to his matter-of-fact acceptance of a life spent constantly at risk of the most hideous death that judicial imagination could devise.

Her own fear shamed her.

And there was something else. She teased it out as she began to punch the stitching holes in the deerskin. It was to do with Traylor and the unexpected side of him that Owen's arrival revealed. She had become less his whore and more his fellow conspirator. If she and Traylor both risked their lives to save others, their relationship was not entirely debased.

When the watch passed on Bankside crying ten o'clock, Owen stood up. 'Time to go.' He gathered up the cloth with the wood shavings so carefully that not one fell onto her floor. He collected his tool bag from the closet.

At the door, he thanked her and handed her a carved wooden apple with a tiny mouse curled inside. 'A rattle for the child you will have one day.'

When he was gone down the stairs, she gave the apple a little shake. Tears pressed at the backs of her eyes, though she had not let herself weep since she left the family house in Stokewell. She closed her eyes and pressed the rattle against her forehead until it dented her skin.

Brother Owen had warmed and frightened her at the same time. Her sleepless night spent listening for his pursuers had shown her what she would have preferred not to see. A harsh and exigent purpose. A terrifying one.

Her urge to flee now seemed selfish and petty. Traylor as a co-conspirator felt more bearable than Traylor as her whore-master. Francis was already lost, even before she turned traitor to England. Rather than run to save herself from indignity and sin, she should do as all good Catholics had been ordered to do by the Pope. She must stay in London, deal somehow with Hugh Traylor, to play her small part in the battle for the true Church.

Francis saw a small figure leaving The Little Rose, though he had missed the arrival. In the darkness he could not see if it was a man or a child. Nor did he know which lodgings the figure had visited. He decided not to follow. When the watch cried eleven o'clock and Kate's candle continued to glow faintly behind her window without further sign of her, or anyone else, he returned to The Elephant to try to sleep. He needed his wits about him for his meeting with Cecil the next day.

40

Francis arrived early. From the cover of a moored dinghy, he watched Cecil's boatman help the Secretary of State up onto the jetty at the warehouse on the Wandle.

A chill trickled down through his chest.

Cecil had a new boatman. A younger, stouter man than the first, with a wide sunburnt face and a smile that sprang to attention whenever Cecil glanced his way.

Well now, thought Francis, wondering if Cecil shared his own conclusion about Bacon's source of intelligence.

What had happened to the first boatman?

In the loft, he told Cecil as little as he could of the truth about just one of the men who wanted to buy some gunpowder. 'Guido.' Almost certainly an assumed name.

He added nothing to what he had already written in his *'tantalizing but incomplete'* letter.

Cecil pounced at once. 'How much does this "Guido" want? A farmer doesn't go to market to buy "a great many cows". He goes to buy seven, or ten, or a score.'

'True, my lord.'

'Now, Quoynt, I'm sure that you are by nature a man of few words, but try to be a little more profligate with me in your future reports. I haven't the time to keep dropping other matters to visit this arsehole of Surrey to prise information out of you. You let me know everything you learn. I'll sift it. How much gunpowder does he want?'

Francis could think of no way to avoid such a direct question. 'Forty barrels. One hundred pounds in each. Four thousand pounds.'

Cecil inhaled audibly. 'Did he tell you what he means to do with so much gunpowder?'

'No, my lord,' said Francis, with relief at being able to speak the unvarnished truth. 'Not yet.'

'Find out.' Cecil pushed himself up from his stool. 'Give him the gunpowder.'

Francis started to speak. Stopped. Spoke anyway. 'I think that would be ill-advised, sir.'

'I see.'

Francis was glad he could not see Cecil's face clearly. The tone of voice was terrifying enough. 'It's too much to trust to an inexperienced handler. Innocent people could be killed, as they were at Bridge House.'

'Do you think this "Guido" is implicated in the Bridge House explosion?'

'It's possible, but I'm not yet certain.' This time, Francis was glad that Cecil could not see his face, even though he had not quite lied.

I'm not absolutely certain, he insisted to himself. You don't hang a man on mere likelihood.

'Give him his four thousand pounds of gunpowder,' said Cecil. 'See where he leads you. Learn who his confederates are. Bring me names. You must be very close to learning names.'

'I've not yet discussed the price with them.' Francis remembered Catesby's bitterness at being without land. 'They may not have the money.'

'If need be,' said Cecil, 'I will pay for it.' He crossed to the top of the loft stairs. 'As for safeguarding the innocent, we must take the smaller risk to avoid a greater one. I depend on you to keep that risk as small as possible.'

Francis pinched his lips together.

'Quoynt? Do you hear me? Do you see a difficulty? The truce did not cancel your licence to make gunpowder.'

'Giving such men gunpowder will encourage their treachery, not prevent it,' Francis murmured. He did not need reminding that his licence could be taken away.

'But I need a traitor,' said Cecil impatiently. 'The King needs a traitor, most urgently. Your task is to find a traitor. I don't think you understand me, after all.'

Halfway down the loft stairs, Cecil paused. 'What did he look like?'

'Who, my lord?'

'Stop playing the simpleton. Guido. Who else?'

Francis gave a brief description. Middling height, handsome enough, russet beard, overeager smile.

'Has he been a soldier?'

'I believe he might have been.'

'Learn if his other name is Fawkes.'

'And if it is?'

'He was my agent once, in Spain. Until he converted and the Spanish turned him. He never knew that I'd learned the truth. Well, well.' Cecil lowered himself down another stair. 'I'm glad I let him run in ignorance. He may yet do me good service.'

Francis watched Cecil's head descend out of sight.

'Give my regards to your father,' said Cecil's voice, muffled by lengths of damp wool.

Listening to the bumping of Cecil's boat against the jetty, Francis thought that his employer frightened him far more than the enemy did. He waited until the sound of oars faded before he went down the stairs.

PART THREE

POWDER SUMMER

'A man must make his opportunity as oft as find it.'

Francis Bacon, Advancement of Learning

41

Brighthelmstone. Summer 1605

Boomer Quoynt leaned back in the sun on a bench in front
of the Ship Inn. Before him lay the sea. To his left, the narrow
ribbon of the market. As a mere village, Brighthelmstone was
proud to have been granted a market charter. Three lines of
stalls and pitches followed the edge of the cliffs above the
beach. At the far end of the market, beyond the Dolphin Inn,
the land tilted down to the low, marshy ground of the Steyne,
fit for nothing but drying fishing nets.

To the other side, on Boomer's right, stood the blockhouse
where local gunpowder and ammunition were stored. Then
the south English coast stretched westward, open and unpro-
tected, to the nearest safe haven at Shoreham, a faint, misty
smudge in the distance.

He gazed past the market at the sea, letting his thoughts
travel onwards. First across the narrow *Mare Britannicum*
between England and France. Then over the *Mare Atlanticum*.
Past the western flank of France. A slice of Spain. The coast
of Africa. The top corner of the southern Americas.

He drank his beer and watched the swaying tips of two
masts on boats moored off the beach below the cliffs, where
fishermen lived in a huddle of cottages.

Though not a sociable man, Boomer believed that the inhabitants of Powder Mote should make themselves seen in Brighthelmstone from time to time. The fishermen and local merchants should be reminded that the Quoynts didn't have horns and tails, even though the estate sometimes smelled of brimstone and the occasional explosion shook the nearby downs.

Boomer also thought it wise to spend money with local tradesmen, however frugally. Sometimes, like today, he enjoyed merely sitting in the sun with a mug of ale in his hand, listening to people being busy around him in the market with nothing more desperate to trouble them than a caterpillar on a lettuce, or a cracked egg. As he was not only suspected of being a wizard but was also the owner of an old local estate, few people approached him uninvited.

He had left his horse up near St Nicholas's Parish Church at the top of the village. Then he visited the nearby black-smith to replace a lost stirrup iron. After that, at the bottom of the hill on the flat ground near the market, he entered the shop of the apothecary, one of the few people in Brighthelmstone who always greeted him with delight.

The Quoynts were the apothecary's best customers. They bought not only large amounts of brimstone, or sulphur as they preferred to call it, but also verdigris, mercury, copper salts, various rosins, and pitch. They bought *aqua vitae,* camphor and linseed oil, both boiled and pure. They bought oil of lavender, varnish and iron scales. Boomer replaced the Muscovy rosin that Francis had burnt up in his rockets and sailed out of the shop before a following wind of flattery and goodwill.

He frowned into his mug now at the thought of his forth-right son in that snake pit called London, but was distracted by a hearty greeting from the apothecary's wife as she passed with a protesting duck under her arm. Then he saw the young fisherman Jem Mawes climbing up from the beach with buckets of the early morning catch.

He hailed the lad. They had met many times on the beach during Boomer's dawn walks. Now Boomer could not help reflecting wryly that young Mawes still worked for his father as a fishing hand on the family's hoggie. Jem had not taken his father's place at the helm.

The young man delivered his buckets to a fishmonger and returned to accept Boomer's offer of a drink.

'How's your father bearing up?' Boomer asked. He himself had lost two sons and an infant daughter.

Jem shrugged. 'He still doesn't say much. He worshipped Shelvy. I do my best, but . . .'

Boomer nodded. They drank for a while in friendly silence.

Jem finished his ale. 'Have to get back. Thank you for the drink, sir.' As he stepped back over his bench, Jem looked at Boomer with sudden concern. 'Are you ill, sir?'

Boomer was staring across the market, his large, craggy face drained of colour.

'Master Quoynt?'

'I'm well,' snapped Boomer. He turned away and rubbed his forehead with his scarred fingers, hiding his face. 'Truly,' he added more gently. 'I was struck by a sudden thought. That's all. Off you go, Jem.'

Jem hesitated.

'Go!'

Jem left, looking troubled.

I've begun to have my nightmares by daylight, thought Boomer.

When he felt that he had his face under control again, he turned back to the market and let his gaze wander idly over the scene before him. The man he had just seen ride up was now dismounting from his horse at the far end of the marketplace, in front of the Dolphin Inn. He handed the reins to an invisible groom then disappeared into the press of bodies.

Don't be a fool, Boomer told himself. You're mistaking a stranger for your private devil.

The man reappeared, a little closer to Boomer. He stood at the edge of the marketplace, near the cliff edge, studying the crowd.

It is he, thought Boomer. There was no mistaking that cold, arrogant face.

Don't meet his eye, whatever you do.

He finished his ale slowly, thinking furiously. He did not know if the man had seen him yet, but he must assume that, if not, he would spy Boomer very soon.

Boomer nodded at a passing stranger, then absently adjusted his codpiece as if it had never occurred to him that he might be observed.

He was asking the wrong questions. Should ask what that man was doing here in Brighthelmstone. And whether he might have come here expressly to find Boomer Quoynt.

Surely not, he thought. Not after all this time.

It made no sense. The man must have known twenty-three years ago that Boomer would discover the lies about the purpose of the raid.

The rough wood of his bench, the wind from the sea, the heat of the sun, all told him that he was awake. He looked up, as if idly, at the seagulls that circled stridently overhead, waiting to swoop on fish guts and discarded offal from the butcher's stall.

He had always felt they would meet again. Now he had to decide what to do.

He rose, knowing that his height would instantly draw the eye. He paid for the drinks. Then he began to saunter among the stalls towards the enemy. When Boomer saw unavoidable danger, he dealt with it at once.

From the side of his eye, he saw the man pause at a stall selling leather pouches. There was no mistake. He was looking at the commander of the raid on the Scottish castle twenty-three years ago, who had cut a young woman's throat and kidnapped her newborn child. And Boomer still did not know why.

He remembered the unarmed boys and old men he had found dead in the castle close. The new mother, the midwife and the waiting woman. All still with him in his dreams.

He could not imagine what would have happened if he had met the man's eyes just now without warning. Recognition would have flashed between them, no matter how quickly suppressed.

Whatever else he might be up to, this man did not leave witnesses alive.

Thank Jupiter, I recognized him after all this time. If he were grizzled and fat I might not have known him until it was too late.

And if Boomer were better known here in Brighthelmstone, it might still have been too late.

He ambled casually, as if a little loose with drink. Near the edge of the market he stopped at a fishwife's stall and stared down in bewilderment at her glassy-eyed wares. 'I'm to buy some sardines,' he said. 'But I've forgotten how many.'

'How many of you at table?' She was happy to help this tall, handsome man with a fearsome reputation but delightful smile.

He gazed at her as if the answer might be read in her sunburnt face. 'Two or three, I believe. Or perhaps it's four.'

She took a net and reached into a barrel. 'Where's your bucket, sir?'

Boomer looked startled, then shrugged. 'I seem to have forgot it.' He smiled again and wandered off. Behind him, the fishwife rolled her eyes a little, as if to say, 'Foolish man!' Nevertheless, she was flushed with flirtatious pleasure.

Boomer reached the very edge of the market, near the cliff edge above the beach, before a low voice said, 'Master Quoynt! I never thought to encounter you here. Are you now turned retired merchant like me?'

There was a challenge in the voice, but Boomer was ready for it.

He turned to the man at his shoulder and stared at him blankly, his expression amiable but puzzled. 'And who might you be, sir?'

And now to continue what I've begun, thought Boomer as his horse climbed the ridge that sloped up from the village to the northwest towards Powder Mote. Jem Mawes most likely thought him ill, though not daft. The fishwife had given him one of those tolerant female smiles.

Who else? The apothecary . . .

He pondered the problem of the apothecary and his wife for a furlong or so. A discreet word, he decided. Without too much explanation. The man would likely say anything Boomer asked, to keep such good custom.

It was just as well that gossip cut both ways. Boomer did not think that Master Hammick, as he now called himself, would be eager to draw the attention of Brighthelmstone to either himself or his past. A 'retired merchant' indeed.

The groom who had returned Boomer's horse at the top of the village had confirmed that a retired merchant named Hammick was said to be the new tenant at Pangdean Place. Boomer went over their meeting yet again in his mind as his mount heaved them up over the lip of the Powder Mote plateau.

At worst, Boomer decided, the man was unsure whether Boomer knew him or not. He must now make certain his story held.

*   *   *

'Who might you be, mistress? What are you doing here in my house?' Boomer frowned at the old woman who had once been nurse to all his children.

Her eyes widened. 'Master Boomer, I'm Susannah White. I'm your housekeeper now. Don't you remember?'

'I don't have a housekeeper,' said Boomer. 'Look around you. Does it look to you as if there's a housekeeper here?'

Susannah burst into tears. 'Oh, Lord help us!'

Boomer patted her on the arm. 'But as you're here, mistress,' he said in kindly tones, 'I'd be most grateful for some supper. Here's for your pains.' He dug into his purse.

'You already paid me for this month, sir.'

As Susannah backed away, Boomer saw a speculative glint come into her eyes. He felt he could read her thoughts clearly.

If he were too addled to remember paying her, what could be the harm in humouring him and letting him pay again? He might not remember that either.

'I'll see what I can find in the kitchens, sir.' She eyed him now with naked calculation. 'If there's anything to be found.'

He had seen her in the market already that morning and hoped she would not reappear to ask for more money to buy food they did not need. He thought her to be an ill-tempered old biddy and a gossipmonger, but also hard-working and very necessary. And, until now, reasonably honest.

When she had left, Boomer fetched a small wooden coffer and a leather sack from his chamber. Then he squatted down in front of the fire and arranged six short lengths of fuse rope side by side in careful parallel lines on the fine but dirty Turkish carpet. Beside the fuses he set three pottery crocks with Latin or Greek labels. He laid a powder spoon, with the edges of its tip bent to form a funnel, beside the crocks.

He rocked back on his heels to consider his work, ears alert for Susannah's return. To the objects on the floor he added some linen strips for shell casings, a wooden casing mould and a wooden stand to hold the casings while they were being filled with explosives. As a final touch, he poured a small mound of salt onto the floor. He thought it unlikely that Susannah would test the grey powder by tasting it.

When he was satisfied with the dangerous-looking arrangement on the floor, he prodded the fire with the iron poker until flames started up brightly from the hot coals where they had been dozing. He added two more logs. Then he went out into the courtyard, leaving the fire roaring and both the hall door and the big front door ajar.

He waited in the courtyard until he heard the housekeeper calling, 'Master Boomer? Here's your supper. Master Boomer . . . ?' Then came a most satisfactory shriek of alarm and then, 'Lord preserve us!' when she saw what he had left in front of the now blazing fire. 'He'll blow us all to Perdition!' She ran back into the kitchen and returned with a basin of water, which she threw on the fire.

Boomer could not have asked for more, not until she went to market the next day. And he was relieved that she had thought the better of asking for more housekeeping money.

Now it was time for another late-night walk on the beach.

42

Kate now waited to learn how God would ask her to serve her faith. She found it hard to believe that Traylor might be His messenger, and even harder to believe that she might once again find something to like in the man. About her decision, she had no doubt.

While she waited, she finished stitching gold lace onto the cuffs of the yellow goatskin gloves. Then she cut out the final hawking glove.

She had lost the knack of sinking down into her well. She felt exposed on the surface like a drowning gnat, tossed by every ripple, waiting for the pike in the depths to strike.

She turned over the pieces of thick cowhide for the hawking glove but left them lying on her table.

She imagined how Francis would back away from her, and his look of horror, if he ever learned, not only about Traylor, but that she was a Catholic. When she was lying naked under him she had shoved such thoughts into a dimly lit, distant corner of her mind.

She could not eat. Her stomach was a tiny clenched fist in her belly.

She was waiting for something to happen, but she did not know what.

On the third day after Brother Owen left, she resumed work on her black widow's gown. Just in case.

A faint tapping on the door made her lift her head from the pillow. She had been asleep for an hour or more. Bankside was relatively silent except for the dogs howling in the Bear Garden.

The tapping was repeated. Three quick taps. Pause. And again, three taps. She sprang up from her bed, ran to the door in her shift and lifted the wooden bar.

A man's dark shape stood just outside the door in the furred shadows of the landing. He was taller than Brother Owen. But not Francis.

'Mistress Peach?' He stepped forward urgently, forcing her back into the room. 'Forgive my uncivil haste,' he murmured. 'I've had someone on my heels all evening.' He dropped the bar of the door, then stood listening. 'Nothing, thank the Lord. But then, I used every trick I know to elude any followers. It would be a poor thanks to you if I . . .'

'I know your voice.' Kate stooped to light a candle from the hot coals of the hearth. Her heart still pounded.

'Did Master Traylor not warn you?' the man asked in dismay.

She stood and held up her candle. The pale golden light glazed his nose and brow. 'Father Jerome!'

A surge of remembered horror made her stagger. The dark hole in which she had kept the past opened like a gaping mouth and swallowed her.

The priest exclaimed in alarm as the candle dropped from her hand and she fell to the floor.

Francis leaned against a wall in Rose Alley with a shimmering unsteadiness under his breastbone. He had just slipped into the side door of the tenement behind a man and followed the careful footsteps to the top floor, to Kate's door.

Francis had glimpsed the man's face as he passed the lantern of The Little Rose. A handsome face – at least what Francis could see of it. Curling beard. Lean cheeks. Too pretty by half.

The rival lover or a Papist traitor?

Perhaps both.

Francis pulled his wool cap lower and waited.

For a time, all was still, except for an irregular fusillade of snores from the tenement above his head. Then a whore and her mark staggered into the alley. They collided with him, cursed and moved on. He listened thoughtfully to their departure. Then he moved quietly back to the mouth of Rose Alley and studied the Bankside for other watchers.

'I'm better now.' Groggily, Kate pushed away the hands that tried to lift her up. 'Let me be.'

She sat up on the floor and dropped her head into her hands, trying to linger in the numbing darkness. But it receded like the tide, leaving her memories bright, exposed and coldly clear.

She saw herself clawing at the wall, locked behind it on the wrong side, a condemned prisoner, breaking her nails and bloodying her fingertips.

She moaned without knowing she did so.

'Hush,' said the priest. 'I'll warm you some wine. I'm so terribly sorry. I asked Traylor to warn you that I was coming.'

Kate began to shiver. A few moments later she felt the quilt drop over her shoulders.

'I never learned what happened after I left your house,' Father Jerome said. 'I confess that I assume the worst on finding you in these circumstances.' He knelt beside her and asked gently, 'Would it ease you to unburden yourself?'

Kate clenched her teeth and shook her head. The memories would blow apart the frail shells of any words in which she tried to contain them.

43

Two summers ago, when her father began to shiver and complain that his head hurt, Kate and her mother had glanced at each other in alarm.

'I feel such fear every time he visits the City,' her mother said.

Summer heat had set its heavy foot on the south of England. Foul airs from the marshes along the south bank of the Thames seeped towards Surrey and Kent. Meat went off and milk turned sour in a day.

'London's a filthy overcrowded place.' Mistress Peach cut another narrow strip of doeskin to trim the cuff of a glove. 'Why can't they keep their contagions to themselves?'

The next day, when she came out of the shared sleeping chamber, she said, 'Swellings have begun in his groin. I must make a poultice. Last summer, Mistress Jackson cured her youngest son with poultices.' Mistress Peach stood uncertainly, as if trying to decide where to walk next. 'We must tell no one until it has passed.'

Silently, Kate finished her mother's sentence. Tell no one, or they will shut us up in our house.

Neither of them uttered the fearful word 'plague'. Every summer, the plague insinuated itself into the City of London and its suburbs. Every summer, the wealthy fled to their country houses, while everyone else stayed put and prayed. Every summer, people died. So far this summer, there had been no cases in Stokewell.

Kate, her mother, her sister, and her brother worked all night by the light of eight candles to finish the five pairs of gloves on Master Peach's workbench. Luke delivered them the next morning, as if nothing were wrong.

On the fourth night of his illness, Kate's father called for her. His breath now wheezed in his lungs. The dark plague buboes in his groin and armpits had bled into the surrounding flesh.

'Here's money,' he gasped. 'To pay for a Mass for me. You know where to go. I've begun to cough up a pink froth.'

They looked at each other.

'Don't tell your mother.'

Kate nodded. She did not tell him that her mother now moved about the house with her eyes pinched in pain and sat heavily on the nearest stool whenever she thought no one saw her.

'And Kate, I would dearly like to make a last confession.' He paused again to struggle for breath. 'If it can be safely managed. But whatever you do . . . don't put yourself at risk.'

Kate put on her stout boots and walked south for two hours, past King's Hill to a small country estate in the shadow of the Brixton windmill. She had come here once before with her father to hear secret Mass performed by a fugitive priest.

A house groom opened the door. He closed it again and left her on the steps while he took away her request to speak to the mistress of the house, a widow in her forties.

The door was opened again. Not by the mistress, but by a gaunt woman with a distracted air, as if she had been asleep or at prayer.

'Mistress Brock is not here. Tell me your business.'

Kate looked at the thin pale face, the cap concealing the

woman's hair, the plain loose gown that faintly suggested a nun's habit, and decided to gamble. She said what she wanted.

'You've come to the wrong place.' The woman began to shut the door.

Kate stuck a boot in the doorway. 'I have the money with me. Please, mistress. My father is dying and fears for his immortal soul.'

'You'll make trouble for us,' said the woman. 'Go away.' She looked fearfully past Kate at the track leading to the gate. 'We're all loyal English subjects here.'

'I beg you.' Kate held out her hand. In her palm lay her rosary. 'In the name of the Holy Mother, have pity.'

'Don't show that so openly!' the woman whispered in horror. 'And don't say such things where anyone could hear.' She wavered, then sighed with resignation. 'Come in.' She barred the door behind Kate.

'Is Father Paul here?'

'Why do you ask about Father Paul?'

'He taught me to read and write, along with my brother. He can vouch for me and for my family.'

'Father Paul is dead.' The woman watched Kate's face suspiciously. 'You didn't know?' she asked in a low voice. 'He was arrested five months ago and taken to London. Died on the scaffold.'

Kate stared, trying to take in this information. 'Have I come for nothing, then?'

'Wait.' The woman left Kate in a tiny parlour to the left of the entrance hall and disappeared.

Kate paced the little parlour. If Father Paul was dead, was this house still safe?

She went to the door and looked into the hall. It might be safest to leave now. Her father might be mistaken in thinking that they still hid priests here.

'I understand that you have business with me.'

An elegant young man in his twenties stood in the parlour at the opposite door. His red doublet had slashed sleeves that exposed a fine linen shirt beneath. His ruff was narrow but precisely goffered and stiffly starched. A pair of close-fitting venetians showed off well-shaped thighs. His shoes were tied with ribbons. He wore both dagger and sword. He had come fresh from hawking and still wore a heavy leather falconer's glove of the finest work.

Kate shook her head. 'No business with such as you, sir.' She began to back into the hall.

'I am a priest, I swear it. I'm Father Jerome.'

The words seemed incongruous coming from a mouth set in such a well-barbered head of fine, curling brown hair. He pulled off his falconer's glove and tossed it onto the windowsill. 'Believe me, I wouldn't last long in England if I were to stroll about tonsured and in a habit.' He gestured to a joint stool beside the unlit fireplace. 'Please do sit down and tell me why you came looking for Father Paul.'

Kate eyed him as she crossed to the offered seat. 'Your disguise is too good.'

He took the stool on the other side of the fireplace. 'Too good is never more than barely good enough.'

'It's just that . . .' Kate still could not believe that this young dandy was a shepherd of souls.

Then, when he smiled again, she saw his gentle good nature. 'It's far worse than you imagine,' he said. 'I'm alive today only because I thrashed a constable so roundly at tennis that he refused to believe I could be anything but a privileged wastrel.' He sat easily on his stool, a hand on each knee. 'I see fear on your face. And darkness. If you are in trouble, daughter, perhaps I can offer solace. Let me try to shine God's light into that darkness.'

*   *   *

Kate then rode back to Stokewell behind him, on what seemed to be his horse, wearing a borrowed hat against the sun. Father Jerome rode as easily as a gentleman, though he had changed into a doublet of plain wool and now wore a leather jerkin and rough wool slops. His communion wafers and oils rode behind her in his saddlebag.

'What if we are stopped and searched on the road?' Kate asked. She felt strange holding a priest by the waist.

'Slip away if you can. It will be me they want.' He stretched forward to brush a horsefly from the horse's neck. 'But we won't be stopped. Not today.'

Odd as the circumstances were, Kate felt eased by his presence. The heavy dread that had weighed her down ever since her father fell ill was no lighter, but she felt more sure of her own strength to bear it.

After a few miles, she asked, 'Don't you fear the plague?'

'Don't you?'

'Of course.'

'Does it stop you looking after your father and mother?'

'No.'

'I, too, care for my family more than I fear the consequences.'

In her memory now, on this ride north back to Stokewell the sun had warmed her bones without oppressing her. The water they drank from a pump at King's Hill was cold and delicious. The comfortable silence, riding behind an attractive young man, even though he was a priest, had been soft with a subdued joy. Even at the time, she had known enough to take what was being offered to her. The journey was too short.

By the time they returned to Stokewell, both Kate's brother Luke and her sister Anne had begun to shiver and complain of a pain in his head. Her mother could not rise from the bed.

'There's two other cases in the village now,' Kate's mother told her. 'The alderman and his wife. Their house is already nailed up. The searchers have started prying. If you go now, you might get away.' She gripped Kate's arm with a hot hand. 'Please go, my sweet. Leave us. There's nothing more you can do. Save yourself, Kate. I beg you.'

'Shortly,' said Kate. 'Don't fuss.'

Father Jerome administered last rites to Master Peach, heard confessions from the rest of the family and granted them absolution. Then he went out to buy bread and carrots, which were thought to help ease the fever. Moments after he left the house, two searchers tapped at the door with their long white wands. They saw at once how things stood and called for the carpenters to nail shut all the windows and doors, with the family inside.

'Leave the door to the yard open!' shouted Kate. 'Or we can't get to our well.'

A stab of pain pierced her left temple. She sank down onto her haunches and wrapped her arms around knees that had begun to shake with a sudden weakness. 'Holy Mother Mary, protect us all.' She lay down, just for a moment, on the cool stone floor of the kitchen, to let the pain in her head ebb a little.

I'll get up again shortly, she told herself. But she did not.

From a distance, she now watched the priest thrust the poker into the heart of the banked coals. He wiped the glowing end on a square of thick leather and stirred it, spitting and hissing, in the jug of wine.

She had come to a hazy gap in her memory, filled with pain and hallucinations; the time when she was ill. The events after that, though still confused in time, were vivid in her memory.

She tried to take the earthenware cup the priest offered, but her hand would not hold it.

'Let me out!' she had screamed. 'I'm no longer infected.'

She hammered and clawed at the door until her nails cracked and her fingertips bled. 'Please let me out!'

By some miracle, she recovered. She did not know how long she had been out of her senses.

Though her father had brought the contagion from the City, he lingered. Her brother died first. By that time, the others were all too ill to help her. Her mother asked about her son, in a moment without fever, and wept when Kate told her. Kate washed her brother and wrapped him in a sheet, ready for the searchers. But no one came to take away his body, though she called and called at the sealed door.

She thought once that she heard Father Jerome in the street outside, but she was not certain. Whoever it was sounded angry, and she had never heard the young priest raise his voice. She knew that something bad was taking place outside the house but her head throbbed so fiercely that she could pay little attention to anything else.

She dragged her brother down to the cellars, where it was cooler than the living quarters if not cool enough to stop the decay. It took her two hours, as the body had stiffened and she was still weak from her own fever. She scrubbed her hands with grit from the floor for half an hour afterwards. The stench of the plague rose through the boards.

She nursed her father, mother and younger sister Anne. She brewed tisanes of rosemary over the charcoal brazier in the room they used as kitchen and parlour. She boiled flour in stale water from the cistern and tried to spoon this soup into the mouths of her family.

'You must eat, or starvation will take you, not the plague. Please. Open your mouth. Keep your strength to fight.'

She cut thin slices from the last onion and ate them slowly, over four days.

'Help us!' she cried from an upper window too high to be nailed shut. 'Please bring us food and water.'

Her father died next. She hauled him to the cellars at once before he began to smell, and laid him beside his son. That day she wept for the last time.

She stood at the door, shouting for food. For someone to take away the dead. Her mother began to keen like an injured cat with every exhaled breath. Kate wiped and washed and dosed, in despair and frustration. She moved from bed to bed, from mother to sister, beside herself with helplessness. They drank the last of the water in the kitchen cistern.

Three days later, her mother and sister joined the two men in the cellar. Trying to make room for her sister, Kate tugged on her mother's hand. The skin slipped off the flesh like a glove. Paralysed, she stared at it, limp and empty in her own hand. Then she threw it down and began to retch.

Back by the sealed front door, she heard a plague cart pass along the street, and the sound of water being sluiced over the track beside the house.

She lost all sense of hunger and thirst and shrank into a small, hard lump of undefined craving. She cut the last slice of bread into cubes and ate them one at a time. She found a half-empty jar of quince preserves. She licked the trickle of water that seeped under the front door twice a day when the street was washed. One night, alone in the house with the four bodies in the cellar, she understood that she would probably die for want of food and water. The miracle of her escape from the plague was to no purpose.

She decided to squeeze through the small loading window in the loft under the rafters of the cottage, and jump. The end would be quicker than starving. But she was now too weak to haul herself up the stairs. Every breath carried the foul stench from the cellar into the centre of her being. She crawled to the front door and lay beside it, persuading herself that a faint thread of clean air crept under it from outside. She kept licking the water that seeped under the door.

When the door was finally opened, fifteen days after it was sealed, Kate was barely alive. A neighbour woman gave her a straw pallet in the loft of her cow shed, and fed her thin gruel. While Kate was recovering, the Peaches' landlord cleared the cottage of all her family's belongings.

'I saved what I could of your stuffs,' said the neighbour, when she thought Kate strong enough to take up her life again. She gave Kate the lease for the cottage, which the landlord had cancelled with diagonal slits, and a letter saying that he had burned all their clothes and sold the furniture to settle the outstanding rent.

Kate quickly understood that her presence frightened the neighbour. Men from London had come asking questions about the handsome young man who had visited the Peaches just before they died. Soon, everyone in Stokewell whispered that he had been a Jesuit priest. She would have to leave, but not before she completed one vital task.

For two more days, she lay weakly on the straw pallet, listening to the discordant bells of the two milk cows below her, preparing herself to rejoin the world. She stroked her father's glove-making tools, the two surviving Italian glasses, a half-dozen pewter plates, a fur-lined cloak, and some iron cooking pots. She asked her neighbour to sell the cloak, the plates and the cooking pots. She would use the money to pay for a secret funeral Mass, even though the bodies of her family had gone into a plague pit.

Then, in the middle of one night, she broke into the empty cottage by forcing her knife blade through a crack in the kitchen door to raise the latch. In the main chamber, she ran her fingers over the wall beside the fireplace until she found a brick that shifted slightly on its mortar bed. Carefully, she worked it loose and lifted it out of the wall. Then she removed the one below it.

She put her arm into the hole, to the elbow. Her fingers touched velvet.

She lifted out the velvet bag that held the family Missal and their rosaries, along with the little silver-gilt patten for the consecrated host, which her father had brought from Italy along with the glasses. She let herself out of the cottage again, looked for a moment at the red cross still painted on the front door, and slept until sunset the next day, using the precious sack as her pillow. Then she took a clear-eyed look at the rest of her life.

She looked up at the two surviving Venetian glasses on the low mantel of her fireplace.

'Can you drink now?' asked Father Jerome. He held the cup for her. 'You're a truly good woman, to come to my aid when I failed you.'

Being called a good woman moved her dangerously close to the tears she had forsworn forever.

'You didn't fail us,' she said at last. 'You were our only solace.'

'My presence may have condemned you,' he said bitterly. 'And I ran, to flee arrest. Before I could bring you food and water.' He retreated to the joint stool by the fire, where Nicholas Owen had sat all day whittling.

Kate shrugged off the quilt. Still sitting on the floor, she began to warm a second cup of wine. The poker rattled against the rim. She laid the poker down and tested the tempera-ture of the wine with her little finger. 'Your coming to Stokewell at all was brave,' she said at last. 'And it saved the souls of my family.'

Father Jerome accepted the wine but did not drink. Instead,

he cupped it as if warming his hands. 'Gossips do as much damage with their tongues as government spies.' He sighed. 'People asked why a stranger was visiting you at such a time. If I had not come, you might have had more charity from your neighbours. I fear that they may have chosen to let the secret Papists die.'

After another moment of silence, Kate drained her own cup.

'I have a pallet for you,' she said brightly. She clambered to her feet. Her knees were a little uncertain. Otherwise, she told herself, she was entirely recovered from her shameful display of feebleness.

'I'm sorry to bring back such evil memories for you,' the young priest said.

'The past is the past.' Her voice was brittle. 'By God's Grace, I survived. And I hope I'm beginning to learn His purpose in saving me. Will you hear my confession tomorrow, Father, before you leave again?'

'Of course.'

'You'll learn that I've become little better than a whore.'

'And you already know that God's Mercy is infinite.'

Kate felt the press of tears behind her eyes again. She poured herself more wine. Pass through to the next moment, she told herself. Everything will make sense in time.

'I'm very weary,' said the priest, when he saw that she was not going to speak further. 'I arrived back in England only today. I have more to say to you, but we have time before I can leave again. Several days if you're willing. And both our minds will be clearer after a little sleep.'

The next morning, in the grey early daylight, Father Jerome sat on the floor with his breakfast ale, leaning on the wall beside the fireplace, out of sight from the Bankside. 'If Master

Traylor didn't tell you I was coming, I hope he did at least warn you of the risk you take in hiding me.'

'I know the risk.' Kate already sat by the window, where she could watch the street. She was stretching the hawking glove over the largest elm-wood hand.

'Master Traylor told you, of course.'

Kate gave a vicious tug at the base of the thumb. 'He lacks your courtesy. But it's no secret that sheltering a Jesuit is as much treason as refusing the oath of loyalty.' She smoothed the cowhide downward to ease out the wrinkles.

Father Jerome looked both startled and horrified. 'You didn't elect to take this course with full knowledge of what you were doing?'

'It's not the first time. I'm Master Traylor's creature, Father. Men like him don't give their creatures the luxury of choice. However good the cause.' She pulled the glove from the mould and dampened it with a sponge. She braced stretcher against the stool seat between her knees again. 'I'm happy to do it. All the more because it's you.'

Distracted for a moment, she looked at the limp, damp-ened glove she was holding in her hand.

He watched her ease the glove back onto the five wooden fingertips. 'You're not afraid?'

'After Stokewell?'

He nodded and scratched his beard thoughtfully.

Kate glanced over at the faint rasping sound. There was enough daylight now to see him clearly. He looked away, as if she had caught him studying her.

He seemed far older than when she saw him last, ten years rather than two, and he had lost his fresh, engaging open-ness. He wore wool slops like a labourer and a leather jerkin. No one would mistake him now for a carefree wastrel of gentle birth.

He set his ale cup on the floor with decision. 'From

Stokewell, I fled to France. I've come back now to do more than conduct Mass and hear confessions. My mission is worth the gravest risk.'

'Preaching treason is always a grave risk,' she said dryly.

He shook his head. 'The Jesuit mission in England is now quite the opposite of treason. We have never advocated rebellion, no matter what our enemies claim. At this moment, we are striving urgently to rein back those Catholics who propose acts of treason . . .'

'But the Pope himself orders all good Catholics to consider themselves to be at war with the English Crown . . .'

'Kate!' shouted a voice from the street.

Kate jumped in guilty terror and dropped the glove. Father Jerome disappeared at once into the closet, taking his mug.

Kate picked up the glove and stretcher. Opened the window. Looked down. Breathed again.

Peg the Pie.

'Broken meats, love. You want first pick of 'em again today?'

Kate hesitated.

Behave as usual.

She nodded. 'I'll come right down.'

By the bottom of the stairs she had her voice under control again.

'Why not tell Cecil, Lord Salisbury . . . and the Privy Council what your true purpose is?' Kate asked, when she had returned and Father Jerome was sitting by the fireplace again. 'They should welcome you, not hunt you down.'

'Men like Cecil would never ally themselves with the Jesuits.' He laughed unhappily. 'After all they've said of us? We're their Antichrist. Satan's hobgoblins. We serve them too well as the source of all sedition. By hating us so fiercely, they can avoid having to hate all other English Papists. Except when it suits them.'

'But surely . . .' She could not follow these political coil-ings. Treason itself was already beyond her understanding. She still did not feel like a traitor. Common sense told her that continuing to worship as every English grandfather had once worshipped could not be as grave a crime as plotting to assassinate the King.

She gave the priest the last of the broken pies and began to unpick a seam of her glove. 'They're mad, then.'

Father Jerome brushed a non-existent crumb from his curly beard. 'Could the purpose of your survival in Stokewell be to help us?' He leaned forward to read her face. 'With more than sanctuary, I mean.'

Kate swallowed. Her waxed linen thread missed the needle's eye. She tried once more, and again failed. 'What would you want me to do?'

'Only to keep your eyes and ears open. To tell me, and others, what you learn.'

'Who would I watch?'

'Other Catholics.'

'You want me to spy on my fellow Catholics?'

'As a benign spy. Our aim is to save hotheads from the scaffold. By persuading them to give up the folly of rebel-lion.'

'But such rebels are good followers of the Pope.' She frowned at Father Jerome. 'How can you, a priest, work against the Holy Father who calls for rebellion?'

'Because some of us care more for our flock in England than we do for Papal Bulls. Because the Holy Father cannot see where his edict will lead.' Father Jerome forgot caution and began to pace.

'It was Father Garnet himself,' he said, '. . . our Superior in England, who first saw the terrible danger. The new King has proved less tolerant than he promised in his early days, but he is not entirely our enemy. Not yet.'

Kate watched him pacing in his workman's clothes.

'But madmen among us want to turn him into a merci-less foe. Many powerful men – Cecil among them, I fear – are waiting for an excuse to wipe out every Catholic in England. One act of Catholic violence now, one attempt on the King's life or on Prince Henry's life, will unleash a slaughter of English Catholics more terrible than anything this country has ever seen.'

Kate turned a skein of fine gold wire in her fingers. 'Do you swear that you don't intend treason?'

'As I trust in my hope of Salvation.'

She laid the skein back with the others in the little basket. She rubbed her forehead with long fingers, then asked, 'Where do I look first?'

At least, she was unlikely to encounter Francis among Catholic hotheads.

'At Master Traylor.' Father Jerome watched her intently. 'I don't think I'm asking you to spy on a man you love.'

'Traylor?' Kate repeated in disbelief. 'Surely not Hugh Traylor. He might arrange things . . . but a hot-headed plotter?'

Did she want to try to save him from the scaffold?

She felt ashamed of this thought at once.

'I never even knew that he was a Roman Catholic until the first time he asked me to shelter a Jesuit,' she said.

'Father Garnet has heard disturbing rumours about him. I hope you can prove them to be false.'

Francis watched through the rest of the night and the next morning but did not see the handsome young man leave The Little Rose.

Just after midday, he finally left his post long enough to deliver a message for Catesby to the Duck and Drake, and to leave another message for Cecil with a goldsmith near the church of St Magnus the Martyr. Then he rushed back to Bankside.

Kate had emerged in the morning to buy broken meats from a pie woman, which she then took to the Clink prison. Then she went to the market, where she bought four early carrots and a bunch of boiled asparagus. After that she went home.

In the late afternoon he saw her standing near the window of her lodgings, apparently talking to herself. Or else to someone in the room with her, but out of sight.

He began to question what he hoped to prove or disprove by this watching. He knew too much already. Kate had led him to Guido. Guido had led him to Robin Catesby. Catesby had rushed to confess his treasonous intent and wanted to buy four thousand pounds of gunpowder for some 'Great Blow'.

Accept the obvious, Francis told himself. Kate is mired in treason.

He wanted to touch her . . . her hand, or neck . . . nothing more . . . He needed to persuade her to speak to him again. Though most likely he would not want to hear what she had to say.

For the first time in his life, he yearned for uncertainty. While he still swilled in uncertainty, he could still hope.

Shortly after curfew, he noticed a shadow between himself and the mouth of Little Rose Alley. Neither he nor the shadow moved for several hours. Francis developed a piercing ache in the heels of both his feet. His bladder grew uncomfortably full though his throat was dry. His stomach begged for food.

A man, who might or might not have been the one Francis had seen earlier in the lantern light, came out of The Little Rose tenements some time after the watch had called two o'clock in the morning. The shadow near the mouth of Little Rose Alley followed the man, who might or might not have been visiting Kate.

As alert as a fox, Francis followed both of them. He nearly walked into the shadow, who was standing in frustration at a corner, looking down first one alley then another.

Francis had no choice but to stagger drunkenly past. He stopped a little further on to relieve himself with noisy, grateful groans against a wall. The other man stayed where he was, as if still trying to decide which way his quarry had gone. When Francis lurched on, the shadow lingered behind him.

Francis decided that it was time to move to different lodgings. He returned by a devious route to his post outside The Little Rose, to watch until it was time to meet Catesby again.

44

'I knew you would agree.'

'You knew better than I, then.' Francis could hardly meet Catesby's eyes, which gleamed with triumph and delight. He enveloped Francis in the glow of his pleasure. They were drinking in The Duck and Drake again.

'I don't like it, but I feel I must,' said Francis.

Which was entirely true.

Guido sat at another table, his head bobbing eagerly at every word uttered by the slouched, lanky figure seated across from him. Both men carefully avoided looking at Francis.

Catesby's eyes filled with concern. He leaned across the table, clasped Francis by the shoulder and shook him gently as if consoling him. 'I've a nose for men's natures, France. And it tells me that you yearn to do the right thing. At times, it's a painful choice.' He lowered his voice. 'Guido over there says you're a mercenary and most likely a spy, and that I shouldn't trust you, but he was born with the vinegar of envy in his soul, poor man.'

'Guido wants to do the right thing.'

'Yes, but from spiritual ambition, not absolute need.' Catesby examined Francis intensely, peering into his eyes. 'You need absolutely to be good. That's why I feel I can trust you.'

Francis was lost for words for a moment. 'I must try to live up to your estimation,' he said finally. And he must resist his sudden hunger to be worthy of Catesby's trust.

'Here's how certain I was of you.' Catesby pushed an embroidered purse across the table. 'For the cost of materials.'

'Thirty pieces of silver?' asked Francis lightly.

Catesby looked at him with concern. 'But you're not Judas. Nor are we traitors. We are surgeons who mean to cut out putrefaction in the body politic. Does your conscience still trouble you?'

Francis nodded with feeling. 'But the pain won't keep me from making you your powder.'

'Look in the purse. It may not be enough. You never told me nor Guido your price.'

Francis hid his face while he pulled open the strings of the purse and examined the gold coins inside. He was grateful that Guido was at a different table. His failure to strike a price would have alerted anyone less trusting than Robin Catesby.

'I'd give you the powder if I could,' he said. 'But you can have it for the cost of making it. Eleven pence a pound for coarsely corned powder of high explosive force, suited for mining . . .'

. . . Or 'close enough', as Robin had said.

'Forty barrels make four thousand pounds in weight. Total cost: one hundred and eighty-three pounds, six shillings and eight pence.'

'I lack so great a sum,' said Catesby. 'But Everard Digby has promised me cash as well as horses.'

Digby, Francis noted unhappily. Another name for Cecil. Another man to offer up for butchery. Which made four, with Guido's companion over there. Not four sketchy, demonic figures called traitors, but four living, breathing, flesh-and-blood people, one of whom he liked very much. And Kate would make five.

'I will get you the rest of the money, I swear.'

Francis tucked Catesby's purse into an inner pocket in his breeches. 'If this is what you have, then it's enough for now. And I'll forgive you the eight pence.'

Even the roots of his hair felt hot with guilt and shame.

'I told Guido you were the right man for us,' cried Catesby. He laughed in a friendly teasing fashion. 'France, my friend, there's no need to blush so modestly at what is merely the truth. I thank you most soberly and sincerely. Are those plain words more comfortable to your ears?'

Francis managed to smile back.

'And we shall have it by the end of September?'

'The end of September?' asked Francis in dismay. 'But that's far too soon!'

'We must have it then.'

'All four thousand pounds?'

'All.' Catesby showed a sudden flash of the ferocity that had propelled him through cavalry charges and made weaker men follow.

The end of September, thought Francis.

On the third of October, Parliament was to open again after the summer break. In his imagination, Francis suddenly saw four thousand pounds of gunpowder exploding under the floor of the Great Hall. Saw the shattered roof of Westminster Palace flying up through a choking cloud of black smoke that spread across the Thames. He saw flames leaping higher than the tower of the Abbey, doubled again by their reflections in the water.

'You've guessed our intention?' asked Catesby, watching him closely.

Francis exhaled sharply. 'I've imagined a blow great enough to satisfy any need for action. If I'm right, it knocks the wind out of me, I admit.'

'Will you still do it?'

Francis looked away from the intensity in Catesby's face, to try to think straight. 'My intent is still firm,' he said finally. 'But my ability lags behind. The time is too short for making so much gunpowder.'

Every word was true.

'Not too short if you are determined enough. As I am. As we all must be!' Catesby waved the other two men to their table. 'He has agreed!' he told them with delight. 'France, you already know Master Guido Fawkes, of course.' He shot Francis a mischievous glance, as if Guido's suspicions were a delicious secret jest that the two of them shared.

Francis and Guido looked at each other with mutual dislike.

You think me a spy and a mercenary, do you? thought Francis. The fact that Guido was right made Francis care for him even less on this second meeting.

And Cecil had been right about Guido's second name.

'Thomas,' said Catesby to the taller man. He took Francis by the arm as if pushing forward a shy child. 'Here is Guido's fortunate discovery, Firemaster Francis Quoynt. Francis, may I introduce . . .'

'Plain Thomas will serve,' the tall man interrupted.

There was one, at least, who understood caution. But the caution was misplaced. Francis already knew the man. Had seen him riding with his kinsman and patron, the Earl of Northumberland. And he had heard the man's reputation: the loose cannon of a noble Catholic family that had managed to retain some position and power. Thomas Percy. He was older than either Francis or Catesby, with a narrow grizzled beard and an air that said he expected nothing of interest or entertainment from anyone.

'We depend on Thomas for his connections in Westminster,' said Catesby.

'Catesby!' Percy frowned a warning.

'France is so much in tune with us that he has divined our intent,' Catesby protested. 'And he is with us.'

Francis saw Guido look sourly at Robin's hand, which clasped his own arm in friendly ownership.

The man was jealous of Catesby's favour.

'You'll find us what we need?' Percy's long face looked surprised.

'Catesby rushes ahead of my words,' protested Francis. 'I said I'm willing. But we've only a small mill at Powder Mote. I need at least two months, not two and a half weeks.'

'Why so long?' asked Percy.

'First we must prepare the charcoal, sulphur and the salt-petre, before even beginning to mix the powder itself.'

'I thought one buys the saltpetre.'

'From Sicily,' Guido added.

'I can't buy three thousand pounds of saltpetre without calling attention to the purchase.'

'Try, France,' begged Catesby. 'Before you tell me you've failed. I am more sure of you than you are yourself. I shall send Guido to the Continent to raise as much money as you need. Thomas will ask his uncle for a further advance on his annuity.' Catesby gifted Percy with one of his smiles of absolute approval, in advance, of whatever the man might achieve. Then he moved on to include Guido. 'I promise you, God will open the way for us.'

'Amen,' said Percy.

'Amen,' echoed Fawkes.

Francis saw Catesby's certainty reflected in the other two faces.

Then with sudden relief he saw that he had no need to make four thousand pounds of gunpowder in two and a half weeks. Once he gave Cecil the names he wanted . . . when Francis could bring himself to report them . . . they would be stopped. Robin, Guido, Percy, Digby, and no doubt several others. Long before the powder could get anywhere near Westminster and the King.

He had only to promise. He would never have to make it all.

'I'll do my best,' he said. 'I can't promise more.'

'My friends . . . my brothers, we have our firemaster!' cried Catesby.

While Catesby and Percy drank to his success, Francis read the warning in Guido's eyes across the rim of his ale pot.

I know what you are. And when I can prove it, beware.

45

'I've had intelligence about you,' said Cecil by way of greeting. 'You're a suspected danger to the English Crown. Congratulations.' The English Secretary of State leaned back deep into the shadows of the wherry's curtains, where his small shape blended into the cushions.

Francis had received the alarming request for this meeting in a letter left with the bookseller outside St Paul's. Cecil's new boatman had picked him up from the tide mill near Horseley Down. Now the man rowed them through the reflections of fat-bellied, ocean-going ships moored in the Pool below London Bridge.

Already on edge, Francis felt a jolt of anger at the glint of glee in Cecil's eyes.

'Who did you set to watch me?' He settled into the unnatural coolness that he felt when preparing to light a fuse, aware that he might be about to die, but with absolutely steady hands.

Cecil wagged a finger in a grotesque parody of playfulness. 'Your power to dissemble is overstretched as it is.'

'Does your spy know who I am?'

'Of course not. And he was watching Fawkes, not you.'

Watched at The Bear Garden, then. Not at The Duck and Drake. And if not The Duck and Drake, Cecil might not yet know about the two meetings with Catesby.

Francis unclenched slightly. Nevertheless, he knew he was being warned.

Cecil grew almost invisible under the awning as they slid into the deep green shadow of an old three-master, a high-pooped, low-beaked galleon. It stank of ordure and human misery. A slaver returned from the West Indies filled with nutmegs or sugar. Then, suddenly, they were out in the bright sunlight again, cutting through water that reflected like a mirror.

Francis decided to bluff it out a little longer. At least until he could talk to Kate.

'What do you have to tell me?' asked Cecil.

Francis glanced at the parcel that lay on the padded bench beside Cecil. 'Nothing so urgent that I could not have written it in my next report, my lord. You summoned me, not the other way round.'

The parcel was the size of two bricks and wrapped in rough sacking that sat oddly on the red velvet padding and silver-gilt fringe of the bench. Francis glanced at it again in apprehension. It looked to him like a pregnant shell deciding whether or not to explode.

Cecil remained silent.

'I agreed to the powder,' Francis said. 'If you still order me to provide it.'

'Why should I change my mind?'

'Before undertaking treason, I would like to be certain that I heard your instruction correctly.'

'Do you need it in writing?' Francis saw the pale flash of teeth, but the voice was icy.

'Your word is more than enough, my lord. And I take it that I still have it.'

'You do.' An irritated glint in Cecil's eye told Francis that his temerity had been noted. 'How much money do you need?'

'He . . .' Francis made certain that he said the right name. He could do no more damage there. The man was already compromised. '. . . Guido still lacks the means to pay for the amount he wants. But as I won't need to make so much . . .'

'Give him all of it.'

'All?'

'You try my patience today, Quoynt. I believe that I spoke clearly enough.'

'My lord, four thousand pounds is too much to make . . .' He was about to say 'in time', but caught himself. He glanced again at the parcel. 'As I said, he lacks the money.'

'All the better,' said Cecil. 'He must therefore draw in more men. Wealthy men. Men of note. Whom you might even know and be able to name.'

Francis heard the edge but kept his eyes steady.

'How much do you need?' Cecil asked again.

Francis told him.

'A box will be delivered to your lodgings tonight. There's your difficulty out of the way. Go to Sussex now and make the powder. Meanwhile, I shall let the rumours of your suspected treachery leak out to certain Papists. To accelerate trust.' Cecil stared past Francis at his own thoughts for a moment. 'Keep me informed.'

'Of course, my lord.'

Cecil laid his hand on the parcel. 'There's something you must know. Kate Peach is a Roman Catholic.'

Francis glowered, to hide the sudden terror that clouded his thoughts. 'But surely not a traitor.' He retreated into stillness. He heard his own voice protesting. 'Your informer was mistaken about me, after all.'

'Last night we arrested a Jesuit priest. He has been hiding with her.'

'A priest risked his virtue in Southwark?' Francis managed a smile. 'I find that hard to believe.'

'A handsome young fellow with a curling beard. You will no doubt have seen him.'

Francis stared back at Cecil. 'Have you arrested her?' he asked, as if merely curious.

'Not yet. It's her other lover who interests me.' Cecil stressed the word 'other' ever so lightly. 'Master Hugh Traylor.'

So that was his name.

Francis believed that he had hidden his terror and confusion, but Cecil added, not unkindly, 'Take your time, Quoynt. I've finished. I suspect you would like to collect your thoughts.' He leaned back on his bench and gave an instruction to the boatman.

There was no point in pretending, when Cecil clearly knew that he was bedding Kate.

'Leave her alone.'

'She hid the priest. And she could be the death of you. The ones we think most harmless often do the most damage.'

The wherry bumped against the dockside at Billingsgate. Francis stepped out onto a slippery wooden ladder.

'Does Bacon know about Kate Peach?' he asked.

'Through one of his own intelligencers? Perhaps. Or, if my informant is serving both Sir Francis and me. Not otherwise. I had no reason to watch her.'

'Has Bacon been watching me?'

The uneven shoulders of Cecil's loose gown rose and fell in what may have been a shrug.

'Most likely. He and I don't exchange all our news. And I'm afraid I can't warn off his maggots . . . Don't look so stiff, Quoynt. I would never deal in person with anyone I considered a maggot.'

'Is this Traylor a Roman too?'

'Lower your voice.' Cecil's voice was edged, though muffled

by the curtains. 'It wouldn't seem so. He reported her to us.
And the priest.'

The earth felt as unsteady as water under his feet. Francis
was certain of only one thing: Cecil had a reason for telling
him about Kate. 'I believe these belong to Mistress Peach,'
he said. His parting words.

Francis looked down at the parcel in his hands. It was
heavy, with square corners like a book.

If only he could read Cecil's thoughts, all murkiness would
clear like the sky after a summer storm.

Men like Cecil seemed to have an extra sense that Francis
felt he lacked, a sense that allowed them to hear and interpret information that escaped him. Such men were like
dogs that prick their ears at sounds their masters cannot
hear.

Does he want me to warn her? Francis wondered. Or to
kill her?

Or had Cecil some other purpose in mind altogether?

Back on Bankside, Francis soon spotted the watcher outside
The Little Rose, propped against the wall. A drunk whose
gaze was just a little too sharp.

And how many more of us are there? he wondered. The
whole world seemed populated by intelligencers and agents.

He bought a mug of beer and went to sit by the drunk.
'Here's to maggots!' He lifted his mug. With grim satisfaction,
he watched alarm flare in the man's eyes and the forced
return to bleariness.

'How long have you been here?' he asked.

The drunk cursed and stumbled to his feet. Francis watched
him stagger towards the water steps. He grinned about him
foolishly, as if inviting shared amusement. An ageing whore
glanced hastily away.

I'm learning, thought Francis. She should be pulling at my sleeve now, instead of sliding into the alley.

Kate's window remained dark.

By dawn the next morning, Francis was certain she was no longer there. Cecil had lied. He had arrested her. If Cecil could pay to make gunpowder for traitors, why couldn't he lie?

While he bought breakfast, Francis tried to gossip with the host of The Little Rose about the arrest, the day before, of a man in the top-floor tenement.

'I hear there was a woman with him.'

'I never saw none.' The man turned away to serve another customer.

Nevertheless, Cecil's men might have picked her up elsewhere.

If her disappearance is Cecil's doing, the Little Toad must beware, thought Francis. He would do nothing else until he found her. If he did not find her, he might kill Cecil.

He searched the crowds in the Long Southwark market. Then he visited the shop on London Bridge that sold imported silk and metal threads. The stall owner had not seen Kate for several days.

Francis stood in the narrow roadway of the Bridge, looking up at the overhanging stories of the houses and *haut pas* bridges, thinking of all the storage rooms and vaults in the pillars of the arches. Then there was the whole of the City. The gaols. The cells and dungeons of the Tower. And the cellars of the big private houses on The Strand.

He turned back into Southwark.

Mary Frith met him in the Paris Gardens, behind the house.

'Why should I know where she is?' she demanded, lighting her pipe.

'She spoke of you as a friend.'

'Ungrateful little trull. I could have helped her many times over. But she was too proud. Too good for the likes of me, la!' She glared at Francis. 'For the likes of you, too, my friend. And I told her as much.'

'I'm glad she chose not to believe you.'

The pipe stem snapped in Mary's fist, but her flat face remained serene. She shook her head regretfully. 'Rumour says that some turd reported the whereabouts of a wanted man. If so, I'm afraid I favour you for it.'

They locked eyes. Francis felt a flush rise in his cheeks. Mary was wrong, but less so than he would have liked.

A nearby fountain splattered like a drunk relieving himself against a wall.

'Go on,' said Mary. 'Protest that you love her.'

'I do.'

'Oh, Lord. My late husband used to say "I love you", long ago. Translated, it means, "Cunny dear, my prick is swollen with lust."' Mary smiled in derision. 'Why do I feel you've missed your chance to "love" Kate? Now, shog off.'

46

But Francis did not 'shog off'. He was certain that Mary had lied. She was too equable and unconcerned. Kate was hiding with her.

The Paris Gardens were open to all. While he waited in the shadows, Francis declined offers to stretch the leather, to beat or be beaten (as he chose), to play at bumfiddle, or merely to have his pickle pumped by a *puto* dressed in a mockery of Jesuit robes. He felt not the slightest twitch of temptation, not even when solicited by a young woman who wore a clean skirt and had an intelligent, knowing eye.

Kate came out for air a little after midnight. Francis followed her. The gardens were not yet empty, but the other occupants were busy with each other. Even so, Kate stayed on the most shadowy paths away from the coloured lanterns.

'It's Francis,' he whispered from the shadow of a tree. 'I had to see you again.'

She cried out in fright and turned to bolt.

'Wait! It's Francis. I must leave London for Powder Mote tomorrow. Had to see you first.'

She turned back. 'You're leaving?'

He took heart from her stricken tone and touched her bare forearm. The touch turned into an embrace. 'Come with me to the warehouse, just once more,' he begged.

'Why must you leave?' she asked breathlessly when they had separated again. But she came with him without protest. 'How did you know I was visiting Mary tonight?'

The implied lie showed how rattled she was. She must know that the arrest of the Jesuit priest was common knowledge on Bankside. And that he would know she was in hiding.

'Why are you walking so fast?' she asked. 'It feels as if you're hustling me away from some danger.'

Instead of the wry, apologetic smile she prayed for, he slowed abruptly. He dropped his hand from her elbow, then looked back over his shoulder.

'What's wrong?'

He shook his head. 'Nothing.'

Few words are more expressive or alarming than that careless 'nothing'. Kate walked on beside him silently, but she glanced sideways now and then to try to read his face. So long as neither of them spoke, nothing terrible could happen.

In the shadows of the warehouse, their kiss was a collision. Nothing fitted. The corners of their teeth cut. She felt his hands press on the back of her head, as if he were trying to force his way through her mouth to somewhere else.

They could not lie down. The carpets had gone. He pulled her with him onto the floor anyway. Kissed her neck, kissed her throat. Then he suddenly released her and fell onto his back with his arm across his eyes. His hands had been as cold as her own.

'Oh, Kate. Oh, my Kate.'

'Francis!' In terror, she leaned over to try to see his face. 'What's wrong? Tell me the truth.'

He swallowed.

'Tell me before you frighten me to death.'

'Soul-sick,' he muttered. He turned with a groan and grabbed her around the waist, burying his head in her lap.

She stroked his short, soft hair and the lean, ruddy column of his neck.

'Because of me?'

She felt icy cold and astonishingly steady. The dead did not tremble.

He sat up, took a parcel from the saddlebag he carried. He set the parcel in front of her on the floor. 'I'm told that this is yours.'

Kate knew at once what it was. 'Where did you get this?'

All answers were equally appalling. She did not like the intensity of his gaze. She touched the wrapped Missal. Taken by the men who had arrested Father Jerome one night as he left The Little Rose and then searched her lodgings.

'Why didn't you tell me that you're a Roman?'

'Would that have changed your feelings for me?'

'Or about Guido and Robin?'

'Who are Guido and Robin? I don't know either of those men.' Hope rose in her. 'There's been a misunderstanding.'

'Or about the priests?'

'Is this a formal examination?' she asked finally. 'Or is it your part merely to report me so that someone else can do the questioning?'

I don't mind if I die, she thought. But there are kinder ways than hanging. 'Is that why you hurried me here, out of sight?' she asked. 'Fear that spies might see you in damning company?'

'No.' He groaned at the irony. 'I'm afraid for you.'

'I'm suddenly afraid *of* you.' She looked down at the parcel again.

'Kate, I would have loved you, Papist or not. I will not believe that you are a knowing traitor. And I will never betray you . . .'

'But there's something you need to say,' she finished dully.

'You know that I'm not smooth-tongued. These are hard words . . .'

'. . . But you'll stone me with them anyway.'

'I can't yet tell you why . . . if I ever can . . . But certain matters are afoot. It would be safer for both of us if we don't . . .' He groped for the softest words. But there were no soft words for this subject. '. . . Safer for both of us if we did not meet again. For a time. But I won't, for the world, have you think that I'm leaving you again. I'll give you money to escape from London and find somewhere safer. You let me know where. I'll come for you when it's safe again.'

'I see.' She sounded very far away. 'And what happens if I'm arrested?'

'If you stay out of sight, I don't think you will be. Please trust me.'

'Why? You were right not to trust me.'

He sprang to his feet in frustration. 'Please God, it will all come right in the end. There's nothing I can say until then.'

'Very well.'

'You must believe me!'

'I accept what you say. Don't fret.' Absently, she stroked the cover of her family's Missal. Why did I survive only to die again now? she wondered.

'How did you get my Missal?' she asked again.

'Kate, I beg you . . .' He was too confused to know what to beg. He leaned down and captured her face in his hands. 'I swear . . .' He did not know what to swear either. Instead, he kissed her, just one more time. She let him.

Their last kiss was tender and dense with feelings still unspent. Then it turned sharp with ending. They both felt the stab of renewed desire at the same time. Their hands tightened on each other's heads. At the same moment, they pushed each other away.

He tried to give her money, but she refused.

'I can survive without your money, Francis,' she said sharply. 'I'm not such a fool that I haven't some idea how you earn it.' She placed her hand on the Missal and looked him in the eye. 'Please, go now. I want to stay here for a time. At this moment, they are torturing Father Jerome.'

'I must see you safely back to Mary.'

'As you just said, it's safer for both of us to be apart.'

'Kate, come with me to Powder Mote,' he said on impulse. 'I'll hide you. We'll sort things out. Manage somehow.'

Kate laughed bitterly. 'Go, Francis. Thank you for returning my lost property.'

He gave her the warehouse keys. He should warn her about Traylor. But then she would know beyond all doubt what he was.

'Trust no one,' he said urgently, hoping it was enough. 'No one. Do you understand me?'

'That's an unnecessary warning, I assure you.'

He left her sitting cross-legged on the brick floor in the midst of the aromatic shadows. He waited outside, across the street where he had waited once before. When she finally emerged, he followed her up Bankside until she was safely inside the female-filled maze of the Holland's Leaguer.

On the way to his new lodgings in Gun Alley, he tapped on a window in Dead Man's Place near the Bank End Stairs to hire a cart for the next day. Back in his chamber, rented from a Dutch whore who leased the entire ground floor of the tenement behind the Gun Inn, he packed his saddlebags. That done, he stared through his reflection in the window, at the dark house-wall across the alley. The sliver of sky overhead was already bleached by the false dawn.

If only he had found the right words, she might have agreed to come with him. Clot! Dolt! He struck his forehead hard several times with his palm.

The self-inflicted punishment did not ease him. He began to pace.

A wrinkle in his knitted stocking filled him with unreasoning fury. He sat on the bed and pulled off his boot.

He had work to do. Saltpetre to find, first of all. Enough to make forty barrels of gunpowder. Three-quarters of it saltpetre. Cecil needed secrecy as much as Catesby. How the devil did either of them think he could come by three thousand pounds of saltpetre without drawing unwanted attention?

There might be thirty or forty pounds at Powder Mote . . . Can't buy from the arsenal storehouse in Lewes, too close to home. Too much risk of gossip . . . He could not think straight.

He circled the room twice, stocking forgotten. Then he suddenly replaced his boot, and donned hat and cloak. He checked in his pouch for the certified copy of the Quoynts' letter of patent, the official permit that gave them the right to make gunpowder for the Crown. And to purchase saltpetre for that purpose. He hoped he could get his mouth around the lie that he had turned from soldiering to working in the mines.

He could have waited until the morning, when he would have both the money and the cart. But he needed to walk.

He snuffed his candle. If he set out now, he could be waiting outside the Royal Armoury in Woolwich by the start of the working day.

Head down, he marched along St Olaf's Street. Past Bridge House. Past the warehouse where Turkey carpets had once been stacked.

'Kate. Kate. Kate . . .' said his footsteps.

He shook his head and muttered to himself. Saltpetre. Saltpetre . . . Where else can I buy some? Have we time to refine our own? Must I swallow my pride and beg my father for help? Kate . . .

Near Deptford Creek, a footpad moved hopefully out of the shadows at the sound of a possible mark. He took a closer look at the size and suppressed fury of the man who approached and sank back out of sight again.

The Dutch whore at the Gun tenements was holding a parcel of shirts for Francis when he returned the next morning on his way to collect the cart. The whore pretended to notice nothing odd about the unnatural weight of the shirts. Between two of the shirts was a heavy flat wooden box.

Francis tied his grey mare to the tail of the empty cart, then hid the box of money under his seat and laid his sword ready by his feet.

Here's an astonishing turn, he thought, as he set off back to Woolwich to collect the first of the saltpetre. The English Secretary of State is paying me to supply traitors with gunpowder so that they can kill the King.

47

Powder Mote's only groom met Francis on the road between Box Hill and Horsham, after the sun had set but while the sky was still light. The youth was riding Boomer's big grey gelding. The horse was wheezing and flecked with foam.

'Master Francis!' shouted the groom. 'I was coming to London to fetch you.'

'What's wrong?' Francis urged the carthorse forward, ice already forming along his spine. 'Is it my father?'

'Yes, Master Boomer, sir.' The boy was torn between fear and importance as he pulled up beside the cart.

'Dead?' Francis felt a terrible swooping sensation in his gut. In spite of their wrangles, he loved his father dearly.

'No. Nor hurt neither . . . or I don't think so. He won't let anyone near him. But you should see the boats! And Master Hammick, that took Pangdean Place in the spring, is saying that he's partly to blame and offers to pay the damages to quiet down the fishermen and settle the fuss.'

'What fishermen. Why damages?'

'Master Boomer blew up their boats, sir.'

Francis drew a deep breath of disbelief. He could not imagine his father blowing up fishermen's hoggies. Either by accident or by design.

And who the devil was Hammick?

'But my father is unhurt?' he asked again. A firemaster is allowed only so many close brushes with death before it gets him. Boomer had used up most of his.

'He's locked himself in his room, sir. All last night and today.'

Francis did not want to ask a groom about the state of his father's wits.

'Who sent you to fetch me?'

'Mistress Susannah, sir. But there's some fishermen at Powder Mote, won't go until they speak with you.'

'I'll ride on as fast as I can. You give that poor beast a chance to breathe, then tie it to the cart and follow more slowly.'

Francis climbed down and untied his own mare. Rather than try to make sense of the tale the boy was trying to tell him, Francis kicked his mount towards Brighthelmstone and Powder Mote.

'You slept last night, so shake your shanks,' he told the horse.

He found three angry fishermen seated on the grass just inside the gatehouse, within the moat. They rose stiffly to their feet when he trotted under the gatehouse arch, as if they had been sitting for a long time.

'Peter Mawes,' said Francis, scraping at his memory for names of the older men. Jem, he knew – Peter's second son, the younger brother who had trailed after the two older boys, Francis and Shelvy. 'And George . . .' The last name of Peter's brother-in-law, the brother of Jem's dead mother, escaped him entirely.

'We don't ask you to take our word, sir.' Jem Mawes, the youngest but most fluent among them, launched into speech as if carrying on with a fierce conversation.

'I would be very happy to take it, however,' Francis replied civilly. 'At least until I've had a chance to wash off the mud.

Won't you come into the house with me and have something to drink?' He wouldn't have minded a few hours of sleep as well, before dealing with trouble.

'In the house with him?' asked Peter Mawes suddenly. He jerked his head in what Francis assumed was the direction of Boomer. 'I'd drink with the devil, sooner.' He sank back into silence.

'We think you'd best come down to the beach to see for yourself, sir,' said Jem.

'Now,' interposed his uncle.

'Before the tide turns again.' The young fisherman was civil but firm.

'My horse has come from London today. She can't stagger another yard.' Francis handed his reins to the groom, who stood gawping nearby, listening to every word.

'You can borrow mine, sir. I'll get up behind my father here. Our horses are back on the other side of the moat.'

In disbelief, Francis surveyed the damage on the beach near the cluster of fishermen's huts that lay under the cliffs, below Brighthelmstone proper.

One hoggie was reduced to charred splinters. A second lay pitched onto its side, its seams gaping, sails and rigging burnt beyond repair. The wreckage of a net hut jutted up from a jumble of rock and mud that had fallen from the cliff behind it.

Francis studied the black crater in the beach.

'We can't afford to replace those boats.' Jem's uncle, George, began to gather verbal speed. 'And even if we could, we'll still lose a month or two of fishing. He's not safe, sir.'

'Are you saying that my father did this?'

'. . . The devil's work,' muttered George, just softly enough that Francis could pretend not to have heard.

Pierce, thought Francis. He's named George Pierce.

The three men showed him a fragment of smooth, curved iron trapped under the debris from the cliff. Like part of a thick-walled iron bowl, which would have been the size of a wash tub.

'First my son, now my boat.' Peter Mawes broke his silence savagely.

Francis squatted down. He scraped away chunks of chalk and clumps of singed grass to show interest, but he did not need a closer look. He recognized the mortar. Or more precisely, the piece of a former mortar. He sighed and stood up.

'I'll pay for your boats.'

'And our lost fishing?' asked Pierce.

Francis's voice took on an edge. 'I'll pay all fair damages. But I must earn the money first.' He did not dare use Cecil's saltpetre money.

'With respect, sir . . .'

'What is it, Pierce?'

'You can't ask us to wait. We have to eat while our new boats are built. That'll take two months in any case.'

'And my son here is getting married after Christmas.' Peter Mawes spoke a third time.

'That's so,' said Jem's uncle. 'The boy's been working night and day to earn money for a house of his own for him and his new wife. And there's Christmas itself . . .'

Francis took a deep breath. 'Let me have a night to think.'

'Master Hammick saw it all, if you want a witness.'

'I don't doubt your word, George Pierce.'

'And how can we trust that it won't happen again?'

Francis rode back to Powder Mote behind Jem, on the back of a plough horse doing double service as transport.

'I don't want your wedding spoilt,' Francis said as they climbed onto the Downs.

'Uncle George tends to get het up, even more since my

brother Shelvy drowned. Sometimes I think he talks all the more to make up for my father. You should have seen Da's face when he saw our boat after Master Boomer blew it up.'

'Is yours the one that's washing out to sea as tinder?'

'Yup.'

'It's a mercy no one was hurt.'

'That's what I said. Boats can be replaced. Though I think Dad loved ours more than he loved my ma before she died. *The Bride of Beachy Head*, she was called.'

'How much is a new boat?'

Francis multiplied Jem's reply by two and added reasonable living costs for the two months. And they should have something for the inconvenience, he thought.

The Quoynts needed to keep their dealings sweet with all their neighbours. The locals already viewed Powder Mote with fear and suspicion. Francis remembered the death at the stamp mill when he was eleven. There had been others. And injuries. And another local man had been blown up in the mixing shed more recently, while Francis was abroad. That the dead man had a reputation as a housebreaker and thief had slightly defused the public wrath.

Even before Cecil had summoned him, Francis was wary of upsetting neighbours with his rockets and other experiments. Now he needed to hire assistants from among the local men if he were even to attempt to make the four thousand pounds of gunpowder.

'I'll give you and your bride a wedding gift to help make it up to you,' he said.

The horse began to wheeze and groan in protest at the extra weight as she tried to keep her hind legs under her while going down a muddy slope. When the track levelled off again, Jem asked, 'Could you do us some rockets, like I saw you setting off a couple of times?'

'I had hoped I was unobserved.'

'Unobserved, shooting those things up? Oh, I see.' Young Mawes laughed when he caught up with the irony. 'Not a chance, anyway, sir. Too many of us up here on the Downs at night, one reason or another.'

'I'm sure I could manage a rocket for your wedding,' said Francis, his humour a little restored.

'Jane would like that very much . . . rockets at her wedding like a fine lady, though she'll only be a fisherman's wife.'

'We must give the women what they want.'

'If we can, sir.'

'There's always that.' His spirits sank again as he thought of Kate Peach.

Susannah White, his old nurse, still did her best against the odds to hold life together for the two bachelors at Powder Mote. Now she lay in wait for Francis in the entrance hall.

'Your father's come out of his room,' she whispered. 'He's in the Great Hall now. Drinking.'

Francis threw his cloak at a peg. It missed and fell into a heap on the floor. He cursed under his breath and left it while he sat on the bench to pull off his boots.

'Our new neighbour at Pangdean Place, Master Hammick that is, sent this letter for you.'

Francis cursed again to himself and reached out his hand. He had forgotten the groom's gabbling of the new tenant at Pangdean Place. Though the residents of Pangdean were called 'neighbours', like the residents of many other scattered Sussex estates, they were in fact a forty-minute ride away, along the coast towards Lewes, on the far side of Brighthelmstone.

He took Hammick's letter into the Great Hall to read by the light of the fire. 'Hello, sir,' he said to Boomer.

In silence, Boomer poured himself more claret.

Francis broke the seal and unfolded the letter. He read it.

Then he searched until he found his silver-rimmed wine cup on a windowsill, where he had left it the night Cecil's letter came. He blew out the dust, and poured himself some wine.

'Are we speaking tonight?'

Boomer turned on his stool. 'It seems that you are. I'm all ears.'

'I've done what I can to smooth feathers,' Francis said. 'But that accident of yours has cost us money we don't have and good will we can't afford to lose. George Pierce spoke of "the devil's work". I ended up offering to pay for both the boats and their lost fishing. And promising a display of fireworks for Jem's wedding in the new year.'

He regarded his father coldly. But as Boomer stared back, the old childhood apprehension crept into Francis's rage. If he had not been so edgy about the problems left behind in London, or so weary from his journey and lack of sleep, he would have curbed his tongue at once.

'By this, however . . .' He held up the letter. '. . . For some reason, our new neighbour Hammick seems to feel some responsibility. Says that he encouraged you. He offers to pay for both boats. We'll have to smile and accept what I'm quite certain is charity on his part. . . . How do you know Hammick?'

'I'm sorry you've been troubled,' said Boomer. He did not deign to ask to see the letter. 'I could have sorted the matter out.'

But last night, thought Francis, according to this letter, you dropped an explosive shell onto a hot coal at the bottom of a mortar. You knew better than that thirty years ago!

Hammick had written to Francis instead of his father, because he thought Boomer's wits were addled. However civilly he put it.

'. . . I should not have encouraged the experiment,' wrote Hammick. 'I was ignorant of the degree to which he had lost much of his former skill . . .'

And I was counting on my father's help in milling the powder, thought Francis.

'Father,' he begged. 'What are we to do?'

At last Boomer looked away. 'Something's going on at Pangdean Place.'

'Please. Don't change the subject. We can't pretend any longer that it's not true.'

'That I'm going mad?' Boomer's voice was icy.

'That you have bad days.'

I'm twenty-seven years old, thought Francis. Why is confronting him still so terrifying?

'And you believe that yesterday was one of the bad days?'

Francis blew out a deep breath. 'I fear that it might have been.'

'I knew exactly what I was doing.'

'Hammick doesn't seem so certain.'

'Hammick knows nothing about ordnance beyond what I tell him. In any case, he was testing me.'

Francis clenched his fists and bit his tongue.

'*Accept my apologies,*' Hammick had written. '*I had no idea that your father had also grown so troubled in his mind.*' The word 'addled' had remained unwritten but it hovered over the paper.

'Hammick's up to something, Francis. I don't yet know what, but I mean to learn. In the meantime, I suggest that you treat him as dangerous.'

'Please leave the man alone, father. I suggest that we treat him as generous.'

'Come with me to Pangdean and see for yourself, you insolent pup.'

'Don't anger him by playing at intelligencer,' said Francis, controlling himself with difficulty. 'We need him to pay for those boats, which, it seems to me, he is not obliged to do. And the sooner it's settled, the better.'

Now Boomer clenched his fists. 'That's how you see it? You can think of no other possible light on the matter?'

'Pluto and hell . . . sir! I didn't drop a shell on top of a hot coal. I didn't bring down part of a cliff and incinerate two hoggies. I didn't stir the local fishermen to near riot.'

'While I, in a fit of senile madness, did all those things? You presumptuous dolt!' Boomer surged to his feet and raised his fist.

Francis held his ground. 'I will not strike you back. But please don't hit me. For a soldier, you were always a gentle father. Don't turn brutal now.'

Boomer dropped his hand. Then he sank back down into his chair. 'Shog off. Take your meddling back to London.'

Francis let out a small sigh of relief. His muscles unclenched, but an angry pulse still thumped in his ears. 'When I was met on the road, I was already on my way to Powder Mote. I have an order for powder. A large order.'

'Do you want me to fall on your neck in gratitude?'

Francis was caught between rage and grief. In former days, he would have confided in Boomer entirely. Cecil, Guido, Catesby, Kate. On the good days, he would still trust him with his life. But he did not understand the dark terrain of the bad days he had seen, nor could he judge the man who wandered there.

He searched for words to soften the anger between them without giving ground entirely. 'Four thousand pounds of powder. Too much for me to handle alone.' And, most likely, too much altogether.

Boomer gave all his attention to the wine jug. Francis noted that his father's hands were shaking, like his own.

'You won't help me?' asked Francis. 'Then tell me at least where to find the book.'

The cold silence lengthened. Francis left the great hall.

*   *   *

'I can't control him, Master Francis. One day, he'll kill us all.' His old nurse Susannah rocked on her stool, twisting her apron with both hands. Bright eyes and a skeletal face above a round body made her look like an unhappy hen.

'I'm too old. I thought I'd be done with work by now. All the babies dead or grown like you and your sister. I was never meant to still be here looking after him! But I'm all that's left.'

'I'm not angry with you.' Francis looked around her modest chamber, which, a hundred or so years before, had been the solar off the original hall. Ivy had almost blocked out all the light from the narrow windows. The corners here were as full of dust and mouse droppings as those in his father's room and his own. The coals of her small fire had almost sunk out of sight into the heap of accumulated ash.

'Can no one else help you?' he asked.

'There's only Peg in the kitchen, up to her eyes without a kitchen groom. And her daughter who pretends to be a maid.'

He remembered that the nurse's voice had always carried a note of complaint, even when she was looking after him as a small boy. A woman who relished difficulty, but only when experienced by other people. She was right, nonetheless. She was too old, and not suited for the task of keeping his father out of trouble on his bad days.

'He left them in front of the fire . . . right up next to it,' she said. 'His powders and jars. While you were up in London. No one could advise me.'

Francis flinched at the possible numbers of that 'no one' whom she had no doubt consulted about his father's lapses.

'I can't sleep sometimes thinking what he might do,' said Susannah. 'Though he's gone and done it now, I suppose.'

With his thumbnail, Francis scraped a puddle of hardened wax off the mantelpiece.

How could he know from one moment to the next which

man he was dealing with? To look at his father tonight, he might still be commanding a company of sappers. But Francis had seen him in his dreams. And there was Hammick's letter. And the inescapable damage on the beach.

He tried to push the window open, but a net of ivy held it closed.

'What will happen when you leave us again?' asked Susannah.

Should he hire someone to watch his father? Francis tried to imagine introducing . . . Who? A fisherman's wife? An unemployed lout from Brighthelmstone? Another soldier, now at loose ends? *Father, this is your new gaoler. My spy, who will be keeping an eye on you . . . Your new nurse.'*

He snorted at the thought.

'Master Francis?'

'Never mind, Susannah. I shall think what to do. You must manage as best you can until then. But please come to me first for advice if you're troubled.'

A flick from her sharp eyes told him that she understood him.

Francis decided to write to his sister. But then he recalled that she already had her hands full on her husband's small estate. And four children . . . or perhaps only three . . . He was not certain of the exact number. And Northumberland was too far.

He had not seen her since her marriage, which had taken place three years after he began to work with his father at the age of eight. They were at either end of the family, the oldest and the youngest. The three siblings between them were bundled in friendly fashion into the crowded family tomb in the parish church of St Nicholas.

'We must all survive for just a few more weeks,' he told Susannah. 'I have a commission to fulfil. Then we can put things to rights.'

After leaving Susannah, he made certain that Boomer was still sitting by the hall fire. Then he searched his father's sleeping chamber. He removed a slow match of tow soaked in spirits and dusted with saltpetre from one of his father's pockets.

When he went back down the stairs, Boomer seemed to have fallen asleep stretched out on the floor, as if the hall hearth were a campfire.

If his father would not help him, then Francis had no choice but to help himself. After assuring himself that his father was truly asleep, he went out through the dark to the old gatehouse, left from the days of the priory.

He climbed the two flights of stairs to the top floor. Working mainly by feel, he tugged at the corner of a section of panelling. Behind the panelling was a niche cut into the thick stone wall, just large enough to hide a man. An outlaw, perhaps. Or a priest clutching the Communion plate while Henry's soldiers raided the priory. Francis had once tried to stand in it but leapt out instantly, with a tight chest and bubble of terror in his throat. It was like standing in a coffin.

He had wondered since boyhood whether his father or grandfather had defied the Crown and secretly held to the old religion. Or whether the niche had been made even earlier, for some other purpose, when the house was still a priory, the cloisters were not yet a chicken run, and the church had not yet been torn down for its stone.

He never asked his father because he did not want Boomer to know that he knew the secret of the hiding place. Because then his father would move the treasure there to a different hiding place, which Francis would have to find all over again.

PART FOUR

LIBER IGNIUM
(THE BOOK OF FIRE)

*'. . . That laws were like cobwebs; where the small flies
were caught and the great brake through.'*

Francis Bacon, Apophthegms

48

Francis lifted the treasure from its hiding place in the thickness of the wall. *Liber Ignium.* The Book of Fire. The Quoynt family book of deadly secrets. Four inches thick.

Boomer still refused to tell Francis where it was hidden when they had finished using it in their work. The fact that Francis had discovered the hiding place for himself did not ease the hurt he felt that his father did not, even now, consider him worthy of such trust.

Or perhaps, thought Francis, he believes the secret must be kept for a deathbed confession, and that in telling me he might set me into his place too soon.

Feeling like a ten-year-old stealing cakes from a stall, he tucked the heavy, ancient leather-bound volume under his arm and took it up to his sleeping chamber, avoiding the Great Hall. In his room, he lit two candles, set them on his little table and opened the book.

'We Quoynts must guard this book with our lives,' Boomer had told him when he first showed the *Liber Ignium* to Francis, his awe-struck eight-year-old apprentice.

Francis now smiled without amusement as he turned the first fragile pages. It seemed incongruous to guard such a book with your life. The *Liber Ignium* held secrets of death. It was a brimming treasury of ingenious ways to destroy, rich in devices for bringing down walls, horses and men.

Here were recipes for fireballs, to fling or to shoot from a mortar (an advance on *ballistae* flinging rocks and dead cows). Countless mixtures of burning pitch and oils. Page after page of gunpowder recipes. Slow and fast, serpentine, mealed and corned. There were different powder formulae for blasting in mines, firing muskets, lifting rockets, setting off squibs among enemy cavalry, or bringing down castle walls.

There were secret ingredients. The alchemical trials. Greek fire, which could not be put out. Notes on failed experiments. All written in the Quoynt family cipher, which Francis, as a child, had learned to read along with the Prayer Book and works of moral instruction.

He found the pages he wanted, the gunpowder composi-tions for producing explosive force rather than smoke, sparks or flames. After marking them with feathers pulled from his lumpy pillow, he turned back to the beginning. He had read the book from cover to cover many times in his life, but it still fascinated him. The *Liber Ignium* was more than a collec-tion of lethal recipes and devices. Among many other things, it defined the inexorable course of his own life.

Once the midwife had seen that Francis was male, the future set rock-hard around his tiny, waving, blood-streaked limbs. Three months later, his hair would turn from black to pale blond, but his future could never change. Francis was to follow his father and the string of fathers before him.

Five generations of Quoynts had flared and died in turn, connected by the long fuse of their shared skills and the secrets passed on in the book now lying on his thighs. Each male Quoynt in turn had lit a spark in a woman's womb, igniting a succession of lives, until the Quoynt flame, through the cock of Boomer Quoynt, had set himself, Francis, alight and fizzing.

Perhaps their first damp squib, he thought wryly.

In the *Liber Ignium*, Francis could also trace the history of his family as it ran in parallel with the history of warfare. The second piece of information he sought lay in that history.

His great, great grandfather had been siege engineer to Harry, Duke of Hereford, who became Henry IV when he returned from France to England to claim his crown from that painted popinjay, Richard the Second. This great, great grandfather had recorded the days of long sieges and short brutal skirmishes. Trials of slow and fast mixtures for mining defensive walls. Diagrams of mines and counter-mines, both zigzag and forked, to be dug right up to the enemy's walls. And the writhing tunnels of the *sinuosi cunuculi*, all designed to prevent explosions from blowing back and killing the moles who lit the fuses. He drew *ballistae*, mangonels and trebuchets and listed a wide range of improvised missiles that could be thrown by them at the enemy. He mentioned kings by name, and dukes. He recorded, without false modesty, how he made the breach at Harfleur.

Then came great grandfather's cramped, faded recipes for cannon mixtures. And for fire-arrows, fire-lances and other incendiary devices to set the enemy ablaze from a relatively safe distance. Here the family fortunes dipped, with a bad decision to back the loser, King Richard III of York, in the dynastic wars eventually won by the Lancastrian Welshman, Henry Tudor. They lost all of their estates. Great grandfather, too, mentioned kings, but no longer of England. The Quoynts had begun to sell themselves to anyone who would pay them.

In the next generation, his grandfather attempted to advance the progress of warfare through a passion for devising exploding shells. At that time, these were used more by the Italians and Chinese than by the English, who were still satisfied with shooting cannon balls of stone or iron. Grandfather must also have served the King, Henry VIII, in a way not recorded in the *Liber Ignium*, for the King gave him the dissolved Augustinian priory that became Powder Mote.

Francis bent close to the page to read the faded brown script in the candlelight. Yet again, he read of his grandfather's repeated attempts to project exploding shells at the enemy without blowing up the gunner. The difficulty lay in firing the propelling charge that projected the shell at the enemy. The first, smaller propelling explosion most often set off the second much greater charge, intended to explode only when it reached its target.

It was a difficulty that Francis himself wrestled with in making his rockets, though on a smaller scale and for more peaceful ends.

His grandfather had designed various delayed fuses to run between the initial propelling charge attached to the bottom of the shell and the second explosive charge at its heart. In ten experiments, he then placed a live coal at the bottom of a mortar and dropped the shell in such a way that the propelling charge came into contact with the red-hot coal. He shattered eight iron mortars and killed four gunners before giving up. Nevertheless, Boomer seemed to have done exactly the same thing when he destroyed the fishing boats. He had used a method of firing a shell that had been given up as too dangerous more than sixty years before.

This curious lapse both puzzled and alarmed Francis.

After a moment, he turned to the page where his father's hand picked up the story. Boomer's square, open script continued his own father's attempts to time a breeding shell so that it would land among the enemy before exploding. With crossings-out and scribbled oaths, he too pursued the perfect fuse. With every word, he demonstrated that he knew far too much to have made that mistake on the beach.

Francis turned to his father's most recent entry to see if

he could detect signs of madness in it. The final entry in his father's hand had been written only a month before, just after Francis had returned from Flanders. Boomer's handwriting had changed while he was still in his prime. While working for the Turks a few years after the siege of Famagusta, he lost the fingertips and some muscles of his right hand to a black shell that had seemed dead but was not. Though he still had use of the hand, his writing now lurched fiercely across the page, full of sharp corners and blots.

Beware, my son and grandsons who may follow me. This book teaches you to play God. Do not take on the role lightly. You must also learn to live with its aftermath. Lately, in my fifth decade, I have begun to dream of finding severed hands in my pockets. Fingers roll from my handkerchiefs. In these dreams, when I thrust my feet into my boots, I find cold, dead feet already in occupation. This weakness appals me, for I am certain that God never feels such mortal regrets. I cannot advise you. I merely warn you to be prepared for that great difference between God and his feeble Image. Man cannot escape his conscience. Having been in the service of princes does not acquit us. The ends of our lives must be spent in search of a peace that we have not earned.

Francis swallowed against a sudden lump in his throat. His father was speaking to him, here, on this page, as they could never talk face-to-face. He had never told his father about his own dreams either.

He lifted his head and stared up at the underside of the roof. His father's words had forced open a door his mind. A horse screamed under a blanket of burning pitch, its hoofs tangled in its own entrails. His hand burned with a flame that would not be put out.

I must try to talk to him again, Francis thought. I need to talk to him. I need his help even more than he needs mine. If he is truly mad, then I'm losing my wits, too.

49

'You meant for me to find the *Liber Ignium*.' Francis found his father before breakfast.

'Do you mean to hide it from me?' demanded Boomer. 'To keep me from blowing myself up, and Powder Mote along with me?' He stood in the entrance courtyard looking up at the ivy that advanced across the roof like a mythological beast.

'Doesn't it resemble a great serpent that has swallowed everything in its path?' he asked bitterly. 'All you can see is the irregular outline of its bulging belly. Those four bumps are chimneys. Best thing, after all, might be to blow the whole place up.'

'I read your last entry, Father.'

'The ivy is holding up the chimneys.'

'You wanted me to read it.'

'So, now you can interpret my thoughts and intentions?'

Francis drew a deep breath, stifled a retort. 'I can, when you write them for me to read.'

'And do you think me as addled in my wits as everyone else does? Babbling of my dreams?'

'Judging by what I read last night, I don't think your wits are addled.'

'That's a pity.'

'What the devil do you mean, "That's a pity"?'

Boomer shook his head. 'The explanation would reverse your new good opinion back again.' He studied the ivy. 'What softened your judgement?'

Francis looked up at the ivy. He looked at the ground. He had rehearsed, but speaking the words was even more difficult than he had expected. 'I dream,' he said at last. 'I too am troubled in my conscience.'

'We're both addled then,' said Boomer with a quick half-smile.

'So I fear.' Francis gazed seriously back at his father.

'They say misery is happiest in company. We shall be happy madmen together then. Two mad eagles flapping about.'

They turned and walked together towards the front door in careful amity.

'Why were you so certain that I would find the book?'

'Use your head, France. It's in the nature of boys to poke their noses into every possible corner. I found that hole the same way you did. Exploring. Looking for hidden treasure. Though it didn't take me so long. I was only seven years old. If I'm right, you were almost nine.'

'Why pretend all those years?' And injure my pride for so long, Francis wanted to add.

'Would you have studied the *Liber* half so keenly if I had thrust it at you like a schoolmaster?'

Reluctantly, Francis laughed and raised his hands in submission. His father's improved humour might make the next part of their conversation a little easier. Even so, he put off his request until they had settled on a bench on the narrow strip of paving behind the house, where they could look south towards the sea. At ground level in the winter, a glimpse of flat wet horizon could be seen through the bare branches of the trees. Now, in summer, only the quality of light and the sense of an empty vastness just beyond the trees announced the presence of the sea.

Four hens came to investigate.

Francis leaned back against the wall of the house and stretched out his long legs to imitate an easy posture. He took a swallow of watered beer.

'Will you help me make the gunpowder?'

'How much, did you say?'

'Forty barrels. Four thousand pounds. In two and a half weeks.'

Boomer whistled between his teeth. 'Who wants so much?'

Francis hesitated. He would have told the old Boomer at once, but a last remaining shard of doubt stopped him now. He did not yet know all that might happen on a bad day.

'A northern mine-owner,' he lied, and felt his cheeks redden under his father's sharp gaze. It was the end of their fragile truce. 'I'm forbidden to say.' He found himself mumbling like a boy caught stealing apples.

Boomer nodded savagely. Then he looked down at his damaged hand, which he opened and closed several times as if loosening his fingers. 'Forbidden by Cecil? Or are you forbidden even to tell me who forbids you?'

'Why did you pretend to make that mistake on the beach?'

'Well, well.' Boomer glanced sideways at his son on the bench beside him. 'We both have our secrets, it seems. I hardly dare trust a man who can't trust me.'

'I would. I will. But not yet.' Francis ached to tell Boomer everything and shift a little of that terrible weight onto his father's broad shoulders.

Boomer nodded. 'I'll tell you in time, too. When I'm ready.' He broke off some bread and threw it to the hens.

Damnation, thought Francis. Now what? He could not possibly manage forty barrels on his own in two and a half weeks. Even with the two of them at work, the odds would be against them. Powder Mote had never made more than a hundred and twenty pounds a day.

One of the hens flapped up onto the bench beyond Boomer.

Even with both of them working, they would still need to hire half a score of assistants to help with the pressing and corning. And with grinding the charcoal, minding the sluices, and cleaning up loose powder, which if allowed to settle too thickly would explode at the first spark.

'How much are you being paid for this gunpowder?' asked Boomer, with his eyes on the hen. 'Or is the honour of serving little Lord Salisbury in such an important, secret cause supposed to be reward enough?'

'There's enough money in it,' said Francis evasively. 'If I achieve all I'm asked. We will be able to put Powder Mote to rights. All of the estate, not just the roof of the house and the broken chimneys . . .'

'A veritable shower of gold, by Jove,' said Boomer dryly.

'We can repair everything,' Francis insisted, unable to look at his father. 'Mill. Barns. Dredge out the moat. Clean out the reed bed that drains the privies. Repair the track. And the estate cottages.'

He decided to say nothing yet about the fireworks display for which Cecil had also promised to pay.

'With only two and a half weeks,' said his father, 'I think you're buggered.'

'I'm caught between a man with absolute authority and a man of absolute convictions.

'We've always been masters of the absolute.'

Francis lifted his head hopefully at his father's use of 'we'.

Boomer gave the hen the last of his bread and lifted her from the bench back onto the ground. 'How much saltpetre did you bring from Woolwich?'

'Twelve barrels.'

'Am I allowed to ask the Crown's saltpetre man in Lewes for more?'

'No.'

Boomer nodded grimly. 'I thought not. So, it's back to scraping stable walls and digging out cesspits. Seeing that we must grow our own saltpetre, for reasons of the very highest secrecy.'

Francis jiggled his foot in irritation, but his relief at enlisting Boomer was greater than his chafing at the gibes that would be the price of his father's help.

'Shall we go look at the heaps in the plantation?' Boomer stood up and brushed the crumbs from his flat stomach and the thighs of his breeches.

They rowed across the moat in one of the dinghies. Then they walked along the fold of the ridge to a flat acre of ground covered with rectangular heaps roughly eight feet long and two feet high. The heaps were built of earth mixed with animal dung, urine, hoofs, bones, and ground oyster shells. The saltpetre plantation was sited away from the house and well downwind.

On the nearside of the plantation stood the leaching shed, with its back against a narrow band of stunted trees. Here they extracted the saltpetre by boiling the crystals formed on the heaps in a lye solution made with wood ash.

Francis bent down and scraped a few salt-like crystals from the surface of the nearest saltpetre bed. 'I'll hire men from the village to start collecting whatever's here. And have them gather wood ashes as well.' He examined another heap. 'But we still won't have enough. Even if we had the time.'

'Will your purchasers test the powder?'

Francis caught his father's drift at once. Counterfeit powder. Passing off chalk ground with soot was a common trick. He dropped the crystals back onto the heap. 'My buyers are former soldiers who know how powder looks and smells. One of them claims to have been a military firemaster in Spain.'

They walked together down a row of heaps.

'I've even considered fitting false bottoms in the barrels,' said Francis. 'Even if we had the time to make it, I hate to trust so much destructive power into the hands of these men.' He told Boomer, with careful omissions, about the purchase of inferior powder, the storing of good powder near a bakery, and the Bridge House explosion.

'Refuse the order,' said Boomer. 'Powder Mote will stand a little longer without being put right.'

'I can't.'

Boomer stared at him for so long that Francis thought he had lost his father's good will again.

'Forty barrels it is, then.' Boomer unlocked the leaching shed and peered into the huge brass kettle in the centre. 'While you go down to the village to hire us some help, I'll ride to Southampton for more sulphur, from my merchant.'

Francis nodded. They could not hope to acquire the ingredients for forty barrels of gunpowder without drawing attention. But some sources, like Boomer's merchant, were less likely than others to report to men who reported to other men, who reported to intelligencers, who then reported to men like Robert Cecil and Sir Francis Bacon, who most likely had managed to turn Cecil's boatman. And then tried to turn Francis.

'Once you've started the saltpetre collection, take a cart to the Weald for charcoal,' said Boomer.

Francis raised one hand in an ironic salute.

50

The following day, after hiring three assistants and before driving off to the charcoal burners in the Low Weald, Francis set his jaw and tackled a duty that he found both galling and humiliating. To pay Master Hammick, his generous new neighbour, an overdue visit of thanks.

From the cliff-edge track that led from Brighthelmstone to Beachy Head, Pangdean Place was invisible behind a solid wooden gate and a high red-brick wall. Even these defences could be seen only when crossing the little valley carved by Pangdean's stream. Francis left the cart on the track and climbed the hillside until he could look down on Pangdean from above like a cruising gull.

Unlike Powder Mote, which was an old religious house adapted for domestic use, Pangdean Place had been built as a gentleman's modest country estate. Though at least a hundred years younger than the original priory at Powder Mote, after twelve years without a tenant it was now crumbling back into the land.

Local opinion agreed that the small estate was part of the widespread Arundel holdings in Sussex, but no estate manager ever visited. No workmen made repairs. For twelve years, local farmers had let their sheep graze onto Pangdean land. Courting couples made love in the overgrown gardens.

Local smugglers used the crumbling cracks of caves in the cliffs beneath the house. All these comfortable freedoms had ended in February with the arrival of the new tenant, Hammick.

'He says he's a retired London merchant,' Susannah White had told Francis eagerly. 'Said to the smith he's tired of fretting about the plague. But he still seems to go to London often enough.'

Her information-gathering was limited by the fact that Hammick had hired no local help. Nor, so she said, had he brought a house family with him from London.

'I reckon he lost all his money,' she had said with satisfaction. 'Maybe his ship went down. That's what people are saying, anyway.' She sniffed. 'He's not married neither. Another bachelor.'

Looking down on the flinty walls and decorative stonework of Pangdean Place, Francis could not imagine what terrible things his father thought were happening there. He saw no suspicious activity. If anything, he saw too little activity of any kind. Pangdean still looked as deserted as it had for the past twelve years. The maze of courtyards and outbuildings at the back of the house was quiet. Francis saw no grooms, no dairymaids at their churns, no laundry hung to dry. No doves flew in and out of the small dovecote under the peak of the roof. No chickens. No dogs.

When the last tenants still lived there, Francis, aged eight or so, had spied on them from this very spot, pretending that they were enemies and the house was a defended castle he must breach.

His father must have done his own more recent spying from somewhere nearby. The idea of that once noble and terrifying man returning to boyhood games of spying made his stomach heavy and cold.

Though Boomer had seemed entirely himself this morning, Francis had to face the truth that his powerful father was growing older. He would die one day, and leave Francis alone in that great rackety place, without even their shouting matches to warm him.

Unhappily, Francis slid back down the hillside to rejoin the track, scattering rabbits and flushing small birds.

'Please don't apologize for not coming sooner.'

Master Hammick led Francis to a small parlour to the left of the Pangdean entrance hall. 'I wouldn't have presumed to expect you any sooner . . . Please do sit down. You must have much to concern you. Calming the fishermen, looking after your father, and so on.'

He was a dark-haired man of about Boomer's age, his manner coolly civil. With a twist of amusement, Francis decided that Hammick dyed his hair. The greying stubble of his chin was a poor match for his head.

'My father and I owe you a debt that may take us a little time to repay.'

Hammick raised a hand in protest.

A swordsman's hand, noted Francis with interest. Hammick was a retired merchant who regularly used his blade.

'You owe me nothing more than this visit,' said Hammick. 'As I wrote in my letter, I fear I led your father on. We'd only just met and I rushed in where I should have judged more closely. There are so few people around here with whom one would wish to spend time. And I wanted to learn more about the intimate workings of ordnance. Now that I'm retired from trading, I mean to turn to study to improve my knowledge of the rest of life.'

'An admirable ambition.' Francis had been looking around curiously but found little to see. The doors to all other rooms off the hall were closed. The parlour held only their two wooden armchairs and some iron firedogs on the hearth. No detritus of a lifetime. No ornaments. No hangings. No signs of a woman's hand. No servants visible inside the house, either. Not even a groom to offer refreshment to the visitor.

Another bachelor, thought Francis. Just as Susannah said. Even so, the house was unnaturally bare.

'My father was wholly to blame for the damage,' he said. 'It's not right that you pay for it all.'

'The truth is that the money means little to me. I've more than enough for my needs.'

So much for Susannah's lost ship, thought Francis.

'However,' continued Hammick, 'my quiet and peace of mind do mean a great deal. I want the matter settled and forgotten as soon as possible. I'm sure neither of us wishes to live among neighbours who are harbouring grievances.'

Francis nodded with a grim smile. Hammick had an air of private amusement that seemed very close to condescension.

'So.' Hammick rose from his chair in dismissal. 'Thank you for coming. We'll now know each other to speak to if we should ever chance to meet in Brighthelmstone market.'

Less than a quarter of an hour had passed. And, clearly, no return visit was intended.

'Our deepest thanks yet again, sir.' Francis wanted to strangle his father for landing him in this galling position. If Hammick wanted nothing more to do with the Quoynts, Francis could not blame him.

Hammick walked him to the front door.

Francis would have left the visit at that, if he had not glanced back over his shoulder while he was descending the front steps.

Hammick stood at the top of the steps watching him leave, with a curious expression of amusement, glee and suppressed ferocity. He was looking at Francis as he would at a fly he was about to swat, or a pigeon in his sights.

He has the eyes of an assassin, thought Francis. A retired merchant with a killer's eyes. And I interest him.

I was wrong. My father is right.

He thought again about the strange bareness of the house. The absence of visible life.

His father was right. Something was amiss at Pangdean.

51

When Francis returned from the Low Weald two days later with a cartload of charcoal, Boomer had started up the water-powered stamp mill.

Francis drove the cart straight down to the mill. After unloading the sacks of charcoal, he watched the three water-driven pestles rise and fall into their bowls. The three assistants were grinding the estate supply of charcoal into a fine, dark grey dust.

Boomer had made Francis draw the mill machine when he was ten. He could still have drawn it. The water wheel in the millrace turned a shaft that worked through a series of wooden gears to turn a camshaft that lifted and dropped three stone pestles into stone mortars shaped like half an egg. Watching now, he could feel the thud of each pestle through the soles of his feet.

Familiar quivers of excitement ran up his spine. Francis had not made gunpowder in large quantities since before leaving for the Low Countries. Abroad, he relied on local producers and on his own ability to reincorporate by hand any decayed powder that had separated during transport. But the process was as familiar to him as the geography of the mill.

First, you loosely mixed the three main ingredients:

sulphur, charcoal and saltpetre. Sulphur and charcoal combined first, before adding the unpredictable saltpetre. Then came incorporation, the close grinding together of all three ingredients. To avoid overheating and explosions during incorporation, you kept the powder moist by adding liquid. Urine, wine or vinegar served as well as water. Then you pressed the mixture into cakes and dried it away from open flames.

Francis watched the assistants begin to feed fresh charcoal into the bowls of the stamp mill.

After drying came corning, or breaking the powder cake into grains of different sizes, depending on the intended use. Catesby would need powder corned to the size of a grain of rice, achieved by forcing the pressed powder through the holes in a parchment sieve with a stick called a 'Jacob's foot'.

Boomer was visible in the distance, beyond the earth ridge that protected the house from the mill, up at the leaching shed with Jem Mawes who wanted work while the new fishing boats were being built.

Francis headed for the leaching shed, then veered away to follow the millrace downstream to the mixing house. He would apologise to his father about Pangdean later, when they were alone.

A high earth bank surrounded the mixing house on all four sides, with a narrow gap left in one corner by which to enter. Francis unlocked the flimsy door and removed his boots, remembering debates with his father on how best to construct buildings that were likely to blow up. Men who handled explosives differed violently in their opinions on the matter. Boomer had the Powder Mote mixing house constructed of light wooden planks, with pegged joints and no nails. The roof was thatched; the floor covered in leather.

When the young Francis had insisted that the building would catch fire far too easily, his father replied, 'Who cares for fire? When a basin full of powder explodes in your face, you want the force to escape. Not to be trapped inside thick stone walls.' The sloping earth banks protected any buildings beyond them and would also deflect the force of an explosion upwards.

The stamp mill had blown up when Francis was eleven. He was in the house, eating dinner with his parents. Suddenly, there was a reverberating thump. Their plates leapt on the table. The ale jug wobbled. The window glass cracked into knife-blade fragments. Francis stared at the glass, which seemed to fall in silence.

'The mill!' White-faced, Boomer had leapt from the table. Francis jumped up to follow.

'No!' His mother, still alive then, grabbed her son's sleeve.

'Let the boy come,' said Boomer.

'He's too young.'

'He needs to see, to learn fear. Fear will keep him alive.'

Running close behind his father, Francis saw a man burst from a pall of thick black smoke, his hair and clothes on fire. The willows in the protective grove lay shredded as if hit by artillery fire. In the middle of the smoke, the remains of the mill burned. The man died a few hours later. It was after that explosion that Boomer built the earth bank to shield the house.

The mixing house was an empty space, the leather floor bare except for two mortars and pestles. Francis sat cross-legged on the floor before one of the mortars. The first small batch of loosely mixed charcoal and sulphur was ready in a separate shed. He would begin the first incorporation of saltpetre after dinner.

He inhaled slowly. Gunpowder hovered as almost invisible dust. It sank into cracks. And waited.

I mean to make you wait a very long time, he told it.

After several minutes, he rose, replaced his boots and closed the mixing-house door. Fear had been a part of his life for twenty-seven years, he could not imagine the flat tedium of living any other way. Other men trudged towards the grave numbed by labour. In spite of his reservations about some aspects of his trade, he knew that he was fortunate. Fear was the price he paid for an exhilaration that was constantly renewed. Each time he finished a task. Each time he walked away unburnt, still able to see and hear. Few other men could possibly gain such intense pleasure from their work. Except for his father, of course.

He would never want to give up the intense delight he felt in eating and drinking, or in the hot flare of a sunset, or the exquisite sheen of a horse's neck. As for the moment of entering a woman's body . . .

He frowned into the millrace.

Kate was walled away from him inside a thicket of thorns.

52

'A visitor for you, Master Francis. A fine gentleman, but he won't give his name.'

In one of the sheds inside the moat, Francis set aside his basin of loosely mixed sulphur and charcoal. On the way back to house he paused at the well in the old cloister to wash his blackened hands and face. Clouds of dark dust rose as he slapped his trousers. The fine gentleman, whoever he was, would have to be satisfied with a dirty host.

In the Great Hall sat Robert Catesby, a mug of ale already in his hand.

'There he is, sir,' Susannah simpered as she emerged from the kitchens, panting slightly. 'Will you take something to eat?'

The Catesby charm had clearly been at work. 'He'll stay for supper,' said Francis.

And not a moment longer, if he could help it.

'What the devil are you doing here?' he demanded when he had Catesby safely out in the orchard away from Susannah's eager ears.

'I came to see how you progress.' Catesby made his visit sound like an enjoyable social duty.

'What if you were followed?'

'Don't be so fearful, France. Aren't you pleased to see me?'

Catesby reached up to stroke a half-ripe apple. 'God's watching over us. Nothing will be allowed to stop us.'

'I'm not so certain.'

'You're a cynic.'

'You're an innocent fool.'

Catesby shook his head. 'I know what I know and believe what I believe.'

'You can't succeed, Robin.'

'Why do you say "you" and not "we"? Are you against me?'

'Of course not.'

'Then trust me, France. We shall be heroes for the Faith.'

'We?'

'Guido. Thomas Percy. Me. And others you will meet. Tom Wintour looks forward eagerly to making your acquaintance.'

Tom Wintour. Another name for Cecil, thought Francis savagely.

'I still wish I knew how you can be so sure.' He could hardly force out the words.

'Take heart, France. We have powerful friends. More powerful than you can imagine. Unthinkable friends.'

'The Spanish?'

Catesby smiled.

Don't tell me! Francis begged him silently. I beg you, don't give me that burden of knowledge. I had to ask, but I don't want an answer.

'You're as sharp as ever, France. And, yes. A Spanish army will wait, hidden on ships standing off the coast. With men, horses, ordnance. Then, the next morning, when they hear the thunderclap of our Great Blow and see our pillar of fire, they will hoist flags and sail up the Thames. But, because of the supposed truce, no one else must know. I haven't told even Guido, who brings me their letters.'

'God's Blood!' Francis turned away to hide his face from

his friend. It was a mercy at least that Guido did not know. Just in case, by any chance, he still reported to Cecil.

'But England and Spain are now at peace,' he protested. 'You yourself said that Spain can no longer support the Catholic cause in England.'

Catesby smiled. 'I've recently had letters. The Spanish cannot show support, but they offer it secretly. The war has merely gone underground.'

Cecil's words almost exactly, thought Francis.

'The sinking of the Armada still rankles,' Catesby went on. 'The English may deceive themselves that Spain is lying down like a lapdog, but that Spanish humiliation is still alive. You should read their secret letters to me.'

With amazed despair, Francis thought that Catesby might even show him the letters, if asked.

'But enough of such weighty talk for now. I've come to give you good news . . . good for you, at least.'

They turned at the end of the orchard and began to walk back towards the ruins of the church.

'Ministers fear a lingering contagion of the plague. Parliament has been prorogued again, from the third of October until the fifth of November. You have a month more.'

If Francis had had any last doubts about what Catesby intended, he could not pretend ignorance now.

'That still is not enough time,' he said. 'Must your blow fall on the opening of the next Parliament? Why not the one after that? Or when they return after Christmas?'

'Our new King once promised us tolerance and freedom. The end of crippling fines. Now he will demand even more savage laws against us, in this next session. To stop these laws, we must stop Parliament. And kill the traitor King.'

'You mean to do it, don't you?'

'By my hope of Heaven, I do.'

They walked in silence for a moment. Francis rubbed his mouth unhappily.

'You must try, France. Surely the extra weeks improve the chances.'

Francis saw his dilemma clearly. Either he must continue to attempt the impossible, or he must betray. As soon as he gave Cecil the true names of Robin Catesby, Thomas Percy and Tom Wintour, they would be arrested, and the need to finish the powder would disappear. The second alternative felt as impossible as the first.

'Won't you think again, Robin? The laws you want to prevent will seem mild compared to what will inevitably follow your "Blow". Why give your enemies perfect cause for a massacre? They are waiting hungrily for an excuse to cleanse England of all Catholics.' Francis felt slightly out of breath, as if he had been running.

'You lack faith, France. There will be a bloodbath only if we fail. And we will not fail so long as we all hold our nerve. And if you provide our powder in time. Can you do it, or not?'

This man means to kill the King, Francis reminded himself. And the Prince of Wales. And hundreds of others. He and his friends. However wronged they might be, they must not do it.

Nightmares of carnage flickered at the back of his mind. He saw Westminster flattened. Black and smoking rubble. Black sticks that were charred arms and legs. He saw badly burnt survivors dying slowing in agony as wounds putrefied.

'I need a traitor,' Cecil had said. 'It's your task to provide him.'

Francis did not need to pretend to agitation as he paced the orchard grass. He stared at Catesby, who stared back.

I will confess who I really am, he thought suddenly. Warn Robin that he will surely be unmasked, that he's as good as betrayed already. Cecil need never know that I have confessed. When Catesby sees that all their schemes are known in advance, he will surely abandon them and flee abroad. And survive. And Guido and Percy and Wintour with him. Even Robin would surely not fling himself and all his friends into certain and pointless disaster.

'Give it up, Robin. I beg you.'

'We have already debated the subject. Can you make our powder in time?' For the first time, Francis saw Catesby's eyes begin to harden.

This extra month was at least breathing space. A second chance to save both Catesby and himself.

'I'm still trying. We have almost eight barrels ready to deliver to London.'

Catesby rewarded him with a glowing smile. 'Why do you look so angry?'

'I would to God you had never asked me to make the powder.'

Catesby bent to pick up a windfall from the grass. A small brown slug clung to the underside. He studied it thoughtfully for a moment. 'I, too, have doubts at times. But I must hide them, or else dispirit the others. Some of them have such a frail resolve and this longer time stretches it even thinner. But I can confess to you, can I not?'

'That you feel qualms about such an extreme and bloody venture? I like you better for it, I assure you.'

'The only other creature in whom I have confided is my confessor. I didn't reveal our full intent, of course. But I asked for his moral judgement on killing a great many men, not all of them my enemies. Because I can't warn them without raising alarm, some friends must also die.'

'Surely, as a man of God, your confessor cried out against murder.'

Catesby set the apple back down in the grass. 'He said that, in time of war, such things happen. Innocent women and children are killed. We must accept that as the cost of war.'

'And did he agree that you are now at war?'

'I didn't have to ask. I know that we are.'

Francis kicked another windfall into the trunk of a nearby apple tree. 'Oh, Robin,' he said in despair. 'You charm even your confessor into giving you what you want.'

But at least Catesby had qualms. With a further month, Francis might yet persuade those qualms to breed and multiply. He must hold Cecil off until he was absolutely certain that Robin could not be turned from his purpose.

'I need you to stand firm beside me, France,' said Catesby.

'I won't give up yet,' Francis said. If he did, he would never sleep peacefully again.

'If you need to stiffen your resolve,' said Catesby, 'you should attend the execution of two Jesuit priests next week in London, when you bring our powder to Lambeth. You will be reminded why we are driven to our drastic cure for the disease you will see manifested there.

'And now to my final reason for coming here.' Catesby gave him a key. 'For the storehouse you will find on the riverbank at my house in Lambeth. I must be elsewhere, alas.' His voice was filled with regret at missing the delight of another encounter. 'Please deliver the finished powder there. I'll leave sacks and so on, to disguise the kegs.' He smiled. 'Discretion, of course, in the delivery. But I don't need to instruct you in such matters.'

'That was the man of absolute convictions,' Francis told his father after Catesby had left. Though he would not yet give up on dissuading Catesby, he did at last have meaty news to report to Cecil. With great care.

During the two days it took Francis to drive the cart from Powder Mote to London with the first eight hundred pounds of gunpowder, he considered how he would present the news of the Spanish treachery to Cecil while still hiding true names.

Once he betrayed the names, it was all over. The executioner would sharpen his knife. The massacres of Catholics would begin.

Late on the Tuesday following Catesby's visit, Francis delivered the powder to the storehouse on the Lambeth estate. As he heaved the kegs and firkins off the cart, he paused from time to time to listen. The night around him felt unnaturally still, as if all the rats, frogs, and insects had fled or crouched in hiding.

He feels me here, thought Guido Fawkes, but he can't be certain.

Fawkes slipped from the shadow of a grain store to crouch behind a low stone wall.

It's not good enough to be uneasy, Quoynt. I could still kill you any time I like.

A single well-aimed bullet would suffice. Or he could slide into the storehouse itself and slit the man's arrogant throat from behind.

When Francis arrived with the cart, Guido had been lodging in the otherwise empty house as he sometimes did while in London. Now he enjoyed the predatory power of stalking an unknowing victim.

Look at him! thought Guido. Who does he think he is? Our new saviour, no doubt. With his good powder. Not that inferior stuff found by poor old Guido and Rookwood.

While Francis was inside the storehouse, Guido moved still closer. He was tempted to reveal himself and make Quoynt wet his breeches at being so blind to possible danger. But such a cheap taunt would demean him. Whatever Robin might now think, he, Guido, was the Chosen One. He did not need petty triumphs. His true mettle would become clear soon enough.

In the end, he followed Francis away from the estate,

hoping to prove a reason for his deep distrust of that hulking pretty boy. But he lost Francis on the river when the wherry man followed a wrong lantern across the Thames. By preference, Guido would have tried to pick up the trail again, but he was due to sail on the morning tide. Duty took him to Spain one more time, to raise money and support for their cause.

Francis returned the cart, unaware of the tracker behind him. Then, as London Bridge was closed for the night, he hired a wherry to cross the river. The St Paul's bookseller came out of his sleeping chamber in his nightgown to take the letter for Cecil. Francis evaded the watch, who prowled for curfew breakers, and took another wherry back to the Bankside, where the watch had given up the struggle.

The Dutch whore had left a letter on his bed.

From Cecil, thought Francis. But he had only just left his own letter. It was far too soon for a reply.

He lit a candle and held the seal to the light. An unfamiliar device. Francis cracked the seal and unfolded the letter. It was from Sir Francis Bacon.

53

'Does my little cousin know that you're making gunpowder? And so much?' Bacon wiped his quill pen on a square of silk and laid it on the table where he had been working. His breakfast sat half-eaten beside a pile of papers.

Francis needed no playhouse skills to look nonplussed. He remembered what Cecil had reportedly said of Bacon. 'The intellect of an angel and the eyes of a hungry ferret.'

The ferret was gazing keenly at him now.

'Why should the Earl of Salisbury concern himself with my actions?' Francis had missed whoever replaced the boatman as Bacon's intelligencer.

'My cousin concerns himself with everything that affects the realm,' said Bacon blandly. 'And so he should. No other single man holds such power to save England, or to destroy her.' Bacon seemed to be hovering like a hawk, waiting for a movement in the grass to tell him where to attack.

'From the little I know of him, I'm certain that the Secretary of State is incapable of letting harm come to the country.'

'Are you quite certain?' Bacon raised his eyebrows. 'Do you not know what they say of men whose bodies are twisted? That there is a consent between the body and the mind. That their souls are likewise twisted. That they seek to free themselves from scorn either by virtue or by malice.'

'I've heard such things said. I don't see them proved in the new Lord Salisbury.'

'But then, as you say, you don't know him.' The verbal stiletto pricked but did not quite draw blood.

Francis nodded agreeably.

'For whom are you making the powder?' asked Bacon, returning to his opening topic.

Behind neutral eyes, Francis considered the situation. If Bacon's intelligencer had been watching Lambeth, he would know about Catesby. In which case, the question would not have been needed. On the other hand, who could judge what Bacon felt to be necessary?

'Since the truce, my father and I are forced to deal with the northern coal mines,' Francis ventured.

Surprisingly, Bacon seemed satisfied with this answer, although he continued to gaze at Francis thoughtfully.'You didn't imagine that you could undertake such a great project and remain unnoticed?'

Francis shrugged, in spite of the jolt Bacon's last words gave him. 'I didn't expect to arouse interest in such elevated quarters.'

Bacon smiled at the sardonic flattery. 'That was an enjoyable volley. But, to the point of our meeting: I called you here to ask if you had reconsidered my offer of employment. If being an intelligencer is not to your taste, I may shortly have work for a firemaster.'

'My answer must remain the same, sir.'

'A poorly judged decision,' said Bacon. 'Perhaps you place your trust in the wrong man. "Let go thy hold when a great wheel runs down a hill, lest it break thy neck with following it." Ask yourself whom Cecil truly serves. His king or himself?'

Francis wished again for Cecil's dog-like ears that could read sounds beyond his own hearing. He felt that Bacon had just made another move in a game, and he, Francis, had no idea even what that game was. He ached for the simplicity of lighting a fuse, then watching his flame take a direct path towards the conclusion.

Though ignorant of the greater game, he had nevertheless learned a little from this meeting. A spy might be watching Powder Mote, though he did not know who was being watched, his father or himself. There might be a traitor close to Cecil. And there was a third possibility, less dangerous for the Quoynts but no more palatable: a spy among the plotters themselves. Guido, perhaps.

Later, standing on some water steps to hail a wherry, Francis admitted his own wish to think the worst of Guido, and rejected him as the possible traitor. The man clearly worshipped Robin Catesby.

Francis could not get a grip anywhere on what had just happened. Only one thing seemed clear beyond all doubt. Bacon hated his little cousin and wanted to infect others with his dislike.

54

The hated little cousin was late. The main door of the wool-dyer's warehouse was locked. The jetty from which Francis had first entered could be reached only by boat.

The rainy autumn evening was unseasonably warm. As he waited, Francis began to steam inside his wet wool cloak. He took off the cloak and his hat and let the rain try to wash him clean. As he tilted his face upward, he wondered how many more such rains he would live to feel.

Then he ventured out along a narrow, slippery wooden walkway that threatened to break under his weight and tilt him into the Wandle. This walkway led to a small, unlocked door at the side of the warehouse. With raindrops hanging from his sun-bleached eyebrows, he pushed open the door.

The drying lines were empty. Bales of dyed wool stacked ready for loading filled the lower floor. The rain drummed on the roof of the loft. The moist air smelled more strongly of sewage, rats and mould than of dye. Francis was still wringing out his doublet when Cecil arrived slowly, step-by-step, at the top of the loft stairs.

One cousin in the morning, thought Francis. And one in the evening.

He reported his meeting with Bacon, leaving out only the discourse on twisted bodies and souls. He had no need, otherwise, to guard his tongue against slips and was almost grateful to Bacon for providing such straightforward matter.

Cecil, seated again at his table, merely nodded as if wearied by the news. 'Envy needs no more reason than its own self.' He gave a dismissive wave of his hand. 'If my cousin Bacon put a fraction of his intellect and ambition to fruitful use instead of detracting his imagined enemies, I might have to fear for my position. Even for my head. But as it is . . .'

'I think you should fear him now, my lord.'

There was an awkward pause in which the sound of the rain wrapped round them in the dusk, closing out the world. Then Cecil said, 'Thank you, Quoynt. I'll bear your advice in mind.' Though dry, his voice held no anger at the presumption. 'And what else do you have to tell me? You called for a meeting before you saw my cousin.'

Francis steadied himself for the lie direct. His first with Cecil, a concocted tale that told some of the truth while leaving out both Robin Catesby and Kate Peach. He had rehearsed it all the way to London.

'I have found a letter, my lord.' He felt his face turn as hot and red as a freshly boiled lobster.

Cecil held out his hand.

'I dared not steal it, my lord, for fear of revealing myself by the theft.'

After a moment, Cecil asked, 'Where did you find it?'

'Hidden among Guido's clothes.'

'Indeed? And who had written to Guido?'

Francis could not read Cecil's tone. 'It was signed "Prometheus".'

'Ah, yes. The fire-bringer. Are these wretches poets then, as well as traitors? And what is Guido's secret name?'

Uneasily, Francis reminded himself that there must be other watchers with their own stories. However, he was committed to his chosen lie. To names without names. 'Dis.'

'The king of the underworld.' Cecil sounded amused. 'And what did fiery "Prometheus" write to our immodest turncoat "Dis"?'

'That the Spanish are promising help for the traitors. Men and horses, on ships standing out at sea, waiting for the signal to attack London.'

'All that was in the letter to Guido from "Prometheus"?' asked Cecil sharply.

'Yes. I fear that the expectation of such support is what drives them on.'

'Good,' said Cecil. 'That's why I wrote those Spanish letters.'

This is the one that will kill me, thought Francis.

55

'I've been intercepting the Spanish Ambassador's letters for so many years,' said Cecil, 'that I believe I could forge a letter from him to his own king.'

An icy hand gripped Francis. He stood paralysed, his mind refusing to deal with what he had just heard.

'Don't look so aghast, Quoynt. I didn't think a firemaster could afford a nice conscience.' Cecil sounded oddly cheerful. 'All's fair in war. We've lived with threats of rebellion and invasion for at least eighteen years. Philip of Spain prepared his invasion fleet, the Armada, with the blessings of the Pope. After the Armada – in whose defeat I believe God played as great a role as our own heroic fleet – Philip then sent yearly invasions until he died. And the rest of Europe stood by. You can't be shocked if we fight back with a few forged letters.'

Francis stood with both mind and body still frozen.

'I'm still trying to undo the damage done when England executed a Catholic monarch.' Cecil slid his small body off the stool and went to peer over the windowsill at the rain. 'I would not have encouraged Her Majesty in that tragic folly as my late father did.'

Francis tried to shake his thoughts loose again.

'Revenge.' Cecil struck the sill with his small fist. 'Mankind lives for brute revenge. First that old fool in Rome took revenge with his Papal Bull for King Henry's defiance in marrying Boleyn. Then Henry revenged himself on Rome by taking all that the Catholic Church owned in England. Then Elizabeth revenged herself on her Catholic cousin for claiming to have a more legitimate right to the throne. None of it makes noble telling. And now the Spanish want revenge for Catholic Mary's execution by her cousin Elizabeth.'

'But what of the truce?' Francis managed to say.

'Bugger the truce!' said Cecil. 'I told you once before. The secret war still rages, and I want it settled.'

'By providing the enemy with gunpowder and false assurances?'

Cecil flung him a glance that cut like icy sleet, then looked back out at the dancing, ragged water that streamed from the eaves.

'Our King needs a respite . . . I need a respite . . . in which to build stability for England again.'

'I see no respite, only risk, if you encourage these men.' Francis began to be able to breathe again, enough, at least, to sustain life.

'You disappoint me, Quoynt.' Cecil turned his eyes from the window onto Francis. 'I took you for a man who can understand the strategy behind the orders he receives. You must be aware that popular opinion is turning against the King. He needs enemies. We have found those enemies. And their terrible intentions must flower for the world to see. His Majesty most of all. In endeavouring to be even-handed – and to increase the number of his friends – he may have compromised himself by promising certain English Catholics favours he cannot be seen to deliver.'

'How far do you mean to let these traitors run, my lord?'

'To the very brink. I want those devils exposed in all their terrifying nakedness, along with any men who may still join with them. I want the nation and her king to feel in every part of all their senses how close they came to obscene disaster. I want them unified in determination that such a thing must never happen again.'

Francis ran a tongue over dry lips. 'What if I fail to make them the full amount of powder before they reach the brink?'

Cecil turned on him in fury. 'They must have it! I depend on you, Quoynt, to do what I hired you to do. You make or find them their powder in time for the Opening of Parliament on the fifth of November. I will see to the rest.' Cecil headed for the stairs.

'My lord, may I ask one last question?'

A renewed downpour drowned Cecil's reply, but Francis read his pause at the top of the stairs as assent. At last, Francis managed to frame his question.

'To whom did you send your forged letters?' The rain disguised the hoarseness of his voice.

If he says Robert Catesby, he thought, I should by reason kill him before he can descend the stairs.

'Why, to Guido, of course.' Cecil braced his hand against the wall and lowered himself down the first step. 'Who else?'

Francis stood, still trembling, with his back against a wall of the warehouse behind a ragged sheet of water that poured from the eaves. In that narrow gap between water and wall, he had an illusion of solitude. He needed to think before he took one more step. His legs needed time to find their bones again.

You ass! You souse-crowned nizzie! he swore at himself. Bad conscience gave you the least little tap and you cracked . . . Just because Catesby said that he had had a letter from Spain.

'*Why, to Guido, of course.*'

Cecil had written his forged letters to Guido, not to Catesby. To Guido, just as Francis himself had said, though he had been lying. Guido must have sent the letters on to Catesby. 'Prometheus' and 'Dis' remained plausible inventions. Cecil had sent his forgeries to the one man whose name Francis had given him.

He regarded his unsteady hands. That little man could make them judder and jump, where a shell filled with explosive could not.

There was no need for his heart to stop, after all. Cecil did not know about Catesby, after all. Therefore, Cecil did not know, after all, that Francis had been lying to him. Cecil was not letting Francis run, as he was with Guido . . .

Francis went around this circle of reasoning one more time. Behind all his thoughts, he kept hearing the insect whine of Bacon's voice. *'Perhaps you place your trust in the wrong man. Ask yourself whom Cecil truly serves. His king or himself?'*

Envy of his cousin did not necessarily make Bacon wrong.

Francis thrust a large hand like a knife blade through the sheet of falling water and watched the splitting of the glassy plane, which never quite mended itself before it hit the ground.

The insect whine began to torment him with a further question. What if Cecil did not mean to pull the plotters back at the brink, as he said? What if he, like the plotters, wanted the King dead in spite of his loyal words? And the Prince of Wales. And the best of the King's ministers. All the men who hold power, dead. All but one.

Whoever replaced the murdered king on the throne would surely need a Cecil to smooth the accession, even more than the newly kingdomed James had done. And by the time it became clear that the Secretary of State had not been delayed but had deliberately avoided the Opening of Parliament, it would be too late.

Cecil might even mean to rule without a king.

A dark blur of movement stirred on the far side of the

watery wall. Alert, Francis watched it pass and fade. A noise on his left made him jump. Then he saw a disconsolate cat compressed into a damp lump under the eaves.

Returning to Cecil, he began to wonder why a treaty with Spain had been achieved only now, not while Elizabeth was on the throne. Cecil might have made secret terms with Spain while the Scottish king was still new to English statesmanship.

Cecil's heritage was slippery enough. His father, Burghley, had embraced Catholicism to please Mary Tudor while she was queen. But behind Mary's back, he began secret correspondence with the next queen-to-be, the Anglican Elizabeth. To please Elizabeth, Burghley then renounced his newly sworn Catholic vows and began to pursue English Catholics viciously with his army of spies. But it was possible that Burghley's old allegiance to the Catholic Queen, Bloody Mary Tudor, still lived on secretly in his son.

Francis cupped both hands. The sheet of water fell too fiercely to stay in the bowl of his flesh. He watched it wash over the dams of his wrists and thumbs onto the mud.

He knew what Robin Catesby and his fellow plotters intended. In spite of the Secretary's professed fervour for peace in England, Francis was suddenly less certain of Cecil. The insect whine in his head insisted that he might be employed by an ingenious and terrifying traitor.

Bacon had been trying to warn him.

On the morning of the fifth of November, Hell would be unleashed in one way or another. The King would be murdered or else Robin Catesby would head for the scaffold, along with Tom. And Guido. And Percy. And the others Francis did not yet know. And those still being drawn in by Catesby, even now.

'I will see to the rest,' Cecil had said.

Oh Lord, Francis begged. Strike me with a sudden faith in

Your Existence. I need advice I can trust. Or else some other form of revelation. I never wanted such power over other men's lives.

When his hands grew too numb to feel the chilly water, he wiped them on his water-logged cloak. He plunged through the falling sheet of water and began to make his way through the dark crevices between the warehouses. Moving away from the industry on the Wandle, he rejoined the south bank of the Thames and walked down river towards Southwark.

His feet beat out the rhythm of his jumbled thoughts. *Cecil lies or Bacon lies. November five, everyone dies. Cecil lies . . .*

He stopped in mid-stride.

Cecil had finally slipped up. When he said, '. . . what I hired you to do,' he had meant making gunpowder, not gathering intelligence.

The rain still blurred all vision. Francis peered through the murky light for the footpads and homeless rogues who haunted the edges of the Lambeth marshes.

There was someone behind him . . . .dark cloak . . . but too far back for alarm.

Alert to the figure behind him but tangled in thought again, he walked on. How did Robin Catesby imagine that England would be governed after his blow had killed every man of knowledge and experience? Being Robin, he would no doubt answer truthfully if Francis simply asked him outright, 'Are you in league with Cecil?'

If so, Cecil had very good reason for absolute secrecy. He had hired Francis to provide powder for traitors. He paid for the traitors' powder. He insisted that they have the powder before the Opening of Parliament. In truth, Cecil was behaving very like a traitor. And Francis was the only man in the world who knew. Except, just possibly, Sir Francis Bacon.

Francis thought again of Cecil's first boatman, who had disappeared. His mind felt like a loose sail in a storm, all corners flapping. He could trust no one.

Except, perhaps, Kate. She had never lied to him, not even at their last meeting, however little either of them cared for the truth. Before returning to Powder Mote, he could try one last time to talk to her.

The more he considered this course of action, the more reasonable it became. This entire nightmare had begun with a request from her. Cecil had given him her Missal to return, and Francis still did not know why. Kate was tangled with him in this dreadful confusion. Even if she refused to talk, she might unwittingly let drop some helpful crumb.

Pausing among some ragged bank-side trees, he bent his head to let the water run off his hat.

He wanted only to talk to her. Nothing more.

But a man can't always stifle his secret hopes.

As he flung himself into motion again, he heard a sound like tearing silk in the air near his head. Something hit the nearest tree with a thud. He saw the crossbow bolt with the side of his eye as he dropped to the ground. He rolled over the edge of the bank into the river and began to swim.

A startled wherryman pulled him out of the water halfway across the Thames and half a mile downstream.

PART FIVE

THE BLACK SHELL

'The worst solitude is to be destitute of sincere friendship.'

Francis Bacon, Apophthegms

'There is little friendship in the world, least of all between equals.'

Francis Bacon, 'Of Followers and Friends'

56

Kate wore her dead brother's clothes, with his hat pulled low, she carried everything she now owned: her rosary sewn into the lining of her doublet, the Missal in the sack slung over her shoulder. She wished it were winter so that she could pull a cloak up around her face, but the weather was too mild. She dared not call attention to herself.

She did not look around her and tried not to think of who might be standing just behind her, watching. Who perhaps had followed her from the Holland's Leaguer. She made herself gaze steadily ahead at the scaffold, where two nooses dangled from a crossbeam and a headsman's block waited near the front edge. No coffins stood ready. The birds would get these bodies.

The early morning crowd in St Paul's Churchyard was small. There had been none of the usual placards, no heralded announcements of the executions. Only street gossip reported that the scaffold had been made ready, as did the whispers secretly passed among Catholics. A whore who had seen the arrest at The Little Rose had told Mary even before Kate arrived looking for sanctuary. Now, a week later, she warned them of the execution.

'You're barmy,' Mary told Kate that morning. 'You go on your own, duck. I'm already uneasy that the news arrived here so smartly.' Mary's eyes were hard, without their former warmth.

Kate kept one hand inside her shirt, gripping her rosary so hard that her nails cut into her palm.

Father Jerome would die that day.

She placed herself near the scaffold, so that the priest would see at least one witness to his death who knew he was guiltless of the treason for which he died. She had never seen an execution, but had heard what they did to Jesuit priests. And she had seen the heads and butchered limbs on the Great Stone Gate.

Please God, let it be over quickly, she prayed.

A fine trembling began to vibrate the cuffs of her jacket. She glanced at the man beside her, his eyes fixed on the scaffold.

You're weak to tremble, she told herself. You have only to watch, while Father Jerome must suffer the agonies.

Steadfast. She must be steadfast.

Holy Mother Mary, help me to be strong, she said silently.

Five witnessing officials climbed the steps to the scaffold platform.

Fools, she wanted to scream. You murder your allies.

Her eyes turned to a disturbance in the crowd. She heard shouts of abuse. A prisoner on a hurdle was being drawn up to the scaffold. At the same time, one of the executioners set up the ladder which each priest would climb to offer his head to the noose.

A stranger was hauled up onto the scaffold.

Kate closed her eyes and kept them shut. She tried to shut her ears to the dreadful sounds. The clatter of a falling ladder. A thump. A shriek abruptly cut off. Around her, some in the crowd shouted in triumph. Others gasped or groaned. Women screamed.

Holy Mother Mary, pray for us.

She felt the darkness under her, everything rushing away.

'Behold the head of a traitor!' The executioner's voice sounded distant.

The crowd around her stank of sweat and high emotion. Their voices turned to a low growl, then a stabbing murmur. A horse whinnied, drawing the second hurdle to the scaffold.

'Will you renounce your wickedness and die in the embrace of the Church of England?'

Kate opened her eyes when she heard Father Jerome's clear voice refuse the invitation. In her thoughts, she put her arms around his waist again to hold them both steady.

'*Pater, filius et spiritus sanctus, misere nobis . . .*' Father Jerome looked straight at Kate as he began his prayer. She moved her lips with his words. He had given his clothes to the hangman, as was the custom, and would die in only his shirt.

He still prayed as he was guided up the ladder with the noose around his neck. The hangman flung him off. He swung in great swooping arcs, kicking like a chicken whose neck has been wrung. The hangman cut him down at once, still breathing. There was a thump.

Kate's sleeve now jumped visibly. *Stay with him. Hold on. Don't look away. Holy Mother Mary . . .*

A man in a butcher's apron flung up the young priest's shirt and sliced off his genitals. Held them aloft.

Behold, said his gesture. This creature is no longer a man. No longer one of us, God's chosen rulers of the world. He is no more than a gelded bullock or shoat.

The executioner drove his knife into the priest's chest, just below the breastbone, and ripped open his belly down to the pubic bone.

Father Jerome made a sound more terrible than anything Kate had ever imagined. He was still just barely alive as two of the executioners pulled out his entrails.

Holy Mother, let him die, Kate begged. She could not tell if her prayer had been answered when the axeman stepped forward and raised his blade. Then he held up Father Jerome's head, the eyelids still fluttering.

Kate staggered. A hand grabbed her by the arm.

'It's me, sweet. We must get you away from here.'

At first she did not seem to see him. Then her eyes found him. Her pupils were black pools. Terror bloomed in her face.

Francis leaned close. 'Hush. Don't struggle. I'm trying to save your skin.'

She attempted to pull away but did not cry out. He could see her trying to decide what to do.

'Take my handkerchief,' he murmured. She stared at it, unable to think why it was there in front of her, then obediently held it to her face as if it were scented with restorative herbs. She let him lead her away.

They stopped on the far side of London Bridge, near the Long Southwark market. She yanked her arm out of his grip. He seemed to be furious with her. It puzzled but also reassured her, though she needed time to think why this was so.

'Why the devil did you go there?' He seemed ready to shake her. 'Don't you understand that the execution was meant to draw you out? All of you. The crowd was full of intelligencers busy writing down names.'

'Draw out whom?' she asked. 'Who are "all of you"?'

'Catholics, you fool.'

'Did you betray him? And me?' She felt very strange, as if she were contracting the plague again. No membrane lay between her thoughts and the world. Nothing stopped her words from falling out unchecked.

She drank an *aqua vitae* he put into her hand. She felt as she had when she woke up that morning in Stokewell after stealing back the Missal. Nothing under her feet.

'I did not betray you, Kate.'

'Mary believes you did.'

'Mary dislikes me.'

'She says she doesn't like spies.'

It was a question.

Francis ran his hand through his pale short-cropped hair, like a cat licking itself in uneasiness. It would be a fair exchange. Her secret for his. But hers would hurt no one but herself, if he could help it, while his concerned a king. And a father suspected of Papist sympathies. And the future peace of England. He might yet find himself charged with treason. He could not weigh her down with so much, even if he were certain he could trust her.

Which, at the moment, he dared not.

'Why did you attend the execution?' he repeated. He glanced around to be certain that no one was watching them.

'Father Jerome was guiltless.' Her face was swollen with unshed tears and disgust. And there was anger as well. 'He was kind to my family when others were happy to let us die. I owed him much more than watching him being butchered. But that was the best I could manage.'

He watched her thoughts race as the numbness of horror began to wear off.

'I think the time has come for you to tell me how you know I'm a Catholic,' she said.

'I told you, I can't.'

'Did you send the pursuivants to search my lodgings?'

'For God's sake, Kate . . .'

'Someone did.'

'Kate, it was Traylor.'

She gave him a scathing look. 'You're lying. He and I were working together. And if by any chance it is the truth, you shouldn't know it. You already know about the search. When they uncovered my past . . . you returned part of it to me. Remember? And when they found my future, which they stole. Perhaps you have that as well?'

Her eyes grew distant as she remembered how the pursuivants upended baskets of silks, threw her father's tools onto the floor, pounded the floor, listening to the dull thuds of the wooden drum. How they smiled in triumph at the sudden hollowness over her secret hiding place. She still did not understand why they hadn't taken her.

The way she lifted one corner of her mouth chilled Francis.

'Did you come looking for me to arrest me after all?'

'Does it seem so?'

After a moment, she shook her head.

'Mary as good as told me to leave you alone. Did you tell her how you suspect me?' He hated to ask but needed to know whether the self-elected Ears and Mouth of Southwark had been told he was a government agent.

Kate shook her head again. 'She didn't tell me you had come.'

'And she didn't tell me she was hiding you.'

'No reason why she should. I left her house. Mary's kind when she chooses, but she's no martyr. I won't repay her kindness by bringing her grief. So tell your hounds to leave her alone.'

'You mean, she threw you out.'

He thought she was going to slap him. Then she said, 'I would have left anyway.'

'To go where?'

She widened her eyes in disbelief. 'Do you imagine I'd tell you?'

'You can't stay in London.'

'I'll find somewhere. Traylor may have another tenement . . .'

'I tell you, Traylor betrayed you!'

'Tell me why you're so certain.'

'Come to Powder Mote. You can hide there until you decide what to do. You'll be safer away from London.'

'Safer with you?' Kate started to laugh then saw that he was in earnest.

57

'What will your father say when you arrive with a Catholic fugitive?'

'My father understands necessity.'

Kate rode numbly. She had felt numb ever since she let Francis lead her out of the crowd around the bloody scaffold. She had mounted the horse he hired for her and followed him down Long Southwark, drained of all strength to fight. Sleep pressed down on her eyelids. She had spent the night before the execution hiding in alleys, not daring to sleep.

Francis insisted that they leave London before midday. They changed horses once, at an estate in Kent where Francis seemed to be known. Now it was close to midnight. Though there was no moon, the chalky track snaked southward ahead of them, pale against the gorse and bracken, just visible enough to be followed. Kate jounced and swayed in the darkness, trusting her mount to keep its nose to the tail of the horse in front.

She kept telling herself that she should have resisted Francis and escaped. Should try to escape even now. Instead, she listened to the irregular rhythm of hoof beats and the snorts and grunts of protest from the exhausted horses as they began their final climb up over the southern Downs.

The truth was that she had no place to go. Even if Traylor could be trusted . . . and doubt had returned in full force . . . she had not seen him for days.

They stopped to rest their horses on the crest of the Downs.

'The void that awaits us all,' said Francis, pointing ahead. He sounded as weary as she felt.

Kate stared into the vast darkness, feeling a little giddy. She could not so much see the sea as feel the absence of land. A soft black line separated the slightly lighter sky above from the darker water below. The lanterns of fishing boats glinted like tiny sequins on a widely-spread skirt.

'There's water enough to put out any fire my father or I can light,' said Francis. He cleared his throat. 'Though I know he will welcome you, the subject of my father is not straight-forward.'

There seemed to be more light here on the top of the Downs than there had been lower in the valleys. Kate could see Francis's head outlined by the pale glow of his hair.

'Francis, you must not shelter me. It was a kind but dangerous offer.'

He waved his hand as if shooing away a horsefly. 'The matter is quite different. I must warn you before we arrive at Powder Mote. My father has good days and bad days. Three years ago, he stood too close to an exploding shell. It seems to have cracked open some of the doors he had locked against his memories.' Francis spoke quickly, imag-ining what his father would say if he overheard this conver-sation. 'Since my return from Flanders, one or two occasions have made me wonder if the damage to his wits is greater than I had believed . . .' He trailed off uncomfortably. He listened to the hollow chomping of the horses on the grass beside the track and to the jingling of their bridles, thinking of his own nightmares.

'What noble company you will keep at Powder Mote,' said Kate. 'A fugitive and a madman.'

'I did not say he's mad,' snapped Francis, more fiercely than intended.

It had just occurred to him that Kate might be able to keep an eye on his father while his father kept her safe at Powder Mote. Leaving Francis free to deal with Catesby and Fawkes and Percy and Tom Wintour. And with Cecil's order to deliver all the gunpowder in an impossibly short time. And with Bacon. And with whoever had tried to kill him with a bird-bolt fired from a crossbow after his last meeting with Cecil.

The horses began to pick their way down the chalky track, which now seemed to glow in the light reflected from the sky.

'You'll be safe here with us,' said Francis, to re-establish his true reason for bringing her here.

'Powder Mote.' Francis held his horse at the edge and pointed down.

Below, just to the right of the shadowy gap carved through the Downs by a narrow river, Kate saw a glinting curve of water wrapped around a cluster of sleeping buildings.

'What is that dark cross-shape on the ground?' she asked, suddenly alert. 'There. Inside the moat.'

'This was once a religious house.'

'You didn't tell me.' She sounded angry.

'Would you have refused to come?' He gazed down with the mixture of pleasure and resentment that Powder Mote always stirred in him. 'It was an Augustinian priory. My grandfather had the estate from King Henry. Most likely to keep him away from London.'

'Did your grandfather tear down the church?'

Francis glanced at her uneasily. 'You'll find a good deal of the stone in many local houses and barns.'

'Have you brought me into enemy territory, then?'

'They made martyrs on both sides down here. And, by God, neither side will let the other forget!' He kicked his horse forward. 'My grandfather did not drive out the Augustinian canons. The place was already ruined when it came to us.'

The gatehouse over the moat was dark and locked. Francis dismounted and disappeared down the moat bank into the reeds and bushes. A startled duck protested. Francis reappeared with a large iron key, followed by an irate quacking.

When they dismounted in the inner courtyard, Kate's legs shook from too many hours in the saddle. Francis pounded on the oak door of the house.

'It's me, back again!' he shouted. 'You're not rid of me yet.'

The light of a candle began to glow behind a window. They listened to the rattle of bars and locks.

'God's blood, Francis! With no more warning than this, I may be forced to let you and your guest both starve.' A tall silver-haired man opened the door and stepped back to admit them. He held up his candle and beckoned them in. 'Welcome, all the same. I can most likely squeeze a few drops of wine from the bottom of the cask.'

Kate gasped.

Francis gave her a curious glance. 'Kate, this is my father, who is also Francis Quoynt.'

'Boomer,' the tall silver-haired man corrected his son. 'I've never answered to Francis.' He peered at Kate intently. 'God's ears! He did say "Kate". You're female!'

'Mistress Kate Peach.' Francis finished the introduction curtly.

'A woman tall enough to look us both in the eye,' Boomer said with satisfaction.

Kate stared from father to son. Francis should have warned me, she thought. So I could have prepared myself to deal with two of them when I'm already having trouble enough with one.

Where she had expected to meet an old man not entirely in command of his wits, she saw nothing but sharp-eyed alertness in Boomer Quoynt – an alertness only slightly softened by late-night alcohol. No more than twenty years marked one man from the other. Otherwise, both were lean, though the father carried more bulk through his chest and shoulders. Both were fair-haired, with skin darkened by sun and wind. They had the same long nose and high brow, the same intense eyes, the same unthinking air of command. And both men were now gazing on her with a concern that startled her and made her suddenly want to weep, a feeling she could explain only by the fact that she was overtired.

'Welcome to Powder Mote, mistress,' said Boomer. 'If my son had warned me he was bringing you to visit, we might have taken a great deal more trouble to put things to rights.'

'When have you ever cared for such niceties?' demanded Francis.

Kate's ears detected an edge in both voices. Still, it was a friendly enough hand that Boomer clapped on his son's shoulder.

'Never before,' Boomer agreed. 'I must be flustered by the arrival of a fine lady from London.'

He looked at Kate's filthy garb and grinned.

She glanced down at her stained breeches and muddy shoes, her grimy hands and black nails, knew that her hair was clumped with sweat and dust, and laughed in polite disbelief.

'That's a nice sound,' said Boomer. 'Not much heard here. Laugh once a day, young woman, and you'll more than earn your keep.'

In the Great Hall, Boomer poured them all wine. Watching him, Kate regained a little of her composure by noting the differences in their hands. Boomer's were broader than those of his son, and the right one was missing three fingertips. If she were to make him gloves, they would be of sturdy calf-skin, cut with a generous gauntlet to protect his long, strong wrists. And without embroidery or lace; just a simple but elegant leather fringe.

As he bent his head over the tarnished wine jug, she noticed also that his hair was a true silver in the firelight, not his son's silver blond. The stubble on his chin was grey, not pale red-gold. There was no trace at all of the doddering, wounded fool Francis had conjured up on the top of the Downs. On the other hand, Boomer Quoynt had appeared to admit them booted and fully clothed in the small hours of the night.

The older man now listened intently while Francis explained where he had found Kate and why they had come.

'Don't fear,' Boomer told his son. 'I'll look after her for you.'

Kate coloured slightly and looked down into her silver-rimmed horn cup. She heard the question behind Boomer's words *for you*.

Either Boomer had not understood that she was a Catholic or he seemed not to care. Past words, too tired to think any further, Kate gazed at a hen clucking absently in its sleep on one of the window ledges.

'She's a pretty punk,' Boomer said later to his son, after Kate had been found a bed that both men deemed worthy and a sleepy, flustered Susannah had shaken free of mice. 'Do you mean to marry her?'

Francis swallowed his irritation. 'I don't know. You must see the difficulties.'

'But you've bedded her?' Boomer raised his eyebrows then answered himself with a nod.

'God's teeth and toenails! What's it to you?'

'You're leaving us here together while you go off on your secret ambassades. I like to know whom I have under my roof.'

'She's not a trull,' said Francis shortly. 'Nor a virgin neither.' He shook out a saddlebag onto the floor and sifted through the heap for a cleaner shirt than the one he wore. 'Nor a dangerous traitor. I'd stake my head on it.'

'You just have. And mine as well.'

'I'm sorry.'

'I'd have done the same.'

Francis pulled off his stinking shirt. The firelight gleamed on his long bare ribcage as he stood turning the shirt in his hands. 'As you've heard a little of her story, I don't need to tell you to treat her softly.'

'No, you don't need to tell me,' said Boomer after a moment of silence.

'I'm sorry, father,' Francis said at once. 'Ten years ago, you'd have clouted me for that.'

'True. I still may.'

Stripped of her filthy clothes, Kate sat up in the narrow, sagging, wood-framed bed, hugging her knees, looking up at the shadowy ceiling and listening to the frogs in the moat. The room was tucked behind the chimney of the Great Hall fireplace. The striped wool and linen coverlet smelled of smoke and mice. The air would have been chilly but for the faint warmth given off by the chimney, like the flank of a great sleeping beast.

A smoky rushlight smelling of mutton fat gave off just enough of a glow to show her that the room served mainly for storage. In the dim light, she saw iron-bound chests, ornately carved boxes, and a suit of horse armour lying in its separate parts like the empty shell of a lobster after a feast. Then she spied, deep in the shadows behind some stacked paintings in ornate frames and a wooden sledge, a painted angel peering out under a furled banner, with a Muscovite fur hat slung on its polychromed halo.

Beside the bed sat earthenware pickling crocks labelled with alchemical signs. A jumble of boots of different sizes spilled out from underneath. A broken bridle finely worked in tarnished silver hung on one of the bedposts, smelling of damp, oiled leather. The scent of hay seeped through the window.

Nothing she feared had come to pass. Yet.

Boomer had listened in silence while Francis recounted the arrest and execution of Father Jerome, and her part in it. He seemed not to care that Francis had brought the taint of treason to Powder Mote along with a fugitive Catholic. When Kate had protested that she could not stay and expose them both to such risk in return for their kindness, he told her most civilly to save her words.

She had seen then, or felt, rather, how father differed from son. Francis burned like a fire, quick and seeking when alert, but able to sink back into the stillness of banked embers and bide his time until ready to burst into flame again. Boomer reminded her of the Thames, running wide, steadily and deep.

Something landed on the bed near her feet. She stifled a gasp.

The cat was as taken aback as she was. They stared at each other for a moment, both of them hunched and bristling. Then the cat turned away disdainfully and curled up on the foot of the bed in what was clearly its accustomed place. After another moment, Kate slid down under the coverlet until her head was on the pillows. She found the creature's indifference to her presence obscurely reassuring.

58

Kate clawed her way up out of sleep.

Danger! Run!

She heard an unnatural silence but could not move or open her eyes. She was blind. Helpless. Exposed.

She prised open her eyelids. Light. She could see again. She blinked up at a strange plaster ceiling. Above her head, a flaking hare painted in faded rust and green stared back down at her from a roundel once outlined with gold. She heard birds. Then she remembered. She was at Powder Mote.

She drew a long shaky breath as she remembered the previous morning and Father Jerome on the scaffold. Then she saw an image of Francis giving her back her Missal in the warehouse. Whatever he might say, there could be no doubt. He was one of the enemy, allied with the pursuivants who had wrecked her room and stolen her future along with her money, tools, the Venetian glasses, and the Missal. She should never have been weak enough to let him bring her to Powder Mote.

She stretched. Though her thigh muscles felt bruised and stiff after the long ride from London, she felt a little restored by a night of sleep and better able to think straight. On the run from London, she had never snatched more than an hour or two of uneasy rest. Even at Mary's hidden among the whores, she was jolted awake by every footstep or slamming door.

She threw off the comforter and limped to the window. In the quiet of Powder Mote every creak of the wooden floor sounded like a gunshot.

A low mist hid the moat. Grey wisps snagged on overgrown box hedges in the remains of a small formal garden. In the middle distance within the moat, the roof of a large barn rose from the mist like the back of a surfacing whale.

Her room faced south towards the distant sea. To her left, brightness was just beginning to push up from behind the curve of the Downs. She saw no signs of life within the moat except the dark blob of a foraging hen on the broad-flagged walk below her window.

Quickly, she dressed in her brother's clothes again.

I would not have minded the chance to wash them, she thought with regret as she sniffed the grubby linen shirt in which she had ridden from London.

Or to wash herself, for that matter.

The previous night, she had been too weary in both body and soul to do more than rinse hands and face at the courtyard pump. No one had suggested a bath. The elderly housekeeper had been thrown into panic enough by the need to find Kate a dry, clean bed. In any case, Kate had already seen enough of Powder Mote to suspect that proper bathing with hot water and clean linen towels was a rare event.

Reeking of horse and carrying her shoes, she tiptoed to the top of the stone staircase. There was no sign that anyone else was awake. Powder Mote seemed impossibly quiet. No shouting watermen, no splashing and rattling of oars on the river. No drunks, screaming babies, barking dogs, watchmen, children, or vendors crying their wares. None of the constant low rumble and mutter of Southwark, like the churning belly of a giant.

Suspended in the stillness, she could hear faint birds and cattle lowing in the distance, but the stone walls of the house deadened all other sounds from outside.

She ran down the silent stone stairs into the hush of the vaulted entrance hall. By daylight, she could see that Powder Mote had once been a religious building, with high ceilings that imitated Heaven. She looked up at fan vaulting and tall pointed window arches edged with stone lace, and an ornate cross carved onto the central boss of the ceiling.

God's house had been twisted to a new use. Even if they had not caused its first destruction, Francis and his father now occupied God's House. They had replaced the holy canons. Their gunpowder had replaced holy water and Communion wafers.

'Those dangerous fellows,' Mary had called the Quoynts.

The first iron bolt of the heavy oak door shrieked as she pulled it back. She waited, heart pounding.

No one came. She set her teeth and pulled back the second bolt. The crossbar squeaked when she lifted it from its sockets. The hinges yelped. Then she was outside in the early morning.

The mist was lifting. A strong smell of wood smoke told her that someone nearby was awake and beginning the day. To her right, behind the house, chickens squawked at the arrival of their breakfast. She pulled on her shoes and pushed her protesting muscles into a run.

The gatehouse that bridged the moat was secured by a heavy iron lock. Kate pushed in frustration at the massive double gate. Then she felt around the edges of the gates, in the gaps between the stones and in the window embrasures. She explored the weeds and nettles on the bank, as Francis had done the night before on the other side of the moat.

No key.

Thoughtfully, she rubbed the nettle welts on her hands. She was a prisoner after all.

Someone or something moved near the barn, which was still indistinct in the mist but growing more solid by the moment. She looked speculatively at the moat, but she could not swim. Furthermore, the dark water was clogged with weed. Shadows glided in the depths. She could not tell how deep the water was, nor how much mud lay under it.

Then she imagined having managed to cross somehow and limping away, dripping wet and hungry, without a penny beyond the few pence left from Mary's last act of charity.

Though the fifteen shillings had not been charity at all, she thought darkly. Merely Mary tightening her grip. Mary had her principles, but they did not include charity.

Kate wavered on the edge of the moat. If, by chance, Francis truly meant his offer to hide her, she would be mad to rush into unnecessary flight.

Then she smelled baking bread. Her last meal had been somewhere in Kent.

'I didn't know you was coming or I'd of baked more.' Susannah White shoved a thick slice of warm bread and a mug of ale at Kate with frail, aged hands that made the younger woman think of dead leaves. 'It'd be better if you wasn't in such a hurry and let it stand a bit.' Susannah covered the cut loaf with a cloth. 'Now clear off and let me get on. There's no one else to do it, believe me.'

'Did Master Quoynt never marry again after his wife died?' Politely, Kate assumed that the woman had died and not run off.

'Does it look like it?' Susannah slammed a kettle of water onto a trivet at the front of the kitchen fire. 'Use your eyes. Look at the state of the place.' She did not offer a second piece of bread to follow the first.

Kate left by the kitchen door and found herself in the walled courtyard that had once been the cloister of the priory. It was now a herb garden of sorts, and a chicken run. She set her ale on the rim of the central well and studied the blocked-up ecclesiastical arches that marched along the side of the house, their filigreed points like silk-lace edging on a sturdy wool collar.

It was no use trying to think she could hide here safely after all, not even for a short time. Not when Francis and his father were the heirs of the men who had destroyed the fabric of her faith. And when Francis worked for the descendants of the men who had ordered it done.

Apart from her own religious qualms, and even if they did mean well towards her, she could not expose them to the penalties for sheltering a Catholic fugitive.

Beyond a gate in the far wall of the cloister lay the ruins of a vast church, outlined by crumbling columns of stone, jagged foundations and the stumpy remains of thick walls.

The priory church. A Catholic church.

Kate walked down the length of the ruined nave trying to decide what she felt. This ghost church had seen bloodshed and destruction. Yet it also embraced her with remembered incense and silent music. When she reached the crossing of nave and transept, she saw the former Lady Chapel to her right. Its walls were reduced and its roof gone, but a small rose window of stone lace still survived in the end wall.

She knelt facing the remains of the altar and recited a dozen *Aves*.

Holy Mother, she prayed. Help me find my path.

As she rose and dusted off the knees of her breeches, she thought she glimpsed movement near one of the broken pillars. She looked again, but saw only a small rusty butterfly hopping from weed to weed.

Beyond the ghost of the vanished high altar stood a small orchard. Beyond the orchard, a row of huts and sheds lined the inner curve of the moat. Some were built of solid brick with slate roofs. Others were of flimsy wood roofed with turf. Thick encircling walls of earth surrounded three of the sheds, to the height of their eaves. The largest had a single chimney and doors in opposite ends but no windows. As she explored, a sharp tang at the back of her nose confirmed Kate's guess that these buildings were where Francis and his alarmingly similar father pursued their explosive trade.

Beyond the sheds, the moat fed a small fishpond, the old monastic stew pond lying within the moat, a watery thumb pointing back towards the house. No Easter carp fattened there now. The pond was as clogged with weed as the main moat. A little farther on, a narrow reed-choked channel filtered the house sewage that flowed out through a large drain half-covered by a broken grille.

An open meadow spread away below the moat bank to the south. Still more small buildings lay beyond a belt of trees on the far side of the meadow. Through the trees, Kate saw the white sparkle of distant water.

'Would you like a better sight of the sea?'

Kate jumped.

Boomer Quoynt stood a dozen paces away, watching her.

'Were you watching me in the church?' she demanded.

He nodded. 'But don't fear. You can pray when and where you like, mistress. So long as your religion goes no further than words and good deeds.'

'I won't lie. It goes as far as sheltering fugitive outlaws. As your own faith clearly does.' She lobbed the challenge like a missile.

'Faith has little to do with it. Come see my church. It might ease your mind.' He pushed aside a thick stand of weeds on the inner moat bank to reveal a moored dinghy. The little boat was in surprisingly good repair.

'Always keep open a back way out,' said Boomer.

As he rowed them across the moat, Kate saw a second dinghy moored in the reeds. If he had not come, she might have found the boats and made her escape after all.

He turned his large head to gauge their approach, then

used an oar to turn them alongside the wooden pilings that held up the far bank. Kate crossed her arms and frowned thoughtfully at her boatman, who looked so much like his son. However amiable he might appear, he seemed also to be her gaoler.

She decided to return that night and see if the boats were still there.

Boomer led her up onto the downs behind Powder Mote. As they climbed, Kate could see to her left the track that she and Francis must have followed the night before, a thin irregular white ribbon running through the dark gorse and bright green patches of grazing land. Then they stepped out onto the edge of a ridge, with the land falling away steeply below them.

'Here's my church. And if I'm damned for saying so, there's no help for it.' Boomer walked to the very brink as if he meant to spread wings and leap off into the air.

Below them, the open arms of the sea spread as far as Kate could see. Near the shore, the water flashed in the sun. At the horizon, a thin band of pewter blue separated water from sky, blurred in places by isolated rain veils.

She gazed farther and farther into the grey-blue vastness, past the tiny shapes of fishing boats, until her eyes lost their grip on the infinite space. She felt dizzy. A lump formed in her throat. A gull glided past, below the level of her feet.

The space! she thought. The space. Unimaginable in the alleys and tenements of Southwark. The Thames gave only a tiny hint of this vastness. The wind that she breathed in swirled beneath her ribs, scouring the weight from her chest until she felt light enough to float off the hillside. She looked down at a pair of cruising gulls. She was above the birds. Eye to eye with the clouds.

As she watched, the morning sun shattered into bright

chips on the surface of the sea. The sky grew darker than the water. A sweet calm began in the centre of her chest and flowed into her toes and fingertips. It eased her shoulders and unclenched her gut. She could not remember when she had last felt such sweetness.

She glanced at Boomer Quoynt.

Surely, standing so close beside her, he must feel the immensity of what was happening to her. But he still looked out, seeming lost in his own thoughts.

Kate knew that her present feelings were dangerous. Nothing in her circumstances had changed just because she had seen the sea for the first time. Powder Mote was still her gaol. That man was still her gaoler.

'May I come up here again?' she tested him.

'Whenever you like,' said Boomer.

'Alone?'

He looked amused. 'With or without a guard. As you choose.'

Kate flushed and turned in confusion to climb back down to the house.

'But you should know, nevertheless, that Powder Mote is a workhouse,' said Boomer's voice following behind her. 'Did Francis not inform you of your sentence?'

Kate stepped on a loose rock and nearly lost her footing. As she recovered her balance, she glanced at him again.

'Five days of heavy labour helping me pull down the ivy.'

He's only teasing me, she thought with a rush of relief and astonishment. And he shares his son's taste for plunging to the heart of fearful subjects.

She tried to think of a light reply but could not. She felt awkward. She had forgotten how to let herself be teased.

'How can you be so eager to leave this place for London?' she asked Francis when she came across him later, sitting in the sun on the bench below her window with his breakfast ale, dressed for riding.

'Wait till you see it in winter. It's not so pretty when the waves are up and the rain's pouring down.' He did not look at her.

Kate shook her head in silent protest but said nothing. 'Pretty' was so much less than she had meant. In any case, she did not mean to stay until the winter, whatever Francis intended.

'I must leave again,' he said. 'For two or three days, on urgent business. I hope you won't mind being left alone with my father.'

'Of course not.'

An uncomfortable silence then fell between them. She stood uncertainly, not wanting to sit beside him on the bench but uncertain where to go instead.

'If you're to use a billhook today, we must find you some boots,' said Boomer, arriving behind her on the broad flagged walk. 'France, where are all your outgrown boots? I've seen them somewhere in the last year.'

'I know where they are,' said Kate.

Boomer might have been teasing her about the workhouse, but he was in earnest about the ivy, as the powder milling had to be suspended until Francis returned.

'It's astonishing how the arrival of a guest makes you see a place with more savage eyes,' Boomer said. 'Can't imagine how the ivy has gone unchecked for so long.'

Francis snorted gently into his ale.

Back in her borrowed chamber, Kate found a pair of boots that fitted her in the heap under the bed. The soles were almost new. Perhaps Francis himself had outgrown them and there was no one younger left to inherit them. She thought she remembered his saying once that he was the youngest and only surviving son.

She explored further, disturbing a large number of spiders. To the right of the angel and under a Moorish scimitar, she found a chest of folded silks, including a length of cloth-of-gold. Behind that chest she found another filled with clothing. Mainly for children of different sizes. Nightgowns. The petticoats and pinafores worn by both sexes before the boys were breeched at five or six. Small, plain wool doublets, well worn. A larger male jacket in black silk, almost new. A girl's bodice, far too small for Kate, alas. A linen overskirt painted in flowering vines, pretending to be crewel embroidery, also too small. All smelling of dusty lavender.

Turning over their clothes, Kate tried to remember what Francis might once have told her about his brothers and sisters. Where were they all now? And who had folded all these clothes away with such loving care?

Near the bottom of the chest she found a suit of everyday clothes for a fully grown youth. Moths had dined on the cuffs, but the doublet was her size when she held it against herself. She shook out a crumpled, yellow-stained linen shirt. The musty smell would fade with wearing. In any case, it was better than old sweat and horse.

When she went back downstairs, Francis had already gone.

'Am I allowed to pry?' On the roof of the lean-to, Boomer gathered up an armful of cut ivy.

Kate stretched up with her billhook and yanked to cut through a thick shaggy stem. Above her on the roof, Boomer pitched an armful of ivy to the ground and began to tug at another tangled mass.

She still felt confused by Boomer Quoynt's similarity to his son. They had the same large heads, the same length of arm and thigh. By daylight, however, she could also see that Boomer had once broken his nose.

'So long as I'm not forced to reply,' she said at last.

'Has my son offered to marry you?'

Go to hell, she started to say. Then she glanced up at the man on the roof above her. He was working with intense concentration as if he had never spoken, frowning at a dark green coil that choked a small chimney in an assassin's grip.

Had he welcomed her in spite of her religion only because he thought that she was to be his daughter-in-law?

The silence grew, filled only with the rustling of leaves and the occasional rip.

'No,' said Kate shortly. 'He hasn't.'

'He's a fool, then.' Boomer cursed as the ivy pulled a roof tile loose. Some time later he asked, 'Would you like to marry him?'

Kate yanked a leafy tentacle from around a lead drainpipe. 'I did hope to once.'

Boomer grunted. A haulm of ivy crashed onto the dirt of the courtyard.

The absence of Francis left Kate feeling curiously free, as if he had carried her London self away with him.

'Gunpowder is his mistress,' said Boomer. 'I fear it may also be his wife.'

'Is it also yours?'

'My mistress or my wife?'

Kate wished she had not asked. While she floundered, thinking how not to sound like a flirting madam, Boomer took pity on her.

'I had a loved and loving wife, who died far too soon. As a mistress, Lady Gunpowder is a wilful slut. I no longer trust her.' He held up his damaged right hand to show Kate the scars and three missing fingertips. 'Francis still dreams of mastering her.'

They then worked in silence until dinnertime.

Kate waved a startled arm when a hen flapped up onto the end of the long table in the hall where she and Boomer sat with their bowls of vegetable stew, set in front of them by Susannah. The hen teetered, then dropped back onto the floor.

Boomer bent to offer the last crust of his bread. 'Chook . . . chook.'

'You let her come and go so freely?'

'Why not? I like to see her about.' Boomer's huge frame lowered itself onto its knees on the stone floor. 'Here, chook.' The hen took the crust from his palm.

'You'll only have to eat her boiled one day.'

Boomer shot her a look. 'But until then she's the queen of my layers. See how her feathers shine. And her comb there . . . like finest coral.'

'If you make a pet of her, won't her stew rise in your gorge?'

'Why not enjoy her all ways?' Boomer ran a finger down the side of the hen's neck. 'Facts of life, chook. A hen lays eggs, then gets eaten. Why should I refuse present delights for fear of the future?' He stood up. 'Take what you can, when you can. I haven't found fate to be over-prodigal with delights. Have you?'

Kate looked out of the window, then at her hands. 'No.'

Boomer suddenly disappeared in the direction of the cloister courtyard. 'Have you ever stroked a goose?' he asked as he reappeared, a hissing head held in one hand, the struggling body trapped under his other arm. 'Go on. There . . . just above the wing.'

The wide-eyed, disapproving face of Susannah appeared in the doorway behind him. She rolled her eyes at Kate then vanished again.

Kate stroked the taut silky hollow with one finger. Through the feathers she could feel the strong body vibrating with life.

'Good, eh?' Boomer ran his thumb across the back of the captive head. 'I discovered that when I was a boy.'

Kate stroked the goose again. 'How you can bear knowing that Christmas must come?'

She heard Boomer breathing quietly as she continued to stroke the goose. 'Poor young Mistress Peach,' he said at last. 'Even Christmas brings grief.' He set the goose down on the floor, where it made its indignation clear with a dropping before it waddled out the door.

'Haven't you ever felt these moments of delight with an animal, which are enough in themselves?' Boomer asked.

Unhappiness clouded Kate's face. 'Yes, I suppose I have. With a bear.'

Boomer looked at her with incredulous delight. 'With a bear?'

59

The boats were still at their moorings the next morning, but by then Kate knew that they would be. Wearing her borrowed work-clothes in readiness for another day of attacking the ivy, she crossed the old cloisters with her breakfast bread and ale, into the ruined church. Sitting on the base of what had once been one of the main columns of the nave, she inhaled the perfume of the newly baked bread and pondered the strange marriage of church and state that was Powder Mote.

On the old Priory walls extravagant carvings, made to delight a sensuous Catholic God, now gave lightness and jollity to the solid four-square stone wing added to the original priory by Anglican farmers. The French Caen stone they had stolen from the church to build it glowed like burnt sugar in the early light. Coppery apples and green-gold pears in the surrounding orchard now replaced the jewelled plate of the high altar. The air smelled of sulphur and chickens, not frankincense.

Though invisible from where Kate sat, the sea lent the sky a luminous clarity.

After watching a rusty butterfly again hopping from weed to weed, she picked some wild flowers and put them in the Lady Chapel. Surely, God did not abandon his holy places when they fell into disrepair.

She tilted her head back and looked up at the sky. It was the flawless vivid blue of the Virgin's cloak, but more translucent than any church painting. She wanted to pray but did not know how to say what she felt. She stared up, trying to see the invisible until she grew so giddy that she nearly fell backwards off her perch.

Before the end of the morning, her unexpected sense of peace was destroyed. Boomer had allowed her up onto the main roof with him, on the condition that she be tethered by a line to one of the chimneys. While he cut and yanked, she took the vanquished ivy and threw it over the edge of the roof.

From so high up, Kate could see the sea again. She paused for breath, gazing out at the metallic grey horizon. Beside her on the ridge, Boomer suddenly leapt into the air, flapping his arms like a terrified hen.

'Take care!' she cried in alarm. Unlike her, he was not secured by a line.

He jumped again then crouched on the ridge and wrapped his arms around his knees.

'Master Quoynt!'

'Boomer,' he corrected her before he dropped his face onto his knees.

'Boomer?' Kate tugged gently at his sleeve. 'What ails you?'

Francis had warned her about possible bad days. But he had not told her how to deal with them.

Boomer shook off her hand. 'Go down now.' His voice seemed as deep and steady as ever, and far gentler than his action. 'Pretend urgency, as if seeking help. I'll follow. There's no need for concern. Take care on the ladder.'

When she hesitated, he flailed one arm at her like a petulant child. 'Go! I'll explain shortly.' In spite of his odd actions, he spoke with his usual authority.

Kate untied the line from her waist, went down the first ladder to the lean-to roof, then down another shorter ladder to the ground. Heart pounding, she looked back up as Boomer uncurled his tall body and walked the high roof ridge like an acrobat at a fair, seventy feet above the ground. For a man of his height, he was both graceful and sure-footed.

He paused at the very end of the ridge as he had stood poised on the down the day before, contemplating flight.

'No!' shouted Kate. She imagined having to tell Francis.

But Boomer turned, saluted the sky, sat, and slid down the roof to the top of the first ladder. While Kate still gasped, he climbed sedately down the ladder, crossed the lean-to roof and descended to the ground.

'Forgive me for that piece of mummery,' he said. 'One must never forget that the watcher can be watched.'

Kate nodded helplessly. She understood now why Susannah had rolled her eyes when Boomer brought in the goose.

He was watching her with a mixture of assessment and something else she could not quite name. She felt suddenly afraid again. She had dreamed herself into an illusion of false safety at Powder Mote. Boomer might not be her gaoler, but neither was he the powerful guardian he had begun to seem. She had been lulled into setting aside thoughts of escape. It would be easiest to go now, while Francis was away.

'I must visit the mill,' said Boomer. 'Please stay close to the house. You don't want to be seen. I'll see you here again at supper.'

She nodded again, puzzled by what felt like grief.

'The watcher can be watched,' he had said.

Secretly, Kate then watched him. After he left the court-yard, he did not turn left across the moat to follow the river down towards the mills, as he had said. Instead, he turned right, up into the Downs.

*   *   *

'You must look after yourselves for supper tonight,' said Susannah, as she served Kate her dinner of potatoes fried with slivers of ham. 'I'm off to see my sister in the village. I'll leave bread and soup. Not that it matters much. Master Boomer won't know if he's had supper or not these days.'

I didn't imagine that astonishing scene on the roof, Kate reassured herself. Others have also noticed that Boomer can behave oddly.

She should not have let him go off alone.

After dinner, she went out into the ruined church to look for him on the downs, but saw no sign of him. Restlessly, she went back up to her chamber, where she shook out her coverlet and two striped linen mattresses. She flung them over the windowsills to toast in the afternoon sun. Then she went down to ask Susannah for a broom.

The old nurse-turned-housekeeper had already left to visit her sister. Kate explored the kitchens and larders until she found the broom, some cleaning cloths and a half-empty crock of beeswax polish. On her way back upstairs, she passed through the Great Hall.

Disorder everywhere. It made her hands itch just to look at it. She decided to put a few things right before she left. To say thank you for the temporary shelter.

Boomer's chamber was on the first floor at the opposite end of the passage from her own. On her way to open the window at the far end of the passage, she glanced through his door. A kind of shyness kept her from taking a good look, but she glimpsed clothing and books strewn on the floor. And an empty wine-stained Venetian glass.

The window was stuck. She shoved the casement several times without effect. Then suddenly it swung open. As she steadied herself on the sill, she saw the man on the Downs above the house. She might not have noticed him if he had not suddenly pulled back into the shadow of a stunted tree.

She made a show of dusting the sill. Then she pulled the window to her a little and began to polish the diamond-shaped panes. Her heart thumped, although there was no reason why a man should not be standing on the hillside above the house. From the side of her eye she could see that he was still under the tree. Not moving. And not Boomer. She was certain, even though he was too far away for her to see his face.

A hat hid his hair. His height was hard to judge. Nevertheless, there was something familiar in his blocky shape and his smooth slide back into cover.

He's watching the house, she thought. He's watching me framed here in this window.

If he had been up there that morning as well, then Boomer really did see a watcher. He wasn't losing his wits after all, however odd his behaviour on the roof had seemed.

She made herself polish the top row of panes while the little hairs stiffened on her neck. When she thought again of escaping from Powder Mote, she had not reckoned on a watcher. From his position, the man would see anyone leaving by the gatehouse bridge. He might or might not be able to see through the orchard to the moored boats on the moat.

Boomer had not returned to the house by the time Kate went to bed that night. She dropped the bar across her door. She also dragged a heavy storage chest in front of it.

60

'Kate?'

She jerked awake. Boomer stood in her room with a musket in his hand. The sky was barely light.

'What's wrong? How did you get in here?'

He pointed to a small door in the far wall behind two stacked chests.

'Can you fire a musket?'

'Why?'

'I think you should learn.' He glanced at the barricaded door.

'Now? Before breakfast?' She fell back onto her pillows and pulled the coverlet up to her chin although she had slept in the linen shirt. Boomer looked very large. 'When I saw you there, I thought Powder Mote was under attack.'

Or that he had gone mad.

Then she remembered the watcher.

'I'll fetch you something to eat.' Boomer leaned the gun against the wall just inside her door and pulled aside the chest. Kate heard the wooden floor of the passage creak under his weight. Then the back stairs announced his descent.

She threw back the coverlet and quickly pulled on her breeches and jerkin.

'I'm sorry if I startled you,' he said when he returned with two mugs of beer and two slightly stale rolls. 'When you rise before dawn, you forget that others sleep.' He looked reassuringly solid and totally sane in spite of his sudden, unexpected arrival in her room.

'I think I saw someone watching Powder Mote yesterday afternoon,' Kate said.

'That's why you must learn to shoot. I was watching him watch you.'

So that was what Boomer was doing instead of visiting the mill.

'Who is he?' Kate's heart began to thump again. 'What's happening, Boomer?'

'Unless my eyes mistake me, his name is Hammick. He's a retired merchant and my neighbour.'

The edge on Boomer's voice made Kate grateful not to be Hammick, whoever he was. And whom she need not fear, as Boomer was dealing with him.

Unless, of course, this was a bad day and Boomer had transformed a curious neighbour into the fantasy of remembered war.

'As for what's happening,' continued Boomer, 'I wish I knew.'

Silently but fervently, Kate agreed.

With a flint, steel and small patch of charred cloth, he first showed her how to light the short length of loosely twisted hemp-rope, previously soaked in saltpetre. This slow match would burn very slowly and seldom go out.

'But in battle, you light both ends, just to be sure.'

They stood in the open field below the moat.

'Hold your match always ready, like this, between the lesser fingers of the left hand, if you favour the right hand. Lighted end away from you.' He demonstrated. Then he handed her the gun, a caliver, long-barrelled and weighing as much as a bale of doeskins.

She balanced it with difficulty across her hip, aware of the hot orange glow of the match-tip a few inches from her fingers.

'Slide open the pan cover here and clean the touch-hole with this length of brass priming wire . . . you do it.'

He pulled a tiny wooden cask from the bandolier slung across his broad chest. 'Now tap a little powder into the pan . . . Watch that match! Keep it well away from the powder . . . In this cartouche, ready measured.'

Kate took the cartouche carefully, filled and closed the pan, blew away any loose powder that might otherwise blow up in her face.

'One question,' she said a little shakily. 'How do I hold this monster level to fire it?'

'I've no doubt you could manage. But I've a musket rest for you. Many men a good deal larger than you have been known to use them.' He showed her a long-stemmed 'Y' of wood, then laid it aside.

'Set the gunstock on the ground now, and pour the rest of the charge down the barrel.'

While she emptied the cartouche, his hand hovered near the slow match, ready to snatch it away if it moved too close to the powder.

As instructed, she dropped the lead ball down the muzzle and rammed the wadding home on top of it with the scouring stick.

'With me so far?' Boomer asked.

Kate nodded.

He drew a deep breath. 'From here on, take the greatest care. You now move the match into your right hand, for the first time. And blow on the tip . . . Keep it away from the gun!'

He watched her closely as she obeyed.

Then he showed her how the match fitted into a curved metal arm called a serpent, which was moved by the trigger lever. When the trigger was pressed, the arm brought the match down to the touch-hole.

'That's it,' he said. 'Do you want to fire it?'

'After surviving so far? Of course I do.'

Boomer pushed the end of the musket rest into the ground and set the caliver barrel in the Y, pointing across the field. 'Sight down the barrel, aiming at that oak.'

The gun kicked her shoulder like a horse. The explosion deafened her. A cloud of acrid black smoke enveloped them both. Her right cheek burned.

'A novel experience,' she said. She wiped the powder residue off her cheek but resisted the need to rub her shoulder.

'You hit the neighbouring tree. Not bad.' Boomer grinned. 'Now clean the pan and touch-hole, and reload.'

She looked at him curiously. 'Do you truly think I need to be able to do all this?'

'I might someday need you to reload for me.'

'In battle?' She could not stop a small smile of disbelief. 'With both ends of the match lit?'

He seemed intensely alert and quick-witted this morning. In fact, she felt she had to scramble to keep up with him. But the warning about bad days still confused her.

'Could you reload in battle?' he asked, a little sharply.

'Yes,' she stammered. 'With a little more practice.' She took the gun from the rest and balanced it in her hands, to avoid looking at him.

'Has my son infected you with his distrust of me?' Boomer demanded without warning. 'I swear I'll thrash him, old as he is, if he has told you my wits are going soft.' He took the caliver from her hands. 'Look at me, Kate!'

She met his eyes, which, unlike his son's, were a clear, cold blue. As sharp as icicles. You could not hide from those eyes.

'By Mars, he has! I can see it in your face.' He yanked the

musket rest out of the ground. 'The lesson's done. My apologies. I didn't mean to force you into humouring an addled old man.'

'Boomer, I never . . .'

'Spare me your kindness.' He shouldered the caliver and strode away among the outbuildings.

Kate felt desolate. There was nothing she could say to him. He was right. She could not lie to deny it.

Why was I so accomplished at lying to Traylor? she wondered. When I seem to be so transparent to the accursed Quoynts?

Then it occurred to her that if he could see mere neighbours as enemies, Boomer might see anyone as his enemy. Then he might become as dangerous as any watcher, with his guns, his explosives and his physical strength, which seemed undiminished by his years.

Those clear, cold blue eyes had looked dangerous. But not in the least bit mad.

Boomer found her not long after, huddled in the ruined Lady Chapel.

'I'm sorry, Kate. I was unfair.' He seemed entirely reasonable. Entirely friendly.

'You were right,' she said. 'Francis did warn me that you might have bad days.'

Go straight to the heart of the matter with the Quoynts.

'Who doesn't have bad days?' Boomer asked grimly. 'My son included.' He looked down at the posy Kate had placed in the Lady Chapel. 'I meant that it was unfair to be angry with you. There's a misunderstanding between France and me . . . he'll come round to my view in time.' He gazed up at the top of a broken pillar in the former nave. 'I was angry . . .' He stopped, then began again. 'Wounded pride. I want you to think well of me. Not as some pantaloon in his dotage.'

He swung round, as if trying to catch her out. 'You're laughing at me.'

'No, Boomer. I'm smiling at the idea of you as a pantaloon. I've never met a man less . . .' She stopped uncertainly, startled by the heat in his face.

'Well,' he said, after a moment. 'Good. And I promise you, I am not mad.'

They both looked at the posy on the altar.

'It has begun to wilt,' said Kate. 'I must pick more.'

'Will you be my gunner's mate?'

'If you need me.'

He turned the cup holding the posy, as if testing it for a better angle. 'France told me a little about you, as well.'

'Told, or warned?'

'Why it was best to get you out of London.'

'Did he tell you about the life I'd been living?'

He turned back to her. 'Not a great deal. But look at you. All hunched up like a hare trying to be invisible under the shadow of a hawk.' Now it was his turn to smile. 'Do you imagine you can shock me? A soldier for more than forty years? We all do what we must to survive. And you weren't trading on the streets.'

'How do you know?'

'I've seen whores enough in my life to know the difference. Poor Kate. Be a little kinder to yourself.'

She inhaled as if he had struck her and burst into tears. 'Don't . . . !' she said, aghast. 'Please go away. I don't know what's . . .' She wiped her face with her shirt sleeve. 'This is absurd.'

Boomer sat beside her on the piece of fallen roof. 'I never saw one of my children,' he said. 'She was born and died, aged two, while I was fighting abroad. What grieves you the most?'

'Gloves!' A cannonade of sobs shook her.

He waited in silence. After a moment, he put an arm around her shoulders and began to search his pocket with his other hand.

'I mean, why I'm making them . . . my father's tools.'

'How did he die?' asked Boomer. He offered his handkerchief.

'P . . . plague.'

Kate told him about the plague house, including the glove of skin that had slipped off her dead mother's hand. The smell. And her own feeble pleading at the crack under the door.

'And I survived. Why? Why should I, alone?'

'There will be a reason.' Boomer gave her shoulders a gentle squeeze. 'Does France know all this?'

'He never asked.' She considered her answer. 'Not really.'

Then she told him about Father Jerome. And Traylor. And saving money to escape by turning widow. And Mary Frith pressing her to turn whore at the Holland's Leaguer. And the freedom she felt when she wore men's clothes. And Caledonian Meg, whose courage didn't save her from being lost.

The sun grew hot as it climbed to its peak. Kate suddenly realized that her tears had dried.

'If we're both out here, there's no one to ring the dinner bell,' she said. 'Susannah says that her elbows ache too much.'

'No one heeds it in any case.' Boomer rose nevertheless and offered her his hand. He kept her hand on his arm as they went into the house. 'Shall we butcher more ivy this afternoon? There's something I must tell you. I wasn't going to, not yet. But after your spy yesterday, I think I must.'

61

Francis returned to Powder Mote in a vile humour. The salt-petre men of Sussex and Kent had failed him. The end of the war with Spain had curbed their sometimes excessive zeal for digging out deposits of the mineral salt. Without an urgent need to supply the Crown, and with lapsed patents, they now met sharp resistance when they tried to dig up the floors of inns, churches and other spots where salt-forming urine might be deposited. They complained that landowners drove them away from barns and barnyard middens. Even private privies were often denied them.

With growing frustration, Francis had listened to these grievances across most of southeast England. Including the complaints of one plump smiling rogue who was, almost certainly, an intelligencer who would report the attempted purchase to the next maggot up the ranks.

Francis had studied every tree along his way for the shadow of an archer. He had a knot between his shoulders from waiting for another crossbow bolt to strike. If he ever caught the man who had tried to kill him beside the Thames, he would twist his head off with his bare hands. As for the man who had hired the archer . . .

Furthermore, he had not slept well, having one ear always awake.

All that frigging way for only another nineteen barrels of saltpetre, he thought, as he unloaded the cart at the saltpetre shed inside the moat. With no hope of more and time running out.

Any number of villains had offered to sell him gunpowder itself. He had never seen so much decayed stuff and hoped that some poor fool's life never depended on any of it.

At least Kate's still here, he thought, watching her pick up windfalls in the orchard. His father had not terrified her into flight during one of his nightmares. While he was away, he had let himself imagine their reconciliation, and what would follow it. In his bed. On a sun-warmed hillside. In the orchard.

He imagined her now, sitting naked in a tree, throwing apples at him, daring him to climb up and subdue her. Then she lay stretched out in front of the fire, with the golden light picking out her ribs, burnishing the smooth curves of her breasts and throwing black shadows around her nipples and bush.

Back in the house, the real Kate avoided his eye and spoke to him as seldom as possible. Her face was pinched as if she, too, could smell treachery in his clothes, on his hair, and carried on his breath.

He studied her covertly during supper. If she were a castle, he would find a way in. She's unhappy, he thought as he chewed on a baked carrot. And he was very likely a chief cause.

Boomer soon excused himself and went out to the saltpetre shed. Then Kate left to feed their scraps to the hens.

We must keep her here at any cost, Francis vowed as he watched her vanish towards the cloisters. He would put things right with her as soon as they had finished with the cursed gunpowder. Until then, there would scarcely be time to piss.

After Francis returned, Kate's spirits plummeted. He thrummed with a suppressed anger she had not sensed so strongly in him before he left. Boomer returned to making gunpowder but would not let her go up onto the roof alone to finish clearing the ivy. The two men disappeared together at dawn and often worked until late at night, leaving her in the house with only Susannah and the ten-year-old kitchen maid as company.

What ails you, you nizzie? she asked herself again and again, when she was not listening for the sound of a distant explosion. In London she had been perfectly happy to live alone. She intended to do so again. In fact, this renewed solitude gave her time to consider her future.

On her first morning alone, she climbed the down to Boomer's 'church' and sat swinging her legs over the edge. The return of Francis had reminded her that she could not stay at Powder Mote. Nor did she dare return to London. She had no money to go anywhere else. She had lost her father's tools and, with them, her means of making a living.

How did Francis and I end up as enemies? she wondered. She must have ignored some dark current running beneath her feet, until it was too late.

She tossed clods of earth and watched them disappear into the spiky, green-black gorse below her.

If only things were otherwise.

She lay back against the short, sheep-cropped grass and looked up at the grey clouds. The warm air around her head smelled of crushed thyme.

If she had not been so certain that Francis was a government agent who had perhaps betrayed Father Jerome (she was certain Boomer could not know this) . . . And if she were not a Catholic outlaw . . . She would not believe that Francis had betrayed her deliberately . . .

Then she might have offered to stay here as their housekeeper.

They needed someone to take a grip. Susannah should have been retired long ago. Once Kate had put the place straight, she could easily keep it so. The two of them would be easy to please. She might even have bought more tools and made gloves again.

She sat up and hurled another clod as hard as she could.

That afternoon, it began to rain. A strong wind blowing off the sea threw water at the windows and pressed it under the doors. Kate stood in the Great Hall for a long time looking down at a trickle of water seeping under a side door that opened onto the terraced walk. She felt herself sliding. Everything was rushing away again.

She turned away abruptly and alarmed Susannah with a search for broom and bucket. Then she attacked the disorder in the Great Hall.

'Did you learn any more of what disturbs my father?' Francis asked cautiously that evening. He and Kate were alone at supper, as Boomer was still down at the mixing house. With a twinge of shame, Francis saw that he was trying to draw her back into collusion with himself instead of with his father.

Kate nodded but said nothing.

He waited.

She ran her hand absently over the table, which now gleamed and smelled of beeswax polish. Then he saw that she was listening to the world outside the house.

'Boomer hasn't lost his wits,' she replied at last. 'You should heed him, Francis. About Pangdean.'

He nodded agreeably to hide the rush of rage he felt at her betrayal. Part of him wanted to shout like a child, 'But I was going to do that in any case.' Part of him wanted to demand how she had arrived at her opinion, but felt a little afraid of her.

Part of him felt a surge of renewed lust.

Her eyes were darker than he remembered. Her hair sparked in the last light from the window. In the open collar

of her man's shirt her strong throat was tinted a faint copper
by the sun. As were her hands and forearms, exposed by
rolled-back sleeves.

Some English sailor may have brought a Moorish wife
home to Stokewell a couple of generations back. Or a foreign
seaman left a child behind. However she had come about,
the Kate who sat across the table from him was keeping him
at a distance while she made him ache with longing.

'Have you forgiven me yet?' he asked on impulse.

'For which betrayal?'

'What penance do you need?'

She gave him an odd look. 'Leave it alone, Francis. You've
made a good beginning.'

Francis was in trouble.

Kate thought about it the next day as she cleaned out the
massive oak pot-cupboard in the Great Hall.

Trouble in London.

For the first time, she considered whether he might have
become entangled almost unwittingly, as she had been. She
wondered how much his difficulties had to do with sheltering
her.

She lifted a stack of dull pewter plates out of the cupboard
and set them on the floor beside her.

For all his uncomfortable openness, he had never told her
the truths she most needed to know. She had asked Boomer
what disturbed Francis, but he had sworn he knew no more
than she did.

At the back of the cupboard she found a silver mermaid,
black with tarnish, hidden on the lower shelf behind the
plates. The mermaid reared up on her tail, arms at her sides,
chin raised, thrusting her breasts forward. A curved handle
grew out of her back. Though she appeared to be a ewer and
could be filled through a hole in the rippling weed-like hair

at the top of her back, she had no spout. Then Kate saw the two holes in her nipples.

The mermaid gave off a lingering sweetness of rosewater. The silver breasts gleamed bright and newly polished against the dark tarnish of the seaweed hair and fishy tail.

Kneeling by the cupboard, Kate imagined the two large, fair men, before this dreadful urgency to make gunpowder had invaded their lives. Sitting among dusty windowsills and flung boots, after a mutton and onion stew, drinking their good wine from silver-rimmed cups and rinsing their hands in the mermaid's scented milk. Then absently stroking her breasts with a finger while they talked.

Which of them hid her when I arrived? she wondered.

She polished the mermaid with an oily cloth and set her on the open top shelf of the cupboard beside the silver-rimmed wine cups made of horn and a silver basin that now gleamed like moonlight.

They won't be having evenings like that just yet, she thought. Both of them were working through the night, barely stopping to eat. But the mermaid was ready for them when the time came.

Later, she listened to them talking urgently on the bench outside on the flagged walk. They had paused for a few moments, in that last fading light when white flowers and the white blazes on the foreheads of grazing horses leap out of the shadows and darker colours fall back. Standing in the side door, Kate could see the two pale heads floating disembodied above the darkness of the bench. Two white clay pipes rose and fell.

Ten feet away, she could smell the gunpowder through the leathery richness of their tobacco.

'. . . convert the corn mill to grind more charcoal,' Francis was saying intensely.

Boomer nodded. 'And rig that small incorporation wheel

downstream from the stamp mill. The frame and shaft are where we left them when the money ran out. But we still won't manage.'

'Let me help you,' said Kate. 'I can boil and strain the salt-petre.'

There was a long silence. Then Francis laughed.

'Not being privy to state secrets, as you are,' said Boomer icily, 'Kate and I don't see what's so funny.'

'Dear God,' said Francis. 'This passes all belief. Oh, Kate, if you knew what you were offering to do!'

'You need her,' said Boomer. 'Or have you given up?'

62

At supper two weeks after he returned from buying saltpetre, Francis put down the spoon he had been staring at and admitted defeat.

'Our mill is too small,' he said. 'Our workers too few. We lack ingredients, and the need for secrecy has closed off all our usual sources.'

'The odds were always against us,' said his father.

Both Kate and Boomer looked at Francis with such concern that he almost told them the whole truth. But he dared not. This was the absolute solitude of the deceiver that he had foreseen that night on Cecil's 'high place'.

'If you can't refuse,' said Boomer, 'why not ask for yet more time? It's not as if we're at war. The army isn't about to sail.'

But we are at war! Francis wanted to shout. More terribly than we have ever been, in either of our lifetimes. England is at war with herself.

After supper, sick with despair, he climbed up onto the downs to chase his thoughts through the web of chalky tracks worn by grazing sheep. He flung himself furiously up the slope while the sun set behind him in bloody splendour.

He had failed, in spite of all their joint efforts.

But Quoynts did not fail. They might ally themselves with

the wrong side. Or they might blow themselves up. But they did not fail.

Dusk found him high above Patcham village and the manor at Preston. He knew he had to take great care what he did next. If he failed Catesby, he also failed Cecil. And if he failed Cecil, he failed England.

Unless, as he had begun to fear, Cecil – The Deep Dissembler – meant to betray England.

It was the end of his hopes for the future, either way. They would all fall together once Cecil withdrew his protection. Francis. Boomer, still suspected of Marion sympathies. Kate, who had hidden Jesuit outlaws. Francis was free to risk his own life if he liked, rather than turn in Robin and the others. But Kate and his father must not go to the scaffold because of his foolish reluctance to betray a man who meant to blow up Parliament and murder his king.

He had to give Cecil names and hope to be forgiven for the shortfall in gunpowder. No more giving in to his liking for Robin Catesby. No more soft-hearted delay. Betrayal was the essence of his contract with Cecil. He must stop trying to pretend otherwise.

God, forgive me, he begged.

After a last steep climb, he reached the charred, flattened site of a signal beacon on the highest point of the ridge, one of a chain of beacons that ran along the coast. Beyond it, the land plunged dangerously into the Low Weald. Far to his right, the tiny lights of outlying farms near Lewes pierced the lowland shadows. Behind him lay the dark void of the sea, pricked here and there by the tiny single lanterns of night fishermen.

The void gets us all in the end, he thought. But some ways of entering it are more terrible than others.

His chest felt tight. His gut quivered as if threatened by the flux. He could not hold firm to any one single thought.

He decided first that he must have an ague coming on. Then he realized. He was afraid.

But the Quoynts were never afraid. They respected danger and avoided it as best they could. Instead of fear, they experienced a cold caution that crimped the hair on their necks and stopped their breath, while their hands still remained steady with the match.

He held his hands out in front of him, but it was too dark to see if they trembled. He descended the way he had climbed, feeling his way in the darkness, following the faint chalky lines of the sheep tracks in the turf.

Halfway down, he admitted the whole shameful truth. He was more than afraid. He was weak with the helpless, flailing terror that he expected to feel only in that fraction of time between firing a charge and accepting that it was the one that would kill him.

Boomer was waiting in the front courtyard when Francis returned long after midnight. Francis saw his father's hair and linen shirt in the darkness near the horse trough.

'France, we need to speak. Openly at last.'

'I can't. I swear, I would like nothing better, sir. But I can't.'

'Sit down.'

Francis hesitated, then perched beside his father on the edge of the stone horse trough.

'You're in trouble,' said his father. 'I've known since you first came back from London, even before you brought Kate. How much worse can it grow if you tell me? Is the danger mortal?'

'Most likely.' Francis leaned sideways and scooped a handful of water from the trickle that splashed constantly from the elm pipe at the end of the trough. 'And not just to me. To you and Kate.' It was a relief to say even that much.

'I might be able to help.' Boomer left a silence for his son's reply. 'Whet your wits against my stone. I'll even forgive you for doubting the state of my wits.'

Francis cleared his throat, which felt swollen with unspoken words. He was twelve years old again and grateful for the calm authority of the man beside him.

'It would be a pity to lose you. I'll help if I can,' said Boomer. 'As far as my aging wits permit,' he added dryly. 'In exchange, I think I may soon need your help.'

Francis told him almost everything. Including his fear of putting so much explosive power into the hands of men he thought to be brave, dangerous and more than a little foolish.

By the time they went to bed, some hours later, they had decided what Francis must do.

'I would prefer to depend more on myself,' said Francis uneasily. 'This hangs on chance. And on the good sense and willingness of other men.'

'So?' replied Boomer. 'Nothing changes.'

63

Five days later, Francis arrived in Lambeth. Though it was after dark, his cart did not carry the lantern required by law, because he did not want to carry an open flame. Twelve hundred pounds of gunpowder, packed into casks and kegs of different sizes, rested on a thick mattress of layered sheepskins.

This load brought the total amount of powder he had so far delivered to twenty barrels. Two thousand pounds, a little less than a ton. Only half of what Catesby had ordered. In spite of the stratagem he and Boomer had devised, Francis was not looking forward to facing Robin Catesby.

A stocky, eager man named Thomas Bates helped Francis unload at the same riverside storehouse where he had stored the first eight barrels. Bates was a Catesby retainer recruited to the plot the previous Christmas. While Bates and Francis worked, Catesby stood watching them, hands on his hips.

As Francis carefully lowered a cask down to Bates, he glanced at Catesby. Catesby was a gentleman, as were most of the others who were coming. Gentlemen did not work with their hands.

Francis could not order Catesby to help. This was not the army. Robin was not a sapper or gunner's mate. But Francis needed for him and the rest of them to work like peasants, all the same.

'How many eyes might be watching us out here?' he asked.

'The gates are locked.' Catesby cocked his head. Then, with the quick and cheerful understanding that endeared him to others, he began to undo the twenty silver buttons marshalled down the front of his silk doublet. 'And I've let the dogs out.' He took off his doublet and laid it carefully aside. Untied and removed his lace cuffs. Reached up to take a barrel from Francis. 'Many hands make faster work . . . eh? You're right, France. We can never be careful enough.'

After Bates had helped Catesby put on his doublet again, Catesby led the way through shadowy gardens into the main house. Bates made them a posset of ale warmed with cinnamon and beaten egg, then left the other two men together in a small parlour with a plate of cold meats.

'When will you bring the rest?' Catesby looked drawn and weary in the candlelight, as Francis had never seen him before. 'Eat, France. You've made a long journey.'

'That's all there will be.'

The welcome faded from Catesby's voice. 'No more at all?' The air in the little parlour seemed to chill.

'I've tried, as you asked, Robin. But Powder Mote can't make or buy enough saltpetre and charcoal before November the fifth without drawing fatal attention.'

'I beg you, France. Don't let us fail.'

'How can I persuade you to see reason?'

'Reason?' demanded Catesby. 'Did you attend the execution of those Jesuit priests and witness that display of Christian forgiveness? I'm resolved, most reasonably, to show as much mercy as my enemies.'

Catesby took a crumpled letter from his pocket and smoothed it on the table. 'We need that powder, France.

We're close to success now. Our allies swell so much in number that I begin to hope that all of England will rise with us. And much of Europe besides.' He tapped the letter. 'But without our Great Blow at the heart, there will be nothing to rally them. And our enemies will remain unshaken. We are depending on you.'

Again, Francis felt a hunger to please Catesby. To be included again in that circle of unstinting approval.

'You're resolved beyond persuasion?'

'Utterly.'

Francis raised his hands in surrender. 'Do you still have the remains of your old decayed powder?'

'The stuff bought abroad by Guido and Rookwood? Still stored in my storehouse where we just put yours.'

'May I see it?'

'But Guido says it's all worthless,' protested Catesby. 'He feels at fault, poor soul . . . still craves absolution.'

'How much was left after Bridge House?'

Catesby shrugged. 'You would have to ask Guido. But he's abroad just now, flinging himself into a final quest for more money and support.'

No general should be so ignorant of the details of his weapons, thought Francis as he found his way back to the storehouse on the river. Catesby could stir men to action, but Francis had begun to see his lacks as a tactician.

Twenty-five barrels lay hidden under stacked firewood and coal sacks at the back of the shed. In the faint light reflected off the water, brightened only a little by the veiled moon, and working chiefly by touch and smell, Francis opened each barrel.

In some, the saltpetre, sulphur and charcoal had separated from each other and settled into different layers. He rolled those barrels to one side.

In other barrels, the powder was lumpy and discoloured with damp. Francis set those barrels on the other side.

When done, he had the twenty good barrels from Powder Mote, along with nine barrels of powder that was damp and useless. And sixteen barrels of powder that was decayed but would nevertheless provide the ingredients, ready prepared for reincorporation, for making sixteen more barrels of good powder. With luck.

A total of thirty-six good barrels. Only four barrels short.

'You could flatten the Tower of London and half the City with thirty-six barrels,' Francis told Catesby.

'Thanks be to God!' The radiance returned to Catesby's face.

'But first, we need a safe house in which to work.'

Catesby nodded.

Francis looked at his friend in his silk doublet, with gold at his neck. 'And as many pairs of hands as possible, attached to men whom you trust. And who are willing to labour at foul and dangerous work.'

'These for one pair.' Catesby held up his own broad, clean hands. 'Bates will provide another pair,' he said with growing excitement. 'I will write at once to Tom and Kit, whom you will meet at last.'

'As for the danger,' continued Catesby, 'I welcome real risk.' He rose and poured them both a glass of canary sack. 'I knew you'd do it, France. You shouldn't doubt yourself so.' He raised his glass to Francis. 'My ingenious friend . . .'

'Our success isn't certain.'

'Then we must pray tonight as we have never prayed before. And trust God to listen.'

Francis imagined that the stink of maggot seeped out from his clothes. He raised his glass to the open friendly face on the other side of the parlour fire. His throat again struggled to swallow.

64

With his hat pulled over his ears, Boomer delivered two hand mills to the empty hay barn on a Catholic estate near Brixton Mill. He also left three mortars for grinding, various wooden tools, five parchment corning sieves, and two casks of wine turned too sour to drink and which Susannah had not yet claimed for vinegar.

'You'll be racked for names if you're seen there,' Francis had protested to Boomer while they talked that night on the edge of the horse trough.

'Who else do you trust to find you your mills and bring them?' his father retorted. 'You stand a far greater risk of the rack than I do, France. Don't put Cecil off much longer.'

'I know. I know!'

'In any case, I have business in London.'

The plotters arrived in ones or twos during the course of a night. First, Catesby and Bates. Then came a burly Yorkshireman, Jack Wright, who had fought like Catesby in the Essex Uprising and wore a gold crucifix nearly as fine as Catesby's own. With him came his brother, Kit Wright. Both men were in their robust prime.

Then came another pair of brothers, Rob and Tom Wintour, both of them shorter and darker than the massive Wrights, with a family estate at Huddington, near Worcester. Then the lean and taciturn John Grant, who had spent the summer gathering weapons at his house at Norbrook. His lined, intense face seemed to brood constantly on painful secrets. At any moment, one felt, he might begin to weep.

Last came Thomas Percy, whom Francis had met in The Duck and Drake. His white-streaked hair and silver beard framed a petulant face. He was thinner than Francis and even taller, but he slouched until his back was as curved as a bill-hook and his eyes seemed lower.

Gentlemen, all of them, thought Francis with dismay, looking them over in the first dawn light. Excepting Bates and myself. And Guido, when he arrives back from the Continent.

Catesby seemed to read his thoughts and came to his aid. 'We are all ready to die for our Great Blow,' he said quietly to the small assembly. 'Does any one of us baulk at labouring first?'

'Surely death is to be preferred.' The tall stooped frame of Thomas Percy lounged against a barn post as if he were observing a game of cards. He was the oldest man there and kinsman to an earl. Francis could not read from his dry murmur how much he was in earnest.

Catesby smiled in appreciation of the sally. 'We all aspire to your noble courage, Tom. You must also, at this moment, be our example in settling for second best.'

Percy nodded his white-streaked head in wry submission.

Though Catesby, in his early thirties, seemed to be the youngest among them, apart from Francis, he was without doubt their commander. Francis ruled this odd little army only as Catesby's man.

'Master Percy will no doubt be pleased to hear that he runs a fair chance of dying here in this barn,' Francis said. Then he explained what they had come there to do.

As he spoke, he felt himself stepping back into the habit of command. Though most of the men had been soldiers, he reminded them of the dangers they faced in reincorporating sixteen barrels of decayed gunpowder, at a rate of one hundred and twenty pounds a day. He told them that they must put aside all knives, swords, daggers and other metal carried on their persons. He explained why he was short-cropped and clean-shaven. He did not, however, risk ordering these gentlemen to shave. As they all seemed set on flinging themselves at death, a singed beard or two seemed a minor matter.

Before beginning work on the gunpowder, Francis had them fill every bucket they could find with water and set one or two on the stone floor of the barn near each of the mortars and hand mills.

'I'll stand the first watch,' Percy announced. He left the barn.

With the high, double wagon doors wide open for light, Francis showed Tom Wintour (in whom he saw a quick, lively wit), Thomas Bates and Robin Catesby how to recombine the separated parts of the decayed powder. They used the large mortars and stone pestles, pouring in drops of wine to keep friction from overheating the mix.

'Trouble, trouble,' Wintour muttered as Francis left him to it. 'Cauldron bubble . . .'

God's balls! thought Francis unhappily. I could grow to like him, too.

Rob Wintour, John Grant and Kit Wright then set to work. By the end of the afternoon, with the exception of Percy, they were stretching painful muscles and binding up blisters.

Percy stood watch in the barnyard until the late afternoon, sometimes smoking his clay pipe. At other times he read a small book, but he was alert enough to any unexpected sounds.

For the moment, Francis left him alone. He was glad for

a sentry. He kept remembering Cecil's warning not to be taken in the company of traitors. He went regularly to check that the estate gates were kept locked day and night by the two elderly sisters who lived in the big house. And that they let the dogs run at night.

Guido returned from the Continent on the evening of their second day of work, in a dark humour. No one abroad was willing to be seen to support the Catholic cause, now that Spain and England were at peace.

'We will do very well with our allies who support us in secret,' Catesby consoled him. 'Don't look so sour, Guido. I'm sure you did everything you could. And the news is not as bad as you fear. I'll explain later.'

'No pipes?' asked Thomas Percy in theatrical dismay.

'No fire of any sort in the barn.'

Percy, with his white-streaked hair, silver beard and languid manner, made Francis feel like an over-earnest schoolboy facing a bored and worldly schoolmaster. But all their lives were at stake, as well as a barn belonging to two courageous women who did not deserve to have it blown up.

Percy touched an ironic finger to his brow and put away his pipe.

'Quoynt knows best,' said Guido acidly.

'God be praised, one of us does,' said Tom Wintour, his round face bright with sweat and mischief.

Guido sank back into himself, looking uncertain whether or not Wintour had lobbed a counter-gibe at him. He glanced at Catesby, but their leader was wiping black dust off his face with a silk handkerchief.

'Loosely mix the sulphur and charcoal.' Francis repeated his instructions again and again.

At Powder Mote they would then grind each batch for twenty-four hours to incorporate the saltpetre. Here in the Brixton barn, Francis asked for only nine hours.

As he expected, Guido protested.

'This powder won't have to survive months in a baggage train,' Francis explained with precise veracity. 'Merely a short cart journey to Lambeth and an even shorter one by boat across the Thames.'

'The grinding time is still too short,' insisted Guido.

Francis shrugged. 'My friend, if you doubt the power of this powder, please feel free to sit on a keg while I light the fuse.'

The other men laughed.

'In any case, I have added a secret ingredient to the wine.' This was untrue, but it convinced most of the plotters.

After incorporation, they pressed the powder then dried it away from flames. Then they broke up the powder cake while it was still slightly damp and forced it through a corning sieve. This corning shaped it into the large grains (but not too large) that burned fast, for the greatest explosive power.

The linen of these gentlemen had never before been so filthy, except perhaps on a battlefield. Their faces held some of the grimness of war.

The two elderly sisters who owned the estate sent kettles of stew and bread but never appeared in person. A serving man brought beer. A groom introduced the two estate mastiffs to the strangers.

Francis offered his hand to be sniffed and hoped that the beasts would remember any new friends when they met them again at night.

'Slowly,' he said, moving again from mortar to mortar. 'Never hurry. Even when you're racing time.'

'What an entertaining interlude this is proving to be.' Tom Wintour glanced up from his mortar, his round face streaked with grey dust. Bloody rags flapped from his hands.

'Wet your powder!' said Francis urgently. 'There's smoke!'

We won't do it, he thought. Not even with their whole-hearted labour.

On their third evening, Francis thought he would go mad if he did not stretch his legs and snatch a moment of soli-tude. Following the inside of the estate wall, beyond a small orchard, he came across the hen house. Behind it stood a small dog mill, intended for grain.

Francis jogged back to the barn. 'Ask the owners if we can use their dog mill,' he begged Catesby.

They could. But the beast that had powered it was long dead.

'The dog mill will be far faster than the hand mills and mortars,' Francis told the men. 'And far more dangerous for that very reason.'

Big Kit Wright offered at once to yoke himself to the dog wheel, where he trudged in circles while Francis fed the decayed powder under the stone. When Kit grew tired, his equally powerful brother Jack took his place.

'I'll take a turn while you eat.'

Francis pressed some powder carefully under the wheel, detected a thread of smoke, poured a little wine. Only then did he look from his low stool into the down-turned, mournful face of the speaker, John Grant.

'There are safer tasks elsewhere,' Francis said.

'I'm content here.' Grant's face reversed itself into a brief, mirthless smile.

On moonlit nights, they worked without sleep. When the night was too dark to work, they slept on improvised beds in the barn and nearby granary, on mattresses from the house, piles of sacking, and the fleeces from the Quoynt cart.

On occasion, Thomas Percy went to lie in comfort at his kinsman's house on the Thames in London. Each time, he arrived back the following morning wearing clean clothes and bearing fine white rolls, a small cask of canary sack and good tobacco.

One afternoon, he announced that he was willing to spread the powder. He also condescended to help with the corning and soon developed a knack for it.

'It's just a pity that I can't smoke my pipe while I watch the powder dry,' he said.

They had to dry the reincorporated powder in the loft of the barn, directly above where they were working. Francis did not like it. If any man, grinding too fast, created too much heat, he might send up the whole barn and ignite the powder in the loft. No one in the barn would escape.

But, lacking a special drying room warmed by the back of a fire in a separate chamber, they made do with a watertight loft designed to keep a large amount of hay from going bad.

In spite of himself, Francis cared whether or not these men died. He admired their passion, however misdirected. He almost envied them their sense of shared purpose. And he knew them now. Good men, if it weren't for their dangerous sense of grievance.

He stopped posting a sentry and trusted to the estate dogs. Every man worked. Any watching spy would think that Francis wanted this powder as much as the others did.

65

One afternoon, Catesby excused himself. He was gone for some time.

'They have a priest hidden in the house,' he told Francis in the barnyard later as they leaned against the side of a shed, eating their supper. 'Happy to hear confessions. I've asked him to come and conduct a Mass for us tonight.'

With a ping of hope, Francis saw the shadow in Catesby's eyes.

'You can turn back even now, Robin,' he said quietly. 'Set a fair example for your enemies to follow.'

Catesby slung an arm across his shoulders. 'You're a good fellow, France. You understand me better than most of the others. And have such a care for my feelings.' Catesby sighed. 'But neither you nor I must falter now. The others need us to lead them. For some, their resolve is terribly fragile. And we can have only one destination.'

'No matter what this priest may have advised?'

'Hush.' Catesby clapped Francis on the shoulder then dropped his arm. 'I was right to invite him to come tonight,' he said after a moment. 'I've no right to stop the others from making their own peace with God.' He turned back to the barn to begin work again.

Francis saw Guido make a sour face when Francis returned at Catesby's side.

Combine. Incorporate. Moisten. Press. Dry. Sieve.
Combine. Incorporate . . .
Black powder lodged in the pores of their faces. Their clothing turned grey and gave off a faint dark haze whenever they moved. The Wrights plodded in endless circles. Percy pressed with the Jacob's foot while Tom Wintour shook the sieve. The others rolled their pestles, dripped wine into their mortars, rolled their pestles. And Catesby worked harder than any of them.

Nine days after they began, in the late afternoon of a fine day, Francis tapped into place the top of the final cask.
'It's done!'
There was a ragged cheer.
They still don't fully comprehend what they've undertaken, Francis thought.
They wiped their grimy faces, flexed cramped fingers and clapped each other on the back in groggy disbelief. 'It's done.' Then they stood dazed in the slanting sunlight.
'Let us give thanks to God,' said Catesby, moved close to tears.
They knelt. Francis too. John Grant spoke the priest's part for the others to answer.
I've done what you hired me to do, Francis told Cecil silently. I beg you to excuse me from the rest.
After praying, Catesby produced a cask of good claret. They swept the barn and set up a trestle table. A little later, the two sisters sent out a haunch of roast pork and five capons stuffed with walnuts.
'It's done,' they kept telling one another, as if they had already achieved their Blow, and not merely the means. 'All

that's left is to carry it across the river and hide it in the Westminster cellar.'

Catesby smiled around him at his companions. 'They're good men, France. I couldn't ask for better.'

'You see the best in men. Then they try to find it themselves.'

Guido stared over his cup at Francis, standing beside Catesby.

Catesby caught Guido's expression and glanced at Francis. Leaning closer, he murmured, 'Even him. Our little Yorkshireman. He has the special fervour of a convert and is growing into a dignity he didn't know he had. You will see.'

He turned to the group. 'My friends . . .' Catesby raised his voice just a little. The others stopped talking at once and drew closer.

'. . . We must speak seriously for a moment, before we are too far gone in wine. The time is now short. We will soon scatter to play our seperate roles in the great venture to come, and some of us will not meet again before the Blow. I have had good news to hearten us on our way.' He pulled two letters from his pocket and held them aloft.

'For the past year, Guido has been bringing me secret letters from Spain. In these we are assured of the firmest support, no matter what cold face the Spanish must seem outwardly to put on.' He nodded to Fawkes. 'Our small numbers will soon be swollen by Spanish armies, our few horses by the cavalries of Spain. In short, our venture has the secret blessing of the Spanish Crown.'

'Quoynt isn't one of us,' said Guido abruptly, cutting through the excited murmur. 'I wouldn't speak so freely in front of him.'

'After the last nine days, do you doubt that France is one of us?' asked Catesby with passion.

'No,' said Percy unexpectedly. 'I have no doubts.'

'Nor I,' said Tom Wintour. 'He's as mad as any man here.'

Francis stared at the letters in Catesby's hand. Almost certainly Cecil's forgeries.

'God sent Quoynt when we needed him,' said Catesby. 'We should accept His gift with good grace.'

Francis forced his frozen lips into a smile.

'Now to the final details of our great venture,' said Catesby.

While still relatively sober, the plotters then rehearsed what each of them would do once the powder was in place at Westminster. They agreed approximate escape routes north through the Midlands and their eventual meeting place in Wales.

'But most of your possible safe houses belong to your families or friends,' Francis interjected.

'Who else can we trust to hide us?' asked Catesby.

Francis caught Tom Wintour's eye and saw his own thoughts there. Families and friends would receive the first visits from officers of the Crown. The known Catholics at Coughton Court and Baddesley Clinton might already be watched.

'In any case,' said Catesby with conviction, 'it will never come to pursuit. Now, who will carry the news of our Blow to our families?'

Most of whom seemed to be unaware of what was planned.

Francis listened with growing disbelief as they spoke next of making a raid on Warwick castle as they fled westward, for more horses and weapons. He looked at Cecil's letters, which were still in Catesby's hand.

'We have young Ambrose Rookwood with his splendid horses still to join us,' said Catesby. 'And I hope to induce Sir Everard Digby to call together a group of gentlemen, armed and ready for a "hunt".'

He said 'hunt' in a way that raised knowing smiles on one

or two faces. 'Our doe is the Princess Elizabeth,' Catesby explained to Francis. 'She must replace her father on the throne.'

'What of Charles, the little Duke of York?' Guido asked. 'He's the other male heir. Should we not choose him over the girl?'

'The little Duke lacks her appeal for the populace,' said big Kit Wright bluntly. 'And he's only five. Too young.'

'We mean to appoint a regent, in any case,' protested Fawkes.

'And he's sickly,' Wright insisted. 'And tongue-tied. He has just learned to walk. He won't do at all.'

Guido looked in appeal at Catesby, who frowned thoughtfully.

'Charles is irrelevant,' said Tom Wintour, as if ending the debate. 'He's a foreigner. Born in Scotland. I say, choose the new infant. She's true-born English.'

'If the Duke is too young, she's even younger,' protested Fawkes angrily.

'I'll see to the Duke,' said Percy.

'We must see which way things fall,' said Catesby. 'And then decide what to do.'

Francis opened his mouth to protest that such loose planning invited disaster. Then he shut it again. Cecil had asked him to assist the traitors by giving them gunpowder. He had not told Francis to offer them military advice.

'Guido, my friend,' said Catesby. 'Don't concern yourself with such details. You're at the true heart of our action . . . as well as Percy who has already hired the cellar beneath the House of Lords.' A quick courteous nod towards the ruthless use of connections, then back to Guido. 'The whole venture depends on you.'

Fawkes looked about uncertainly, his fur still bristling.

'Come, Guido, stand here by me and instruct us.' Catesby's

voice held not the slightest hint of irony. 'How will you proceed? We're all ears.' His gaze collected up the others in assent.

Still flushed with anger, Guido rose from his upturned box. Watching him, Francis felt a twinge of envy at Catesby's power to inspire others. Even Fawkes, born with vinegar in his soul, basked in Robin's attention.

It was the last rich course in a feast of pickings for an intelligencer, but Francis could take no more. He would stand down, for one night. For just a few hours. He had done what he was truly hired to do and Cecil could go frig himself for just one night. Francis would decide in the morning how to deal with what he was learning tonight.

He watched Robin's face while Fawkes explained how, on the night of the fourth of November, he would lay a powder train through the Westminster cellars from the hidden barrels of gunpowder. Catesby was nodding in approval as if he saw nothing wrong.

But Francis did, on two counts. With sudden clarity he understood why such an excessive amount of gunpowder was needed. They could not mine their target with precision, so they meant to flatten all of Westminster rather than miss their aim. These gentlemen were willing to kill a thousand people to be sure of just one.

Francis turned back to Fawkes who, as a former sapper, must surely see the other difficulty. Guido avoided his eye.

'It will be a very long powder train for such damp conditions,' said Francis, unable to contain himself any longer.

'Have you been in the cellars below Westminster?' demanded Fawkes. '. . . I thought not. I have been there. I have studied the conditions there. I assure you, what I propose will work.' His eyes shot at Francis a gleam so dark and malevolent that Francis felt a little shock under his ribs.

Suddenly Francis knew who had fired the bird-bolt. And knew that every smile Robin Catesby gave him, every mark of favour, made Guido's hatred burn even hotter.

Keep your damned mouth closed, Francis ordered himself. Not one more word! He raised his hands in concession and leaned back against his post with his arms crossed.

'Quoynt does speak from great experience,' Tom Wintour offered quietly.

'As do I,' snapped Fawkes. 'Enough that you trust me with the "true heart of your plans", as Robin called it. Perhaps you now want to change your minds and replace me with Quoynt.'

'Julius Caesar himself could not have arranged a campaign better,' said Catesby soothingly. He raised his glass to Guido and invited the others to join him.

Fawkes nodded, softening in the warmth of Catesby's approval.

'Now we must celebrate.' Catesby refilled his glass from the cask. 'My friends . . . my brothers-in-arms, this is our last night together before battle begins.'

Francis lifted his glass with the others.

'Smile, France!' cried Catesby. 'We're not all dead yet.'

Francis forced a smile. 'To the triumph of Right,' he said, gazing around their circle.

'. . . The triumph of Right,' the others echoed. But Guido lifted one corner of his mouth in sour derision.

I hear your evasion, said his eyes. I hear what you do not say.

'A special toast to Guido Fawkes, your gallant firemaster,' Francis added. 'I wish him well.'

'There you are, Guido,' cried Jack Wright. 'An offer of truce between firemasters. Clasp his hand and thank him for your powder.'

'There's a good fellow,' said Catesby. 'We're all brothers tonight.'

Fawkes held out his hand. 'And may we still be so tomorrow.'

'As much as ever we were,' said Francis with a smile.

66

Francis resolved to forget Guido's animosity for just one night. Until morning, he would pretend that these men really were his friends and colleagues, not traitors and would-be murderers. That they had worked together, and triumphed, for a purpose that he shared.

Alcohol, the end of effort and lack of sleep soon tilted them towards a feverish good-fellowship. Like the rest of them, Francis grew drunker and drunker. When Tom Wintour begged him, he dug his little wooden boxes out of his saddle-bags. Outside, well away from the barn, he showed them tricks with gunpowder; squibs that leapt and spat sparks. Then a 'Ground Rat', a small rocket that dashed in wild zigzags along the ground. Useful in battle to frighten horses.

There was wild applause. Demands for more. He showed them the pipe trick he had used in Kingston. Then the popping stars used on Kate's window.

'Let me!' cried Tom Wintour.

John Grant turned one over in his hand thoughtfully, then gave it back.

'May I throw one?' begged big Kit Wright.

As Francis listened to the soft popping and watched the little flashes of light, his humour threatened to darken. He shook it off and drank more wine. No Cecil, not tonight. Not even Kate. A man can take only so much darkness without a little respite.

He remembered other evenings almost like this one, in foreign inns, around campfires. But there were no whores here. Seen through a veil of drink, these men were the priests of revolution. They were Isaacs, offering themselves up without a prompt from Father Abraham. These were men who believed they could make a difference. They feasted. They anointed. With wine by the cask, they washed away sins and memories alike. They stripped themselves clean to face the future, which might be short, and they trusted in an Afterlife, which would be glorious. Tonight, they would not think about the painful road that led between the two.

Instead, they sang vile songs in Latin, French and English. Guido raised his glass and cried, 'To be a martyr!' But he was smiling now, with Thomas Percy's arm draped over his shoulder.

'A pissing contest!' cried Tom Wintour with hectic good humour and a desperate look in his eye.

They lined up outside the barn, wavering like trees in a high wind.

'I'm the winner by a yard!' (Har, har, har!!)

'We all piss by our yards, you pixilated sot!'

'He's the Ajax of pissing . . . !' (Hoo! Haw! Haw!) 'A . . . jax!' (Whoaaahawwr!)

'He's drunk as an owl . . . *Whooooo! Whooooo!*'

'. . . Writing my name . . . my namie . . . '

'Take care! That's my best doublet you just doused in your holy water!'

'Put your weapons away, lads. There's not one big enough to frighten a flea!'

'I have fleas!' This mumble from the prostrate form of Jack Wright was ignored.

'Bring your great pikestaff over here, then. And wave it at

my hat to depopule . . . Depol . . . deep . . . popple . . . popple
. . . Hang the fleas!'

'Aye. It's the headsman's itch you must scratch.'

Arms slung over shoulders. Francis between Kit and Robin.
Tom Wintour with Guido. They fell into heaps like puppies.
Wilfully numbed.

There's nothing like it, thought Francis, not quite as drunk
as he pretended. No closeness like that shared by warriors
who might die the next day. He could not renounce it forever
to be a mole, a snout, a smooth-tongued liar, when he had
once been a man of explosions and fire.

Catesby bumped him like an affectionate hound. Eyes
gleaming like damp grapes. Hair hanging over his face.
Crumbs in his beard. 'I love you, brother! I love them all, all
of us. But you most of all!' Arms gripped him and hugged
him close. 'Another like me. Others look to us and wait for
a command. I sometimes grow weary . . . .weary tonight.'

They staggered together into the barn, watched by Fawkes.

'Give it up,' said Francis.

'Oh, but you see, I chafe at commands from any other
man.'

'Robin! Listen to me.' Francis stopped suddenly, causing
Catesby to swing round him in a country-dance figure. Francis
caught him in both arms. 'Give up this venture. Give up your
Great Blow!'

Catesby kissed him on the lips. 'Can't stop now. Nothing
else to be done.'

Francis felt an urge to weep. 'You're a fool, Robin! You're
all marked men. I tell you, Cecil knows. He's drawing you
on.'

'Don't care. Must do something. Can't sit any more. The
King's a liar . . .'

'Your men may care. Or their wives may care about losing
husbands. Their children . . .'

Catesby hauled him onwards. 'Shut your face, Quoynt. Brother mine. Need to sleep. Where's the bed gone? Here, beddie, beddie, beddie! Come to Robin! Sweet bed!'

They staggered together up the loft stairs.

'I'm Cecil's man!' Francis fell with Catesby onto the nearest mattress.

'Know it. Guido said. From the first. But not a bugger. Keep me warm then, brother. Need friendly arms around me tonight. Cold road. Cold road . . .' He began to snore.

Francis groaned and rolled over. He had not been as drunk as he pretended last night, but he was drunk enough for his head to be teetering perilously now on the feeble trunk of his neck. Catesby still slept beside him, boots sticking out from a tangle of woollen cloak to dangle over the side of the mattress.

Slowly, Francis sat up. At least no one had cut his throat in the night.

A hand clamped onto his arm. He looked down. Catesby was awake.

'Thank you, brother.'

'For what?' asked Francis cautiously.

'Your confession.'

'In the light of day, I was hoping you were too drunk to remember.'

'I told Guido we could trust you in the end. "He's a soldier, not a courtier," I told him.'

'But what I said is true.'

'And you also worked like a man possessed to make us our gunpowder. I take deeds as my witnesses, not words.' He smiled up at Francis. 'And see now how your honest words prove me right yet again.'

'How can I persuade you to give up your terrible project?'

'You can't.'

'Not even if I promised betrayals? Arrest and execution?'

Catesby shook his head, then groaned. 'How did I carouse like that every night just a few short years ago?'

'I shall clout that thick head to make you listen!'

Catesby lay with his eyes closed. 'You're the one not listening, France. We will not be turned. And we will succeed.'

'You should be terrified of Cecil!'

'Believe me . . . Sweet Mother Mary, my head is beating like a drum! Don't fear. I don't tell you everything. Did you think I did? It's best for you as well as for us.'

While Catesby was saying farewell to the owners of the barn, Francis unbuckled Catesby's saddlebag. He still felt the warmth of Catesby's arm across his shoulder and the heat of their shared laughter. When the first saddlebag offered nothing of interest, Francis searched the other.

The letters were in Catesby's Missal.

Robin was a trusting fool. Unless he had set a trap for Francis.

Francis went to the top of the loft stairs. The barn below was quiet, except for some snores. One of the estate hounds slept in the sun just inside the barn doors, curled like a bread roll.

In the first letter, Count Alva in Spain promised horses, armed men, and support for the Catholic uprising that would follow the Great Blow. Francis recognized Cecil's hand. The one he used in his secret letters to Francis.

Francis cursed. He would rub Robin's heroic nose on these to make him see how false they were. That his supposed allies were a fiction created by his enemies. He had to make Catesby see the horror he was bringing down on his fellow Catholics.

He turned over the second letter, also purporting to be from Spain. It was written in a different hand from the first.

At first he thought that Cecil was entertaining himself with variety. Then he read the final sentences.

'... *Have no fear for the success of your venture. We shall provide the promised horses ... four ships standing off the English coast near the place in the south that we both know ... that Devil in Whitehall, namely that twisted imp called Cecil, lately made Lord Salisbury, we shall confound him. Already sending him false news which he swallows whole, so eager is he to sniff out any who oppose his purpose, which, we do sometimes believe, is to rule England without even the show of speaking through the King.*
    Your Brothers in Christ.

Cecil never wrote this, thought Francis. Someone else is urging Catesby on. And this support, these horses and armies, may be real.

His father was right. Francis had to tell the full truth to Cecil at last.

67

Francis turned to wait with his pistol in his hand. The rider behind him was Fawkes.

Guido reined back when he saw the gun. 'Steady, Quoynt! I thought I might ride with you.' He smiled.

Francis said nothing. He was considering his dilemma.

'If my company's not too tedious.'

Francis nodded and replaced his pistol in his belt. Then he turned to make some adjustments to his saddlebags. When he straightened, Fawkes was watching him alertly.

'I seldom carry so many tools of my trade on horseback,' Francis explained. 'Let's see if she settles now.' He took up the reins with one hand and patted his mare on the neck with the other.

No weapon in either hand. He saw Fawkes relax slightly.

They rode on for a few yards. Then Francis's big grey mare bucked and sidled off the track. Francis pulled up again.

'She's still not happy.' He dismounted, removed the wrapped mortar balanced on the horse's rump, retied the bundle at the back of his saddle, then opened a saddlebag and made a show of repacking his bottles and crocks, talking to the mare all the while.

Fawkes watched from his bay gelding.

'She thinks I'm making a carthorse of her.' Francis gave

Fawkes a wry smile as he took a wooden tube loosely wrapped in parchment from the bag and buckled it onto the outside. He replaced the mortar and lashed it down.

'Let's try again.' He remounted. The horse walked on as if it had forgotten any earlier ill-temper.

The track narrowed to follow a stream. Both men tried casually to make the other go first.

Don't force his pace, thought Francis. There was only a short distance before the track widened again. He let Fawkes drop behind. His shoulder blades tightened.

'Those were ingenious tricks you showed us last night,' said Fawkes when Francis waited for him to ride up alongside again. 'Impressive to the ignorant.'

'And you're not ignorant, are you, Guido?' Francis turned his head to look at his unwelcome but not entirely unexpected companion. A long stretch of open track lay ahead before they next entered the trees.

'You think you're the only one among us who's not a fool,' said Guido tightly. 'I watched you while Catesby spoke last night.'

'And I was listening to you. You may convince Robin, but not me. You won't escape from those cellars in time. You know that.'

'I do know.'

'Then you mean to die?'

'How else can I be absolutely certain of the explosion? As you yourself pointed out, with your superior experience and knowledge, no powder train or fuse can be trusted over such a great distance in such damp cellars.'

'But to choose certain death . . .'

'It's certain for us all. What difference does a year or two make in the end?'

To keep him talking, Francis said, 'I took you for a cynic, I confess.'

'You mistook me then.' Fury blazed in Guido's eyes. 'Many men do. And then make the mistake of discounting me. Faith found me in Spain. I'd rather die for a cause I believe in than while fighting another man's war. A swift death in the cellars will be far better than rotting in the mud of some battlefield. Or a traitor's death on the scaffold.' He crossed himself. 'Don't you ever want to redeem your worthless, pitiful life, Quoynt?'

Francis inhaled sharply.

'A palpable hit,' said Fawkes. 'Don't bother to deny it. I know the stink of Cecil's men. I suspected you from the start.'

'Like knows like.'

Guido shook his head. 'No longer. I despise how I once lived. As I know you still despise yourself.' He smiled with bitter dignity. 'It's far easier to choose a swift, glorious death. And then . . . who knows? At worst, I'll be remembered as a Catholic martyr. At best, in time, I could be made "Saint Guido" when England once again embraces Rome.'

'That will never happen.'

'God assures Catesby that we will win,' said Fawkes. 'Do you speak to a higher authority?'

'Catesby mistakes God.' Francis ignored Guido's underlying challenge.

They were halfway to the trees.

'Cecil is watching you,' Francis said quietly. 'Robin knows that you're marked men. Yet he persists in this Blow, while you, Tom, Rob and the others follow him even though I see questions in some eyes. Now he has brought in Rookwood and means to recruit Digby, who is little more than a boy.'

'A child,' Fawkes agreed. 'Who yearns only for some grand venture. I promise you, he and Rookwood know nothing of the Blow itself. They're recruited only for their horses and men. If young Digby succeeds in kidnapping the Princess, or Percy captures the Duke of York, all the better. If not, who cares? The Blow is all that matters. The rest is mere after-math. Details.'

'It will be a shambles,' said Francis. 'And not just in Westminster.'

'I know the odds against us as well as you do,' said Fawkes furiously. 'I too can see the flaws in our greater design. But because I am ready to die I have the power to make those flaws irrelevant.'

He leaned towards Francis. 'No one expects me to be willing to die in the cellars. When Westminster explodes into flames, and bloody fragments of the King and Prince Henry are flung into the sky, along with those pompous villains who claim the right to govern England, who will care whether Digby has kidnapped the right royal pup? How many of us live or die won't matter a devil's fart.

'So long as I set off that gunpowder, nothing will rob us of our fame. That beacon of wonder and terror, which I will light, will be read as far as Heaven. The English people will rise up behind us. Our Glorious Blow will be remembered as the moment that the True Church returned to England.'

'You're all blind fools,' said Francis. He reined his mare back, just a little.

Guido matched his pace. 'I'm no fool. And I won't let us look like fools by risking failure in the cellars. Our cause can survive oppression and martyrdom. It won't survive ridicule.'

Fawkes now reined back harder so that he began to drop behind Francis as they approached the next narrowing of the track.

Here, Francis decided. Before reaching the trees. 'I think that ridicule is the demon you fear the most.'

'And it's not yours?' Fawkes's voice rasped with suppressed fury. 'Poor Francis Quoynt. Lost in a hell of uncertainty. But though I pity you, I can't let you betray what you learned last night to your twisted little imp of a master.'

'You fired that bolt.'

'Which bolt?' Guido faltered, sounding genuinely surprised. 'An attempt on your life? Don't be an ass. We needed your powder . . . until now. Drop your pistol and sword on the ground. You know how to do it.'

Francis raised his open hands slowly to his side and half-turned his horse with a kick.

Fawkes was pointing his pistol at him.

'Mine is not loaded.' With one hand, Francis pulled his gun from his belt and tossed it into the grass at the side of the track. 'I would fear for my balls if I carried a loaded pistol on horseback.'

His difficulty was that he could not kill Guido, but must let him live to run to the very edge, as Cecil had ordered.

'Now your sword.'

On the other hand, he could not let Guido kill him. Not even to oblige Cecil.

Francis drew his blade slowly, then leaned over and thrust the point into the soft earth of the track. The sword quivered but stood upright like a crucifix. As he straightened, he whipped the wooden tube from the side of the saddlebag.

There were two triggers on the ignition device. One pull snapped the flint across the striking surface. One pull released the spring coiled inside the tube. He ducked and kicked his horse sideways. No need to aim exactly. Not like Guido.

The tree above Francis rattled as the lead shot from Guido's pistol shot punched through the leaves. Guido was falling. His gelding screamed and reared away from the half-dozen Ground Rats jumping and spitting sparks around its hoofs. Then it turned and bolted, leaving its rider on the ground.

'That's a trick to impress the ignorant I didn't show you last night.' Francis kicked his mare forward again and snatched his sword. He hated to leave the pistol but dared not retrieve it.

Guido rolled out of the way and crouched on the verge, fumbling to reload. As Francis rode at him, his eyes widened. He scrambled in panic away from the mare's hoofs and the upraised sword.

At the last moment, Francis wheeled his horse away into the tunnel of trees. 'You look ridiculous cowering down there in the dirt, Fawkes,' he called over his shoulder.

Francis was around the first bend in the track before he heard the second pistol shot. Fired more in frustration than in serious intent. He hoped that Guido would be too shaken to wonder why Francis had not finished him off. Robin, on the other hand, would consider such mercy as yet further proof of good will.

Jogging north towards London, he touched the pouch where he carried a copy of that second letter. For once, he might have a surprise for Cecil.

PART SIX

LIGHTING THE FUSE

'We know diseases of Stoppings and suffocations are the most dangerous in the body; And it is not much otherwise in the Minde.'

Francis Bacon, 'Of Friendship'

'Eat not the heart.'

Francis Bacon, quoting Pythagoras.

68

'I replaced the original where I found it.' Francis gave Cecil a copy of Robin's letter. 'In a saddlebag.'

His tongue tried to shape the name of Robert Catesby. He felt it contract and flatten against his back teeth. The tip curved upwards. He made a strange sound, as if trying to clear his throat, then fell silent. His employer did not notice.

Cecil's oddly stretched face was turning grey as he read. The small body went very still.

'A cruder style than my own. I would have liked to see the original hand.' The voice remained steady and dry. He met Francis's eyes blandly. 'I assume there were no others.'

Francis shook his head. He glanced past Cecil at the boatman, leaned forward and lowered his voice still further. 'Only your own last letter. Is this one truly from Spain?'

Cecil ignored the question. 'What do you make of it, Quoynt?'

'Not one of ours.'

'Oh, thou paragon of perception!'

As Cecil read the letter a second time, Francis watched the twin daggers of his eyes stab again and again at the same place. Whoever had written '*that twisted little imp called Cecil*' was surely being pricked down among the damned.

'It has an English turn of phrase.' Cecil turned the copy

over as if further information might lurk on the back. 'Not a mistake I would make. Nor is it in Alva's style, which I have learned to imitate so well.'

He folded the copy of the letter with finicky care, flattening the creases between stubby finger and thumb. 'I must determine who wrote this. Bring me the original, or another letter in the same hand.'

'Stealing the original might be impossible, my lord.' Although Robin Catesby, so blindly set on his destructive path, would doubtless find a reason why the theft of a secret, damning letter was a further sign of God's special favour.

'I must see the original hand,' said Cecil impatiently. 'To compare with those I know. I fear we may have a new player. Bring me the letter itself or learn who sent it.'

Francis sat by the water steps at Horseley Down long after Cecil's boat left him there. It was now the twenty-fourth of October. Eleven days before the Blow. He hailed another wherry to take him upriver to Lambeth.

It was no surprise to find Catesby's house locked and dark. He could not get access to the storehouse to see if the powder was still there or had already been moved to Westminster.

Now where?

You're up to your neck in shit, my friend.

He walked back to the nearest water stairs. As he crossed the Thames to the City, he tried to recall the drunken conversation of his last night among the plotters. Coughton or Bath? Or Baddesley Clinton? No shards remained in his memory to tell him where Robin had intended to go next.

Francis frowned at the back of a fellow passenger on the wherry. It was possible that Robin had suspected him even before his confession. That he had believed Guido's first warnings after all.

All that open talk, that evening of good fellowship, might have been as false as Cecil's forgeries.

Remembered warmth turned to bile.

Back in the City, Francis went to The Duck and Drake. None of the plotters sat drinking in the low-ceilinged room. When the host saw Francis, he moved swiftly to block the way.

'Get out. We don't serve your sort.'

'No maggots,' was what Francis heard.

He was finished. The letter Cecil wanted was now beyond his reach. His part was over.

It was his own fault for his drunken candour. For not being able to live with being a liar and having to prove himself to be an honest man.

For lack of a better idea, he went back to Southwark to reclaim his horse from an ostler near The Gun. As he put on the bridle, he suddenly wondered whether Robin and the rest might, like himself, have been false from the very beginning. The uncertainties unleashed by that possibility made him lean his forehead against his horse's neck for the comfort of its warm animal smell.

But however hard he tried, he could not see Robin Catesby as a successful Machiavel. Guido must have gone back after trying to kill Francis and convinced Catesby to cut the connection, now that they had the powder.

In Robin's boots, that's what he himself would do. In Robin's boots, he would also order someone to kill Francis Quoynt.

The stables were quiet except for the stamping and blowing of the horses.

Here I am, if you want me, he shouted silently. But beware.

He wanted to strike out, to slash with his sword, to ride his horse at a chasm.

His mare stepped out eagerly, fresh from a day in the stables. Though it was past midnight, Francis turned her south across the Lambeth marshes. One way was as good as another. He almost hoped for the attack of a footpad or homeless rogue.

Quoynt or no, he had failed. Lost Robin off his hook. Deceived Cecil, and must now also fail him.

He considered turning his horse and galloping back to confess everything to Cecil and beg for mercy. To give Cecil every name, every detail that he could scrape from his memory. But a canker of doubt stopped him. It was just possible that Bacon's silvered venom might be true. And that Cecil wanted the Spanish letter, not to learn who wrote it, but because he wanted to destroy it as evidence of his own double dealings. Cecil might, as his cousin Bacon had hinted, intend for Catesby and Fawkes to succeed.

And had hired him, Francis Quoynt, to make it possible.

A searing wash of understanding suddenly flooded him.

That's why Robin was not afraid of Cecil!

Cecil was a traitor.

And Francis a dead man.

He had provided the powder. He was the only soul alive who knew that Cecil had paid for it and urged on the plotters.

As for what might happen to his father and Kate . . .

He rode south for an hour before he was able to think more calmly again. Reason regained a small, if precarious, finger-hold on his thoughts. A plan began to take shape. A test for Cecil. Protection, however fragile, for Kate. It would be a small act, but better than nothing.

He carried on southward to Powder Mote. At the lowest point of the night, he rested and watered his horse while he slept for an hour or so on a riverbank. He arrived at the estate shortly before midday.

69

25 October 1605

Kate felt a rush of relief mixed with apprehension when she saw Francis safely back, crossing the wide flagged path on his way from the stables. When he vanished up the stairs towards his chamber without calling her name or seeking her out as he passed, she bent back to Boomer's glove, which had split between forefinger and thumb.

A few moments later, he came to her chamber, still wearing his riding clothes and carrying an inkpot and quill pen.

'Do you know where the writing paper is?'

'That's an unusual greeting.' She laid the glove in her lap. 'You look dreadful. What happened in London?'

'Hollow blasts of wind and secret swellings of the seas before a tempest,' he said a little wildly. 'Discords and quarrels and factions . . . Do you know how to write?'

'I was taught my letters,' she replied stiffly. 'With my brother.'

He thrust the pen and ink into her hands. She heard him slam the cupboard doors in the Little Parlour next door. He returned with some paper.

'Please sit here at your table and write what I say.'

She lodged her needle carefully in the glove. 'For what reason?'

'I beg you, Kate. No questions. The matter will explain itself.'

'No, my dear Francis. I've done with "no questions". My life is too much in your hands already.'

'That's what troubles me. God's Blood, Kate! Please. I've been thinking most of the night. Events are unrolling that put you in grave danger . . .'

'What has happened?' The glove slid from her lap onto the floor as she rose to her feet.

'Please write. Then I'll answer your questions. I don't know how to begin, else.'

She watched him go to the window. 'Don't fear. The dogs warn us when anyone comes.'

'So my father lets them run loose now?'

'He thinks it best. We've had a watcher on the Downs.'

He stared at her oddly, as if trying to force together two ill-fitting ideas. Then he took back the inkpot and added water from a jug on a tray, his eyes passing distractedly over the two wine-stained glasses that she and Boomer had used the night before.

'Sit!' he ordered her.

She pulled her stool to the table.

'"My Lord . . . "' Francis began.

'Which lord is this?'

'Any lord. I'm still considering which one is best. Write. Then decide whether or not to trust me.'

Kate gave him a long look, then bent her head to the paper. 'I'm not accustomed to the pen,' she said after a moment of scratching. 'A pox on it!' She glared down at an inky splutter of small blots.

Francis fetched another sheet of paper. 'Do the best you can. I'm not accustomed to forming gentlemanly phrases.'

Kate began again, with great care, fighting her hand's desire to jump and tremble. '"My Lord . . . " There. That's achieved.'

'" . . . Out of the love I bear to some of your friends,"'

Francis dictated. '"I have a care of your preservation . . . " Do I speak too fast?'

He waited for her to catch up. '"Therefore, I would advise you . . . "'

Advise you . . . Advise most fervently . . . Would urgently advise . . . I must leave no doubt, he thought.

'" . . . advise you as you tender your life . . . "'

Yes. That expresses the threat clearly.

'" . . . to devise some excuse to shift your attendance at this Parliament . . . "'

Kate raised her head.

'" . . . this Parliament,"' Francis repeated, looking away, '" . . . for God and man hath concurred to punish the wickedness of this time."'

He made a restless turn around the room while her quill scratched. The words still seemed too mild.

'"And think not slightly of this advertisement, but retire yourself into your country where you may expect the event in safety."'

'Francis . . .'

'Hush.' He stood behind her, where he could watch the set of her shoulders and back of her neck. '"For though there be no appearance of any stir, yet I say they shall receive a terrible blow this Parliament; and yet they shall not see who hurts them."'

Kate's hand, reaching down for the inkpot, froze in midair. He watched her shoulders move gently with her breathing while she thought. Then she dipped the quill into the inkpot and wrote again.

'"This counsel is not to be condemned, because it may do you good and can do you no harm . . . " Are you with me still?'

After a moment, she nodded.

'" . . . for the danger is passed as soon as you have burnt the letter . . . "'

How can I prod the fellow into doing what I want him to do?

He thought for a moment, then resumed. '"And I hope God will give you the grace to make good use of it, to whose holy protection I commend you." Be certain to write "make good use" very clearly.' He read over her shoulder and wondered if he should have her underline 'make good use'. She smelled like fresh air.

'That's the end,' he told her.

'Am I not to sign it?'

'No.' He leaned to take the letter.

Kate pinned it to the table with her fingertips. 'Not yet!' She slipped from under him, still with the letter, even now aware of the heat from his body. 'You said in St Paul's Churchyard that you wanted to save my life. In spite of all reason I believed you. And you should know that, even if you are my enemy, I would save your life if it were in my power. But I must know who will have this letter.'

She held the letter towards the fire as if to throw it onto the flames.

'I'll tell you when I know myself.' Francis paced the room distractedly.

Who indeed?

For certain, the man must be a minister who would be attending Parliament. He must be a Catholic but not a recusant rebel. He must be well-placed but fear to lose his position. Above all, he must be loyal to the Crown.

Not Northumberland, who was going to suffer in any case for his kinsman Percy's treachery. Not Tresham, who might protect the plotters . . . might even know of the plot already . . . and who no longer had a position to lose. Perhaps Monteagle, who was already close to Cecil . . .

'Lord Monteagle.' He watched her face closely. Sweet Lord, it was even more beautiful than he remembered.

'A Catholic lord!' In her agitation, Kate kicked over the

inkpot, unnoticed. 'Why do you, of all people, want to warn a Catholic lord?'

'Because he is also a loyal English subject.'

It took a moment for his implication to hit her.

'You mean him to take this letter to Cecil?' She frowned in confusion.

'I fervently hope so.'

Kate shook her head slowly as she began to understand. 'You mean to betray someone through Monteagle. And are using me!'

'And you don't know whom?'

She stepped forward and slapped him hard. 'You do think me a traitor!'

'No, Kate. You're not the traitor here.'

She slapped him again. 'You brought me here to Powder Mote only to test me. Why don't you just deliver me to that vicious little lapdog of the King?'

She raised her hand to strike again. He stared at her but did not move.

'Mother of God, forgive me . . .' She reached up and rubbed at the red marks of her fingers on the pallor of his cheeks. 'I didn't mean . . .'

'I believe you to be loyal,' he said. 'And I'm staking a great deal on being right.'

She read the letter again. 'I can't betray my fellow Catholics,' she said after a few moments.

'Those madmen would betray you. And many others who are far more innocent than either of us. I hope this letter will prevent rather than betray.'

Father Jerome had used almost the same words, thought Kate.

'I think you must tell me how I am tangled in your double games.'

'I would if I could.' He looked at her unhappily. 'I hope

this letter will force Cecil to head off what he can no longer pretend not to see.'

'I can't betray,' she repeated.

'I believed that I could not. I don't know any longer what I have or have not done.'

She had never seen him so distraught, not even in the warehouse the night they parted.

'I'm groping blindly through a cave,' he said. 'The floor could disappear from under all our feet . . . at any time.'

'Am I in the cave as well?'

'You know that you are. And so is my father.'

Kate nodded. 'I manage to forget for hours at a time down here. It feels so distant from London. Safe. Most of the time.' She shrugged. 'Well. There it is.'

'Will you give me the letter?'

She held it out to him. 'Why did you have me write it?'

'Even the best outcome will be brutal.' He folded the letter carefully. 'As you saw when you wrote, an act of terror is threatened.'

'The "terrible blow".'

'No matter how it unrolls, there will be terror and retribution.' He took her hand and she let him keep it. 'It's best if you don't know all. But, no matter what happens, think what it might mean that a letter of loyal warning is written in your hand. It's not much, but it's the best I can think of at the moment to help keep you safe.'

'You're staking all on Cecil to emerge alive from that cave of yours. Do you trust him?'

'Never.' He looked at her wretchedly. 'I've staked my soul that he truly wants peace for England, but I don't trust him.'

Kate watched Francis ride away again with the letter for Lord Monteagle, on his father's borrowed horse, without even sleeping the night at Powder Mote. If she were to be jealous over Francis, Cecil would be her chief rival.

She returned to mending the glove and tried not to listen for an explosion from the shed where Boomer was working.

When Francis had driven away to Lambeth with the last of the gunpowder, Boomer had not returned to taming the ivy. Instead, he set about extracting the last crusts of salt-petre from their plantation. They re-boiled used liquor, then leached and strained it again and again. Boomer bought more sulphur. He kept on two of the assistants at the stamp mill, and Jem Mawes. He still spent long hours in the incorporation shed.

Then he told her why.

'I'm not so ambitious as Francis,' he said. 'We'll manage with no more than four hundred pounds this time, not four thousand.'

'Will Francis help you?' she asked, with a stab of fear.

'When I know exactly what needs doing.'

She often heard him leave in the middle of the night to go and watch Pangdean.

Kate finished the glove, laid it with its mate on Boomer's bed, then put on her boots and breeches. As there was nothing more to do in the saltpetre shed, she found her gloves and billhook and climbed up onto the roof of the kitchens to continue stripping away the ivy.

Though the days were shortening, she still had more than enough light. From the roof ridge she searched the Downs with her eyes, looking for their watcher. She had seen him only once more after that first time but whenever she left the house the back of her neck told her he was up there.

She saw movement at the crest of the Downs. A cart came into view.

70

The cart was travelling dangerously fast. As it got closer, Kate saw, to her disbelief, that Mary Frith was the driver, sitting on the bench with a pipe clenched between her teeth, her whip flying like a flag. The cart carried something huge and square-cornered, covered with a canvas sail. From under the sail came angry roars that dwindled, from time to time, into whimpers.

Kate sheathed her knife and climbed carefully down the ladder from the kitchen roof. The cart rumbled across the moat bridge and burst out from the gatehouse arch.

'Hellish roads, duck!' shouted Mary. 'You'd best have plenty of goose grease ready to soothe my aching arse . . . Whoaa!' She hauled on the reins. 'Where's Boomer Quoynt? He owes me for this.' She swung down from the driver's seat and grabbed the bridle of the nearest sweating, jittery horse.

'Quoynt?' she yelled. 'Brought your parcel.'

The parcel snuffled.

Kate ran past Mary to the cart. Heart thumping, she began to tug at the knotted ropes holding down the sail cover.

'All's well!' she crooned as she struggled with a knot. 'Don't fear. All's well.'

She abandoned her struggle. 'Apples,' she cried to Boomer, with whom she collided as she ran into the house just as he was coming out.

By the time she returned with her pockets full of apples, Mary's groom was holding the horses and Boomer and Mary had untied the ropes securing the cover. Kate seized the canvas and hauled it off the cage on the cart. Caledonian Meg peered with watery eyes from a reeking, unhappy heap on the floor.

'Kate, take care,' cried Boomer before he could stop himself.

She climbed onto the cart and thrust her hand between the bars, holding an apple.

The bear stood up, weaving slightly like a sailor grown used to a heaving deck. Staggered forward, pigeon-toed. Her moist nose searched the air from top to bottom and bottom to top. Then it sniffed delicately at Kate's wrist.

'Oh, my darling queen,' murmured Kate. 'I thought you were dead. Sweet Meg. Oh, my sweet, brave, noble Meg.'

The long tongue wrapped around the apple. Caledonian Meg gave a moan of what sounded like delight and swiped a second apple from Kate's hand.

'The horses tried to run away from her the whole way from London,' Mary said to Boomer as they watched Kate reach in with her other hand to scratch the bear behind the ears. 'Cut three hours off the journey.'

'I thought we could put her in the old cow barn. Fence in that bit of paddock behind,' said Boomer.

'Tracked her all the way to bloody Colchester for you.' Mary began to rummage in her pockets for her tobacco pouch.

Meg wedged her bristly snout between the bars of the cage, offering it to Kate's scratching. Boomer walked over to the cart. 'Are you pleased, Kate?'

'You know that I am.' Still dazed by astonishment and joy, she turned to look down at the half-familiar face with its alien scars and lines drawn by time. Boomer smiled back up.

He looks as happy as I feel, she thought. She wanted to

leap down and hug him. This thought and the open delight in his smile suddenly made her feel shy. 'How did you know?' she asked.

'You told me. I heard.'

The magnitude behind these simple words made her unsteady.

'When?'

'The day you stroked the goose.' Boomer held her gaze. 'Now, ask anything else you like.'

She had to look away. 'Within reason, of course?' She pretended to find a flea on Meg's snout.

'I don't see why reason need come into it.'

71

In London, Francis lurked outside Monteagle's house, well-wrapped in his cloak, his hair covered by his hat. Monteagle himself walked right by him, returning from dinner elsewhere, but the Catholic lord was accompanied by four chattering acquaintances and their serving men. Francis considered merely shoving Kate's letter under the door. But he could not be certain that a dog might not chew it to pieces or a careless foot might not kick it aside. Just before the watch grew suspicious enough to ask him his business, he thrust the letter into the hand of a startled serving maid who had emerged to empty a chamberpot.

After returning to Powder Mote and digesting the news that the estate now included a bear, Francis slept for two days. He woke on the second evening and rode down to the coast. Here, he stripped off his clothes and swam in the sea to wash himself clean. After the summer, the water was not yet icy. The late October air was kinder to him than his own thoughts.

He sat on a fallen chalk boulder to let himself dry in the last of the sun. A cold heaviness still dragged at his throat. He stared at the shallows where waves churned up a muddy cloud of sand and shingle.

Too much could go wrong. Guido might unaccountably

escape capture. The powder made in Lambeth might be better than Francis had intended. Monteagle might not take the letter to Cecil.

Or the unthinkable might be true, as Bacon had as good as said. That Cecil intended for things to go wrong, so that he would be left as the only surviving minister. And he had needed a traitor, not to expose as the King's enemy, but to carry out his own bloody work.

If so, Francis would have helped to unravel England.

I would have to shoot myself, he thought. But first, I would kill Cecil.

'Here you are,' said his father from behind him. 'Waving your prick at the mermaids?' Boomer squatted down on the shingle. 'It's no time to lose your grip, France . . . Don't give me that murdering stare. I can see how things are with you . . . Jem Mawes has just told me that someone landed a load of provisions and equipment at Pangdean two nights ago.'

'Why would Jem Mawes tell you that?'

'Because I asked him to keep an eye on the place.' Boomer held up a warning hand. 'Don't risk a single word, or I swear I will clout you, even if you are near dying of self-reproach. Come to Pangdean to see for yourself before you pass judgement on the state of my wits.' Boomer stood up. 'Come with me now, France. I fear the matter is growing urgent.'

'Mars help us,' murmured Francis, 'if we were ever to take on that crew.' Sliding into place beside his father, he could barely see him in the darkness, a mere three feet away. 'Forty-two warhorses, give or take. It's a wonder they remain undetected.'

'Not entirely undetected,' Boomer allowed himself to murmur.

Before joining his father on the hill, Francis had made a clandestine survey of the Pangdean stables. Pangdean was a modest gentleman's house. Forty-two horses were too many for the stables to hold. Some were tethered in empty store sheds and other outbuildings. But there were only two grooms, his father said, both of them no doubt now asleep in the hayloft, exhausted from doing the work of ten.

Boomer continued to study the faint points of light below them. He turned his head to listen to a rustling in the grass. 'Rabbits . . .'

They eased themselves back from their observation point. Motionless again in the shadows of some gorse, they listened to the hillside above them before moving away.

Solid walls, locked gates, thought Francis. At least forty armed soldiers hidden inside. And Hammick. And an unknown number of serving men.

They moved in silence for a quarter of a mile.

'What are we going to do about them?' he asked his father when they were far enough from Pangdean to talk freely.

'There's one piece of good luck,' said Boomer, ignoring the question. 'You will have noticed. No external sentries. In all the times I've watched the place, I've never seen a sentry outside the walls. If they're who I think they are, their need for secrecy is even greater than their fear of enemies.'

'Who the devil are they?'

'Wait for daylight. There's someone I want you to see before I say more.'

His father was the general again. Francis tried to accept his role as lieutenant with much grace as he could muster. It was too late to change a working relationship of nineteen years, but the two years abroad with his own command made him restive.

'I've already seen Hammick,' he said. 'When I went to grovel. Have you forgotten? I told you then I thought him an unpleasant rogue.'

'Not Hammick. A man you've not yet seen.'

They wrapped themselves in their cloaks and slept in a hollow carved out of the gorse by grazing sheep.

'That's Hammick sure enough,' murmured Francis.

'Look at the other.'

They had circled around to the east of Pangdean Place so they could use the spyglass without catching the morning sun on the lens.

'Quickly!' said Boomer. 'He's turning back into the house.'

The tiny figure of Hammick stopped to look up at the downs behind the house, where they had lain the night before.

'You feel us out here, don't you, you murdering get?' said Boomer under his breath. 'As a viper feels the tread of a foot through its belly.'

Francis moved the glass. Got him! A face leapt into clear view for an instant before it turned away. He kept the glass trained a little longer on the dark red head lit by copper glints. Then he lowered the glass in astonishment. That was not the companion he expected for a retired merchant with a swordsman's hands and assassin's eyes.

So young, barely more than a handsome youth.

And over-splendid for the south English coast near the fishing village of Brighthelmstone. The youth wore a white silk doublet and ribboned shoes to take the air in a stable yard.

'Can a retired London merchant afford such a well-garnished *privado*?' he murmured.

Boomer showed his teeth briefly. 'You've a shallow mind, France. I fear that Master Hammick means to use him far worse than that.'

'Must be his son, then,' said Francis.

They followed the cover of a gully down towards the sea. The cliff-top peeped and rustled. Below them the shale clattered softly as it fell back after the retreating waves. They climbed down the cliff and walked, out of sight from the track above, in the direction of their horses, left grazing near Brighthelmstone.

'Who is he?' asked Francis.

'I want you to tell me. To prove I'm not mad in truth.'

The two of them leaned forward, cutting across the offshore wind.

'I fear that she's back,' said Boomer. 'They can't lay her ghost now that she's dead any more than they could while she was alive. He could have been his grandmother in disguise.'

'I may clout you.'

'Just wait.'

When they reached Powder Mote, Boomer left his horse in the forecourt. 'Kate!' he shouted from the entrance hall. 'Kate, are you here?'

'Of course, I'm here.' She appeared from the service range, wearing breeches and an apron.

'Good,' said Boomer. 'That's good.'

'More to the point, so are both of you. Back safely.' She looked from father to son. 'What did you find?'

'Wait.' Boomer disappeared up to his chamber.

Francis and Kate waited. To soften the uneasy silence, Francis scratched the golden stubble on his chin. He had rolled up his sleeves.

Kate watched the long muscles moving under the browned skin of his forearm. 'You still distrust me, don't you?'

How dark his eyes were today. So different from Boomer's.

While Francis was still struggling to think how to explain, Boomer jogged back down the stairs.

'She gave me her portrait,' said Boomer. 'As a token, but that's a tale for another time. I was the piper who got paid – that'll do for now. Tell me now in all honesty that she's not back, crying "Vengeance!".'

He held out a miniature portrait in a golden frame studded with red stones, smaller than the broad palm on which it lay. 'Look at that face, France. Don't tell me you didn't just see it at Pangdean.'

Francis took the small oval frame between finger and thumb and held it to the window. As he studied the face in the portrait he felt his thoughts begin to settle. Not yet into full understanding, but with a first trickle of clarity.

'That's Mary, Queen of Scots,' said Kate.

Boomer's hand hovered possessively over the jewelled miniature still in his son's grasp. 'Whose followers would have made her Queen of England. A legitimate Catholic queen, in place of Elizabeth, the Anglican bye-blow.'

Boomer took back the picture. 'Then Elizabeth had her beheaded . . . It's all in the book. Best if you read it, then we'll speak further.'

He took the portrait back up to his chamber.

72

In the top room of the gatehouse, with Kate looking on, Francis prised away the false panelling over the secret hiding place. The folds of the wrapping around the *Liber Ignium* were not as he had last left them.

How my father must have enjoyed making a fool of me all those years, Francis thought as he unwrapped the book. However much Boomer might deny it. Laughing at Francis while his son was despairing at his soundness of mind.

Francis knew that he owed his father an apology, but he still wanted to clout him.

The page after his own final entry was newly written in his father's hand. When Francis began to read, he felt his discomfiture change to an icy stillness.

My son,

I have written to you that a man cannot escape his conscience. Now I must tell you some of what lies behind my nightmares and midnight ravings, loath as I am to relive a single detail of that day. Twenty-three years ago in Scotland, a newborn babe was kidnapped. I found his mother with her throat cut, still dressed in the birthing gown, with the bodies of her women nearby. I had found no sign of the men whom I thought I had come to help kill.

*After a further search of the castle, I saw that my employers
had lied when they hired me. I had not come to wipe out a
nest of vipers plotting to murder Elizabeth and set Mary of
Scotland on England's throne. I had not helped to deliver a
warning to all other would-be traitors. I had helped murder
old men, boys and mothers of newborn babes, for reasons I did
not understand. However, I had begun to have fearful suspicions.*

*It is easier to write of the rage and shame I felt than to
speak the words to your face. War requires hard deeds. A
soldier makes his peace with himself as best he can. But that
massacre of innocents still haunts me.*

*I had been too eager for the fee. Or perhaps I was merely
driven by a restless need to be in action. I have forgot now.
Whatever my reason for carelessness, I had scanted my usual
checks. Not only had I been taken for a fool, I feared that I had
been duped into what might prove to be a dangerous association. If they had not come to kill traitors, the men I had accompanied might themselves be traitors.*

I had to decide whether to finish my work or to flee.

*If I fled leaving the castle intact, my employers, who were
then standing off the coast in boats, would know for certain
that I had baulked. And they would ask themselves, 'Why?' I
would be in danger for the rest of my life and never know from
what quarter it might come.*

*As I could do no more harm to the poor souls in the castle, I
elected to finish. It was not a challenging task, for the cliffs
beneath the castle were honeycombed with small caverns. You
will understand how simple it was to knock the castle's feet
from under it and drop it into the sea. It would have been an
elegant and pleasing piece of work, had I liked the reasons for
it better.*

*I had agreed with the leader of the raiding party that unless
the condition of the sea or the debris of the castle prevented it, a*

boat would collect me from the shore. I was now certain that whoever might come for me in that little cove would instead smash my skull. I preferred to let them think I had been injured or died in my own explosion.

The more I thought, the clearer it became. The child was the sole purpose of the raid. All witnesses to the kidnap were then murdered. Then, by destroying the castle I was to erase the evidence of the murders.

I also asked myself why the raiders had also wrecked the castle, methodically and with deliberation, room by room, tearing away panelling, hacking at the floors, hauling down hangings – but then suddenly stopped, leaving half the cushions in a parlour untouched on their stools while the others lay gutted and strewn across the floor. I concluded that they had found whatever they were looking for.

They took the child. And also some necessary object. Some talisman. Some testimony. Some proof.

Proof of what? Who was that child?

You must know two more things:

Set into the floor of the secret Catholic chapel in the cellars, I found a stone, newly carved with the Latin inscription: 'Hic inhumator corpus Davidi Alexanderi Stuarti'. In case you have forgot all your Latin, this means: 'Here is entombed the body of David Alexander Stuart'. Dead only a few months, by the date on the stone.

The Latin was followed by a line in Scots, which I will not try to remember. But the meaning was clear. 'This son of an earthly queen has gone to join the son of the Heavenly Queen'.

I believe that the dead David Alexander Stuart was the father of the kidnapped babe. And I hardly need tell you who I believe to be the mother of David Alexander, though his father was no king. His birth was never acknowledged openly by the Queen but rumour had often spoken of him. The babe, his son, Mary Stuart's grandson, was of no use to anyone without proof of his lineage. With this proof, the babe had claim to the English throne as lawful as any Elizabeth ever had.

And, lastly, the man now known as Hammick was the Englishman who led that raiding party and carried away the child. He knew me at once when we first met again earlier this summer in Brighthelmstone. I have gone to great lengths to ensure that he believes I do not know him. There is some use, after all, in being taken for an addled old fool.

73

'But Catesby and his crew hope to make James's daughter, the Princess Elizabeth, their new monarch,' protested Francis. 'Not the grandson of Mary, Queen of Scots. Robin Catesby is an honourable man, if nothing else. He wouldn't deceive his followers about his intentions.'

'A man who intends as he does has no honour,' said Boomer.

'You and I are both guilty of deeds almost as savage.'

'But not in peacetime. Not against our own countrymen,' Boomer replied viciously. 'And I, for one, do not lay claim to honour.'

That night, after napping briefly in the late afternoon, Francis and Boomer then waited in a crevice in the cliff below Pangdean. Some time after midnight, the forty-two horses were brought down to be exercised on the beach.

From their cliff crevice, the two Quoynts listened for more information, but the riders' voices were as muffled as their horses' hoofs.

After a time, the horses passed by again and began to climb back up the steep path from the beach. There was a scrabbling and the sound of falling rocks.

'*Quedado!*'

'*Hijo de puta . . . !*'

The voices were hushed at once. But not before Boomer and Francis had turned to each other in the faint light.

Spanish.

'Would you dare call your horse the son of a whore?' whispered Boomer when the riders had disappeared over the top of the cliff.

This must be some of the Spanish help promised in the letter to Catesby that Cecil did not write.

'They may be preparing to move out,' Boomer murmured, after they had watched Pangdean for three hours in the grey early morning light. They were back at their vantage point above the house. 'I've never before seen so much activity. Nor so many signs of the numbers hidden in the house. I wonder how long we have.'

'Today is the last day of October,' said Francis. Five days before Catesby's 'Blow'.

'They're perfectly placed to march on London,' said Boomer. 'A night's march away from a position just south of the City.'

With the young man Boomer believed to be the grandson of Mary, Queen of Scots. Another Stuart pretender to the throne of England.

Francis could not imagine Robin in league with a man like Hammick. But here was Catesby's Spanish support. Real, not just forged promises. Therefore, those disguised ships off Gravesend might also be real. There might be other houses like Pangdean Place, all along the English coast, concealing still more Spanish soldiers. Here was the likely reason for Robin's stubborn faith in God's Will.

Francis had a sudden image of Westminster exploding, a hole gaping where the Hall had been, like the fiery mouth of Hell. An image of Digby holding the Princess at sword-point. Of Percy slitting the Duke of York's five-year-old throat.

Of the King and all his ministers raining down from the sky into the flames.

'We must watch again tonight,' murmured Boomer. 'Decide just how soon we think they mean to move.'

'And then alert the Sheriff in Lewes to bring the militia.'

Francis waited for the third sighting before he let himself believe his eyes. His first glimpse of the figure crossing the rear courtyard to the stables caught him off guard. Hammick walked beside the man, talking with intensity. The man listened, but all the while his head turned like a hawk searching for quarry in the grass.

Francis willed himself to steadiness until the man came out of the stables again, still walking beside Hammick. But both he and Hammick went into the house without turning their faces to the watchers on the hillside.

If the man did not emerge again until after dark, Francis might never be certain.

If the man wore his hat pulled low he still might never be certain.

Francis and Boomer shared a bottle of watered ale and two bread rolls as their breakfast.

But the man came out into the stable yard again in mid-morning. He climbed onto the mounting block, holding his hat. While the man waited for his horse to be led up, Francis risked a flash of light off the lens of the spyglass.

There was no longer any doubt. Even with the glass, Francis could not see the hazel eyes clearly, but the full lower lip, pushed forward between the curving moustaches, was unmistakable, as was that sudden hawk-like turn of the head.

However, Francis also knew that it had just become impossible to alert the Sheriff in Lewes, or any other Crown official.

'The man in the overcoat and long, slashed sleeves is Sir Francis Bacon,' Francis murmured.

He felt unexpected joy.

Cecil was not a traitor. Merely a clever man who used any means to achieve his ends. Devious and dangerous. But not a traitor. Bacon spoke with political precision as well as personal venom when he said that Francis was serving the wrong man.

Bacon, not Cecil, meant to become the highest-ranking statesman to survive. Bacon, with the family position and the intellect to become the new Chief Minister to the new Catholic king.

The wily Cecil had fallen into the trap of thinking himself more cunning than anyone else. More cunning even than his own brilliant, dark-souled cousin.

Try to think like Cecil, Francis told himself now. Would he want his cousin arrested as a traitor and the entire family thrown into question? Cecil's own role would be examined. The Spanish truce would be threatened and the populace alarmed when Cecil did not offer either a solution or revenge.

Cecil would want the matter solved quietly, Francis decided. And for the Pretender, like the gunpowder at Bridge House, to cease to exist.

Then, with absolute certainty, Francis changed his mind. Beyond all doubt, Cecil would want to keep the Pretender alive, in reserve, as a counter in his game of diplomacy with Spain.

'What shall we do now?' he asked.

'Robert Cecil's cousin,' muttered his father thoughtfully. 'I fear we'd be unwise to call in the Sheriff just yet.'

'I must ride to London to warn Cecil.'

Boomer shook his head. 'Stop Hammick and Bacon first. Then take good news.'

That same night, in London, a shadowy boat slid away from the Lambeth shore of the Thames. It carried no lantern.

Hidden under the apparent cargo of bundled firewood, were eighty pounds of gunpowder.

The man who called himself Guido let the current carry him silently while two wherries crossed a little farther downstream. Then he bent and pulled at the oars, pointing his boat at the Westminster shore. A fierce joy fuelled his strokes. He had already ferried two loads of powder across the river and stowed them in the great cellar under Westminster Palace. Still more powder waited in the waterside storehouse on Catesby's Lambeth estate. He had at least four more crossings to make but he felt that he could row all night. Could row to France, to Spain, or even to Cathay if his purpose required.

The others might plot and scurry about, but in the end, it would come down to him. He was their secret weapon in a way they did not yet fully realize. Not even Robin.

At his back, the dark silent bulk of Westminster Palace waited for him. He looked over his shoulder as he pulled at his oars. How he would change that place. Like God sending fire to Gomorrah.

Morning. Tuesday the fifth of November. The first day of the new Parliament. The sun would be bright.

He pulled again on his oars and closed his eyes for a moment to let imagination shine more brightly behind his eyelids.

The golden royal barge, its pennants snapping in the breeze pulling up to Westminster Steps. The King stepping out, followed by his oldest son, Henry, Prince of Wales. Courtiers jostling to catch the royal eye, men who had sold estates to cover their backs in silk and velvet just for this day.

I will save them all from bitter disappointment, thought Guido. If the King is allowed to live, he will disappoint all his subjects just as he has disappointed the Catholics. He will lie. Promise favour, then snatch it back. Promise freedom, then persecute more harshly than before.

Guido lifted his oars and let his boat drift silently again while a coal barge crossed his path heading upriver. The only sound he made was the small dripping of his oars. When the barge was safely past, he pulled again towards the dark Westminster bank.

In his mind, he saw himself hold the slow-match to the fuse. Because he was only rehearsing the great deed in his head, he could take time to admire his handiwork. He watched the flame leap from match to fuse. He watched the hot spider of flame scuttle along the fuse and disappear into a crevice in the stacked firewood that hid the gunpowder barrels.

I'm doing this for all of you, he thought. For all English Catholics. And for you most of all, Robin.

He saw the flash, heard the dull thump that shook the earth under his feet and made the water jump out of the Thames. He felt the heat of the flames flash along his bones and melt the ice that had settled long ago on his heart.

The floors burst upwards as if punched from below by a giant fist. Black smoke uncoiled and spread in a choking cloud across the surface of the Thames. The shattered floors of Westminster Palace flew up and up, through the roiling smoke, taking the roof with them. Then the wreckage began to fall back into the inferno below and with it fell the bodies of most of England's most powerful men.

Outside the precinct of Westminster, people watched in horror and disbelief as the smoke flowed towards them through the alleys and avenues like a black tidal wave. Then they turned and ran. Some waited too long. The black cloud rolled over them and squeezed the air from their lungs.

And bodies still fell out of the bright sky into the cellars where he had set off the blast. Ministers, lords, Anglican bishops, Members of Parliament. A wondrous downpour of enemies tumbling into the fiery gaping jaws of Satan. He saw hands, boots, arms and legs, hats. The King's severed head, turning like a ball, looking astonished, the crown still in place.

Well done, my son. God's voice reached his ear like a whirlwind. He stepped onto the vast outstretched hand and was lifted away to safety. *Only you and I have the power to change the world.*

It will happen, he thought. Very soon.

The little water steps at Westminster were dark and silent. With the roar of the coming flames in his ears and the awe-struck faces of his fellow conspirators warming his thoughts, he swung the first powder keg up out of the boat as if it were a feather pillow, to hide with the others already in the great cellar.

74

'Most straightforward. Bring down Pangdean with everyone in it.' Boomer turned his wine cup in his large hand, then rubbed the silver rim on his sleeve. 'Easy enough to do. But not yet. Not without proof of what they intend. Unless we want to hang for wanton destruction and murder.'

'Cecil will want proof that Bacon was there with Hammick and that young man who looks like Mary, Queen of Scots,' said Francis.

They pushed away their empty plates, the appetite raised by two nights on the downs finally subdued.

'We must get inside the house,' said Boomer.

'And out again,' snapped Kate, who was listening with horrified disbelief in her dark eyes. 'Sweet Mother Mary! Won't one of you say it? "And out again!" After the two of you – if you just happen to feel so inclined – have dealt with Master Hammick, your mysterious red-haired man and forty armed Spanish soldiers.'

She banged down her own cup. Wine slopped onto the table as she refilled it from the jug. The silver mermaid stood near her elbow, but these were neither the meal nor the circumstances Kate had imagined when she knelt beside the cupboard with her oily rag.

Boomer laid a soothing hand on her arm. 'We know who

the young man is. The mystery is what he expects to gain from being here.'

'Kate made a fair point about getting out of the house again,' said Francis sharply.

'I know it, France! For the love of God and all the saints! D'you think I don't know?'

They left their horses grazing high on the downs and climbed to the beacon where they could be certain they were not overheard.

'The odds are twenty to one against us,' said Francis.

'Mad,' agreed Boomer. 'But less mad than allowing Hammick and his Spaniards to march on London.' His hair showed like white smoke against the night. 'And we're not calculating straightforward battle odds. We're firemasters, not common soldiers. We have our own weapons.'

They stared into darkness that was thick and phlegm-like with sea mist. At last, Boomer sighed.

'Stealth and deception, France. We must fight with those. Hammick already thinks my wits are addled . . . I hope. And don't forget that I'm a suspected Roman. We must use both rumours. We must astonish them so that they don't begin to fear us until it's too late.'

They collected their horses and rode down to the sea. Up to their knees in the breaking waves, the horses were in far better spirits than their riders. Boomer and Francis rode along the water's edge to a stretch of open shingle that offered no cover to listeners. They reined in their mounts and stood looking out into the fallen cloud that covered the sea.

'We have a siege,' said Boomer quietly. 'But no besieging army that we dare call on. There's no point breaching the walls if we've no army to send in afterwards. Therefore, we can't simply mine Pangdean, although I have already prepared a few wormholes in the caves below the house, just in case. Nor do we want to kill our quarry. Reason says that we must get inside the house and survive long enough to do whatever we must.'

Francis tried to wait as he had done in his apprentice days, for his father to lay out all his thoughts first. But his imagination darted around Pangdean Place, testing for weakness. 'Like the Greeks, we must "burn the topless towers of Ilium",' he said thoughtfully.

'It's vital that we take both Hammick and the young Pretender alive . . . Whoa, boy . . .' Boomer steadied his gelding, which had decided to test its chances for a swim in the sea. They stood again, listening to the slap and clatter of the waves. 'Once in, we can reduce their numbers enough to improve our own odds.' Boomer tossed the idea to Francis with a questioning glance.

'But as soon as we've killed the first few, the rest will withdraw to a defensible position,' replied Francis.

'Just so.'

'Even if we reduced them by ten . . .'

'Still desperate odds. But eagles don't need to hunt in flocks. We must think like eagles.'

'Noble words, sir,' said Francis lightly. 'But not so easy to act on.'

'We need a stiletto, not a broadsword,' said Boomer. 'You're the subtle mind, France. Put it to work at once. We've not got long.'

They had ridden on twenty paces before Francis realized that his father had asked his advice. And seemed prepared to accept it.

The first fragile edge of an idea was just slipping into his mind.

When Kate went up to bed that night, she heard someone in her room. Boomer was rummaging in a corner by the light of a lantern, near the painted angel in the fur hat. He pushed aside a chest and vanished deeper into the shadows.

'Have you seen a lion?' he asked Kate over his shoulder.

'How large? Have you looked in the attics?'

She lit a candle and followed Boomer and his lantern up a narrow flight of wooden stairs to the attics, a series of unfinished chambers under the roof in the wing set at right angles to the large attic room that Francis occupied. House grooms had once slept here on pallets. Now the chambers were the edge of a sea where time had washed up an astonishing range of flotsam and weed.

Kate spied a glint of gold behind a set of wooden golf clubs and a pierced metal Moorish lantern. She climbed over a musty saddle made for some creature not shaped like a horse.

'Is your lion wearing a crown?' she called to Boomer.

Together, they wrestled the creature out into full view. It was made of gilded leather stretched over a wooden frame, a little larger than life-size, *couchant*, on a gilded base, with its forepaws extended neatly in front like a dozing cat.

'The Venetians know how to design a triumph.' Boomer dusted the beast's gilded leather hide with an old saddlecloth. 'And their fireworks aren't bad.'

'It's beautiful,' said Kate. 'Fierce. How did it end up at Powder Mote?'

'Satisfied princes like to show their gratitude. This one was unfortunately short of cash. He gave me a bridle inlaid with ivory as well. Sold that a few years back.'

He bent to examine the joint where the lion's haunch was attached to its flank. Then he walked around to peer into the lion's half-open mouth. He ran his thumb down one of the ivory fangs.

'He'll do,' he said.

*   *   *

'France's idea. Persuade the soldiers to gather in one place,' said Boomer when the three of them had wrestled it down into his sleeping chamber. 'The lion will be our *ducdame*.' He pronounced it '*duke-dah-may*'. 'As Master Shakespeare would have it. A device for drawing fools into a circle.'

Francis gave his father a sharp look. 'I didn't know you frequented the playhouses.'

'I told you, France, there's a great deal you don't know.' Boomer straightened up. 'Is that someone down in the hall? I asked Jem Mawes to stop here before he rides home tonight.'

'Did your brother ever carry contraband?' Boomer asked Jem, while Francis went down into the cellars in search of another cask of claret.

'That would have been against the law, sir.' Jem glanced uneasily at Kate, who made an excuse to leave the two men alone.

'Are you saying my brother was a smuggler?' asked Jem when Kate had gone.

Boomer shook his large head impatiently. 'I'm not a prosecuting judge, Jem. I want to know how he died. There were no underwater rocks at that beach to account for the dent in his skull.'

'Perhaps he did land a few strange catches,' Jem admitted.

'Did he ever land goods at Pangdean?'

'It's near where he was drowned.' Jem looked at his tightly linked hands. 'I believe he did, sir. Yes. At Pangdean.' His voice was so low Boomer could barely hear it. 'They paid well. He gave me nine pounds towards a boat of my own.'

'How certain are you that he earned the money at Pangdean?'

'I KNOW! Because I helped him land it there! All right?' Jem looked startled to find himself shouting at Boomer Quoynt. 'Sorry, sir.'

Boomer waved away the apology. 'Shelvy had the misfortune to work for a man who kills all his witnesses.'

'They never saw me,' said Jem, turning pale.

'And it's just as well for your father that they didn't. . . . and for you, of course.' Boomer gave the young fisherman a little time to take in what he had just heard. Then he asked, 'Will you help us avenge your brother's death? I believe I know who killed him.'

75

After Jem left, Boomer and Francis retrieved the *Liber Ignium* from the gatehouse and took it to the Great Hall.

Kate tried to read over their shoulders without being detected. Having already been allowed once to read the book reserved only for Quoynts, she did not want to press her luck. She glimpsed the words:

Compounds:

To Make Sparks
To Make Fire
To Make Smoke
To Make Force

'Aha!' cried Boomer.

Kate found a reason to walk past again to see where he and Francis had bent their heads.

Greek Fire . . .

Boomer glanced up and smiled. Kate smiled back although she was sick with terror at what the two of them meant to do. Even though her knowing it proved beyond all doubt that they both trusted her.

'To project flames . . .' muttered Francis, leafing through the pages.

Boomer blew out a gust of air. 'Three days,' he said. 'At least it's not four thousand pounds of powder.'

Francis suppressed a flinch and gave a half-smile. 'I know you've made the necessary powder already. I saw it in the shed.' He was damned if he would let Boomer announce the stuff at the last minute with a flourish of triumph.

'It's so late that it's hardly worth going to bed,' said Kate. 'But I think I'll go anyway.'

'Kate, tomorrow, would you be kind enough to clean the lion?' Francis asked. There was a beat of silence, then they all laughed.

'Lions, bears . . .' She pulled an imaginary forelock and backed out of the room in a servile hunch.

I could lose both of them in a single day, she thought.

The next morning, they explored, looking for a base closer to Pangdean Place. They decided on the deserted village of Telscomb, to the east of Pangdean. They hoped to work there undetected. Local rumour blamed both the marauding French and the great Black Death for the desertion of Telscomb. Regardless of the truth, local people still avoided the place for fear of a lingering contagion by either ill luck or the plague.

From their return after dinner until long after dark, Boomer and Francis huddled over scraps of paper on which Francis made sketches of Pangdean. He sketched the shape of its outer walls, the courtyards they had stared at for so many hours, and all that he could remember of the interior from his single humiliating visit.

They discussed where they might set charges.

'Even with Jem, we're too few.'

'Use me.' Kate held the lion's crown up to the fire to inspect her new gilt paint for any bare patches.

'No,' said both Quoynts in unison.

'How safe will I be if you're both dead?' She pretended to be engrossed in the crown during the thoughtful silence that followed her question. 'I can reload a musket.'

'Enlisting Kate would solve the problem of tactics,' said Boomer. 'We could put her here on the west wall, with Jem to the east, closer to the stables.'

'But she must have a horse, to get away,' said Francis. 'Even at the risk that it might alert the others.'

'Did I say she could not have a horse?'

Francis set off into the dark with a load on his back. Boomer went up to his chamber and closed the door.

Kate stood for a moment in the great hall. Then she took the crown upstairs to the lion, which was now in her chamber. Boomer had removed its rear haunches at the joints and taken them away. Kate peered inside the beast at the stout wooden framework and the bent iron nails that held it to the base.

Suddenly it was no longer a lion but a lion-shaped void. Inexplicably, the interior felt larger and more filled with mysterious corners than the outward beast. In that void the future for all of them would rest.

She found her cloth and began to polish the gilded leather hide. She had already polished it twice that day and had to take care that she did not rub the gilding entirely away. But she was not merely helping to prepare a modern Trojan horse. She was readying a magic talisman to protect the two creatures she now loved best on earth, though she had not yet admitted it, even to herself.

*   *   *

The following morning, Francis reported that the preparations at Pangdean suggested that Hammick would march within two or three days.

'He'll want to arrive at London just after Parliament goes up,' Boomer judged. 'In his place, I'd wait until the people begin to recover from their first blind terror, decide the world hasn't ended after all and start looking around for someone to tell them what to do next. They'll march all night on the fourth, I reckon. Then wait south of the river for the Spanish ships to sail up the Thames when they see the smoke. I reckon we have two days.'

He explained their tactics to his small army: Francis, Kate and Jem. His finger traced lines on the sketched maps as he showed them where to run after firing their fuses.

'Count aloud to thirty as you run. That's how long you will have to reach safety. Here, for you, Jem.' Boomer moved his finger over the map that Francis had drawn. 'Kate, you'll be here.'

He made Kate practise running and counting over a comparable piece of ground near Powder Mote and showed her how to move through the dark.

Francis dragged a handcart to an unused sheep shelter at the deserted village of Telscomb. The lion's intended contents then made the same journey on the backs of Francis and Boomer, wrapped in oiled cloth. And finally, Boomer finished mining the caves below Pangdean.

On the night of the second of November, Boomer took Kate to Pangdean to show her exactly where she must go and what she would find when she got there.

On the last day before they made their move, Boomer made Kate and Jem repeat the sequence of actions each must follow:

Jem was to wait to the east of Pangdean Place. Once Francis

and Boomer were inside the house, he would move into position to free as many of the Spanish horses as he could. Both Kate and Jem would listen for the first large explosion in the house. Jem was to fire his charge first, then Kate.

'There's little risk to Jem or me,' protested Kate. 'You fret about yourselves.'

'Just don't call out our names,' said Francis.

In London, on the night of Sunday, 3 November, 1605, Thomas Percy summoned Catesby and Tom Wintour to an urgent meeting at The Duck and Drake.

'I've just heard from Tresham,' he said. 'Monteagle's had a letter warning him to stay away from the Opening of Parliament.'

Tom Wintour glanced fearfully at neighbouring drinkers.

'Does the letter say why?' asked Catesby.

'The details don't matter,' said Wintour. 'It's enough that a Catholic lord has been warned to avoid the Opening. We're undone.'

'Steady, Tom.' Catesby laid a hand on Wintour's arm. 'Hold your nerve. The men-at-arms haven't yet knocked on our doors.' He turned back to Percy.

Percy shook his long silver head. 'The letter warned only that a terrible blow would punish the wicked and advised Monteagle to make some excuse to stay away from London.'

'A vague warning received by a single Catholic lord is no reason for us to falter,' said Catesby.

Wintour groaned between clenched teeth.

Percy rose to his feet. 'I'll go to Syon. Northumberland's still trusted at court, Papist or not. I might learn more from the gossip in his household.'

Catesby and Wintour watched him go.

'It doesn't matter what more he learns,' said Wintour. 'The damage is done. You must see that. We must pull back now.'

'On the contrary, there's nothing left for us but action. I persevere, with or without you, Tom. But I'd fear nothing if you were at my side.'

After a moment, Wintour slumped down on his stool. 'I'm too far in,' he said to the tabletop. 'We're all too far in. It's too late to pull back. You're right in that. Nothing but the details are left to be decided now.'

'You must have faith in God and in our friends abroad.' Catesby stood up and tugged his cape over his shoulders. 'It's time for me to ride north to meet Digby. Dear Tom, will you come pray with me first?'

On the night of the third of November, Jem picked up the lion in an unlit boat from the beach at Hove just below Powder Mote, and rowed to a small cave near Pangdean. The three men hauled the lion up the cliffs to the sheep shelter for final loading and priming.

When the lion was ready, Jem stood watch, as he had only a short, easy run to his position for the next day. Boomer and Francis curled up in their cloaks and slept for two hours until time to set off.

After the men had left Powder Mote, Kate loaded the caliver and other guns too heavy to carry at a run. Then she wrapped them lightly in oiled cloth, with cartouches of powder, unlit slow matches, flint and steel, wadding and charred cloth squares.

She could not sleep. Before dawn, she would leave the guns at strategic points on the estate, the big caliver last, at Boomer's 'church'. Then ride to the downs above Pangdean, hide her horse, and slip downhill into position.

76

Monday, 4 November 1605

Dawn.

The first faint glow. A strange apparition moved along the cliff-top path towards Pangdean Place. A handcart pulled by a tall, fair-haired man jolted over the rutted mud. A second man, equally tall, with a head of white hair, pushed the cart from behind, with one hand steadying the cart's passenger. The passenger was veiled, like the statue of a saint carried in a procession.

'Shit!' muttered the younger man, pulling the cart. The passenger swayed dangerously.

'Don't fret. I've got a hand up his arse,' said Boomer.

The cart jolted back up out of the rut and began to run easily again.

Francis lifted his head. 'Where are the sentries? We could use some help.' He spoke loudly enough to be heard on the hillside above them.

They advanced unchallenged until they turned in at the Pangdean Gate.

'Bell rope's gone,' observed Boomer. He shook the locked gate. 'How do they expect to receive unexpected guests?'

'Unexpected guests aren't welcome.' A man wearing a leather jerkin and carrying a musket stepped out of the shadows beside the gate. Though his English was good, he spoke with an accent.

'It's the cook!' cried Boomer in an ecstasy of feigned recognition.

'Please forgive my father,' said Francis, rolling his eyes. 'I'm the firemaster Francis Quoynt and I've business with Master Hammick.'

Boomer took off his hat and bowed deeply to the sentry. 'Be kind enough, cookie, to tell Master Hammick that Master Boomer Quoynt has brought a gift for his guest.'

Let Bacon not be here, prayed Francis. He would have the lion dissected before letting it near the house.

The Spanish soldier looked at the lion, then at the steps leading up to the front door of the house, and waved for them to follow him around to the back.

From her hidden vantage point on the down, Kate saw Boomer, Francis and the lion disappear. Then they reappeared again in the courtyard at the back of Pangdean Place, escorted by three soldiers.

Holy Mother Mary, keep them safe.

Her heart thumped so hard that her vision was blurred by a beating in her eyelids.

One of the soldiers went to back door of the house. Francis and Boomer waited on the far side of the courtyard.

A man came to the door to speak to the soldier. She knew him . . . his shape . . . the set of his dark head.

It was the watcher Kate had spied on the Downs, close enough now to recognize. She blinked to clear her eyes.

It was Hugh Traylor.

The soldier returned from the house and lifted the canvas shroud, then the cloth of gold, to inspect the lion. Another reached up and tapped the crown.

'Real gold? Real pearls?'

'All real,' said Francis earnestly. *'Oro verdadero.'* He glanced at his father. Twelve Spanish soldiers were with them now in the courtyard.

'Que pasa?' Other curious voices asked what was happening.

The soldier jerked his head for Francis and Boomer to follow.

They pushed the lion through a narrow, tunnel-like passage, with the first three soldiers in front of them and a growing tail of men behind. The procession emerged into the large drawing room.

There, two dozen soldiers were busy polishing armour or tack, under the eye of Hammick.

'What time must we set out tonight?' someone was asking in accented English, 'Do we know for certain that the ships will arrive off Gravesend?' The speaker was the tall young man with rich red hair, whom Francis had seen on their exploratory raid.

At short distance, his beauty caused that brief shock of recognition and wistful envy that greets the occasional visiting angels who drop to earth. He had fair skin, clear, heavy-lidded blue eyes, a long straight nose, a wide elegant mouth with a full, slightly sulky lower lip. His jaw was just strong enough to keep him from looking girlish. He was almost as tall as Francis and had exceedingly fine legs, displayed in a pair of tight-fitting velvet breeches.

Today he wore a sea-green slashed velvet doublet embroidered with pearls. A heavy gold jewelled cross weighed down a chain of linked gold hearts.

'By Christ, he's the image of his grandmother!' muttered Boomer.

'You say you bring me a gift? Who are you?'

'Distant neighbours, your majesty,' said Hammick.

'Your loyal subjects, the Masters Quoynt,' said Boomer. 'And good Catholics . . .

'Kneel,' he added under his breath. 'Dammit, France. Just kneel. I reckon he expects it.' He fell to his own knees. 'We dare to hope you might honour us by including our gift in your triumphal procession.'

'What the devil are you two playing at?' demanded Hammick. 'Quoynt, shouldn't your father be tied safely to his bed?'

Francis saw the speculation in Hammick's eyes and their quick flick towards the nearest soldiers. The man was not going to take any chances with the two Quoynts. They would have to move fast.

'Our gift was first made for the accession triumph of an Italian prince, Your Majesty,' said Boomer to the young man. 'And has been in retirement *en mi casa* waiting for such a moment to come again.'

'How do you know who I am?' asked the young man.

'Get up, Master Quoynt,' snapped Hammick. 'The pair of you. I don't know what you imagine you're doing.'

'Surely His Majesty should give me permission to rise,' said Boomer.

A spectacular suit of ceremonial armour, of leather and gold, was laid out, being polished. The device on the golden shield carried both the Stuart unicorn and the English lion. Silver and gilt armour for Stuart's horse hung on a large wooden frame. Such armour was now outdated in modern warfare as it was cumbersome and gave little protection against ordnance, but it would strike awe into the popular heart when Stuart rode across London Bridge in his triumphal procession.

We were right, thought Francis. They're almost ready to march on London.

No Sir Francis Bacon. But no more acting, either, to judge by Hammick's predatory expression.

'Did you promise Robert Catesby Spanish support?' Francis asked Hammick.

Hammick shook his head in disbelief at the question.

'Your venture is doomed,' said Francis. 'Catesby and his fellow plotters will be stopped. Your pretender will meet a healthy king in London, and an eager executioner.'

Hammick smiled. 'I don't care whether those hotheads succeed or fail.' He lowered his voice and glanced at Stuart. 'There's no lack of willing assassins.'

'What do you mean?'

'Only that the King should take care when next hunting, if he manages to survive this Parliament. The Prince of Wales, too. If Catesby fails, I have arranged a failsafe.'

'Now?' asked Francis. 'Or after the intended Blow?'

'You'll have to die in ignorance, Quoynt. Missed your chance to join the winning side. Arrest them.'

'*Momento!* Wait!' Stuart interrupted. He had been looking increasingly puzzled. 'Do you know those English rebels, then?' he asked Francis.

'Yes, Your Majesty. I know them well.'

'What manner of men are they? Why did they kill my cousin and all his children?'

'Not the Lady Elizabeth, Your Highness.' Hammick spoke soothingly, as if to a fractious child. 'Remember? She is to be your wife.'

Stuart rubbed his left hand with the thumb of his right. The rings on his fingers winked in the firelight. 'I wish they had not killed them all.'

'They're not dead yet, Your Highness,' said Boomer. 'Señor Hammick is lying . . . *el miente*. And they will not die, if you do not wish it.'

'My personal wishes must be set aside.' Stuart smiled sadly, parroting what he had been taught. 'I can have no wish but my duty. I am to be the next king of England. That's what I was born to.'

'You can choose to prevent the death of England's present king . . . your cousin James.'

'Shut him up,' cried Hammick.

'Wait,' cried Stuart again. He held up his hand to stop the soldiers. He crossed to Boomer. 'How do you imagine that I can prevent it? He is already dead.'

'And I assure you that he is not. You need do nothing to save him. Only refuse to obey your gaolers.'

'His Highness is not our prisoner,' said Hammick furiously. 'He is the next king of England.'

'We all know that he has been your prisoner ever since you kidnapped him at birth and cut his mother's throat. He has been your prisoner ever since you tore him from his mother's breast and smuggled him out of England.'

'His mother gave birth to him in Spain,' cried Hammick. 'And trusted him into our care, after making us swear to restore him to his rightful throne.'

'I was there when you took him, Hammick. As you know. I heard his first cries. I saw what you had done. And it was not the cause for which I had enlisted.'

Boomer turned back to Stuart, who was staring from one to the other, dumbfounded. 'Your Majesty, your grandmother Mary, Queen of Scots was beheaded for treason because others wanted to use her to build their own power. I would not have you suffer the same fate. But you will surely die like her if you allow these men to persuade you that you can ever be king of England.'

'He lies!' Hammick glared at Boomer, just beginning to understand how far he had been duped. 'He is what he has just warned you about – a man who would use you to build his own power. But I won't let him leave here alive to endanger Your Majesty.'

'I saw her,' said Boomer. 'After this man killed and left her. A beautiful woman, your mother, and newly widowed. You would have been her chief joy and consolation. But she was not allowed to keep you and love you.' *El matara su madre!* This man murdered your mother!'

Stuart rubbed and rubbed at his hand with his other thumb.

77

Hoof beats drummed along the edge of the cliff. The freed horses stampeded without riders, running towards Telscomb, where sweet hay and water waited for them. Jem counted thirty-six before he moved on to his next task.

Kate took out the pistol that Boomer had given her and looked to see that it was loaded. She laid it on the ground near her hand.

Whatever Traylor was doing at Pangdean, this time Kate would kill him.

'Go out of the main door and through the gate,' Boomer told Stuart. 'Turn left . . . *izquierda, entienda?* . . . east along the cliffs. Do not stop below the walls of the house.'

'Stay where you are!' roared Hammick. 'You are the next king. You do not obey the orders of pigs.'

'How do I know which of you is lying?'

'Go,' said Boomer. 'If Master Hammick tries to stop you, he will prove that you are not the next king, merely his prisoner.'

The rings flashed as Stuart rubbed his right hand with the thumb of his left.

'May I reach for my pouch?' asked Boomer.

Stuart nodded.

Boomer pulled out a square of folded yellow linen. 'I found this in your mother's needlework basket. Take it. She was making it for you.' He bowed as he offered it.

Stuart unfolded an infant's gown, fragile with age.

'Flummery,' said Hammick. 'It could be anything . . . a rag he bought in a thieves' market.'

'But you know that it isn't.' Boomer waited.

Stuart stood gazing at the embroidered hearts intertwined with the letters 'R.S.' on the bodice of the gown. Then he clamped his lips tightly together. Holding himself balanced like an overfilled wineglass, he nodded at Boomer, turned and walked out of the hall.

'He won't get far,' said Hammick. 'You!' He pointed to three soldiers. 'Stop him, but keep him away until I finish with these two.'

'Forty,' said Francis under his breath. 'All here.'

'*Perro, es el rey!*' Boomer said.

The soldiers hesitated. '. . . *El rey nuestro*,' they muttered to each other.

'They say that Stuart is their king,' Boomer explained to Hammick. 'They hesitate to lay hands on him.'

'As the King, he should be spared the unnecessary sight of bloodshed,' said Hammick. 'Go! Do as I tell you.'

The three soldiers began to move towards the lion and the main door beyond.

Boomer laid his hand on the lion's rump, under the cloth of gold, and gave a minute nod. The lion quivered, then began to belch a stream of Greek fire. A burning sea lapped around the ankles of the advancing soldiers.

They leapt back, shouting, into the melee already fighting to escape the flames. The lion belched again. More fire fed the burning lake and set alight the clothing of a man who had been knocked to the floor.

Francis tried not to think about the man on the floor. All that mattered now was a steady hand. With controlled urgency, he launched the four earthenware grenades hidden inside the lion, their linked fuses already sparking, their bursting charges pregnant with thick, black, throat-clawing smoke.

Boomer loosed a plague of Ground Rats that raced across the floor, leaping up under cloaks, setting stockings on fire, herding back any man who still tried to escape through the large door to the Great Parlour.

Cursing, coughing and screaming, the soldiers jammed themselves into the narrow passageways behind them. Burning clothing set other clothes alight. Weapons caught. Armour snagged.

'Take care, France!' shouted Boomer. 'Hammick's coming round on your right flank . . .' He seized the gold-trimmed bridle from its block beside Stuart's ceremonial armour, then backed towards the entrance hall. 'Oh, shit. *Mierda!* Where's Hammick?'

'One,' said Francis, still beside the golden lion. He coughed in the spreading black smoke. '. . . four . . . five . . .' he went on, not losing a beat. He grabbed the Stuart standard leaning beside the door.

'OUT!' bellowed Boomer from behind him in the hall passage. 'Now!'

Kate heard the explosion. The lion's last roar. A puff of smoke leaped up into the early morning sky like an acrobat springing out of a chest. It tumbled upward, then uncoiled and began to spread, seething like the front edge of an advancing wave.

Kate blew on the end of her slow match and moved it towards the fuse. Her knees could shake all they liked, but not her hand.

Jem's charge went off almost at once. The far wall of the

estate collapsed into a second swelling cloud of black smoke, taking with it the attached range of outbuildings.

Kate held her hand steady until the tiny flame flared into life and began to race along the fuse. She counted aloud as she scrambled out of her hiding place. '. . . four . . . five . . . six . . .'

Running now. To the west. Towards the shelter of the dip in the land.

'Keep the fuse short to be certain,' she had insisted to Boomer. 'I'm a fast runner.' Now she wished the fuse were several hundred feet long.

'. . . fifteen . . . sixteen . . .'

She could not help snatching a look back over her shoulder as she neared the top of the little ridge.

Was that a fair head on the cliff-top track, beyond the house?

'. . . twenty . . . twenty-one . . .'

She dived and hit the ground rolling, through gorse, over stones, falling down, down, down as far and as fast as she could go.

The earth jumped under her. She covered her head with her arms.

Please, Holy Mother, get them both out in time.

'I lost Hammick!' shouted Boomer.

They were still running when Kate's charge exploded. Debris thumped to the ground around them.

'I'll go back,' panted Francis. 'We need Hammick. You go for Stuart!'

'Stuart will wait.' Boomer turned and ran back towards Pangdean with his son. 'Get Hammick! I thought the whoreson was trying to attack my flank . . . led him on . . . didn't think he would run.'

*   *   *

When dust and rubble no longer rained down from the sky, Kate rose shakily and sent up a small signal rocket to say that she was clear. The she began to climb the side of the down towards the scrubby thicket above Pangdean where she had hidden her horse.

She was still disorientated by the explosion, a hundred times more violent than the one that had struck her on London Bridge. The jelly in her eyeballs still trembled. Her heart skipped and danced in time with the echoes. Somewhere, she had lost the pistol.

She felt rather than heard someone scrambling up behind her, dislodging still more stones and clods of earth. Just in time, she remembered not to call out.

No names.

Jem would have run the other way, east towards Telscomb. If all had gone well, Francis and Boomer should be on the cliff-top track, on the far side of the ruins where Pangdean House had recently stood, with the beautiful red-haired youth in their custody. Leaving her with the shortest run for home.

The footsteps were still following. A man coughed violently.

'Francis!' screamed Kate, in spite of herself. 'Boomer!'

Traylor staggered out from behind a broken wall.

Uphill . . . her horse was uphill.

Kate threw off her heavy leather jerkin and ran.

78

On that same morning of Monday the fourth of November, on the north bank of the Thames in London, Sir Thomas Knevett stepped from his boat onto the little landing at the back of Westminster Palace where Guido had landed the gunpowder. Carefully briefed by Cecil, Knevett made a quick search of the small paved yard and the palace cellars that opened off it.

He stayed only a short time, during which he examined the outer storage rooms but glanced only briefly at the huge stacks of firewood in the echoing vaults of the main cellar chamber. As his eyes passed over a figure lurking in the shadows of the yard, he shook his head minutely at the constable accompanying him. Then the search party left.

Guido Fawkes, the man in the shadows, knew beyond all doubt that the hand of God had cloaked him in a divine invisibility. God had stopped Knevett on the threshold of the main cellar, where 4,000 pounds of gunpowder lay hidden under the firewood. Though it had escaped a quick glance, a closer search would quickly discover it.

He must continue to escape arrest for only twenty-three more hours. Then he would change the shape of England's future.

*   *   *

'Kate's safely away,' cried Boomer. 'There's her signal rocket.' He pointed at the puff of pale smoke hanging in the air to the west, beyond the black clouds rising from the ruins of Pangdean.

The ruins were still on fire, but from what they could see, most of the soldiers had been caught by the second blast as they struggled in the narrow passageway. A few had fled down over the cliffs towards the beach. Boomer dispatched another whom he found blinded and missing most of his skin.

'We need to take Hammick,' he said bitterly. 'I let him escape.'

'At least we have Stuart, if he's still there. We must find him,' said Francis. 'Before anyone else does.'

'We must let him go.'

'I'm taking him to Cecil. To prove the plot.'

Boomer shook his head stubbornly. He bent to pull a dented gold equine breastplate from under a pile of smoking bricks. 'You'll take him to certain death. He goes free. '

'You have lost your wits now!' Francis glared, disbelieving. 'I'm meant to be the one with a tender heart.'

'Help me salvage this armour. Worth a king's ransom, so to speak. I owe him a life, France.'

'He's no less a danger now,' protested Francis. 'I refuse to face Cecil without him. What happens when the next ambitious schemers get their hooks into him? Or he himself decides to raise support?'

'I don't think he will.'

'You can't simply let him walk away.'

'I doubt if he's gone very far.' Boomer pointed with his sword down at the beach. Four of the Spanish soldiers were swimming out to sea.

'Take your armour off, you dolts,' muttered Francis.

As they watched, one head sank. The other three kept going.

'It's a long way to Spain.' Francis searched the cliff-top with his eyes. 'There he is,' he shouted.

Robert Stuart stood at the cliff edge, looking down at the swimmers.

'I thought you'd made off by now,' said Francis.

Stuart arched his eyebrows at the sword-point aimed at his elegant throat.

'Where would I go?'

'Back to Spain?'

Stuart shuddered. 'Never.'

Francis and Boomer glanced at each other and exhaled in unison. Francis lowered his sword.

'Where to then?'

Stuart shrugged. 'I have no idea.' He glanced at their faces and smiled wryly. 'Someone has always decided for me. Although most politely.'

The Quoynts studied him for a moment. Francis was unsure whether Stuart was mocking them.

'I'm here because you told me,' Stuart added. 'The others are dead?'

'Your old life is over,' said Boomer gently. 'You must begin to make your own decisions.'

'What do you want most to do?' Francis asked. He watched the young man's face closely.

Stuart looked blank for a moment. '*Andar . . . solo*. To walk alone,' he said at last. 'Without a guard.' He gave Francis a suspicious glance. 'Why do you ask me?'

'I want to know.'

There was a flicker of something in Stuart's eyes that might have been either humour or a quick understanding.

'I would like to go to a market. And buy rabbits.'

'That's all?'

'Perhaps also a loaf of bread and a garlic sausage to go with it.' He looked Francis straight in the eye.

Then he grew uncertain again, glancing anxiously about as if for instruction. He rubbed his left hand with the thumb of his right. Looked at Francis thoughtfully. Looked at Boomer.

He lifted the jewelled cross on the heavy gold chain over his head and gave it to Boomer. 'I don't think that I will be needing this now.' He considered the many rings on his fingers but seemed to know the fine line between a statement of political intent and a bribe.

'How do you mean to set free this caged bird of yours?' Francis asked his father. 'As it seems that he doesn't know how to fly?'

'How many in England know your face?' Boomer asked.

'Only Hammick and Señor Bacon. And the men dead in the house. Many more in Spain, of course.'

'House servants?' asked Francis. 'Grooms?'

Stuart shook his head. 'Here, Master Hammick keeps me closely mewed up. I am not going to address my troops until tomorrow, when they gather at London.'

'They will not be gathering, sir,' Boomer said gently.

'No. Of course not. I forget. I think I am a little . . .' Stuart's hands urged the elusive word to spring from the air. He shook his head and looked back down at the sea, where only one swimming head remained afloat.

Boomer rubbed his broad forehead, squinting in perplexity. He hefted the gold chain in his hand. 'You'd best come back with us to Powder Mote while we all decide what to do. You can't stay here wandering on the cliffs.'

His father's fierce look made Francis close his mouth again. He nodded in temporary resignation.

'We must finish bringing the place down,' said Boomer. 'Leave nothing. Drop it all into the sea. Would-be looters and the merely curious will be flocking soon.'

Francis nodded again.

If Stuart had said that he wanted to avenge his grand-mother, or had demanded that diplomatic negotiations begin to secure his release, Francis would have killed him, father or no. He still could not go free, no matter what Boomer said. That young man was too subtle by half.

Then Francis looked at Boomer with sudden horror. 'The failsafe!' In the press of battle, he had forgotten about Hammick's failsafe assassins. 'I must ride to London at once to warn Cecil!'

79

Kate wore breeches. Traylor was at least twenty-five years older than she, and wore a sword and heavy leather boots. Jem had freed Traylor's horse among the rest. By the time she reached her horse, he was twenty yards behind her, without a mount.

After a short, terrified sprint over rough ground, she pulled her gelding back to a safer pace.

Neither Francis nor Boomer was at Powder Mote when Kate arrived, although she was almost certain she had seen them both clear of Pangdean. She decided to leave the gate-house locked to keep Hammick out. She was certain he would try to kill her before he vanished to Spain, or wherever he meant to flee.

She hid her horse in a shed near the mill and rowed across the moat. There was no sign of Traylor, but any of the shadows among the trees could have been a man.

The other boat! she thought in terror. Where is it? Then she realized that it made no difference. Traylor could easily swim the moat if he wished.

Inside the house, she barred the big front door, then ran from room to room securing windows and other doors. The ways to enter the house multiplied until Powder Mote seemed as transparent as a sieve.

She ran through the scullery, down into the cellars. The narrow windows there, half below ground, had no shutters, but they were small and already barred with iron grilles. She could secure them no further. Back in the kitchen, she hauled the big scrubbed table across the door to the cloisters, although she had already locked it.

She found a carving knife, remembering how she had imagined thrusting her scissors into Traylor's heart. The knife would be little use against his sword but felt better than nothing in her hand.

She went back to the Great Hall and listened. Susannah White was still visiting her sister. The kitchen maid slept at her family's cottage across the moat. Kate was alone.

That's wind, Kate reassured herself. That's a mouse. That's an old house shifting in its sleep. Nothing more.

The remains of their final preparations lay on the hall table. Among these were a flint and steel, a box of charred linen squares and four slow matches. These reminded Kate of the guns she had loaded and left for Boomer and Francis around the estate.

All but the big caliver.

In her haste to leave for Pangdean, she had forgotten to take it to Boomer's 'church' and left it in the barn after feeding Meg.

To get it, she would have to leave the house. Go back outside with Traylor.

Gripping the knife, she unlocked the side door that led from the Great Hall onto the narrow terrace where Francis and Boomer liked to sit. Then, with a rush of terror, she locked the door again. After a moment, she left the key in the lock.

Drawing a deep breath, she went upstairs and searched both of the men's bedchambers, but she found no other weapon.

The knife would have to serve.

She went back down to the Great Hall to wait for the two Quoynts to return. She imagined the joy and relief with which she would run to answer their knock.

And if they didn't return?

For the first time since she had arrived at Powder Mote, she was back in passing-through time. She felt herself sinking back into the depths of her well, away from an unbearable present.

Hugh Traylor was a demon with magical powers to follow and torment her. She felt that she would never escape him. He was too strong. She could only sink deeper and deeper, shrinking smaller and smaller, until she was gone. Safely somewhere else.

She stirred the fire and put on another log, more for the company than for the warmth. She sat on the floor beside the fire, laid the knife close by her knee. Listened. Only then did she notice that her hands and face were bleeding from the gorse.

She lifted her head, in the middle of picking out a splinter.

That was not the wind. Not a mouse. Nothing like the harmless sounds with which she had alarmed herself earlier. That was a foreign body in the fabric of the old house. Moving. In the passage leading from the kitchens.

She did not even try to persuade herself that it might be Francis or Boomer. They would have arrived like a wave. Pounded on the door, calling her name, and filled the house suddenly with their size, their voices, the sound of their boots.

Traylor came a little way into the hall with his sword drawn. His jerkin was charred. Blood ran from his scalp into his face. His hair hung in wet ragged clumps. His clothes dripped water onto the floor.

'My sweetest Kate.'

She picked up the knife and rose to her feet.

He wiped the blood out of his eyes. She could now see their cold gleam of anticipation.

'Bitch,' he said. 'You do know that I mean to kill you this time?'

'How did you get in?'

'A rusty grille on the jakes pit, if you must know. They should keep this place in better repair.'

He had swum the moat, as she feared he would, then broken into the cellars through the sewage drain. In the cellars, she had not even thought of the drain grille, hidden behind a closed door in a side passage.

'That's how much I want to kill you,' he said. 'After showing you the butchered bodies of your two cock-peddlers. Or are they your new pimps?' He leaned forward to see her better. 'Which one is fucking you? Or is it both?'

Give him nothing, she reminded herself. Never again. Even if he does kill you. As it seems likely that he will.

'You'll never take the two of them.'

'Could they watch me cut your throat?'

They were still alive then.

Traylor stepped closer. 'Lay that knife on the table . . . I suppose I'm obliged to fire this place. I always return favours.'

She set down the knife. Picked up the flint and steel. Opened the little box that held the charred cloth squares. 'Why were you at Pangdean?'

'I'm the new tenant.'

'Hammick is the tenant.'

'And I'm Hammick.'

Traylor took another step towards her, close enough now for her to smell the acrid sewage and rotting water-weed on his clothes. 'Your two firemasters should be here soon, unless they were caught in their own blast. I saw one of them run back into the house at Pangdean . . . not certain which.'

He lies, she insisted to herself. He lies, for pleasure.

She could not begin to think yet how all the strands knotted together. His betrayal of Father Jerome, which she now believed. And his betrayal of her. His presence at Pangdean with the Stuart Pretender.

With the table between them, she struck steel on flint, caught the spark on the square of charred cloth, and lit the match at both ends.

'Do you hope to set me alight?' he asked with amusement. 'But we must celebrate our reunion first. What welcome will you give me before you send me up in flames?' He reached for her. 'Why don't you bend over the table?'

Kate overturned it instead. Heard him shout in pain. She opened the side door, sprinted across the terrace. With the lighted match in her hand and Traylor cursing behind her, she ran towards the musket in the barn.

Meg growled when Kate hauled the door open.

'Good girl,' murmured Kate. She looked back. Traylor had slowed, limping but confident.

'Good Meg,' said Kate. 'I know you still feel uneasy here. Most of all tonight.'

The bear reared uncertainly onto its haunches.

The musket was leaning on the wall where Kate had left it. To reach it, she would have to pass Meg.

'Steady,' she said softly. She had no apple nor any other offering to calm the beast. 'It's me, sweet. It's Kate.' She did not think that Meg would ever attack her, but life at the Bear Garden had left the bear edgy and unpredictable, like a dog that has been severely beaten. And Kate smelled of blood from her scratches.

Traylor reached the barn. Kate could hear his harsh breathing.

Meg grew agitated again. She swung her head from Traylor to Kate.

'Let me past, sweet Meg.' Kate offered her empty hand for the bear to smell. 'If you let me past, I'll bring you a peck of apples.'

The nose explored her hand and wrist. Then Meg licked her hand.

'Kate!' Traylor cried in mock astonishment. 'Another tame bear. You seek out your own kind! And I've never buggered a bear.'

Kate took a step towards the musket.

Traylor looked around the barn. 'Stay away from that gun.' He advanced a few feet. His sword swished through the air like the tail of an angry cat. 'Or I'll have your head off before you can insert the match into the serpentine. I find that I'm not so hungry to service you after all.'

Kate stood still.

Meg lumbered two feet forward, then stopped and sat back on her haunches again.

'Good girl. Good girl.' Kate backed away from the musket until she was standing beside the bear. 'And now?' she asked Hammick.

Hammick hesitated. The bear looked placid in its stillness. He raised his sword. With one eye on the bear, he made a teasing lunge at Kate.

She leaped back. Meg turned her head with interest, following their movements.

'Do you enjoy the sport of baiting, Kate?' He feinted at her again with his blade. 'You stand a better chance than most bears. You're not chained to a post.' He made a tick-tock movement with the tip of his sword. 'But then, this bout is to the death. I'm afraid you won't be retired to do damage another day.' He took a sliding step forward, preparing to lunge. 'To her, boy. To her!'

Kate screamed. '*Sa! Sa! Sa!*'

Meg uncoiled in a blur of speed, reared up on her hind

legs and swung her paw at Hammick's head with the full weight of her body behind the blow.

That same Monday, Digby's 'hunting party' gathered at The Red Lion Inn at Dunchurch, ready for a glorious adventure. Before telling his eager friends the royal nature of the doe they would hunt the next day, Digby invited them to join him in numerous pints of ale and a fine supper.

80

4 November and 5 November 1605

Francis set off for London at a gallop as soon as he and Boomer finished bringing down Pangdean. A cart would follow more slowly with Hammick's body. Francis carried with him the royal Stuart standard, furled. In his saddlebag he had the gold-trimmed bridle from Pangdean and the golden cross that Robert Stuart had given Boomer on the cliff-top.

He should have been bringing that bastard Stuart as a prisoner in irons. Or else his head in a bucket. Francis could not think what ailed his father, to turn so soft.

Although they did have Hammick's body . . . Traylor's . . . The man's identity would be hard to prove either way, after the clout the bear had given him.

Nor could Francis believe that he had thought he was bringing Kate to safety when he forced her to come to Powder Mote.

He kicked his horse into a longer stride.

Others things, too, stuck like thistles in his throat.

Barring a miracle, Robin Catesby was going to force him to accept that a man he liked better than any he had met in many years was a traitor to his country. Willing to shed innocent blood. Blind to the consequences of his actions, careless of his friends and family. Was a worse traitor, even, than Francis himself.

He changed horses at Crowborough and Orpington during the night. Once, riding on the grassy verge of a wide carriage road, he fell asleep in the saddle and woke just in time to stay on his horse.

He and Boomer had made a quick search of Pangdean before bringing it down, but found no letters, no documentary proof of what was planned there. Nothing from Sir Francis Bacon, although Hammick must surely have insisted on a letter. For protection, at the very least, in case Bacon found his conscience at the last minute.

Long after midnight, while Francis was riding for London, Guido lifted his head abruptly in the darkness. He heard a faint scraping, as if a boat had docked outside the cellars. Then footsteps gritted on the stone floor of the vaulted passage.

The searchers were back. He waited a few thudding heart-beats for God to intervene again but he already knew that this time was different. He heard a purpose in the approaching voices that was missing before.

He did not hesitate. His action would not be what they had all planned, but it would be enough. A different glory. Enough of the enemy would die – all those now asleep in chambers above his head, the approaching search party. Hell would still gape. He knew that Robin would still be proud and would tell the world what he had done. For him, it would be swift, a quick spasm as his soul escaped its husk. Far better than a soldier's common fate, his life oozing slowly from a mangled body into the mud of a battlefield. Far, far better than if he were taken.

He ran to the back of the main cellar, knelt on the cold stone floor and lit the fuse train. Then he walked out to meet

the search party, smiling. He needed to delay them in the
passage for only a few heartbeats. Then they would all be
dead.

As Francis pounded into Long Southwark on Tuesday
morning, the fifth of November, the orange light of bonfires
flickered over the roofs of the houses. The streets seethed
with people. Words flew thickly through the air. Murder.
Outrage. Assassins. Papists. Fiends. Miracles. London was in
an uproar.

'"*The Devil of the Vaults*",' bawled a ballad-seller. 'Come buy!
"*The Miraculous Escape of the King*".'

Francis left his horse at The Elephant and elbowed his way
across London Bridge. Only his urgency to reach Cecil kept
him upright. Halfway across, he saw a gang of youths
smashing the shutters of a shop that sold Spanish oils.

On the City side of the Bridge, he pushed through the
excited populace gathered around St Magnus the Martyr and
turned towards The Strand.

As he walked, he muttered the story he had rehearsed on
the way from Brighthelmstone. Enough of the truth to satisfy
Cecil and convince him of the grave danger the King was in,
still, even now, with the rejoicing at his delivery already
begun. But not so much of the truth that Francis put a noose
around his own neck, or Kate's, or Boomer's. He would not
tell Cecil, for example, that Powder Mote now sheltered not
only Kate Peach, guardian of Jesuit priests, but also a Stuart
pretender to the English throne.

At the Cecil family's house on The Strand, he demanded
to know where Lord Salisbury might be. To his surprise, the
Secretary of State was at neither Westminster nor Whitehall
but would be returning shortly from the Tower of London.

'How shortly?'

'Soon.'

'Which way can he be met?'

'You must wait like everyone else.'

Francis hovered in the forecourt with a press of other peti-
tioners, wondering if he should run to Whitehall and try to
warn the King directly, without terrifying him.

This threat needed a Cecil.

One advantage of his great height was that Cecil saw him
in the crowd and beckoned for him to follow the horse.

Francis grabbed the Secretary's cloak. 'Don't let the King
hunt!' he said urgently, not waiting until they were alone.
'Or the Prince. My lord, send men to protect them at once!'

PART SEVEN

LADY GUNPOWDER

My L. I am informed for a certaintie that a Mr. Tho:Percy was mett this morning about eight of the clock ryding toward Croydon: by one Matthew my Hoast of ye George in Croydon with which ye said Pearcy having good acquaintance demanded of ye Hoast; what newes . . . So quoth he: All London is up in Arms.

Yo'r L. R. Cant.

Richard Bancroft, Archbishop of Canterbury

81

'There's no body? You don't have the Pretender?' The rage and disbelief in Cecil's face made Francis take a step back.

'No, my lord. You'll soon have the corpse of the chief conspirator, but Robert Stuart was unfortunately buried in the ruins of Pangdean.'

'You blundering arsehole.'

That's noble gratitude for you, thought Francis. He had been waiting for several hours in Cecil's chamber at Whitehall, without food or drink, still in the clothes he had been wearing all night.

Cecil had immediately sent men to guard the King and the Prince of Wales. Others now watched the Queen and infant Princess. Soldiers were riding towards the estates occupied by the Princess Elizabeth and the little Duke of York. Several discreet arrests had been made, and a man who claimed to be a waterman looking for a place to sleep had been quietly removed from the Westminster cellars.

Cecil had ordered the gunpowder to be taken at once to the safety of the Tower, to avoid any further attempts to set it off. He also passed a discreet but urgent message to the Spanish ambassador about the disguised ships standing off Gravesend. He had a private audience with the King. Only then was he free to listen, in total stillness, to Francis's full account of the confrontation at Pangdean.

'How can I prove anything of this to His Majesty without the Pretender, either dead or alive?' he demanded. 'How can I keep Spain at heel? I can't threaten to expose this despicable perfidy . . . in our supposed allies . . . if I don't have either letters or the body of the man they sent to usurp our throne! What am I supposed to do with the faceless corpse of some *soi-disant* London merchant?'

He's badly shaken, Francis thought with astonishment.

Cecil fingered the gold-trimmed bridle angrily. 'These are playhouse props.' He held the gold crucifix close to his eyes to study it again. 'Are you certain there's no one left alive to be examined. No one to make a confession.'

'There is one man whose word might be taken as proof,' said Francis carefully. 'Even at the highest level. But I don't think he will be eager to speak.'

Cecil wheeled round. 'Who?'

'Sir Francis Bacon.'

For the first time in their acquaintance, Francis watched Cecil shrink. The vital force that gave him the presence of a much larger man suddenly drained out of him. He seemed to deflate. The skin of his long cheeks sagged. He turned away and gripped the windowsill with his stubby fingers while he gazed out into the precinct of Whitehall.

'How much does Bacon know?'

'I can prove nothing, my lord, but I would swear he knows all that I just told you. That Guido Fawkes was a mere decoy, as was the blow against Parliament. That you were meant to drop your guard and pursue the Parliament traitors north into the midlands, thinking the King saved. I think Bacon knows that assassins were in place to kill both the King and Prince of Wales as soon as you lowered your guard. He knows that the Stuart Pretender would march on London from the south, to reassure the populace and claim the now-empty throne.'

'Do you have any letters proving Bacon's knowledge of these things?'

'No, sir.'

'How would he know all this?'

'He was at Pangdean, my lord.'

Cecil's face contracted with pain. He and Francis looked at each other through the cloud of words Francis had not spoken.

The King and Prince Henry murdered, even as Cecil triumphantly announced the arrest of Fawkes and the uncovering of the Gunpowder Treason. Cecil's failure to protect the King. His gullibility in swallowing the trailed bait. The failure of his intelligencers to see the traces of the Stuart plot for what they really were.

And then, Cecil's certain humiliation, his possible execution for treasonous neglect. And his cousin Bacon as his replacement at the helm.

'Then my cousin knows how close I came to letting England out of my grasp,' Cecil said dully.

Francis almost felt sorry for him.

Cecil sank into deep calculation. 'Can we prove him a traitor?' he asked at last.

'So far as I know, my lord, there's only my word as a commoner against his. Which of us would the Privy Council believe?'

Cecil scowled, but his rage was directed at the subject of his private thoughts. 'I shall deal with him,' he said, as if to himself. 'Can't yet think how, but I will.' He stared out of the window, biting down on his lower lip. 'What could you say against Sir Francis if asked?'

'That I saw him at Pangdean.'

'In the company of the Pretender?'

'No, sir. In intimate conversation with Hammick four days before they were to march on London. He slept at Pangdean for at least one night, where the preparations for the march were clear to see. Robert Stuart was then at Pangdean.'

'Who else saw him?'

'No one.' Kate and Boomer did not need the attentions of Robert Cecil.

'Do you swear that you saw my cousin there?'

Francis felt the nape of his neck begin to crawl at the icy calculation in Cecil's eyes.

'To you, my lord, I swear it. As for anyone else, I wait to learn what you want me to say.'

Cecil sank into absolute stillness again.

'You killed them all, you say?'

'All the principals. Stuart. Hammick. The Spanish officers. Most of the soldiers.'

'You did not do this alone. Who helped you?'

'Simple men, sir. Who did not understand anything beyond my orders.'

Cecil weighed this information.

'. . . and who want only to be left in peace,' Francis added. 'One or two of the Spanish soldiers may have escaped, but I doubt if they survived for long. We cut off the serpent's head. That's all that need concern you.'

'I will overlook your presumption in instructing me how to govern. Nevertheless, there are serpents left alive in Spain.'

'But without their Scottish poodle of a pretender.'

A flash of irritation told Francis that Cecil had already considered this subject and moved on.

'And with Philip still waving our Treaty to dry the ink,' the Secretary said thoughtfully. 'And Spain wanting our trade.'

Then he startled Francis by smiling. 'Without proof of what happened at Pangdean, I must be content with the lesser victory. We took Fawkes neatly enough. He walked into my trap. I shall write his confession, which I am certain he will eventually sign.'

Francis made an unwitting movement of protest. Poor Guido, to have his self-sacrifice so twisted.

Cecil walked around the creaking, panelled room with growing resolve, as if ice holding him had begun to crack and shift.

'The King is snatched from the jaws of death by Divine intervention and his own inspired understanding of that warning letter . . . or so His Majesty now begins to believe.

'Parliament still stands. The jaws of hell have not gaped and swallowed us. The Catholics are in rout. The people cry outrage on behalf of their king and overflow with thanksgiving at his escape. In time, we will have confessions to implicate the Jesuit Superior, Garnet, and prove Jesuit perfidy. We have achieved a triumph of intelligence-gathering and statesmanship.'

'If you say so, my lord.'

'Indeed, I do say it.' Cecil turned a cold stare onto him. 'It's the truth and must stand as such. Does it seem otherwise to you, in any way, Master Quoynt?'

Francis hesitated for only a fraction of a heartbeat, holding Cecil's stare. 'The truth is that which best serves the good of England,' he said. 'I'm a simple man, willing to settle for that. Truth needs a university of philosophers to tame her.'

Cecil snorted. 'That's not a simple man's answer, Quoynt. You're grown as devious as any Whitehall conniver.'

'No, my lord,' said Francis hotly before he could clamp his teeth on the words. 'I am not.'

Shut your mouth, ass, he told himself. But he was too weary and too drained to take his own advice. 'If to be devious is to act with a cold, calculating heart, I am not devious. But I am confused. My heart is sore.' He dropped to one knee.

'Have my neck now, my lord, and be done with it. I've done my best and am racked by it. I serve you as well as I can, but I will not say I like it.'

'I didn't mean to offend you.' Cecil sounded more surprised than angry.

'I beg you, release me from your service.'

'Are you still enough my creature to be trusted with one last, needful embassy?'

Francis looked up warily. With him on his knees, they were almost eye-to-eye.

'To my cousin Bacon. I'm sure I can devise some shift to bring him to heel.'

'As a favour, my lord, I will. Not as paid service.'

Francis rose when Cecil waved him to his feet. What he now wanted most to know, he did not dare to ask.

82

After leaving Cecil, Francis went to the barber-surgeon's shop
at the top of Fish Street. There he found a knot of other men
listening eagerly to a member of the night watch, who sat
on a stool with his feet in a basin of steaming water.

'. . . a great confusion at Essex House in the middle of the
night,' the watchman was saying.

The steamy air was thick with the smells of wintergreen
and wine.

'. . . Soldiers, constables, swarms of 'em. A warrant had
been signed for the arrest of Thomas Percy, who was staying
at Essex House as a guest of his patron and kinsman,
Northumberland.'

'For what crime?' Francis ventured through the murmurs
of the others. Hard as he listened, he heard only the name
of Percy mentioned.

'Plotting with his Papist confederates to kill the King, the
Prince, and all of Parliament.'

'Is Percy taken?' asked the man on the barber's stool.

'Not yet,' said the watchman. 'He fled north, they say. But
with such a pack of a *posse comitatus* on his trail that he can't
escape for long.'

A pack of vigilantes that he would lead straight to Robin
at Holbeach.

Francis suppressed a groan of despair. 'Who are these supposed Papist confederates of Percy?' he asked.

'One was arrested last night, a desperate devil found lurking in the cellars of Westminster. Gave the name John Johnson. "The Devil of the Vault" he's already being called. Taken with one thousand barrels of gunpowder.'

'So they say,' the barber interrupted dryly as he wiped his razor.

'I swear it,' insisted the watchman hotly. 'That treacherous, murdering fiend meant to blow up the King and Parliament in the name of Rome, and regrets only that he failed.'

So, Cecil had linked Guido and Percy. Without the help of Francis.

Back in the street, Francis jammed his hat on his head and marched savagely along The Strand.

'Ballad, sir? New minted! "The Devil of the Vaults." Be the first to sing it.'

Francis pushed the vendor out of his path, then, changing his mind, swung round to toss him a coin and snatch the offered paper.

> *. . . Satan supplied these fiends with powder,*
> *But Mounteagle sang God's warning louder . . .*

He crushed the paper in his fist and aimed it at a heap of horse turds steaming in the street.

83

Francis found it impossible to leave London as Cecil had advised. Instead, he wandered the streets, tight-limbed and with stones in his belly. Past bonfires, mock executions of the Pope and other frenzied jubilations that followed the arrest of 'The Devil in the Vaults'.

It was a desperate fall for Saint Guido.

He saw gangs of apprentices breaking windows of Catholic houses and, just for good measure, the windows of any foreigners who might have been Catholics. On the fourth occasion, Francis could bear it no longer and routed the gang with shouts of 'Watch coming!' and a shot from his pistol.

Drawn by distant howls of rage, he watched from conceal-ment while the Spanish ambassador threw gold coins down from his window to try to assuage the baying crowd.

He witnessed two arrests of Catholics. In the alehouses, he heard how informers were rushing to spew out tittle-tattle about who had been seen drinking with whom, and at which tavern, and where the host might also repay a closer look. Though The Duck and Drake figured more than once in these rumours, there was still neither mention nor news of Catesby, the Wintours, the Wrights, Keyes and the rest.

Though he listened everywhere, Francis heard no whisper of Pangdean either. Hammick and the Spanish plotters might never have existed. Robert Stuart might never have been born. Meanwhile, the Spanish ambassador to England was fulsome in his public rapture at the miraculous preservation of King James, ruler of the newest ally and trading partner of Spain.

Francis also heard the growing public glorification of the King – wise, forbearing, judicious. His Majesty, in a stroke of divinely inspired genius (as soon became widely known), had understood at once the true meaning of a mysterious letter delivered to one Lord Monteagle by an unknown 'tall man'. His omniscient Highness had seen at once the truth that had somehow escaped all his ministers – that the letter warned of an attempt to blow up Parliament with gunpowder hidden in the Westminster cellars.

The miracle of His Majesty's escape was cited in the streets as God's final, inarguable stamp of approval on his reign.

In all of this, Francis clearly read the work of Cecil, creating his 'triumph of intelligence-gathering and statesmanship'.

On Wednesday, the day after Guido's arrest, Cecil summoned Francis and asked him to take a small packet to Bacon.

Francis weighed it in his hand. It seemed a light device for dealing with a treacherous, ambitious cousin.

'May I visit Fawkes in the Tower?' Francis asked as he was leaving.

'You mean John Johnson,' Cecil corrected him sharply. 'The man is nothing to do with you now. Stay away. Though he still admits to nothing but the false name of John Johnson, he'll confess to everything we need. In time. You don't know him. Go back to Powder Mote.'

Cecil said nothing about the reward he had promised to Francis. Nor did Francis. At that moment, escaping with his life was enough. That and the fact that neither Kate nor his father had been mentioned again.

Nevertheless, curiosity sent him to lurk in the jumbled

alleys and courts of Whitehall, to observe the results of Cecil's message to Bacon. Nothing happened for two days after he delivered the packet. Then, as Francis lounged against the chequered stone and flint of the Holbein Gate, he saw, at a distance, crossing the wide public carriageway that split Whitehall, the figures of Robert Cecil and Sir Francis Bacon walking together in apparent amity.

Francis stared. Then he spat onto the ground as if he tasted tainted meat. As a mere firemaster, he could not have known that he was watching a most refined statesmanship at work in that stately progress of mutual blackmail.

On Thursday, the seventh of November, Francis bribed an old acquaintance, now an officer of the Tower, for news.

'Percy's still at large,' said the officer. 'But there's another chase on. Sir Thomas Walsh, the sheriff of Worcestershire, is hot after a party of night raiders who attacked Warwick Castle. His warrant's for a band of Catholics. Robert Catesby, Thomas Wintour, a pair of brothers named Wright . . .'

Francis listened to the list of names with disbelief. Surely Guido had never gabbled out their names when he was arrested. He refused to give even his own name.

It was too neat. Men pursued for a lesser crime when they were not yet wanted for a greater one. But soon would be.

The mood at the Tower was subdued. Francis swallowed a sour belch of nausea when he was told why. 'Johnson' was refusing to talk.

The examiners had begun to torture Guido on the rack.

The next day, Friday, Francis went again to the barber-surgeon. Sitting on the barber's stool, uneasily aware of the lethal blade sliding over his throat, he wondered how the man came by all his information, and who might pay him to tell it.

Two customers recovering from a sweat bath gossiped in the window.

'Quoynt, this is your line of country,' said one. 'Did you hear that they moved the Westminster gunpowder into the Tower yesterday? Most of it had decayed. That poor devil in the cellars was sitting on a damp squib.'

I judged it right in Lambeth, thought Francis dully. Guido was right, of course. The incorporation time was far too short. He felt the barber's warm breath on his face.

Why didn't he feel more pleased?

'That's it, then,' said the barber, wiping his razor on a napkin.

Francis stared blindly at the barber. If Guido refused to talk, how did Cecil know so precisely which men the Sheriff should pursue?

Francis had seen night raids. He knew how hard it was to give a name to every raider when all were wearing cloaks and hats. In the dark.

The madness, the incompetence, the little spider in his web, all came together in his head.

'Sir?' the barber asked. 'Anything else?'

'The success or failure of those hotheads is of no importance to us,' Hammick had said.

Hammick's assassins were not his failsafe. They were his chief players.

Francis had almost seen it earlier. That Robin and his crew were not the allies of Bacon, Hammick and the Spanish party. They were the sacrificial pawns. Under any of his names, Hammick had never hesitated to sacrifice his pawns.

Neither Catesby's enemies nor his allies had ever intended for him to succeed.

Hammick had given Cecil their names for the warrant. Hammick, or one of his agents, had betrayed the plotters to Cecil, just as he had betrayed Father Jerome and Kate.

Betraying Kate and Father Jerome bought Hammick distance from the Catholics, proved his loyalty to the Crown, and gave him immunity from suspicion while he plotted a coup.

Catesby and his fellow conspirators were sacrificed to create a diversion. To draw all attention, first to Westminster and then to the country north of London by filling it with fleeing traitors. Everyone would be looking northwards. No one watching the King, now believed to be safe. No one would be watching Sussex and the march on London of the new Stuart king.

Small wonder that Catesby did not fear Cecil. The credulous, soon-to-be-discredited Cecil.

Francis imagined Francis Bacon seated at the front of the spectators watching the small shape of his hated cousin mount the scaffold. Oh, how England would then cry out for a new hand at the helm to help the new Catholic king steer the ship of state. Poor Robert Stuart – young, inexperienced and misinformed, with no practical knowledge of his new realm. Who would be left to serve him but the hungry, intelligent cousin of the former chief minister?

Francis suddenly swayed as his legs became jelly.

'You look like you've just seen the devil over my shoulder.' The barber pushed him gently back down onto the stool and put a pot of ale into his hand.

Francis still stared unseeing at the barber. For how long had Cecil known all those names before the warrant was proclaimed?

If Cecil knew the names, he had been having the men watched.

Therefore, no matter what he said, he was also having Francis watched . . . it seemed clear to Francis now. Cecil had never needed him as a spy but only to provide the powder, so that the plot could go ahead. Even at the very beginning,

Cecil had understood him far too well.

He imagined what he would have said to Cecil when they first met . . . when he still imagined himself to be a man of at least a little honour . . . if the Secretary of State had asked him baldly to connive at arranging treason.

'More ale?'

Francis drank whatever was in the pot.

Cecil had known exactly what Guido and Robin wanted but left Francis, all white-hot to save the King, to discover it for himself.

The barber refilled the pot without waiting for an answer. Then filled it again.

Francis drank whatever was in the pot.

If I was watched, he thought, Cecil must know how often I met Robin. He must know about the days in Lambeth restoring the powder. And our drunken evening. He knows that I must know their names. And never told him.

Beyond all doubt, Cecil knew that Francis had lied to him.

As Francis walked with careful, ale-induced deliberation back towards the Elephant, the ballad-seller by St Magnus the Martyr told him that Robin Catesby had been killed at Holbeach.

'A single bullet passed through him and Thomas Percy both. What a fine song that will make.' He again offered Francis 'The Devil in the Vaults'.

'Do you, by chance, work for Cecil?' Francis asked, waving the ballad away angrily. 'If not, he could use your services.'

Well, Robin, he thought, as he waited for a wherry to take him across to Southwark. I'm sure that you made a heroic stand. Back-to-back with Thomas. Valiant to the end and a swifter death than on the scaffold.

On Bankside, he turned with snarling ferocity on a whore who pulled at his sleeve. She swore and ran, stumbling over the black skirts in which she had dressed as Lady Gunpowder.

He dragged himself back to The Elephant, to which he had returned for the sake of its beds.

Take Cecil's advice while you still can, he told himself blurrily. Go back to Powder Mote and pray . . . oh God . . . oh Jupiter . . . whoever's listening . . . that in the press of more urgent business, Cecil will forget his less-than-candid agent.

But Cecil had not forgotten him yet. A letter was waiting for him at The Elephant, in the safe-keeping of the host. Francis took the letter as if it were a black shell deciding whether or not to explode.

He laid it on his bed while he unbuttoned his doublet. He could smell his own fear rising from the sweaty linen shirt.

Throw it away unread, he thought. As you should have thrown that first letter at Powder Mote.

And then what would he do? Flee the country? How long was Cecil's reach?

He picked up the letter with resignation and snapped the heavy blood-red seal. The message was in the familiar cipher. Although a little fuddled, he unscrambled it in his head.

'Fawkes has confessed. We have them all, on his publicly sworn testimony. I am a man of my word. Light your fires. As promised, I am also good for the company. Please petition for patronage in the usual way, and in plain English, through my secretariat, so that we may speak openly.'

There was no signature. Folded inside the letter were bearer's bonds for two thousand pounds.

He's letting me run, thought Francis. Just like Guido.

84

Francis rode south to Powder Mote before dawn, with five gold nobles in each boot, one hundred pounds divided between his saddlebags, ten pounds in his purse, and the rest of Cecil's money lodged securely with a goldsmith in Clerkenwell. Cecil was letting him run with a full purse.

For the length of Long Southwark and some way beyond, he thought about the use that Cecil had finally made of Fawkes.

What pain of the soul it must have caused Guido when pain of the body forced him to name his friends. No one would ever remember that the names on the warrant came before Guido's confession.

And Cecil wasn't done with Fawkes yet, any more than he was done with Francis.

Even in November, some trees clung to their leaves. His horse kicked up the orange, gold and brown carpet on the track. As the sun rose, Francis lifted his head at the fanfare of a distant cockerel and felt profound relief at leaving the fever of London.

To his amazement, he recognized in the gradual deepening of his breath and a sudden intense awareness of autumn smells, the gift of being alive. He heard every snort of his mare and the faint clinking of the buckles on the bridle. He felt her steady rhythmic movement between his legs and let his weight follow each tiny falter as her hoof slipped on a stone. The air tingled in his lungs.

He took off his hat to feel the air on his head.

When, in the early evening, he reached the top of the southern downs, he rested for a short time, sniffing the salty air. Today the sea merged with the sky. With his eyes half-closed, the horizon became a layer of low-lying cloud broken only by the bright hot slit of the setting sun.

He could not help a small ping of pleasure at the thought of arriving at Powder Mote with the means to start putting the place right. He looked to the east, but the ruins of Pangdean would not have been visible even if most of the house had not fallen into the sea.

We did avert a great disaster there, he thought, even if no one but Cecil and Bacon will ever know. Which led him on to thoughts of the pyrotechnic display that was his reward.

He had to decide where to launch himself in his new role, with all of England to choose from. And choose an occasion to be the excuse for celebration. He'd be damned if he would pretend to celebrate the preservation of His Majesty.

He kicked his horse onto the track that curved down towards Brighthelmstone. The answer came to him like divine revelation, though, unlike St Paul, he did not fall off his horse.

He would ask Kate to marry him. At last. To make up to her for leaving her the first time. What better occasion for fireworks than a wedding? And if he refused to confess to whatever charge Cecil might one day decide to bring, he would at least protect his estate from confiscation and make her a rich widow.

The more he thought, the more the idea pleased him. His spirits soared as he had feared they never would do again.

And there was Jem, who wanted fireworks for his new bride.

Francis had almost forgotten that promise, given casually as he balanced on the back of a carthorse behind Jem after viewing the wrecked boats. It gave him great satisfaction to think that Cecil might pay for his father's politic error.

One boot for me, one for Boomer, he thought.

Even with only half the money, he now had something to offer Kate. If she still wanted him.

She can't leave Powder Mote, he thought with sudden terror. The estate needs her. We all need her.

A surge of lust reminded him how much he needed her. He rode for some time imagining their reunion in bed. Kate stood naked by the bed with her hands on her hips, then prodded him gently with one bare foot . . .

A worrying thought intruded. Jem was to be married in January or February. That was very soon. Fireworks took time to design and make. And even more time when you didn't yet know exactly what they would be. He had inventions to test. Recipes to adjust.

He began to calculate how many rockets he could he make in a day. And how many hundreds he would need. He would need assistants . . .

The horse now knew its way. Francis let the reins go slack and began to dream again.

Tempests.

Lightning.

Comets.

What more could a man say to the woman he had chosen to be his wife? He would die happily once he did all this. And if his rockets flew high enough, perhaps Robin and Tom, and the others when they joined them, would look down from Heaven and wonder.

All of these marvellous reflections had one terrible flaw.

If he made his display for the double wedding, it would take place in Brighthelmstone. A long day's ride from London.

Two days for ladies in carriages. If carriages could get through at all, in January or February . . .

Cecil promised to bring guests, but to Whitehall, to St James's Field, or even to Greenwich Park, thought Francis in anguish. Not to bloody Brighthelmstone on the south English coast. In January or February.

He could see it now: Francis Quoynt, Firemaster, Master of Pyrotechnics to fishermen, shopkeepers, two particular young women and sheep. Laughing stock of his former military comrades.

Ah well, he thought glumly. Cecil would no doubt think him a fool.

Then he pictured how the water would reflect the rockets as they burst above the sea. And how the Downs would echo with the noise. He must remember to warn the farmers to move their livestock and to tie up their dogs. Thank Mars, the rockets would veer away into the offshore winds.

When he arrived at the gates of Powder Mote, he had managed to forget for a short time the unfinished business of Guido, also known as John Johnson, also known as Guy Fawkes, who had been racked until he signed away all hopes of sainthood.

85

Francis invited Kate to walk beside the moat after she finished feeding Meg, and plunged in at once before he could lose his courage. 'Kate. You give this place a sense of living being done.'

At these words, she went suddenly still.

Francis faltered at the coolness of her face. Even so, he thought, she's the fire at which both my father and I warm ourselves. Even when she just sits or stands there, as she does now, breathing quietly.

'My father once said that women turn the world. Men run it, but women turn it.'

He looked at her again. He could not speak for terror.

This Kate was very different from the woman he had known in London. She had swum up out of her well. And Kate, in full view, almost overwhelmed him.

If she leaves, he thought, neither Boomer nor I will survive.

'Though Cecil may yet have me arrested . . .' he began again.

A miserable way to begin a happy subject.

He launched himself yet again. 'You must know, Kate, that my years as a soldier have not trained me to woo . . .'

'You can stop turning yourself inside out, Francis.' Kate glanced away, smiling slightly though her face looked strained.

Francis went icy with apprehension.

'I'm going to marry your father.'

'My father?'

'I'm going to marry Boomer,' she repeated steadily.

Francis suddenly looked dangerous.

'Is it your dream of becoming a respectable young widow?' he asked when he could control his voice. 'But you've decided to suffer the inconvenience of having a husband first?' Breathing hard. 'At my father's expense? I won't let you make a fool of him.'

'Take care,' she said levelly. 'I'm not after your inheritance. Powder Mote will be yours. We've discussed it, he and I.'

Francis felt he had been slapped. And no doubt deserved it. 'I didn't mean . . .'

'Then say what you do mean and don't do careless damage to our ability in the future to speak to each other at all.'

They stood side by side, staring into the moat.

You can't bed him, he wanted to shout. Can't let him touch you . . . You can't want that!

He drew a jagged breath. 'I meant to say that you're young, Kate. You'll be alone again. You know it.'

And be forbidden to him forever as his father's widow.

'Yes,' Kate said quietly. 'I must learn to accept. But until then, I'll always know where he is. And I won't be living in up-and-down hopes of sharing old age, always wondering when he might decide to disappear for a year or two.' She sighed. 'It's a truth of life that people leave you. What matters is how you live together while you're both alive.'

Francis swallowed.

'And Boomer's not so old,' she added fiercely.

Together, they watched a bubble burst up through the floating weed.

'I understand something of his nightmare journeys,' said Kate more calmly. 'He has begun to speak of them to me.' She smiled to herself. 'Your father is an extraordinary man.'

'So I've been told all my life.'

'If I outlive him, I'll be a widow with warm memories.'

She shot him a sideways glance but decided to ignore what she learned by it. 'And I love him. I didn't mean to love him. I'm as surprised as you are. But I do. He and I are better suited for marriage than the two of us would ever be.'

Her smile convinced him. It was thoughtful, contented and a little wry.

At least she'll still be here at Powder Mote, he thought. He must do nothing to drive her away.

'The evening is getting cold.'

She nodded. Together, they turned to walk back to the house.

'Kate,' he said intensely.

She turned in alarm. 'What?'

'Must I now call you "Mother"?'

She looked startled, then laughed when she saw that he was trying, through gritted teeth, to tease. 'I'm certain that Mary knows some well-born gentleman who would pay dearly for that very pleasure.'

He offered his left arm. She hesitated but took it. 'Confess,' she said. 'You're secretly relieved to be let off.'

He put his right hand on top of hers where it lay in the crook of his elbow, and held it against his flesh, feeling her warmth through his shirtsleeve. 'Confused,' he said at last. 'It's too soon for relief. At this moment I want to strangle you.'

Kate nodded as if he had said something entirely amiable. 'I feel that we're going to survive this, you and me. And I vow that neither you nor Boomer will ever have cause to regret the marriage.'

'You speak for Boomer, if he's willing. Leave me to decide on my own regrets.'

I'll throw her down here on the grass, he thought. Remind

her of what we've had. Show her one last time what she'll be missing.

'Do you mind that I'm happy?' she asked.

'How could I mind?'

Liar!

'You're a good man, too.'

'No,' said Francis. 'I'm not. If only you knew.'

'He and I might disagree about chickens,' she said. 'Time will tell.'

86

After a sleepless night, Francis knew that he must give Kate and Boomer the fireworks as their wedding gift. To show that he bore them no ill will.

When, in fact, he thought he would drown in it – a great, evil-smelling sea of bitter self-mockery. A deep well of cold, green-black bile.

Though they had clearly discussed the need to protect his *amour propre*, his predator eyes pounced on every secret brush of their hands, every quick look they shared.

They had already agreed on a double wedding in mid-February. Jem Mawes and his Jane. His father and Kate.

You waited too long to speak, Francis berated himself.

But when, before? With all else happening?

He knew that he was the most at fault. He had brought Kate to Powder Mote in part to help look after his father. He had no right to complain when she did it too well.

He fled to the mixing shed, where he did not have to watch them together. Here he set to work with less joy in his heart than he had anticipated, and only two and a half months in which to prepare his masterwork when he needed a year.

What kind of time for a wedding was February, anyway? The day would be cold, dark and no doubt wet. The fact that no one knew of his intended fireworks when they chose the day did not improve his humour.

He wrote to Cecil explaining his intentions. Then he claimed the mixing house for filling rockets and the stamp mill for incorporating seven hundred pounds of gunpowder. He set up a long trestle table in his chamber under the roof, where the heat from the back of the main chimney let him work without an open fire but still keep his fingers from freezing.

When he returned from London, he had found Robert Stuart still at Powder Mote, transformed to 'Richard Seaborn'. The young Pretender had not dyed his hair as Francis suggested before he left. Instead, it had been cropped short like Francis's own hair and his father's.

While removing his cloak, Francis glared at his dangerous royal cuckoo and wondered how they could be rid of him. Apart from slitting his throat. Then Francis remembered the story of the young man's birth and felt a little ashamed.

'Mistress Peach says I have no need to change the colour,' Stuart-now-Seaborn explained. 'Not while I remain at Powder Mote. In this fashion, she says, I might appear to be a cousin.'

Though more slightly built than either Francis or Boomer, Stuart did have the same long limbs, strong jaw, ridged nose and bright, though slightly darker, hair. His eyes were Boomer's blue rather than the changeable sea-green of Francis. Only the heavy eyelids and full lower lip set him apart.

A cousin, then. Why should Francis protest when Kate and his father had clearly already decided? A visiting cousin was as plausible as a chance stranger.

Francis had himself under perfect control. He would not hit the young man standing warily in front of him. Even though he had every reason to hit him, and reserved the right to do so in the future. When Cecil's agents arrived at Powder Mote, for instance.

'Has he learned to dress himself yet?' Francis asked Kate later. 'Which of you cuts his meat for him?'

'He's most willing to set his hand to everything,' said Boomer. 'If a little untrained.'

'Master Quoynt?'

Francis looked up from the lists and drawings on his worktable.

Robert Stuart stood in the doorway. '*Se puede entrar?*' He corrected himself at once. 'May I enter?'

Francis threw up his hands as if to say, make yourself welcome. You will in any case, whether I agree or not.

'Rockets,' said Stuart, looking down at the papers on the table. 'I admire rockets very much.'

'Do you now?'

'I ordered many rockets for my twentieth birthday, in Spain.'

'Did you?'

Stuart glanced at him. Then turned back to the papers. He picked up a drawing.

Francis resisted the urge to snatch it from his treacherous, royal Scottish paw.

'What is this?' asked Stuart. 'I never saw nothing like it in Spain.'

'You wouldn't have done,' said Francis reluctantly. 'It's my own design.'

'*Es magnifico!* . . . I mean to say . . .'

'I understand Spanish,' said Francis.

'How large is it? How does it work?'

Half an hour later, Francis had moved on to explaining to Stuart his difficulties in packing the stars around the breaking charge in a rocket.

Before the end of the week, Stuart proved to have a knack for fiddling with ingredients and for experimenting endlessly with the fine adjustments that drove Francis mad with impatience. The broad sweeps and grand designs still filled his mind. In the end, Francis left entirely to Stuart the arrangement of stars in the garniture for the rockets in the finale. Meanwhile, he himself wrestled with the awesome difficulty of designing linked fuses in a very long train that would withstand English weather in February.

England will have seen nothing like it before, he thought. If it works.

He asked Stuart to try to discover how to make red stars.

Boomer also offered his help. 'It may be a wedding gift, France, but you'll not do it without me.'

Francis knew he had no choice but to take all the help he could get. Gratefully, he handed over to his father the part of the display that was to be on the top of the Downs.

Kate and eight fishermen's wives set up a factory in the Great Hall to make paper and canvas shell-cases of every size, from the diameter of Kate's thumb up to that of a large melon. They filled basket after basket with the finished shells. Kate also supervised the soaking of fuse rope in a solution of salt-petre and other ingredients that Francis refused to reveal.

Everyone who worked at Powder Mote was sworn to secrecy, but the manufacture of more than one thousand shell-cases soon leaked out into Brighthelmstone. When Francis advertised after Christmas for assistants to help set up his show and light the fuses, he was astonished by the rush of volunteers.

However, when he told these eager volunteers that all assistants must shave their beards, abstain from drink for forty-eight hours before the display, and be capable of a good burst of speed in a sprint, the numbers fell rapidly. Leaving Francis with a team that satisfied him, of ten able-bodied, quick-witted men willing to take possibly fatal risks for the wedding of Jem Mawes and the glory of Brighthelmstone.

*   *   *

In mid-December, Cousin Richard Seaborn announced one night at supper that he wished to travel to Scotland to visit his birthplace.

'There's not much left to see,' Boomer warned him.

'I must go there all the same.'

At last! thought Francis. As grateful as he was for Stuart's help, he would be relieved to see the back of him. Forever.

'The rockets are finished,' Stuart assured Francis. 'I've made several sets – enough for you to test many times.'

'Why go now?' asked Kate. 'In the middle of winter?'

'This is a good time,' Stuart insisted, with the quiet, deferential stubbornness that had emerged as part of his nature, as his previous mix of uncertainty and tutored imperiousness fell away in the company of Boomer and Kate.

Kate at last dyed Stuart's hair dark brown with walnut juice. In a little more than a month, he had learned many of the practical details of English daily life – money, shopping in markets, ordering food and drink in an inn, hiring a boat, how to approach strangers, and when to leave them alone. He adopted a faltering manner of speaking that largely disguised his Spanish accent.

Back in late November, Boomer had gone to London to sell Stuart's rings and the amethyst buttons from his doublet. He now gave the proceeds to Stuart, along with detailed directions for journeying north and how to find his destination once he reached Scotland.

'God go with you, Richard. You'll find your corner somewhere. The Scots are your people, after all. But take care. Don't talk Spanish in your sleep!' Boomer gave the young man a clap on the shoulder.

They all stood in the courtyard, where Stuart was holding the reins of his horse.

'I thank you, Master Quoynt, for . . . everything.' He smiled at Boomer, who smiled warmly back. 'Against all odds, you have made me welcome.'

A sudden sharp spasm of awareness shook Francis, who was standing a few feet away having already said farewell. He looked at the two of them, his father and Robert Stuart, son of that illegitimate son of Mary Stuart. Robert Stuart, whom his father had defended against all reason.

Never! he told himself fiercely. In no way is it possible.

But it could be possible. As my father said, there's a great deal I don't know about him.

Just before Seaborn – as he must now forever be known – mounted his new horse, Boomer embraced him.

Francis, Kate and Boomer walked beside the horse as far as the gatehouse over the moat.

'At last, we can breathe easily again,' said Francis, as Seaborn vanished onto the track up over the Downs. 'Perhaps I should ride along, to ensure that he's really gone.'

'He's a good enough lad in spite of being so badly reared,' Boomer protested mildly. Then he turned and saw his son's face. He flushed.

'Ah, France . . .' he said. 'Och, aye,' he added wryly, after a moment. 'You may be right. Who knows? How can any man truly know? I don't, and that's for certain.'

One day before the end of January, 1606, Francis left his varied assistants to get on with the preparations. He could not afford to take the time. He did not want to go to London. He knew he must.

It was painful, but also a relief to leave the children. For Boomer and Kate seemed like children in their shared lightness of spirit and the fervour with which they greeted each new day of delightful labour together on the estate. Feeling as old as the Downs, as juiceless as a gnarled, twisted, leafless tree, Francis rode away from Powder Mote, headed for London to watch Guido Fawkes die.

87

31 January 1606

Francis pushed through the mob crammed into the Old Palace Yard in Westminster. It was still dark, and cold, at eight o'clock in the morning on the last day of January.

With a playhouse sense of occasion, Cecil had chosen the day and time, deep in mid-winter, when the world and souls were dark. And all hope lay in the promise of new spring beginnings.

Francis looked at the wooden stands built for the official witnesses, important spectators, and families of the condemned. These stands were already full, with Cecil and Sir Francis Bacon among the other witnessing dignitaries. Cecil's sharp eyes spied Francis, then moved on, casually surveying the crowd.

The deaths of the Gunpowder Plotters had been cried on every corner. England, or as much of her as could squeeze into St Paul's Churchyard and the Old Palace Yard, would witness and rejoice at the fitting end for her enemies – who were all the more vile for being Englishmen. Their deaths, hideous in proportion to the crime, would demonstrate the power of the Crown to punish all threats against its king and its people. The sure descent into hell of the traitors, promised by the Anglican clergy, would tilt even higher into the light the Divine preservation of the King.

A man tried to sell Francis a tract explaining how this day of reckoning had come about. Then the hawker looked into Francis's eyes, muttered an apology and backed away.

With placards and proclamations, Cecil had ensured a baying mob in the Old Palace Yard. Today, the Devil of the Vault himself would be sent to his master in Hell.

The day before, his co-fiend, Sir Everard Digby, had died in St Paul's Churchyard, with Rob Wintour, John Grant and Tom Bates.

While they died, Francis had been riding north from Brighthelmstone to London, sick from drinking himself senseless the night before. By Long Southwark he had vomited himself inside out like a pulled-off glove, but a nugget of vileness still hunkered down in his belly.

Bile welled up into his throat again.

The first horses appeared, drawing the condemned men after them on wicker hurdles. Tom Wintour, Rob Keyes, whom Francis had never met, and poor young Ambrose, who thought he was joining a great adventure. Guido was to be the last.

Not the swift and glorious death he had imagined.

Francis wrapped his wool scarf more tightly around his neck, shouldered his way to the front and hugged his hands under his armpits. Heart thudding, he had to look away as Tom Wintour was dragged up onto the scaffold. Around him, eyes glistened and gaping mouths bellowed in rage and triumph at the events he was refusing to watch.

He braced himself against the screams, unbearable sounds.

Thank God Robin was killed at Holbeach.

One . . . two . . . three . . . Tom. Robert. Ambrose. Done for.

At last, Francis lifted his head, his eyes skittering away from the charnel heap on the platform.

One noose still hung on the beam. Beside it dangled three limp ropes from which the nooses had been cut. As Francis looked up, one of the executioners slipped on the blood. Someone laughed.

Only a single line of spectators stood between Francis and the scaffold platform. He saw the head of another horse moving through the crowd, hauling the last hurdle.

Guido.

On the scaffold, the quartered limbs and haunches of men who had thought him a friend were now being cleared away to prepare the stage for the arrival of the arch-fiend whom Cecil had chosen to represent them all.

Not one of the landed gentlemen, thought Francis with ferocious clarity. Nor Percy, the kinsman of nobility. But the mercenary soldier from York who prefers to use a foreign name and dared to choose, of his own will, to turn Papist when reason told the English to desert Rome. Cecil had chosen the rebels' firemaster to play the devil. The outsider who dared to think he could outmanoeuvre God.

But Francis had chosen him first. Given him to Cecil.

Fawkes had to be lifted from the hurdle and helped up the steps to the scaffold. After the rack, he could barely stand. His head trembled.

Fawkes flinched at the cries of rage that greeted him and gazed with astonishment at the size of the crowd that had come to see him die.

'Do you repent your crime and beg forgiveness of the King and the State for your bloody intent?'

Francis's heart seemed to climb into his throat and suffocate him.

'Do you repent?' repeated the clergyman on the scaffold.

Painfully, Fawkes lifted his right hand and made a defiant sign of the cross. Then he met Francis's eyes. The crowd howled with fury.

Through the fog of pain in Guido's eyes, Francis saw the spark of challenge. He nodded in acknowledgement.

One man tried to climb onto the scaffold to tear Fawkes apart with his hands. Quickly, the hangman drew Fawkes to the ladder.

Go with God, you stupid bastard, Francis thought, as Fawkes began to shuffle up, rung by rung. You got what you wanted, after all. Martyrdom. You chose this of your own will. And I may be the only man here who knows it.

Fawkes turned his head from his intense concentration on the rungs. He found Francis's eye again, then jumped into space.

The mob howled with rage. He had escaped them. His neck snapped and he was dead.

It was over. England could sigh with relief and look forward to peace, at last. King James could return safely to his hunting. A male heir to the throne survived. Though the Prince of Wales was to die of typhoid seven years later, his five-year-old brother would become Charles the First.

Cecil could take an even stronger grip on the reins. Francis Bacon could, at last, begin a slow, and apparently well-behaved, climb towards position and power, first as Attorney General, then as Lord Keeper, and finally as Lord Chancellor, but he would have to wait for all these appointments until after the death of his cousin, the Little Toad.

Francis, however, could not yet sigh with relief. He had a debt to pay in Brighthelmstone and a reputation still to make. The next weeks would also test just how far Cecil was a man of his word.

He feared that The Deep Dissembler might be playing a hideous game of cat-and-mouse. The man had promised patronage. He was making good his promise. But after that, what?

He's letting me run, thought Francis yet again. To serve him later, as Guido has just done.

GARNITURE

88

February 1606

With one eye on the weather, Francis watched the last decorations being hung on the wooden stand built in the marketplace for the most exalted guests. Cecil would bring with him, among others, the Spanish Ambassador, and no doubt take subtle pleasure in rubbing the poor Spaniard's nose in these celebrations.

Francis should have been beside himself with joy and gratification. Instead, he was filled with multiplying terrors.

The miraculously clear weather might not hold. Sudden rain would drown the fuses. The wind would rise and blow all the rockets off course. Boomer and his crew would never finish in time with their mammoth task on the tops of the Downs. Kate would lose her grip on the village children. His own devices would fail.

It was like battle. Too much hung on fragile means. On a length of powdered string, a handful of grey dust, a tiny spark of fire.

He feared misfires, accidents, being blinded or maimed. The wilful, capricious nature of Lady Gunpowder herself, who could turn sullen and erratic even when all else was perfect.

And the fear of Cecil still gnawed.

The spectators' stand in the market reminded Francis of those built for the witnesses at executions.

As darkness fell, the wedding guests and foreign visitors gathered in the Brighthelmstone marketplace, swaddled in cloaks and scarves. The locals milled about excitedly and stared at the fur-wrapped strangers seated in the stand. On the beach below the cliff edge that ran along one edge of the market, shadows scurried.

'This'll give Chichester and Lewes something to talk about,' Francis heard one man say.

'Where are all the children?' a woman's voice asked. Her question spread through the crowd like the murmur of a retreating wave.

The two inns, The Ship and The Dolphin, one at either end of the long marketplace, sent boys out into the crowd with trays of ale, spiced wine and hot pies that exhaled steam when broken open in the cold air.

The last daylight faded. The moon claimed the sky for a short time, then slid behind a fist-shaped cloud. The smells of cinnamon and clove blended with those of damp wool, leather and fish. Dogs sniffed for fallen pie crumbs. Five or six voices started a song, then died. People stamped their feet against the cold and braced themselves for the first bang.

Francis stood in a green coat of laurel leaves, down on the beach amongst his green-clad assistants, peering up past the crowd in the marketplace into the darkness. Cecil was forgotten. All his thoughts were now for the show.

Please, he begged whatever gods controlled the night. Let the wind not rise. Let every fuse fire. Safely. At the right time.

Get it right, he silently begged his assistants. For Kate and my father. For me. For the ghosts of Robin, Kit, and Guido. And poor Ambrose . . .

A single rocket suddenly soared up from Patcham Down and shivered silently into sparks.

'Look!' cried the new young Mistress Mawes, eager to lay public claim to her wedding gift. 'It's beginning!'

On the dark surface of the down, small cool stars appeared, like glowworms, by twos . . . tens . . . dozens . . . scores, until the slopes looked like a fallen starry sky.

The crowd grew hushed. Then a woman's voice exclaimed, 'There's the children!' The crowd began to laugh and buzz, passing on her words.

Suddenly, each star became a fiery serpent, twisting as if alive. The down seethed with silent light.

With a whoosh, a fountain of brilliant white light rose as high as a house on the crest of the down above the serpents. On the beach below, Francis gave a gratified sigh. Boomer had timed the fountain perfectly.

As the fountain climbed against the sky, the crowd cheered. As it subsided, so did they. In the darkness that followed there was uncertain applause.

'That was a strange beginning,' one of the London visitors whispered to another. 'Where are the machines? Where is the battle?'

Francis blew on the end of his slow match and signalled to his three assistants.

A streak of light climbed into the sky. There was a heartbeat of silence. Then . . . Glory! The thump of God's fist against the bowl of the universe. A sun burst out of the darkness and died again, leaving behind a sense of exhilaration mixed with loss.

Then, oh joy, in the length of a gasp, came another thump. This time a pale moon floated down through the sky. It shivered, dissolved. Thump, thump, thump, thump, thump, thump. Six more moons floated down to meet themselves rising up beneath the surface of the sea. As the twined moons kissed and died, a gentle melancholy sucked at the hearts of the crowd.

But, then! Thunder! A boisterous stampede of bangs chased each other across the night sky. Whoopee! Hats in the air. Lungs filled. Chests swelled. The air beneath arms pushed them up as if the bodies were about to dance.

Bang! Bang! Chests vibrated. The jelly in eyeballs shook. Hair quivered. Oh, glorious, liberating SOUND!

Francis sprinted feverishly across the shale, wishing he had a hundred arms and hands, intent, his mind empty of everything but the need to make the darkness bloom with light.

Now. Oh, oh, oh. Too fast to track. Comets burst everywhere. There. No, there. There! Overlapping like rich embroidery. Their light frosted the downs with silver snow and turned the folds of the land into crisp black shadows.

Suddenly, there was silence again. Everyone waited. Hoped. Staying afloat.

'It's over,' said a fisherman heavily.

They began to wake. Bodies settled back onto feet. Trying to re-enter the world.

But, not yet, after all. A miracle! More!

Sweet Lady Gunpowder! thought Francis. You beauty! You glorious thing! Favour me now.

The sea, the downs, the beach threw still more comets up into the sky. It seemed that the heavens would shatter. The stars were tumbling down. The moon, out from behind its cloud, stood amazed. The earth trembled in anticipation. The sea shivered. Dogs whined and flattened themselves against the ground. Cats ran beneath beds and bushes. A toddler screamed but looked up, its open mouth drinking the falling light as if it were rain.

Now! Francis begged silently and set his match to his final fuse.

There was a deep thud. A single plain shell soared like a

bright arrow up through the falling sparks. At the apogee, a simple explosion. The stars spread, hovered against the blackness of the sky, modest in number but forming the shape of a rough letter 'K'.

People began to cheer, a little uncertainly.

Kate turned to Boomer, who stood behind her on the crest of the down near the dying coals of the fountain.

'Watch!' he said breathlessly, embracing her tightly from behind. 'It's a linked fuse.'

A second shell chased the first, with two more on its heels, burning onto the after-vision, leaving the word 'K . . . A . . . T . . . E . . .' hanging in the sky.

The startled crowd below them cheered wildly. Kate began to laugh and cry at the same time.

'Now!' Boomer bellowed to the two fishermen on the far side of the gully. Then he kissed Kate.

Before the cheers could die, fire began to grow again on the ridge to the east of the town. It climbed the wicker forms, until 'JANE' burned in letters taller than one man standing on another man's shoulders. Then, on the next ridge, the word 'BRIGHTEMSTON' grew until it flamed large enough for God and all his angels to read in Heaven, let alone in Lewes.

The crowd went mad, shouting, weeping, laughing and calling for Francis Quoynt. To shake his hand, toss him into the air and pour ale down his throat.

On the top of the down, Boomer stood with an arm around Kate, murmuring, 'There. There. It's all right, my love,' as he wiped her wet cheeks with his thumb.

Francis was standing on the beach, panting, at the foot of the cliff, staring in horror at the figure he had spied hidden in a shadow.

Before he could speak, he heard Cecil call his name. Looking back in disbelief at the man in the shadows, he scrambled up to the market-place to face his patron.

'Good work, Quoynt,' said Cecil, drawing him aside from the mob of eager well-wishers, who fell back respectfully. 'The Spanish Ambassador is incoherent with delight. I shall present you later, to him and to some others.'

'And you, my lord? Are you satisfied with your bargain?' Francis asked cautiously. This is the moment for the reversal, he thought. Do I live or die?

'Yes. I am,' said Cecil. 'I've achieved what I wanted. The King and his heirs still live. His Majesty's subjects have never loved him more. England might now enjoy at least a hundred years of peace, with the help of God and constant vigilance.'

Francis listened to every nuance of Cecil's voice. His future, his life rode on a falling tone or expressive pause.

He glanced back towards the beach, praying to be mistaken in what he thought he had seen there.

Just stay where you are! he begged the shadow.

Cecil paused while two men hung a lantern on a nearby post.

'I have more employment for you,' said Cecil when the men had moved on.

Francis knew what he meant. 'No, my lord.' He lowered his voice. 'No more. I'm not cut out for it.'

'On the contrary, I thought you did rather well.' Cecil's amusement was open. 'In fact, your gift for duplicity must have astounded you.'

Their eyes met in the orange light of the lantern.

'There's no more successful rogue than a man with the reputation for being honest,' said Cecil. 'And I trust a man who's a bad liar, I know where I am with him.'

He laid a small hand on Francis's arm, in a gesture instantly read at large in the crowd as a sign of the highest favour. 'In the meantime . . .' He raised his voice for all to hear. 'I'm certain the King will want you to present yourself at Whitehall when he has heard reports of tonight. The Princess Elizabeth celebrates her birthday soon.'

He gave Francis's arm a final pat and turned away. The interview was over.

Francis found that his legs were trembling. But it was too soon to feel relief. The crowd closed in again at once. Francis begged an urgent need to see that everything had been properly extinguished on the beach and he slid back down chalky cliff. The shadowy figure was still waiting.

'What the devil are you doing back here?' Francis demanded under his breath. 'Do you know who's up there in the crowd?' He was almost incoherent. 'Do you know how many guards are posted? How many agents may be watching?'

'I had to see my rockets fired,' said Robert Stuart. 'They worked perfectly, did they not?' He pushed down his scarf so Francis could see his smile. 'You're better than anyone in Spain, you know. I've never seen the sky come alive like that before.'

'God's teeth! I thought we were rid of you. You death-bent noddy! You risk your life coming back here. All our lives . . . You risk everything I've won . . . by the skin of my teeth, I may add.'

'Robert Stuart would be a danger to you. But he's dead. And though I found much of interest there, Scotland has no place for Richard Seaborn.'

'And you think that England has? I may kill you myself.'

Stuart smiled hopefully. 'But won't you be needing an assistant at Powder Mote, if what I just overheard is true? And we must still learn how to make true red.'

Francis could only stare, beyond words for that night. With a sense of both defeat and rising elation, he recognized a fellow soul.

AUTHOR'S NOTE

This story might be true.

The Firemaster's Mistress is grounded in the historical facts of the infamous Gunpowder Plot of 1605, so far as they are known. Everyone 'knows' that Guy Fawkes tried to blow up the English Parliament. As a result, we have bonfires, fireworks and children cadging 'a penny for the Guy' every 5th of November. After that, for most of us, the story grows hazy. For historians, the details mount but so do the differences of opinion. I explored the gaps. I speculated.

Supported by enduring family legend among descendants of some of the historical figures involved, I wrote the story that might very well lie behind the known facts of what is already a real-life thriller.

Robert Cecil, the then English Secretary of State, was a consummate manipulator of information – a seventeenth-century spin doctor *par excellence*. Without doubt, the official version of the events as passed on by the government of the time is full of highly unlikely precision. It is also, almost certainly, not the full story of this seventeenth-century act of political terrorism.

The Places
Brighthelmstone is an old name for Brighton, West Sussex. Those who know the modern city will recognize fragments

of my Brighthelmstone glimmering beneath the surface of the Regency preservations and modern concrete. The (real) market-place ran along the seafront between East and West Streets, while Western Road was a mere track through crofts and fields. The Dolphin Inn was where the Queen's Hotel now stands. Powder Mote (fictional) lies more or less on the rising route to the Devil's Dyke, though anyone who loves Michelham Priory as I do will recognize my pillaging and transposition. The river that feeds my moat, though now suppressed, still regularly floods the London road. Pangdean Place, fictional but named for a real vanished village northeast of Brighton, stands in a cleft in the chalk cliffs not far from Roedean School. No equating of these last two places is intended.

In London, The Little Rose and other inns were all mentioned by Stow in his survey of 1588. Shakespeare personally recommended The Elephant in Southwark as 'the place in London where it is best to lodge' (*Twelfth Night*). The Bear Pit probably stood pretty much where I have put it. So far as possible, the placement of water steps, the shops and buildings on London Bridge, and the Bridge House warehouses is historically accurate. All major buildings stand where shown in the maps and engravings of the period (notably Visscher) or in the best compromise position when these sources disagree (often). I also spent several days walking the streets and alleys of Southwark, whose names evoke and roughly map the now-vanished inns, bear garden, fishponds, theatres, markets and pleasure grounds. St Olaf's Street is now Tooley Street.

GUNPOWDER PLOT:
THE HISTORICAL CHRONOLOGY

1603

Death of Elizabeth I on 24 March. James VI of
Scotland (son of Mary, Queen of Scots) inherits
the English throne.

The plague delays royal entry into London.

Treason of the Bye and Treason of the Main (set a
precedent for 'The Blow' and an alternative
monarch).

1604

20 March   Meeting at The Duck and Drake of the first five
conspirators:

Robert Catesby, Warwickshire gentleman, aged 31

Tom Wintour, back from Flanders, aged 33

Jack Wright, aged 36

Thomas Percy, cousin of the Earl of
Northumberland

Guido Fawkes, mercenary soldier from York, in
his mid-thirties

Percy then rents a private house in Westminster
precinct, with Fawkes disguised as his servant
'John Johnson'.

| October | Robert Keyes joins the plot. (Cousin-in-law to Ambrose Rookwood.) |
| December | Thomas Bates joins the plot. (Retainer to Robert Catesby.) |

1605

February	Parliament postponed to 3 October, for fear of summer plague.
25 March	New recruits to conspiracy: Robert Wintour (aged 37, brother of Tom) John Grant (aged 37) Kit Wright (aged 35, brother of Jack). Lease to cellar 'secured'. [Storehouse at ground level.]
April	Birth of Princess Mary – the first royal heir to be born in England.
May	Cecil made Earl of Salisbury. Public christening of Princess Mary at Greenwich.
July	Fawkes has '36 barrels in place'. Rowed from Lambeth in batches. Parliament prorogued by proclamation, to Tuesday 5 November, due to '... *dregs of late contagion.*'
August	Secret meeting near Bath. Catesby to *'call in whom he thought best'.*
Late August	Fawkes back in London from support-seeking mission to Continent. Discovers that powder in cellar has decayed.
29 September	Ambrose Rookwood joins the plot.
14 October	Catesby recruits Francis Tresham
21 October	Catesby recruits last conspirator, Sir Everard Digby, 24 years old, wealthy, handsome, naïve and gallant. Raised as a Protestant but converted. Happily married to a rich young wife,

he was to abduct Princess Elizabeth, whom the plotters meant to make Queen.

26 October   Monteagle Letter delivered by 'a tall man' to Catholic Lord Monteagle at Hoxton House in London, ten days before the 'terrible blow'. Monteagle takes the letter to Cecil. Cecil decides not to 'trouble' the King until the last minute.

2 November   Cecil has alerted Parliament to 'some danger'.

4–5 November   Evening: King James finally warned by Cecil. Search of cellars under House of Lords by Sir Thomas Knyvet, a Westminster magistrate. Fawkes found and arrested. Hauled before the King.

6 November   King orders torture of 'John Johnson'.

7 November   Fawkes reveals his true identity. The gunpowder is taken to the Tower, and discovered to be decayed.

8 November   Fawkes signs confession giving names of fellow conspirators. Catesby and Percy are killed. The Wintours are wounded in round-up at Holbeach. Thomas Wintour, Ambrose Rookwood and John Grant are captured at Holbeach.

1606

30 January   Execution of Everard Digby, Robert Wintour, John Grant and Thomas Bates in St Paul's Churchyard.

31 January   Execution of Tom Wintour, Guy Fawkes, Ambrose Rookwood and Robert Keyes in the Old Palace Yard at the Tower. Fawkes was the last to die. Though very weak from torture, he managed to jump from the ladder and break his own neck in the noose.

The Other Boleyn Girl

Philippa Gregory

Two sisters competing for the greatest prize . . . the love of a king.

Mary Boleyn catches the eye of Henry VIII when she comes to court as a girl of fourteen. Dazzled by the golden prince, Mary's joy is cut short when she discovers that she is a pawn in the dynastic plots of her family. When the capricious king's interest wanes, Mary is ordered to pass on her knowledge to her friend and rival: her sister, Anne.

Anne soon becomes irresistible to Henry, and Mary can do nothing but watch her sister's rise. Anne stops at nothing to achieve her own ambition. From now on, Mary will be no more than the other Boleyn girl. But beyond the court is a man who dares to challenge the power of her family to offer Mary a life of freedom and passion. If only she has the courage to break away – before the Boleyn enemies turn on the Boleyn girls . . .

'This compulsively readable novel is a wonderful account of the Tudor court. This is the finest historical novel of the year.'
Daily Mail

'The very believable dialogue and detail takes you all the way into the claustrophobic privy chambers of the royal palaces.'
The Times

ISBN 0-00-651400-6